Revealing Angel

Revealing Angel

Julia Maclean

ST. MARTIN'S PRESS
New York

Design by Judy Dannecker

Library of Congress Cataloging-in-Publication Data

MacLean, Julia.
      Revealing angel / Julia MacLean.
         p.   cm.
     ISBN 0-312-05874-8
     I. Title.
    PR9199.3.M3316R48   1991
    813'.54—dc20   90-27077
                              CIP

First Edition: June 1991

10 9 8 7 6 5 4 3 2 1

To my mother

Acknowledgments

Special thanks to Enzo Fulco for providing me with an insider's view of Rome.

Revealing Angel

Prologue

SHE looked as if she had fallen asleep after a fevered bout of love-making, naked on the rumpled silk sheets with her face half hidden by her tangled hair.

When the maid discovered her in Rome's pale morning light, her first impulse was to straighten the primrose yellow sheet and to smooth the blond curls back from the lovely face. But the old woman hesitated.

By the time the police arrived, the hysterical woman couldn't remember what had alerted her to the truth. The empty pill bottle on the floor beside the bed, the pile of ashes in one charred corner of the thick white rug, the swollen bruise that marred the beautiful young woman's left cheekbone, or the man's silk tie draped almost too casually across the oak headboard. In the end, she insisted it was the unnatural quiet that had made her scream so loud that the usually sedate neighbors ran out of their luxurious apartments in the exclusive building on the Viale Parioli to pound on the door. "It was too quiet," the old woman offered as her explanation, exhausted from crying and questions. "She was there, but I knew I was all alone. Do you understand? Angel was gone. *Stavo sola.*"

A photographer, perched dangerously on a narrow ledge on the fourth floor of the building across the street, managed to capture the broken old woman as she poured her story out to the police. In the background the shadowed outline of the naked corpse could be seen. With that picture—the elderly maid's claim to immortality—the photographer made a small fortune. The next day it appeared on the front page of every newspaper in Italy. The headline in Rome's *Il Messaggero* was the simplest and, somehow, the most moving.

È Morta. "She Is Dead."

1

STEVIE Templeton hoped she was dreaming. It was the only acceptable explanation for her discovery that she was fondling a naked man who had somehow materialized in her bed.

Unfortunately, the dream hypothesis was put in doubt by the man's steady breathing, the warmth of his arm against her bare breasts, the firm presence of his—

She yanked her hand back.

He didn't move. She squinted in the dark room, but the heavy curtains blocking out the nighttime lights of central Rome made it impossible to see. Perhaps it really was an unusually vivid dream.

There were plenty of reasons for her subconscious to be disturbed. She was alone in a strange apartment in a foreign country. The last year had been rough: first her father's death, then the news that her teaching position in Boston had been declared redundant. Terrified at the prospect of unemployment and poverty, she had finally accepted her best friend's advice to take a teaching position in Rome, but such a bold move went against her grain. Like her father, she was a creature of habit and would have preferred her usual lumpy bed in her cramped Boston apartment to this enormous, canopied creation in the plush apartment that belonged to her friend Toni's mother.

After all that stress, a bizarre dream was perfectly understandable. In the morning she would laugh about it.

The dream cleared his throat. "Did you have to stop?" he asked in Italian.

She lay motionless for a few seconds while the truth sank in. Then she scrambled out of bed, snatched up the top blanket to cover herself, and screamed as loud as she could.

"Get out of here!" She spoke to him in Italian to be sure he understood.

"Pardon?"

It was an odd thing to ask her to repeat. What else would she have said? She pressed her back against the wall—unfortunately the door was somewhere on the other side of the huge room—and decided to try to outwit him.

"I have a friend coming back in a few minutes," she said as steadily as she could. "When he finds you he'll call the police and have you arrested. If you're smart you'll get out of here as fast as you can."

"Have me arrested?" the man asked. "What for?"

She tightened the blanket around her body. She didn't usually sleep in the nude, but the airline had lost her luggage.

"I think we both know what you could be charged with," she said coolly. "There's no need to go into the details."

"Please," he said. The sheets rustled as he sat up. "Give me details. What have I done?"

"You . . . well, to be blunt, you molested me. Or tried to."

"My dear Signorina, as I recollect, *you* were molesting *me*. And I didn't threaten to call the police!"

"You—" She tried to make out the features of this incredibly presumptuous man, but the darkness was impenetrable. To accuse

4

her of molesting him! Although, to be honest, her hand had been, well, active when she woke up. But she couldn't be held responsible for her behavior when she was asleep. He was the one who had snuck naked into her bed.

"You had no right to come in here! I was sound asleep. You could have done anything to me."

"Please," he replied, sounding both offended and amused. "I don't have to force myself on anyone, and when I make love to a woman, I expect her to be something other than comatose, if only to ensure that she'll be appropriately grateful afterward. Usually, they give me small tokens of their esteem, gold cuff links, occasionally a car. Nothing too ostentatious. The Maserati Biturbo rather than the Quattroporte . . . so you can rest assured that I wouldn't have done anything while you were unconscious. I am not a man to waste my talents."

Stevie shut her eyes. It had been a long night. The plane had been three hours late, and then there had been the fruitless wait for her luggage. The cab driver must have taken her through most of Italy before he dropped her in front of the apartment building and demanded an astonishing sum for the ride. That had been followed by the self-administered tour of the Contessa Barberini's enormous apartment that was so opulent she kept expecting to bump into Robin Leach and his camera crew. And now she had to deal with this arrogant man.

"I knew it was a mistake," she said. "I should never have come to this country. I should have got a job as a bank teller or a file clerk, something really exciting. I should have told Toni—"

"Toni?" the man in the bed interrupted. "You're a friend of Antonia's?"

"Yes," she sniffed, struggling to subdue the self-pity that had hit her. "I'm from Boston. Toni's my best friend. Her apartment is next to mine. Or was until I came here."

"Now I understand the confusion. I moved in a few weeks ago, before Laura, Toni's mother, left for her holiday in Portofino. But Toni wouldn't expect anyone to be here during her mother's absence."

Toni had described her mother as beautiful and wild, but Stevie hadn't believed her. Without a firsthand model—her own mother had died when she was a baby—she tended to imagine all mothers as prim and perky, like the ones on television commercials. But this was obviously the Contessa's latest boyfriend. Italian men! He discovers a naked woman in his girlfriend's apartment and is corrupt enough to hope for some action. That was a hell of a lot worse than the bottom pinching Toni had warned her about.

"That only explains why you're in this apartment," Stevie said, tightening her hold on the blanket. "Not why you climbed into my bed."

"*My* bed. This is the room I use."

"But when you discovered I was already in it you should have left! Instead of—"

"Instead of letting you molest me?"

"I did not."

"In case you haven't noticed, it is a large bed and a very dark room, and I was exhausted. I didn't notice you until you were . . ." He chuckled. "Well, I certainly thought you were molesting me. And quite nicely at that. Why should I look a gift horse in the mouth?"

Stevie sighed. She would never win an argument with this man. "You're not by any chance a lawyer, are you?" she asked.

He roared with laughter. "As a matter of fact I am. I didn't realize it was so obvious. And I'm also a gentleman. Since my presence disturbs you, I will happily move to another room."

She could barely make out his shadow as he freed himself from the bedclothes and slipped out of the bed on the same side as she was. She blushed. Darkness or not, a naked man was standing right in front of her.

"Sleep well, little one," he said softly. His tone was intimate and sexy. "I hope we see each other in the morning. And it won't be necessary to bring along your imaginary friend for protection. Or the police."

He strolled to the door, a shadow moving through darkness.

"I . . ." Her voice caught. "I'm sorry. I mean, I think I had every right to be frightened. But I shouldn't have carried on like an outraged virgin."

He laughed again. "Don't worry. Believe me, you didn't act *anything* like a virgin."

The door opened, and for a second he was silhouetted in the light from one of the other rooms. And then the door shut behind him.

For the first time, Stevie noticed that the temperature had dropped several degrees. Shivering, she slipped back into bed and huddled under the covers. She was still cold. Without thinking, she slid over to the indentation her recent bedmate had made. She curled up in the warm space and buried her face in his pillow, inhaling the lingering male scent.

When in Rome, she thought, amused by the uncharacteristic impudence of her action. Waking up in the same apartment as that man would be interesting. But their second meeting had better be less intimate than their first. Rome or not, she was still Stevie Templeton.

2

"Buon giorno."

Stevie stretched and blinked in the warm sunlight. A young woman in a pretty blue uniform was anchoring the heavy silk curtains back from the window. A silver breakfast tray was on the table beside the bed, and the incomparable aroma of coffee and fresh bread filled the room.

The maid moved away from the window and disappeared into the adjoining bathroom.

"Your clothes have been cleaned and pressed, Signorina, and laid out for you," she called out in her softly accented English. "It is one o'clock in the afternoon. The Signore asked me not to disturb you until now. I tried to find your suitcases to unpack, but—"

"Lost," Stevie supplied. "The airline promised to call when and if they find them."

"That's horrible! Some of Signorina Barberini's clothes are still in her room. I'm sure she wouldn't mind if you wore them."

Stevie pressed her cheek against the gold satin pillow. Languishing in an oversize bed while a servant tended to all her desires was a memory she would cherish for the rest of her life. "It's all right," she called to the maid, who was still in the bathroom, probably fluffing the towels and opening up a new bar of soap. "I was planning to buy some dresses after I arrived. I'll go shopping this afternoon. But thank you for everything. You mentioned . . ." At the memory of her nocturnal encounter with "the Signore," her skin flushed. The details of the event were foggy, but she was pretty sure she had made a fool of herself. "The Signore? Is he still here?"

"He had to leave after breakfast. I would have stayed last night if I had known you were coming, but Signorina Barberini didn't tell us what day to expect you."

"I was fine." Stevie pushed her loose blond curls back from her eyes. She pulled herself up to a sitting position, tugging the sheet up to cover herself, and surveyed the room. In the light of day, it was even more impressive. An ivory and blue silk rug, antiques that had to be priceless, the huge bed with its glistening gold canopy, windows stretching up to the towering ceiling . . . Toni's insistence that her family would be considered average in modern-day Italy where every other person had a title appeared to be overly modest.

"I'm glad the Signore was here to welcome you," the young maid continued from the bathroom. "He is such a wonderful man."

"He and the Contessa are . . ." Stevie searched for an inoffensive term, "close?" she finally concluded.

The maid came out of the bathroom and went to a small desk near the bedroom door where she had left a mass of daffodils. "Oh yes," she replied, as she arranged the flowers in a crystal vase. "The Signore is her closest friend in the whole world. She says that without him she would be completely lost."

Stevie raised her eyebrows. Her assumption that the mysterious Signore was the Contessa's boyfriend had obviously been correct. Yet that hadn't kept him from seizing an opportunity for a good time with a stranger, even if it was in one of the Contessa's beds.

The flowers arranged to her satisfaction, the maid turned to face Stevie, a broad smile on her pretty face. "He—"

Her welcoming expression froze. "I—" she sputtered. "You—"

Stevie's mind was still on the handsome stranger. Well, she didn't know that he was handsome. To amuse herself, she imagined him as toothless and bald, with a huge paunch and bony, stick legs. But actually he had seemed quite lean and muscular when she had awakened and discovered him beside her. At the memory, a warm sensation filled her body. She shut her eyes and started to slide back down in the bed.

No. She pulled herself back up. She wouldn't get involved in a situation out of a low-budget Italian movie. He was the lover of her best friend's mother. And, if that weren't enough, a rat.

She glanced up at the young maid, who was still standing at the end of the bed. The girl looked shocked. Was she a mind reader? Maybe she was already suspicious about what had happened when Stevie and the Contessa's boyfriend found themselves alone together. After all, this *was* his usual room. What if this girl confided her suspicions to the Contessa? How could Stevie ever face Toni's mother? Even the truth was humiliating.

"Your name," the maid whispered. "Signorina Barberina did not say who you were. I don't . . ."

"I'm sorry. I should have introduced myself. I'm Stevie Templeton."

"Ave, Maria, piena di grazia," the girl murmured, her face white. She backed toward the door.

"Maria?" Stevie said. Her confidence in her Italian wavered. Even after a three-month immersion course and Toni's extensive coaching, the maid's full name sounded more like a prayer to her. "Thank you, Maria, for everything."

The young woman had reached the door. While she fumbled with the knob, she stared back at Stevie with wide eyes. Then, without saying good-bye, she slipped out and slammed the door shut. Rapid footsteps faded into the distance.

Stevie shook her head. The maid was actually running to her next task. "And some Americans think Mediterranean people are lazy," she observed to herself as she turned to the breakfast tray. "That's the most eager worker I've ever seen."

ONE entire wall of the bathroom was a mirror. Stevie decided that the Contessa Barberini must be extremely beautiful. Less fortunate women presumably shared Stevie's taste for small mirrors with dim but flattering lights, like the one in her old apartment. This one was cruel.

She received quite a shock when she caught sight of herself as she stepped out of the sunken marble bath. Even naked, she looked like the classic image of a schoolteacher. Her pale hair was neatly tied back, she wasn't wearing makeup, and her hunched shoulders did a good job of hiding her surprisingly full figure.

No one would call her ugly; in fact, she was often complimented on her large green eyes, the only inheritance from her dark father. But she was definitely on the plain side. Toni had offered to transform her with expert makeup and a new wardrobe, but Stevie usually felt comfortable the way she was. Beauty wasn't worth the trouble. Who was she going to impress: the seven-year-olds she taught?

Still, when she slipped into her tailored navy dress with its high collar and long sleeves the results were even less flattering. She looked twenty-five going on eighty. She might as well put on a hair net. Was she really going to step out into the streets of Rome looking like this?

She yanked the elastic from her shoulder-length hair and fluffed out her natural curls. Then she undid the top two buttons on the dress and rolled the sleeves up to elbow length. A little more makeup than usual, and she looked . . . like a schoolteacher. But at least a moderately attractive schoolteacher.

She slipped out of the apartment to avoid disturbing the maid and cook. The maid's attentions were a little embarrassing. Growing up in a modest house in suburban Boston near the elementary school where her father taught hadn't prepared her for breakfast on silver trays. And there was no point in allowing herself to become spoiled, since in a week or two she would be settling into some drafty, dingy apartment that was all her budget could accommodate.

She had a map of Rome and a guidebook in her shoulder bag, but she decided to wander around for awhile before choosing a particular destination. She wanted to get the feel of the city. The view from her bedroom window had taken her breath away. Every building looked like a museum or palace. Rome obviously wasn't the kind of place that could be mastered with a three-day bus tour.

At street level, the city was almost overwhelming. Cars and motorbikes careened at terrifying speeds with no regard for traffic laws. People of every shape and form were hurrying along the street. Dark-eyed beauties with glistening hair and long legs, middle-aged women with sharp, alert faces, thin, handsome young men in well-cut suits . . . She smiled, enjoying the spectacle. Maybe Toni had been right to force this change on her.

She turned left and started down a slight incline and then, on a whim, turned off onto a narrower street. She had heard that the plumbing in these exquisite, golden buildings was dreadful, but that seemed a small price to pay for living in a work of art.

Suddenly an old woman moved in front of her. Stevie stopped and smiled at her. Her crinkly gray hair was wound in a tight bun. To Stevie's surprise, her eyes were full of fear.

Stevie smiled reassuringly. In Boston she was often approached by confused older women who wanted directions. Their choice made sense; her appearance couldn't frighten anyone. *"C'è qualcosa che va male?"* she said, asking if something was wrong.

The old woman slowly extended her wrinkled hand and placed it on Stevie's bare arm. Her thin voice was barely audible. *"Non è possibile."*

Stevie bent down to bring her face closer to the troubled woman. *"Cosa non è possibile?"* What isn't possible?

The old woman didn't answer. Her frightened eyes searched Stevie's face. With her free hand she reached up and stroked Stevie's cheek. Then her cold fingers tightened around Stevie's wrist.

Stevie didn't know what to do. She didn't want to be rude and walk away, but she couldn't spend the rest of her day with someone who was obviously disturbed. Perhaps a passerby would help.

Two aging men in black suits were approaching along the narrow street. Stevie waved to attract their attention. They stopped. One of them nudged the other with his elbow. They whispered something. Then they both pointed at Stevie.

A middle-aged woman in a flowered silk dress was hurrying along the other side of the street. When she saw Stevie, she also stopped. And covered her mouth with her hand.

Stevie slowly straightened up. There was something wrong with these people. The old woman was still clutching her wrist. Her fingers had tightened like a clamp.

"Excuse me," Stevie said in Italian, "you're starting to hurt me." She tried to twist free, but it was impossible. The woman was surprisingly strong. Stevie stepped back hoping the woman would let go, but instead she followed her. Stevie continued backing up, moving uphill. The three bystanders kept pace with them.

"Could someone help me?" Stevie cried, lapsing into English. Two young women wearing jeans and T-shirts turned onto the street. Stevie smiled with relief; they certainly looked sane. She waved and called out. *"Scusi!"*

They both looked up. Their bored expressions disappeared. They gasped.

Stevie wondered if she had wandered into a neighborhood populated by mental patients. She had to get away before things got worse.

She turned to the old woman. Her thin lips were moving, but Stevie couldn't make out the faint words. "I have to go now," Stevie said, remembering to use Italian. Then, with all her strength, she tried to jerk her arm free. The woman dug her thick, yellow nails into the skin. Blood sprang to the surface. Stevie tried to ignore the pain. She pulled free and jumped back several steps. The woman clawed at the air, trying to grab her again. She crept forward, her yellowed eyes still on Stevie's face.

"Angel," she whispered. *"È Angel."*

13

Stevie realized that the surrounding group had grown. There were at least fifteen people staring at her. They all had the same dazed, mad look.

A little boy cried out. "Angel!" The people nodded and started to move toward her.

Stevie turned and ran. Suddenly people were coming at her from all directions. She couldn't remember which street led back to the apartment, but somewhere in this enormous city there had to be at least one normal person who would help her. She ran as fast as she could. But the mob was growing. People were coming out of doorways, cars screeched to a halt and the drivers and passengers tumbled out to join the chase. Everyone was trying to grab her, to stop her. She kept knocking arms away as she ran faster and faster, her feet flying over the rough stones. Footsteps thundered behind her. She didn't know where she was. People were even leaning over their balconies, stretching their arms out, trying to grab her from above.

"Angel, Angel, Angel." Everyone was chanting it, but what did they mean? And the Italian phrases. *"È ancora viva. È un miracolo."* She is alive. A miracle.

She twisted her ankle on a broken cobblestone and nearly fell, but she had to keep running, she had to get away from them. She turned down another narrow street. Her chest hurt and her leg throbbed. Hot tears stung her eyes. She was tired; she couldn't keep going.

"Help me," she gasped. "Someone help me."

"Angel, Angel, Angel," was the only response.

And then there was a light in front of her and a clearing. She stumbled out of the narrow street, praying for help.

A fountain was at the far end of the square. Statues of ancient gods cavorted in pulsing water. A small crowd was clustered around it. They turned, as if one body, when they heard the approaching mob. And then their eyes focused on Stevie. And widened with horror.

She spun around. The people who had chased her poured out of the narrow street and filled the square. They were everywhere. The same look, the same cry.

"Angel."

And now she was their prisoner.

"I don't understand," she whispered. Tears spilled from her eyes. Her chest heaved as she tried to catch her breath.

For a moment, the crowd seemed confused, as if having caught her, they didn't know what to do. Then an old man in front of her sank to his knees. She was afraid he had collapsed. But then he stretched his arms out. His fingers touched the tips of Stevie's shoes.

"Angel," he cried. *"È un miracolo."*

Stevie rubbed her wet eyes with trembling hands. A miracle. Why did they keep saying that?

Then, one by one, the others followed his example. They lowered their bodies to the rough stones and stretched out their arms in supplication. They were worshipping her.

"Angel, Angel, Angel," they chanted. The rushing water merged with their voices. "Angel, Angel, Angel. *È un miracolo. Un miracolo. Grazi á Dio.*"

Finally she was the only one standing. She looked around at the people who were on their knees before her. Her shoulders shook. Her tears wouldn't stop. She covered her face with her hands. She didn't know what was happening. She only knew that their adoration was the most humiliating thing she had ever known.

3

"ANGEL Concelli, you are a star."

Angel leaned back and inhaled on her cigarette.

"It's amazing what a blow job will get you these days."

Her reflection in the large mirror grinned back at her. She straightened the midnight blue, sequined dress that had taken most of her paycheck for the movie. Since it was slashed to the navel and slit to the hip, the couturier obviously didn't charge by the yard. It was worth every penny: it made her look like a star. She fluffed out her wild mass of blond curls and batted her long lashes.

"What marvelous green eyes, darling," she said, knocking cigarette ashes onto the marble floor. "They look just like emeralds. They must have been the reason my husband picked you for this part."

She laughed out loud at the memory of her encounter a few minutes earlier with the producer's wife. The old bat would have fainted if Angel had told her the truth. Angel would never forget the details of that day eight months ago, when Aldo Guerritore, the fat, bald producer, had made his offer. She could have the part—small but pivotal—in a big-budget Italian movie, the kind of role that could make a beginning actress's career. But there was one catch. "*Bella,* you've got a great mouth," Aldo had said, his cigar still planted firmly between his teeth. "How about a little blow job? Nothing fancy. You don't even have to take your clothes off."

Angel had crossed her legs, sat back in her chair, and realized a profound truth about herself.

Armed with this truth, she had slowly stood up, put her hands on her hips, pulled back her shoulders so that her already tight sweater pulled even tighter across her breasts, and said in as charitable a tone as she could manage, "If you'll enjoy it more with my clothes off, I'll be glad to be oblige you."

The profound truth, she reflected a few minutes later as she crouched naked between his legs, was that she really understood the poor slob's point of view. If abusing a position of authority ever became the only way she could get laid by someone young and desirable, then she would probably do it, too. As her mother used to say, "Anyone who says sex isn't the most important thing in life needs hormone treatments."

When the cigar finally dropped out of the producer's mouth, Angel knew she was going to go a long way in show business.

Tonight was payoff night. Earlier in the evening, the movie's premiere had been held at Rome's Teatro Sistina. People had cheered and stomped their feet. It wasn't art, but it had money written all over it, something Romans like just as much and maybe a little more. The movie, a big-budget sex farce starring the beautiful Sophia Moro, had a plot that was embarrassingly thin. When Sophia discovers that her husband is having an affair with a young waitress, she decides to do him ten better by working through a selection of handsome young studs. Complications ensue, naked men pile up in the apartment, hiding under beds and in closets. Everything in the movie was stale except the waitress.

Angel Concelli.

An overnight star, that's what everyone at the post-premiere party had been calling her until she finally escaped into the washroom to catch her breath. You have that special something. Magic, several had said. Like Marilyn Monroe, Brigitte Bardot. Hollywood will be banging on your door tomorrow. Four agents had already tried to sign her up.

Angel butted out her cigarette in the sink and took one last look at herself in the mirror.

"I want it all," she said, leaning forward to stare into her large, green eyes. "I want money and fame and parts other actresses would kill for. And nothing's going to stop me. I'm going to be the biggest star that ever lived."

She pulled the front of her dress down another inch, took a deep breath, and opened the door.

"Angel, there you are!" someone shouted. "This wonderful man from California has been dying to meet you!"

Aт three in the morning, the party was still in full swing. Although it was a cool night, Angel slipped out onto the palazzo's terrace for some fresh air. She walked to the edge to view the sculptured gardens below. She couldn't remember whose house this was. The horny producer, the gay director, or maybe Sophia Moro herself, who had been jealously glaring at Angel all evening.

Leaning on the stone railing, she gazed up at the sky. A thousand stars glittered above her, but she found the distant sparkle of Rome even more impressive. She was a city girl; even though this house was only a few miles outside of Rome, she felt as if she were visiting a strange and exotic place where grass had mysteriously sprung up instead of the more natural pavement. Like a drink of water, the countryside was all right from time to time, but she wouldn't want it every day.

Suddenly she sensed that someone else was on the terrace. A powerful urge to run back inside took hold of her. But there were hundreds of people only a few feet away. Shrugging off the irrational fear, she turned to see who her unexpected companion was.

He was standing alone, his hands in his pockets, at the side of the house, as if he had been waiting for her to arrive. His face was hidden in the shadows.

"Angel can't be your real name," he said.

"Almost," she said. "Angela."

"And you don't seem Italian," he continued.

He stepped into the light. He was tall and extremely handsome. A broad, intelligent brow, riveting eyes, sculptured bones, thick black hair—no Italian actor looked that good. There was something ominous about him—he reminded her of a restless panther on a thin leash—but that had never stopped her before. She liked an exciting man.

"I was born in Rome," she told him, her curiosity growing. "But my mother's American. We spoke English at home. Concelli is, if I recollect correctly, the name of my fourth stepfather. That was before my mother settled for just fucking them. I am, as we native Romans like to say, *una bastarda*. And you are?"

He slowly walked toward her. His impeccable black suit had to be the creation of Rome's finest tailor. For a moment she felt that he was going to keep walking until he reached her and then pull her into his arms. But he stopped just before their bodies touched. A thin gold watch glittered briefly as he raised his hand to the terrace railing. He placed his fingers a fraction of an inch away from hers.

"You don't know who I am?" he asked.

"Should I?"

He smiled, amusement in his dark eyes. "I am Gian-Carlo Cassieri," he said.

The door to the terrace opened, and the sound of drunken chatter and bad music spilled out. But someone immediately shut it, restoring silence.

"And?" Angel said. "Gian-Carlo Cassieri is?"

He stared down at her, his face impassive. "I am in politics, Miss Concelli."

"That explains my ignorance. I don't have time for politics, Mr. Cassieri."

"And I don't have time for movies. But, if all reports on your debut are correct, then I am to politics what you will soon be to movies."

She grinned. "You're a star?"

"In Italy, I am the sun."

"In Italy, as I understand it, there is usually a star on the right and a star on the left and forty-seven stars in the middle. How do we know which one is the sun?"

"The one who brings warmth and life to everyone is the sun. I am *l'amico del popolo,* the friend of the people. My only aim is to serve."

She threw back her head and laughed out loud. "Excuse me," she said, carefully wiping the tears from under her eyes so she wouldn't smear her makeup, "but I've never heard of a politician who was out to serve anyone but himself."

His eyes darkened.

"But you've never met me before," he whispered.

She swallowed. "That's true."

He reached out and lightly touched her bare shoulders. He was standing so close her breasts almost brushed against his chest. Her heart was pounding.

"You're the most beautiful woman I've ever seen."

Angel laughed nervously. "Without mascara I only come in third or fourth."

He traced a small circle on her shoulder with his finger. "Angel," he whispered, "I'm serious."

"Maybe I'm not," she said. "Maybe I'm not interested."

He smiled, a confident smile. He was not a man who wasted his time on games. With appreciative eyes, he studied her face, her elegant neck, her pale breasts. She liked the flattery. It made her skin tingle.

He moved his hands from her shoulders and took her wrists. Then he gently pulled her arms up around his neck. Their bodies finally touched. He ran his hands over her bare back, to her narrow waist, up to the exposed sides of her breasts.

She sighed. Her nipples were hard, so she couldn't claim she wasn't interested. And although something about him made her nervous, she didn't want to go home alone after her triumph.

She stood on tiptoe, ready to kiss him. But just as his lips were about to touch hers, she whispered, "You're not the kind of man who'll want to own me, are you?" She kept her tone flirtatious.

His eyes were surprisingly serious as he considered her question. "I think the greatest danger is that you're going to own me, Angel."

She smiled. She liked that scenario.

She kissed him, tightening her arms around his neck. His mouth was hot and strong. He slid one hand down to the base of her spine and held her close. His kiss was both hungry and gentle, as if he wanted to kiss her forever. No man had ever felt this good.

Finally he pulled his mouth away. He pressed his lips against her hair. Breathless and limp, she fell against him. Remembering where she was, she looked back at the palazzo. She had completely forgotten the party.

The revelers were dancing and drinking. Two people embracing on the terrace meant nothing to them. By now countless couples would be rutting in the palazzo's many rooms. She hoped he would invite her back to his home instead of just joining the search for an empty room.

Then she noticed a woman standing alone at one end of the large room, almost hidden by the drapes, looking out at the terrace. She was tall, erect, her black hair swept high with diamonds. Angel couldn't make out her features.

"Someone is watching us," she whispered. "A woman."

Gian-Carlo kept his eyes on Angel. His fingers slipped under the sequined silk of her dress. He began a maddeningly slow caress of her full breasts. His mouth was on her cheek, moving along the curve of her jaw, his breath warm on her neck. His hand strained the thin material of her dress. When he finally spoke, his voice was a low whisper into her bare shoulder.

"My wife is watching."

4

ANGEL sat cross-legged on the wood floor in the tiny living room of her fifth floor walk-up apartment. Clippings from newspapers and magazines were spread all around her. She couldn't stop grinning. They were all about her!

In the two weeks since the movie's premiere, her wildest dreams had started to come true. She was definitely on her way to stardom. Every review said she stole the movie from Sophia Moro. Sophia had to be going insane with all the remarks about how old and faded she looked next to the exquisite young Angel Concelli. And the media were begging Angel for pictures and interviews. She had been photographed flashing her thigh at the Colosseum, revealing ample cleavage at the Forum, looking demure at St. Peter's, like a schoolgirl at unpretentious coffee bars, chic on the Via Veneto . . . And the public kept demanding more. She had already received twelve hundred fan letters. Twelve hundred people had actually sat down to write her!

She cursed that bastard producer, Aldo Guerritore. The small print on her contract included a clause stating that she had to make her next five films for him. Which meant she had to turn down the offers pouring in from the Hollywood talent scouts who were particularly thrilled when they discovered her flawless English. Not that Americans were offering her leading roles—no Italian starlet is that lucky—but some of the parts were in major pictures. Aldo had finally promised that when she finished his next movie—which started filming in three days—he would think about loaning her out to an American producer. But he was the one who would get rich on the deal. Her paltry salary would remain unchanged.

"Slavery," she had spat at Aldo.

He had smiled placidly. "Remember, Angel, I'm the one who discovered you, who gave you your big start. Show some gratitude. Why don't you think of me as your father?"

"Because my father wouldn't have made me suck his goddamned cock!" she had screamed before storming out of his office.

But a lawyer she consulted told her she might as well shut up and finish the movies as quickly as possible. "Take some consolation from the fact that Aldo Guerritore isn't known for his painstaking, artistic productions. His movies take about three weeks to make."

It was only a slight exaggeration.

She picked up the script for the one she was starting on Monday. At least she was the star this time, playing a beautiful young woman who marries a wealthy but elderly family friend for security and comfort after the sudden death of her parents. But, restless and unsatisfied, she takes up with the virile, young chauffeur. A situation that—after considerable humping—ends in tragedy. Angel yawned and flicked through the pages randomly, reciting bits of dialogue.

"Oh, Paolo, we mustn't, we mustn't! . . . My darling, you're the only man in the world for me . . . No, no, Giorgio, put the gun away! . . . Why must I always bring tragedy to those I love the most . . ."

Angel threw the script across the room. It was trash, but trash that would help her career. Lingering scenes of her disrobing in the back of a limousine, in a haystack, in the pantry, in a meadow.

Someone banged on her door.

"God, not more presents," she moaned, pulling herself to her feet. She yanked down the long cotton shirt that was all she was wearing. Since the night of the premiere Gian-Carlo Cassieri had deluged her with gifts. Flowers first, then, when that didn't work, expensive clothes, jewelry, even, the day before, the keys to a red Ferrari that was waiting downstairs—an unusual sight in the seedy neighborhood where her two-room apartment was. She had refused everything, scrawling Go to Hell! across the accompanying cards.

On the night of the premiere party he had looked as if he wanted to kill her when she had pulled free, slapped his face, and run away. She had gone home without saying good-bye to anyone. She couldn't bear the thought of bumping into his wife. Angel shuddered as she remembered Cassieri's hands on her body while his wife stood at the window watching them.

The knock was repeated. She sighed as she opened the door. "Tell Mr. Cassieri—"

His arm lashed out, forcing the door to remain open. "Tell me what?"

She stepped back, shaken by the force of his presence. He was even more handsome than she had realized on the dark terrace. A magnificent animal, in a silk shirt open at the neck and tailored gray pants, he was hard to resist. He hadn't shaved. Without wanting to, she imagined his rough beard against her skin, her nipples rubbing against his broad, bare chest.

As if he had read her mind, he smiled with the confidence of someone who usually got whatever he wanted.

But he wasn't going to get her. Quickly composing herself, she answered coolly, "Tell him that Angel Concelli is not a whore."

He raised his eyebrows. "She isn't?" His voice was insinuating.

Her face flushed as she remembered kneeling between the knees of Aldo Guerritore. But things were different now. "Don't you read the papers, Cassieri? I'm a star now. A star only fucks for love."

He stepped inside the room and kicked the door shut. "Then fall in love with me, Angel."

His words surprised her. What did this game have to do with love? Her heart was beating fast.

The arrogance had left his face. His voice dropped to a whisper. "I keep thinking about you." His words came slowly, as if she were forcing him to make this confession. "I can't sleep. I stay awake in my office until dawn. I think of touching you, of taking you in my arms." His eyes moved from her disheveled blond hair down her slender body to her tanned legs. She knew he was imagining making love to her.

She could imagine it too: her long legs around him, her hands sliding across his broad shoulders, his face only a fraction of an inch from hers as his mouth searched hungrily for hers.

"Your wife . . ." she whispered.

His eyes held hers. "What about my wife?"

"She . . ." Angel cleared her throat. She didn't know what to say. "I didn't like her watching us."

"She's not watching us now." He took a step toward her. She held out her hand to stop him. They both waited for her decision.

Angel knew she had to have him at least once.

Her hands moved to her hips. In one easy move she yanked off the loose shirt. She stood naked in front of him, conscious of her own beauty. "Now it's your turn," she said.

But he was on her already. For two weeks she had been trying to forget how good he felt. She tore at his clothes, wanting to equalize them.

As the two of them fell to the floor amid the newspaper clippings, she remembered him stepping out of the shadows the night she became a star. From now on, everything in her life was going to be exactly the way she wanted it.

5

"ANGEL, Angel, Angel."

Retreating into the bedroom where she had spent the previous night, Stevie huddled in one corner of the small sofa. She covered her ears to dull the sound of the insistent chanting outside the window. Her face was sweaty and tear-stained, her arms and legs were scratched and bruised, and her throbbing ankle had started to swell.

Thank God two policemen had finally come to her rescue. They had rushed her away from the hysterical crowd that had trapped her in the square and returned her, by police car, to the Contessa's apartment. The two young officers were curious but polite. Although they stared at her on the way to the apartment, they didn't ask questions. She wouldn't have known what to answer.

But somehow the crowd had managed to follow her. They filled the piazza outside, chanting in unison. She had pulled the thick curtains shut, but nothing could stop their voices.

Who was Angel?

She heard a noise. It was inside the apartment and coming closer. They had broken in!

The bedroom door swung open.

She cried out in terror, covering her face with her hands.

"Get out of here!" she screamed.

"Every time we meet you're so rude to me."

She sighed with relief when she recognized the voice she had first heard in bed the night before. She lowered her hands and looked at the man in the doorway. "I'm so glad it's you."

His grin was boyish. He was nothing like the fat, bald man she had conjured up. His cinnamon-brown hair, unruly and in need of a trim, framed a handsome tanned face with an open, easy charm. His body was as lean and sexy as she had remembered. In his mid-thirties at most, he had to be considerably younger than Toni's mother.

"A much better greeting," he said. "The maid telephoned me about your predicament. May I come in?"

"Of course." She didn't care how embarrassing their first encounter had been; she was overjoyed to see someone she could talk to. Since he was the Contessa's boyfriend, she felt she could trust him.

He sat next to her on the couch. Then he leaned back, unbuttoned his tan corduroy jacket, and stared openly at her face. "The resemblance is amazing."

"Who is she?" Stevie asked.

The sound of the chanting crowd—"Angel, Angel, Angel"—seemed to rise up.

"*Was.* An actress. Angel Concelli died last week. Italy is still in mourning. And—" He held out his hands. "You appear. Looking like her ghost."

"But I've never heard of her."

He shrugged. "Sometimes goddesses are a local phenomenon. And she was young. She would probably have become an international star if she'd lived. She was in movies." He gave a slight twist to his mouth, indicating that they weren't significant movies. "Why does the public worship one person and not another? I don't know. But Angel was—" He waved his hand, searching for the right words. "Beautiful, of course, but that isn't enough. Vulnerable, tough, fascinating, magnificent. Adjectives cannot possibly do her justice."

"Then how could she have looked like me?"

He laughed, a rich, relaxing sound. "If you were a more sophisticated woman I'd think you were searching for a compliment. You are very beautiful. Not the same way as Angel, I admit. But the difference isn't in the features, the bones. Angel knew she was beautiful. You don't. And that made her more beautiful. The day you discover your charms you will become a very formidable woman." He grinned at Stevie's crimson blush.

To change the subject, she asked, "When will the crowd go away?"

"Eventually, word will spread that you're not Angel. And they'll have to get on with their lives. It'll probably be a week at most."

"A week!"

He smiled at her reaction. "It might speed things up if you issued a statement to the press."

"The press?" She stared at him. She couldn't imagine doing anything of the kind. She was Stevie Templeton, a nobody. "What would I say?"

"To tell you the truth, the resemblance is so strong I find it hard to believe you aren't related to her. Are you sure you don't have any relatives in Italy? Cousins? Which reminds me. We haven't introduced ourselves. Our meetings have been too dramatic for such social niceties. I'm Domenic Funaro. Nick."

"Stevie Templeton. With absolutely no relatives in Italy."

"You should contact your parents," he recommended. "There might be something they've never mentioned to you. An aunt who ran off with some wild Italian. A story they considered unsuitable for a nice young girl."

"My mother died when I was a baby and my father ten months ago. But they were both only children. Like me."

"Then I suppose all you can do is issue a short statement saying the resemblance is merely a coincidence. People will bother you

28

for awhile. But they'll lose interest once the initial shock is over. Right now they want to think she is alive. You feed that fantasy."

Stevie shivered. She didn't want to feed anyone's fantasies, and certainly not those of a mob. It was eerie to think of someone with her face. "Do you have a picture of her?"

He rose to his feet and left the room with an easy, relaxed stride. A moment later he returned carrying a newspaper. Stevie took it from him. The headline was huge.

È Morta.

Half the page was taken up by a blurred photograph of an old woman talking to a policeman, the body of a nude woman in the background. Stevie turned the page.

She choked back a sob at the face in the photos. Angel Concelli seemed to reach out, larger than life. She was beautiful, and yet she was remarkably like Stevie. Stevie a thousand times better. With her cascading blond hair, luminous eyes, wide, sensuous mouth, she was a star, a goddess.

Stevie looked at every photograph, several pages dedicated to Angel Concelli. Some were cheesecake, others portraits. In every one, the camera loved her. But there was something seductive about her, something that pulled you in, made you want to touch her, to know her, to become her . . .

Stevie understood the chanting mob. She understood why they needed her.

She thrust the newspaper back at Nick. "Take it away." Her hands were trembling. "If I look at it any longer I'll go mad."

"Stevie, being chased by that mob must have been a terrible shock for you. You have to try to relax."

"How did she die?" Stevie asked.

He sighed and looked down at the front page of the newspaper. "It's very complicated. But it was probably suicide."

"Probably?" Stevie leaned forward to look over his shoulder. There was a small photograph near the bottom of the page of Angel with her hair covered in a scarf, sitting in a car with a strikingly handsome man in a three-piece suit. She looked desperately unhappy; the man's face was closed and angry. Stevie read the caption. Angel and Gian-Carlo Cassieri.

"The politician? Isn't he running for prime minister of Italy?"

"He prefers to say that he is willing to serve in whatever manner the people wish," Nick replied dryly. "But yes, he is running for prime minister. The election is in less than two weeks."

Stevie skimmed through the article that accompanied the pictures, but most of it was a fawning tribute to Angel's beauty and charm. The death was attributed to suicide, an overdose of pills.

"Why did you say *probably* suicide? And what connection did she have with Cassieri?"

Nick folded the newspaper and put it beside him on the couch. "There have been rumors, gossip in the cafés, that the whole story of her death hasn't been disclosed. But I don't know anything. And Cassieri? It took guts for the paper to print that picture. Especially on the front page. It's probably the only photograph of them together, except at parties, premieres, things like that. But there's been talk about the two of them almost as long as there's been talk about Angel. EARLY ON IT HELPED Cassieri's career. It made him look potent and attractive, the man who could win the heart—and body—of the magnificent Angel Concelli. But at the same time people, hypocrites, as usual, expected a married man with children to be discreet."

"Why do you say it took guts for the newspaper to run the picture?"

"Gian-Carlo Cassieri is a very powerful man. Lately, Angel had become a hindrance to him."

"Why?"

He smiled. "Why, why, why. I can't answer all your questions. Does it matter? Yesterday you'd never even heard of Angel Concelli."

She looked down at the photograph of Angel's body sprawled on the rumpled bed. Someone should have had the decency to cover her with a sheet. "Because . . . now that I've seen her, when hundreds of people are chanting her name when they look at me . . . I'm curious. I feel . . . drawn to her."

Nick leaned forward. He put his hand on hers. His fingers were cool. "Stevie, please, you're tired, you need to sleep. You've been through a nightmare. We can discuss this tomorrow. For now, take my advice. Just relax and—"

He frowned. "What's that?"

Voices could be heard outside the bedroom door.

The door flew open and two men rushed into the room. They were dressed almost identically in ill-fitting gray suits and dingy white shirts. The young maid came running in after them.

"Signore Funaro, I'm sorry. I tried to stop them."

The smaller of the two men stepped up to Stevie. He was thin, with pockmarked skin and small, knifelike features. The large one remained in the doorway. He wiped his pink sweaty face with a large handkerchief.

Stevie turned to the man in front of her. His eyes were cold and blank. He stared at her for a moment before he spoke. He chose English for her benefit, pronouncing each word slowly and carefully in a colorless voice. "I am Paolo Garelli of the Rome police department. My colleague, Giovanni Maltesta, and I would like to question you about the death of Angel Concelli."

6

THE young maid set the tray of drinks down on the table. Stevie gave her a weak smile. "Thank you, Maria," she murmured.

Nick poured a large brandy and handed it to her. "Drink all of it. That's your lawyer's orders."

Stevie grinned at him over the brim of the huge glass. "You were magnificent."

As soon as the police officer had announced his intention to question Stevie, Nick had turned on him and shouted in a thousand Italian words a minute that a physical resemblance to a famous person was not a crime, and if they persisted in harassing Stevie he would contact the American consulate and create an international incident, which would prominently feature both officers' names.

Surly but cowed, the two men had finally departed.

"Why would they want to question me?" Stevie asked now, as

the warming brandy went to work on her tense muscles. Nick poured himself a glass of water.

"If I were in their shoes I'd want to question you too, if only because hysterical crowds are following you. It would be reasonable for the police to demand some schedule of your expected activities so they can prevent rioting. But their curiosity must go beyond that. Given the striking resemblance, they assumed you were related to Angel. They thought you flew in when you found out about her death. They wanted to know if you'd been in contact with her lately, if you had any information that could help their investigation, and so on. To tell you the truth, I doubt those two are really with the police. They probably work for Franco Uccellini, one of Cassieri's people. He likes to know everything that's going on, especially if it concerns Cassieri."

Stevie rubbed her forehead. It was all too much for her. She gestured at the window. The crowd's chanting continued unabated in the piazza outside. "The neighbors will want me to leave."

He laughed. "Don't worry about the neighbors. Or the police, or anyone else. I asked the maid to bring in some of Toni's things. Your clothes have suffered quite a beating."

She looked down at the torn, sweaty dress. It was only the second time she had worn it. She remembered picking it out in downtown Boston to wear on her flight to Rome. That seemed a thousand years ago.

"Sleep is the best thing after an upset like yours," Nick continued. "You should lie down."

Stevie sipped the brandy. Her mind was spinning; she couldn't hold a thought. The chanting grated on her nerves. But the alcohol—which she had never had a head for—was doing its job. Her eyelids were getting heavy. Nick was right, she needed to sleep.

Suddenly she remembered something she had wanted to ask him before the police had interrupted. He smiled when she looked up at him. His friendly face made him very approachable.

"Did you ever meet her?" Stevie said. "Angel?"

His smile disappeared. He rose abruptly and walked over to the window. Pulling the heavy curtain back a fraction of an inch, he peered out at the grieving crowd.

"Yes," he said finally.

She waited for him to continue.

He cleared his throat, still staring at the people in the street. "Once. At a party. I only spoke to her briefly. She was . . ." He ran his fingers through his thick hair, then tried again. "Every woman in the room wanted to change places with her. I mean literally. I think if you had asked each one if at that very moment she would have given up her whole world to become Angel Concelli, she would have said yes."

He stopped. His eyes were still on the crowd. Or on his memory of Angel.

Stevie swallowed. She didn't know if she wanted to hear more. But they couldn't leave the story half told. "And the men?" she prompted, giving him permission to tell her.

"The men?" His voice was harsh, a strange mix of desire and suppressed rage. "Every man wanted to make love to her right then, on the spot. Love isn't the word. I'm being polite. They wanted to possess her mystery, to destroy it, and make her just like everyone else." He shook his head. "But it wouldn't have worked. Not with Angel Concelli."

Then, as if shaken by the violence of his own words, he turned to Stevie. His eyes were tense.

Stevie slumped back on the couch. She felt insignificant, as if the large brandy glass in her slim hands carried more weight than she did.

Nick's eyes relaxed. "All the men but me, little one," he added quietly. "She wasn't my type at all. Now it's time for you to get to bed."

THE silence woke her. Stevie lay with her eyes closed for several minutes, afraid to face reality. The chanting had finally stopped, but nothing else had changed. She was thousands of miles from home, caught up in a confusing, frightening situation, her only guide a man who had, on their first meeting, proved himself to be an opportunist.

She took several slow, deep breaths to calm her jagged nerves. It didn't help. But there was one solution. The perfect solution, which would take her away from this nightmare forever.

A plane to Boston.

Beautiful, familiar Boston. Home. She could get a job in an office, take some evening courses, stay up late talking to Toni about clothes and boyfriends and the latest movies. There would be no surprises, no hidden terrors, no crowds of people grabbing at her, tearing at her clothes, screaming, chanting . . .

Angel.

She slipped out of bed and pulled on the robe that Maria had left at the end of the bed. The newspaper was still on the couch. Sitting down, she spread it out in front of her on the small marble table, then slowly turned the pages, studying each picture of Angel Concelli. What was it about this woman? Was Stevie succumbing to the same spell that had apparently afflicted most of Italy? But she had never been intrigued by celebrities before.

Yet Angel wasn't just another celebrity. She had Stevie's own features. Stevie's unruly blond hair that she tied back in a desperate, often doomed, attempt to control it. Stevie's own body, small boned but well developed. And yet, on Angel everything was different. Angel was magnificent. Stevie was ordinary. It had to be more than the clothes and makeup, although they were part of it. Not for what they did, but for what wearing them told you about Angel. Stevie couldn't imagine decorating herself like that. Wearing clinging, gold lamé gowns, brief satin slips, exquisite spike-heeled sandals, ropes of jewels sparkling on her neck, gold sequins on her eyelids. She would feel like a child in her mother's clothes.

But they belonged on Angel. Angel was the grown-up woman little girls long to be. The one they wait and wait to become, until they discover when they're forty that they've somehow missed out on the transformation, that wrinkles and middle-aged spread have followed directly upon pimples and baby fat. But it wasn't just the dresses and cosmetics. There was Angel in a plaid flannel shirt and jeans, her hair pulled back in a pony tail, her face scrubbed clean. She was a vision. She was sex itself.

Stevie felt as if she were disappearing, fading into the wallpaper, destroyed by Angel's image. How could she ever look at herself in the mirror again? Angel's ghost would taunt her for the rest of her life.

She flung the paper onto the floor, wishing she had never seen it. She had a sudden, stupid urge to go out and spend all her savings on clothes and jewels, to pay a Roman beautician a small fortune to make her gorgeous.

Sighing, she picked up the newspaper again and smoothed out Angel's crumpled image. "At least I'm alive."

Her voice startled her. Then she realized why she had spoken out loud. She needed to prove she was alive. She needed to feel the blood coursing in her body, her heart pounding, another beat, another second of life. That woman, her double, was dead. She studied the blurred picture on the front page. The naked corpse, stretched out, helpless. She wished she could enter the room and cover the poor exposed girl.

Poor Angel. How had it happened? How had that magnificent woman come to such a horrible end? She was only twenty-three. What misery had made her gulp down the contents of a bottle of pills, passing on a nation's obsession like a relay runner's baton to a thin shadow, a cowardly woman from Boston, Stevie Templeton.

Although Stevie didn't know the details of Angel's life, she suspected the rumors of murder resulted from the almost unbearable pain of the truth. Who wanted to believe that a woman who seemed to have everything, a woman loved by masses of people, would end her own life? It was easier to believe that she had gone out screaming and kicking, greedy for more time. If such a woman couldn't be happy, then who could?

But in the end, murder was even more unthinkable. Who could have killed an angel?

Stevie got up and walked to the window. She was restless; the crowds had made her feel like a prisoner in this opulent apartment.

The piazza was deserted. Its emptiness was jarring after the tumultuous activity of the day before. The sun was just rising; they must have gone home to sleep. But if she ventured out, she risked being trapped on her way back.

While she leaned against the window, a lone car, a black Cadillac, turned into the piazza. Slowly it moved in a half circle and then came to a stop directly below her. A uniformed chauffeur stepped out, walked around the car, and opened the back door. An elderly woman in black, her face covered by a heavy veil, stepped onto the pavement. She spoke briefly to the chauffeur. Then her erect figure moved toward the apartment building.

Stevie knew. Somehow she knew that the woman was coming to see her. She pulled Toni's robe tight and ran barefoot to the main entrance. It seemed an eternity before the doorbell rang. Stevie pulled the heavy door open.

The old woman stepped into the hallway. Her face was still covered by the heavy black veil. Then, her wrinkled hands bare of rings, she slowly raised the veil.

She had been crying; her cheeks were still wet. Her brilliant blue eyes studied every inch of Stevie's face. Finally she held out her hands. Stevie took them into her own and squeezed them tight.

"Stephanie," the woman cried. "Thank God you're here."

7

A HALF dozen pastries were on the coffee table in front of the television set in Angel's cluttered dressing room at Cinecittà Studios. She dipped her finger into the whipped-cream topping on one of them and then slowly licked it clean.

"Angel, you're doing that to drive me insane!" Aldo Guerritore snapped. The producer was sitting beside her on the vinyl-covered couch. "And put some more clothes on." He dragged his fingers through his sparse gray hair. "I can't believe this! I'm alone with the most beautiful woman in the world, and I'm begging her to get dressed."

She crossed her bare legs. "If this damned negligee is considered adequate as a costume for your movie, then I don't see why I can't wear it in mixed company."

Filming on her second movie had just finished for the day, and she and Aldo were in her dressing room watching Gian-Carlo Cas-

38

sieri's televised rally in Rome's Piazza Venezia. The politician was one of four candidates for the leadership of his party.

"Angel, you're going to make me pay for that blow job for the rest of my life! Every time I see you, you try to make me hard and then you won't let me do anything about it."

She scooped up the rest of the pastry's whipped cream. "You're not paying for the blow job, Aldo, but for telling every damned guy in Rome about it." Her voice hardened. "You even told Gian-Carlo."

Aldo held up his hands. "Can't a man brag? Is that so unreasonable?"

"Shut up. I want to hear the rest of the speech."

Angel focused her attention on the television. The press had forecast that no more than a few thousand would attend the rally, but the commentator estimated the crowd to be over a hundred thousand. With a private television station covering the speech, countless more would be watching at home and in coffee bars.

Gian-Carlo stood in the middle of the stage, speaking without notes. Tall and elegant, he wore a dark blue suit, the jacket open, his tie loosened at the neck.

"We're cynics, we Italians," he was saying. "We don't trust any politician. And with good reason. We've seen enough of them come and go."

His approach—a man addressing his friends in a local coffee bar—was working with the crowd.

"So how can I convince you that I'll be any better than the rest? How can I even know myself until I'm tested in the fire? We all have illusions about ourselves. Every young boy thinks he'll grow up to be the greatest lover in the world. And every girl thinks she'll become as beautiful as—Sophia Loren, Angel Concelli, Laura Antonelli. But it doesn't happen, does it?"

"He's gorgeous," Angel said, licking the cream off another pastry. "And he even mentioned my name."

Gian-Carlo hesitated before the silent crowd. His voice dropped to a whisper that managed to reach every ear. "I can't promise I'll be better. No one comes with a guarantee, not a politician, not a husband, not a wife. But I can tell you this—" He leaned forward and gripped the podium. "I love Italy. All of it. All the hundreds of bits and pieces that were fused into this country. It disgusts me when I see our country ridiculed by the rest of the world. Our people have accomplished more than any other civilization since the dawn of time. In my heart, in my soul, I respect, I honor this country. I don't see easy answers or simple solutions to our problems. I can't, I don't have a simple mind. But although I see enormous difficulties, sacrifices we'll all have to make, I also see—"

He searched their faces, as if he needed to confirm his belief. "I see greatness! I see—"

Aldo groaned. "This is such shit. There's nothing worse than fake sincerity." He got up and turned the sound off.

Angel sighed. "I wish I could fuck him right there in front of all those people."

"And in front of Lucia Cassieri."

Angel's face fell. "Thanks, Aldo. I needed that."

"I'm sorry, *cara.*" He patted her bare knee. "But you can't pretend she doesn't exist. They've been married for years. Gian-Carlo's had hundreds of mistresses, but he always goes home to Lucia. And not just because of his career. He wants to. They're two of a kind. Like Macbeth and his wife, if you ask me."

"Come on, Aldo," she said. "You've never read *Macbeth.*"

"And you have? I read a synopsis once. I was thinking of making a movie of it with Marcello Mastroianni and Laura Antonelli. It turned out to be all wrong for them, though Laura would have been good in the sleepwalking scene. That girl has a great body. I was going to have her do it nude. You can get away with more when it's art. It's the only chance cultured people get to see tits."

Angel ignored him. Her eyes were still on the television set. As the camera scanned the wildly cheering crowd, she realized that Gian-Carlo would probably achieve his dream. The party leadership now, a steady building of popular support, plenty of deals and compromises with the other parties, and then, perhaps in an election or two, prime minister. What could stop him? Certainly not principles or ideology: he wasn't a fanatic. The man she was in love with could actually be prime minister someday. And, no matter what Aldo thought, he couldn't live without her. They had been seeing each other every day for almost four months.

Gian-Carlo was on screen again. He gestured for someone in the audience to join him. The crowd roared its assent.

Lucia Cassieri stepped onto the stage. Gian-Carlo took his wife's hand and pulled her close to him. Together they received the crowd's adulation.

Aldo touched Angel's wrist. "I'm sorry I set you up with him, Angel."

She clenched her jaw. "I'm not."

"He'll never leave her, Angel. Never."

She shrugged, pretending she didn't care. "I get the best part anyway. Who wants to wear a hat and gloves all the time?"

Angel watched the regal dark woman calmly acknowledge the crowd. Gian-Carlo couldn't prefer that cold fish. Their marriage was dead. Or else Lucia would have confronted them on the terrace instead of watching from the shadows.

She glanced at Aldo. "What did you tell him about me? What made him come to the party after the premiere?"

Aldo squirmed. "Angel, please, men say such stupid things to each other. Don't make me repeat it."

Gian-Carlo was hugging Lucia. Colored dots embracing another set of colored dots. She could turn off the set and make it disappear. "You might as well tell me," she said quietly. "I'll only imagine something worse."

"I said you were beautiful, of course." He cleared his throat. "And available."

She raised her eyebrows. "Available? Come on, Aldo."

"All right. I said you had great tits and you were an easy lay. And that you had the most beautiful face I'd ever seen. But I sold you short, Angel. What I didn't tell him was how special you are. I didn't see it myself. I've spent the last twenty-five years surrounded by gorgeous women with fantastic bodies. Even my wife is gorgeous, although I have to pay a fortune to a plastic surgeon to make her look as if the embalmer did a great job. I didn't see

41

your magic, Angel, not till the premiere. I needed the audience to show it to me. Will you forgive me?"

"Will you let me out of my contract?"

"Angel, *bella,* what's five little pictures? This one's almost finished. Give me a break, okay? And I promise you, you'll do one in America soon. I'm listening to offers already."

Gian-Carlo and Lucia were leaving the stage. Bodyguards held back the surging crowd. They were rushed into a dark blue limousine.

"I'm not sure I want to leave Italy."

Aldo snorted. "Don't throw away your career for him. He wouldn't do it for you. And he'll never leave Lucia."

Angel jumped up from the couch and ran behind a screen that blocked off one end of the dressing room. Yanking off the sheer negligee, she tossed it onto Aldo's lap and pulled on tight jeans and a black sweater. She came out from behind the screen, slipped her feet into a pair of high-heeled sandals, and looked around the messy room for her purse.

"Where are you going?" Aldo asked, although he already knew the answer.

"Gian-Carlo said he'd come by my apartment after the speech."

"He won't come. Not tonight. Not after that."

Angel stared down at the overweight producer.

"Aldo, you found out at the premiere that I was special. I knew it as far back as I can remember. Gian-Carlo knows it too. He's not stupid. I'm just as important to him as his career."

Aldo shook his head. "His career is everything. It's his life."

"Well, he can have his career and me too."

"Don't be naive."

She shrugged, but to the producer she looked less confident than usual. Aldo continued gently. He was genuinely fond of the girl and wanted to correct the damage he had done by bringing the two of them together. "He won't come tonight. Go out dancing, go to a party. Let me buy you a nice dinner. Don't be alone."

"He will come." She tossed back her loose mane of blond hair. "He has to. For himself, not for me."

Snatching up her purse from a cluttered table, she opened the door and then looked back over her shoulder to deliver her parting line. Earlier in the day Aldo had watched the director teach her the same move, the same expression, for a major scene in the movie.

She dangled her shoulder bag from one finger. "After that speech Gian-Carlo's going to want the best fuck of his life. You think he'd go to Lucia for that?"

ANGEL stared at the luminous clock on her bedside table.

Four thirty-two.

Four thirty-three.

He will come.

Four thirty-four.

She rolled onto her back and pulled a pillow over her face. A split second later she flung it across the room.

The phone rang. She grabbed it. "Yes?"

"I'll be there in twenty minutes."

People were talking in the background. She heard music, laughter, someone arguing. "I'm ready and waiting, darling."

She slumped back down on the bed and smiled. She ran her hands over her body. When dawn hit Rome, he would be in *her* bed, not Lucia's.

The jangling phone slashed through the silence again. This time she waited before picking it up.

Please don't say no. Please don't change your mind.

On the sixth ring she raised it to her ear. "Yes?"

There was only silence. She knew enough not to say his name. "Who's there?"

The silence continued.

Someone in the city was holding a phone, listening to her breath. She imagined Lucia, that impassive face, her long red nails curved around the receiver.

"Fuck you, bitch," Angel whispered. Then she slammed the phone down and got out of bed. She needed to prepare for her lover's arrival; his wife would have to find her own way to kill the time till morning.

8

"ANGEL Concelli: The Complete Story."

Angel cleared a large space on the rickety wood table in her living room. Then she opened the Sunday edition of *Il Messaggero* to its feature story. She picked up her half-finished cigarette and started to read the public version of her twenty-one years.

"Nice work, Aldo," she muttered. She knew her producer had paid six writers to create it. "One day you should try investing this much money in a movie script."

ANGEL: THE EARLY YEARS

The beautiful two-year-old slipped her chocolate-covered fingers into her mother's cool hand.

"Please, Mommy," she begged, her lovely face radiant with excitement, "can we go to the movies again tomorrow? When I grow up I want to be a big movie star, just like Sophia Loren. She was so pretty in that picture."

Angel's mother smiled down at her daughter. She knew the little girl was very special. Although Rosalie Concelli was already working at two backbreaking jobs to support herself and her child, somehow she would manage to find the money to take Angel to all the movies she wanted. Her daughter's happiness would always come first to Rosalie.

Angel pressed her fingers into her ears, but it wasn't enough to kill the drunken laughter of her mother and the strange man. In the small alcove where she slept in the one-room apartment, she huddled under the blanket and prayed for sleep, or even death, to blot out the scene that was taking place.

"Jesus, Claire, you're a great broad. I really love your tits."

"Yeah? Well you've got a pretty good body yourself, Jack."

"What's a nice American girl like you doing in Rome?"

"*Cherchez l'homme,* honey. Fifth or sixth one back. But I like it here. American blondes are popular this season."

"What do you do for money? Do you have a job here?"

Claire's already slurred words acquired a bad Southern accent. "'I have always depended on the kindness of strangers.' And a little waitressing when the kindness dries up. I'm a practical woman."

Jack's laugh was cruel. "Just don't expect too much kindness from me. I've only got about twenty bucks to spare."

"Twenty bucks is twenty bucks."

"Are you sure your kid won't hear us?"

"Angel? Sleeps like a log. Come on, let's pull out the couch."

"You're really ready, aren't you? You're one hot broad."

"You're going to find out just how hot I am, Jack. Now get out of your clothes before I have to rip them off."

Angel started to cry, but her mother and the man she had picked up were already making too much noise to hear her . . .

THE article in *Il Messaggero* next described a touching bedtime scene in which little Angel asked her mama where her papa was.

45

"He's in Heaven," her saintly mother told her. "He died in a car accident just before you were born."

"Why did he die?" the little girl asked.

"Because he was such a good man that God needed his help," Rosalie said, bending forward to kiss her precious daughter goodnight.

"Who's my daddy?"

Claire squashed the remains of her cigarette on the cracked plate. The butt was caked with red lipstick. She glanced around the nearly empty restaurant where they had gone for a cheap spaghetti dinner.

"Daddy?" she said then. "Couldn't you at least use *father* or some other less guilt-ridden term?"

Angel was fourteen. It had taken her a long time to work up the courage to ask this question. Her biggest fear was that her mother would say she didn't know, that she had only been able to narrow it down to the men of that particular season, which would probably make him one of ten or twenty. Angel shut her eyes for a second, hoping it would be one of the men her mother claimed to have actually married.

"Don't sit there with your eyes shut, as if you expect me to announce it was an entire soccer team. Sluts are made, not born, Angel darling, as you might find out yourself in a few years, especially with a body like that."

Angel felt the burn of vomit rising in her throat. She coughed, choking it down, then pulled a crumpled tissue from her pocket and held it to her lips.

Claire sighed. "I guess I have to tell you." She stared at her chipped red nail polish. The lines around her mouth deepened. Her usually attractive face looked old and bitter. "He had a wife and kid so I never told him about you. I just went away. Believe it or not, it seemed like the honorable thing to do."

The older woman fell silent, her eyes glazing over as she relived her memories. Angel waited for her to continue.

Suddenly, Claire's face softened. She looked vulnerable and

young. Angel realized with something very close to fear that there must have been a time when her mother had had all the normal dreams of a life that offered love and a real home.

Claire jerked herself back to the present. Her expression hardened into its usual mask as she stared defiantly at the daughter she had raised alone. "If I'd told him about you, he would have just offered me fifty bucks toward the abortion. I can give you his name, but he wouldn't want to see you. You'd mess up his tidy little life. Christ, he probably doesn't even remember me."

As the words pounded into her consciousness, Angel grabbed the edge of the table. She thought of all the nights she had lain awake praying that her father would suddenly appear and tell her how much he loved her, how much he wanted her, how happy they would finally be. She hated Claire with a loathing that was strengthened by the realization that her mother had been young once. If Claire was human, then she had no excuse; she should have known enough to lie. Why couldn't she have said he was dead? It would have hurt less.

Forcing herself, Angel managed to shout out her final questions, forgetting the other people in the restaurant. "So why didn't you take the money, Claire? Why didn't you have the damned abortion? Why didn't you save me from all of this?"

And Angel sat impassive as her mother began to sob, the tears streaking the thick makeup that no longer disguised her age.

"Has it been that bad, honey?" Claire finally asked, searching her daughter's face for some kind of reassurance. "Haven't we had a few good times together?"

The fourteen-year-old girl stared with disbelief at her mother. "It's been hell, Claire."

"THE world is full of clichés, Aldo," Angel whispered as she closed the magazine. "You should have asked me what the truth was. I'd have given you a better story than your damned overpaid writers."

9

THE afternoon sun was hot and harsh in the bright, spacious room. As her hostess rose to shut the curtains, Stevie studied the frail figure wearing a simple black silk dress with a long loose string of pearls.

Not that frail, Stevie observed when she saw the strength with which she pulled the curtains. But the mysterious woman was at least seventy and possibly older. Despite the sadness and pain in her face, it was obvious that she must once have been a great beauty. The years had been kind to her: her skin was surprisingly smooth and her pure white hair was twisted into a dazzling crown of small precise braids. Stevie trusted her. That was why she had, at the woman's quiet insistence, accompanied her to this lovely small villa on the Via Appia Antica outside of Rome. During the drive neither of them had spoken. The woman had held Stevie's hand in silence, squeezing it as if she were afraid Stevie would slip away. She had fought, sometimes unsuccessfully, the tears that filled her eyes.

Now the elderly woman returned to sit in a large chair across from Stevie. A maid, a handsome woman in her early forties with a competent, quiet manner, slipped into the room and placed a tray of tea and cakes on a low table.

"I hope you will excuse my eccentricity," the old woman said. "I lived in England for some time and never got over the habit of taking tea in the afternoon. I love Italy"—she gently waved her hand, and Stevie knew she was indicating all the splendor of Italy, caught even in this modest but beautifully preserved villa—"but I never would have expected to end my life here. For most of my days, I couldn't have imagined such a thing. But, finally, I think of it as my home."

Stevie took the dainty flowered teacup that was offered.

Sitting back, the woman stared at Stevie. Her intelligent eyes, although kind, examined every detail of the young American's features.

"You don't look exactly like her."

Stevie sighed. She had been hoping that Angel Concelli had nothing to do with this, that this person had come for Stevie herself—Stephanie Templeton. Ever since her father's death, she had had moments when she was filled with such a powerful longing for family that she actually wondered if there could be long-lost relatives she had never met. Although she recognized that her feelings stemmed from the loneliness and fear of being the last member of her family, that insight didn't make them disappear, and this woman's dramatic arrival had stirred her hopes.

"Your face is slightly longer," the woman continued. "And you're thinner, of course. About five pounds. Although she lost weight near the end. And she dyed her hair a shade lighter when she started acting."

Stevie tapped her fingers on the china saucer, irritated by the ghoulish inventory. She considered getting up and walking out of the villa, but the woman was old and obviously harmless. Another minute of polite patience followed by a gentle but firm good-bye would only cost her a little discomfort.

"You resemble your mother more than she did," the woman continued, leaning forward for a better look. "It's more than the features. Angel appeared strong, but she wasn't. The poor child needed more than the world could ever give her. You're different. You're a survivor, like Claire."

Claire.

Stevie's hands jerked up. Hot tea splashed onto her dress, scalding her thigh. It hurt. This wasn't a dream.

Her mother. *Claire Templeton*.

The woman pulled herself to her feet. "I'll show you." She went to an antique desk in one corner of the room and returned with three photographs. Stevie's hands trembled as she reached for them.

The first one was of Angel. It wasn't like the newspaper photographs, which, except for the blurred snapshots taken by paparazzi, had the calculated air of an actress presenting an image to please her audience. This was Angel laughing naturally, a dripping slice of pizza in her hand, her beautiful face free and joyful. She looked no more than sixteen.

"It's my favorite picture of her," the woman said, tears filling her eyes again. "It was so unusual for her to be happy—to want only what she had at that moment."

Tears also came to Stevie's eyes as she looked at the laughing girl. The same young woman who had been presented as a naked corpse in the public press only a few days earlier. "I'm so sorry she died," Stevie whispered.

The woman cleared her throat, struggling to maintain her composure. "Look at the next one."

Stevie slid out the second photograph. She gasped. It was Claire Templeton. And she was at least forty years old. Stevie shut her eyes. Her mother died when she was one year old. When Claire was twenty-five. With her eyes still shut, Stevie made herself remember every detail of the pictures she had seen of her mother. The lovely pale face, the large eyes, the wide full mouth. Stevie's face. And Angel's.

She looked at the photograph in her hands again. Claire Templeton. But older. Years older.

Quickly she pulled out the last photograph.

It was Stevie. It had been taken on her twelfth birthday. She was standing in front of their small house in Boston in a pink cotton party dress. She remembered her father holding the camera, shouting "Cheese."

With shaking hands, she spread the three photographs out on the table in front of her.

"It's the last photograph I have of you," the woman said. "After I received it, your father started returning my letters unopened. I understood why. You were reaching the age when you would ask too many questions. He wanted to protect you. But God, I hated him for it." She took a deep breath. "I lost my daughter, I didn't even know that Angel existed. And I was cut off from you."

The elderly woman knelt at Stevie's side, her black silk dress rustling in the quiet room. She took Stevie's hands and squeezed them, just as she had at the Contessa's apartment. "Don't leave me, Stephanie. I've already lost Angel. You're all I have now. Come live here with me. Please."

Stevie stared into the woman's eyes. Then she turned back to the three photographs on the table. "Who are you?" she whispered.

"I'm your family, Stephanie. I'm your grandmother." Her voice broke. "Please don't leave me all alone."

She held out her arms. Stevie hesitated. She looked down at the photograph of her mother. The wide blue eyes frightened her. She wanted to destroy it, to protect her memories. Instead, she opened her arms and accepted the older woman's powerful embrace.

10

At the window of the library in Contessa Barberini's apartment, Stevie watched the cars speeding through the small piazza. She had been afraid that the mob would return, but, except for several policemen, everything seemed back to normal.

"I don't know how she did it," Stevie said to Nick. She had found the attractive lawyer working there in his shirt-sleeves when she had returned from the old woman's villa. "She said she'd keep the crowds away, and they're gone."

"What did you say her name was?" Nick asked.

"Ellen Brenner. Brenner was my mother's maiden name. But both my grandparents died before I was born. Or at least that's what my father told me."

"Come sit beside me. Let's go over this carefully."

Grateful for his interest, Stevie joined him on the brown leather couch. She was comforted by the books lining the walls, and she started to relax. Safe in this room with Nick, she didn't have to worry about any startling new revelations that would turn her world upside down.

"She says she's your grandmother, and that your mother lived longer than you were told? And that Angel was your sister?" Nick asked.

"Half sister, since she couldn't possibly be my father's daughter. I can only assume that my mother and father were divorced, and he decided I'd be better off thinking she was dead. But I can't believe he'd do that. We were so close." Stevie shook her head. "Yet Ellen Brenner has those pictures. The one of me had to come from my father. No one else could have given it to her."

"You didn't ask her any more questions?"

Stevie shook her head. "I couldn't. She needed to rest. The conversation was very hard on her. She sent me back here to get my things. And just before I left she promised to stop the crowds from pestering me." Stevie turned to him. "Nick, she really expects me to move in with her. Her driver is waiting downstairs. I don't know what to do."

"If we assume she's telling the truth about being your grandmother—and I don't see why she would lie—wouldn't you want to stay with her?"

Stevie shrugged. "I don't know. I'd love to have family again. It's strange. When I saw her get out of the car, somehow I knew she was coming to see me. Not Angel, me. But everything is happening too fast. What I'd really like is time to think."

Ever since her conversation with the old woman, memories of her childhood had been surfacing, memories of the years she lived alone with her father in their small house. When he had died of a heart attack ten months ago, she had felt desolate and abandoned. There was no one else she could completely trust the way she had trusted him. Had her troubled fantasies of mysterious relatives been true? But in many ways, that was more frightening than being alone, because it meant the man she had trusted so much had lied to her. And not just any lie. He and her mother had played a monstrous, evil trick on their own child, and then he had lived that lie every day of his life.

Tears slid down her cheeks. It couldn't be true. But the pictures, and Angel's likeness—

Nick's comforting arms slipped around her. He pulled her gently against his chest. Her cheek touched his crisp white shirt. "Don't worry, *cara*. Everything will be clear in the end."

The steadying beat of his heart was soothing. She was so glad she had someone to help her. The tension was disappearing from her body as his hands gently stroked her bare arms. She felt his lips on her hair.

Then his finger was under her chin. He raised her face until her eyes met his. "Stevie," he whispered. His lips grazed against hers. He looked at her again to see if she wanted him to stop. She hesitated, then raised her mouth to his. He kissed her slowly, his mouth soft and comforting. His arms tightened around her.

Suddenly a shrill voice filled the apartment. "Nicky! Nicky! Where are you, darling?"

Stevie broke out of the embrace and turned toward the open door. Spike heels clicked across the marble floors.

"Stevie," Nick whispered urgently. "Stevie, listen to me. I want you to know that—"

Contessa Laura Barberini appeared in the doorway. Stevie had never seen anything like her. The woman's black-and-silver-streaked hair was frizzed out in a fashionable version of the Bride of Frankenstein's hairdo. Her skintight black leather pants and braless red sweater revealed a figure that belied her forty-eight years. Rhinestone-studded sunglasses hid half her tanned face.

She put her hands on her hips and pouted. "Nicky darling, where's my kiss?"

Nick hesitated. Then, smiling stiffly, he got up and lightly pecked her cheek.

"Is that all I get after three weeks away?" the Contessa complained. She grabbed Nick's tie and yanked him closer, then planted a loud kiss on his mouth. Nick wiped off her scarlet lipstick with a handkerchief before turning back to Stevie.

"I suppose I should make the introductions." His face was flushed. "Laura Barberini, Stevie Templeton. Your daughter's best friend."

The Contessa clapped her hands. "Stevie, you're the reason I'm here! All my friends have been phoning me about this mysterious double of Angel Concelli who's attracted thousands of people to my apartment on some kind of bizarre pilgrimage. And there I was in Portofino, missing all the fun. I came back as soon as I heard about it."

Laura thrust her sunglasses up into her mass of hair and stepped closer, squinting. "My God, it's true. You look so much like her. You'd think Toni would have mentioned it."

Nick spoke up. "Toni's been in Boston for over two years. Angel's first movie would have come out after she left Rome."

"Oh, Nicky, you're so clever. I don't know what I'd do without you." Laura waved Nick forward and slipped her arm around his waist. "Isn't he wonderful, Stevie?"

Stevie gave a weak smile. *Wonderful* was hardly the word for a man who had first tried to seduce her before they even exchanged names, and who had been making a pretty successful second attempt until his lover interrupted him. Thank God the woman had made plenty of noise instead of slipping in quietly.

"You must tell me everything that's been happening since you arrived in Rome! I love gossip. I couldn't believe Angel Concelli died. Nicky, do you think Gian-Carlo had her murdered? Or did his wife do it? Or maybe it was that nasty man who works for him. This is so exciting, with the election only ten days away."

Nick shrugged. "I don't know any more than I read in the papers."

"Nicky, that can't be true. You always know everything. You don't want to tell me because you think I'll be on the phone to all my friends." She giggled. "And you're probably right."

Being in the same room with the couple made Stevie uncomfortable. There was no mistaking their relationship; the Contessa couldn't keep her hands off Nick. At least it settled the question of where she would stay.

Stevie stood up and smoothed her borrowed dress. "I'm sorry to leave so quickly, Contessa, but I'm afraid I have to be going."

Stevie glanced at Nick. She expected him to look guilty, but his steady dark eyes held hers as if he had nothing to be ashamed of. Angry, Stevie looked away. Even if they were one of those sophisticated couples who tolerated infidelity, he shouldn't assume she wanted to be part of their little game.

"But where are you going?" the Contessa cried.

"I . . . I have an invitation to stay with someone. I think it's best."

The Contessa frowned. "But I thought you didn't know anyone here."

"It's a long story, Laura," Nick said. "I'll explain later."

"If you don't mind," Stevie said, "I'd like to borrow this dress. It's Toni's. The airline mislaid my luggage, but Maria told me they called and said I could pick it up tomorrow morning. I'll send this back to you."

"Keep it, keep it," Laura said. "And take anything you want. Toni will never wear them again. Is Maria the woman you're going to stay with?"

Stevie was puzzled. The Contessa thought Stevie was going to stay with her maid?

Nick's booming laugh suddenly erupted. The two women stared at him. "Through some misunderstanding," he explained, "Stevie has been convinced that the maid's name is Maria. She's been going through so much we haven't had the heart to correct her."

Stevie felt her face turning red. She hated being made fun of by this pair who were obviously too sophisticated for their own good. "I'm sure she introduced herself as Maria," she said, defending herself.

Nick grinned. "Americans always think that all Italian maids are named Maria, and all French ones Marie."

Getting angrier by the minute—as soon as she was out of the apartment they would probably have a big laugh about her reaction to finding Nick in her bed—Stevie pressed on. "But surely her name must sound something like that. I'm not an idiot. What is it?"

He smiled. The Contessa was already giggling.

"Sally," Nick finally supplied. "Around the time of her birth, her mother liked to watch 'The Flying Nun' on television."

His answer was so unexpected that Stevie finally succumbed and smiled at her mistake. "I'll apologize to her before I go. If you'll both excuse me, I'd better get my things now. And thank you for everything, Contessa." After a moment's hesitation, she shook Toni's mother's hand warmly. The woman might be a little extreme, she realized, but she was also generous and friendly. And there was a good chance she didn't even know about Nick's infidelities.

Ignoring Nick, she walked toward the door. She was being rude, but she didn't know what to say to him. Although he had been a great help to her, she couldn't excuse his attempt to seduce her while the Contessa was on holiday.

When she reached the library door, she heard Nick's footsteps behind her. He grabbed her arm and swung her around to face him. She looked down at the floor to avoid his eyes. She was uncomfortable standing this close to him. Her life would have been much easier if the Contessa's helpful boyfriend had been fat and bald instead of sexy and good-looking.

"Stevie, are you sure you really want to go?" Nick said in his seductive, low voice. "Why don't you stay here for a few more days and think things through? You can visit this Ellen Brenner without promising to live with her."

Stevie shook her head. She couldn't imagine sharing an apartment with Laura and Nick.

"I'm going."

He sighed with exasperation. Then he pulled a white card from his pocket and held it out. "My office number is on here, and I've written the one for this apartment. Call me if you need me for anything. Call me if you just want to talk. Call me if you *don't* want to talk and tell me that. Promise?"

To be polite, Stevie took the card and slipped it into her purse. "I can't imagine what I'd need you for," she snapped.

"Ah, you're always flattering me." Smiling, he reached out and pushed a lock of hair back from her eyes. His voice dropped to a

57

whisper. "The more I see you, the more I come to realize that you're even more beautiful than Angel was. See me again, *cara*. Please."

Stevie glanced at the Contessa, who had sprawled on the couch and kicked off her sandals, then turned back to Nick. "Thank you for everything," she said coldly, "but I really don't think I'll be needing you again, Nick."

As she walked away, she knew he was standing in the doorway watching her leave. Then the Contessa's shrill voice summoned him back. "Come here, Nicky, and sit beside me. You promised you'd tell me everything that happened while I was away! Now don't start keeping secrets from me. You know I hate it when the men in my life do that."

11

ANGEL held out her arm to block Aldo.

The two of them were about to enter an enormous palazzo where a society party was in progress. Angel had been invited on the strength of advance word on her second movie, which was opening in a few weeks.

"Tell me the truth," she said. "Is there any chance that another woman will look better than I do?"

Aldo, grateful for the excuse, looked her over. She was wearing a skintight black dress, the front cut low enough to expose all but a sliver of each breast. Her hair was swept up in a mass of curls, and her only jewelry was a pair of diamond earrings Gian-Carlo had given her a few weeks earlier. She spun around. The back of the dress dropped below her waist. Elbow-length black gloves enhanced the overall effect of a spectacular, nearly naked body.

Aldo shook his head. "God was very kind to you, Angel."

She snorted. "Like hell he was. Up to now, anyway. But come on. I'm about to conquer Rome."

Angel walked calmly to the top of the staircase that led down into the crowded room. She paused for a moment, pretending to adjust her gloves. Aldo was impressed. She really knew how to make an entrance. By the time she looked up, the room had fallen silent and all eyes were on her. Turning to Aldo, she smiled sweetly and took his arm. Together they slowly descended the wide marble stairs, Angel stepping confidently in her black high-heeled sandals.

Before they had reached the bottom of the stairs, Angel had spotted her target about halfway across the crowded room. "Introduce me to Gian-Carlo," she whispered.

Aldo followed her eyes and saw him standing with his wife and several other people. He groaned. "Since you've been bragging all morning that his back is covered in scratches from your nails, I suspect the two of you have already met."

"Come on," Angel said, pulling him forward.

"Angel, not when he's with Lucia. You'll be making a big mistake. You've got to follow the unwritten rules."

"Like hell I do," she snapped. "You don't understand. He's crazy about me. He spends every night at my place. The poor bastard has to get up at three in the morning to go home to change."

"But he always goes home," Aldo said.

Ignoring his advice, Angel moved swiftly toward Gian-Carlo. Aldo felt sorry for the girl. She was about to meet her match. Even Catherine the Great would have been cowed by Lucia Cassieri.

Gian-Carlo and Lucia were talking to two members of the government and Gian-Carlo's principal assistant, Franco Uccellini, a man Aldo considered a cold fish. The group also included one of Italy's leading industrialists and a handsome thirtyish man in a dapper blue suit. Three other women—wives or girlfriends—completed the group, but Aldo knew Angel didn't care about them.

"Gian-Carlo, Lucia, I'd like you to meet Angel Concelli. And this is Daniele Valante, the industrialist, Dr. Uccellini, Gian-Carlo's assistant, and— Hey, aren't you Ron Blackstone?" Aldo asked in English.

The handsome American who had starred in a series of internationally successful spy movies modestly bowed his head.

"I love those Brad Bradley movies!" Aldo cried.

"I understand your performance in your new movie is impressive, Miss Concelli," Daniele Valante said, eyeing her breasts. He leaned dangerously forward, trying to determine if her nipples could be spotted.

Angel smiled. "Why thank you, Mr. Valante."

Across from her, Gian-Carlo cleared his throat. It was the moment she had been waiting for. When her lover would show his wife that he found Angel Concelli more attractive than he could ever find her. Angel turned to meet the eyes of the man who had sworn he couldn't live without her.

His face was polite but blank, as if it really were their first meeting.

While Angel stared at him, Lucia spoke. The woman's silky deep voice had the knowing, proprietary edge a wife uses with her husband in a crowd.

"My husband and I haven't had an opportunity to see your movie, Miss Concelli, but we understand that you're a very talented young lady."

Gian-Carlo smiled lovingly at his wife before turning back to Angel. "Yes, I was telling my wife just the other day how lucky we are to have so many bright young actors and actresses for our film industry."

Angel looked directly into Gian-Carlo's eyes, trying to force him to acknowledge their feverish, violent lovemaking, which lasted for hours at a time. No matter how late his meetings and social obligations went on, he always arrived at her door desperate for her love.

But he continued to look at her as if she were a stranger.

Finally, she tore her eyes away from Gian-Carlo to study her rival. Lucia was less attractive in person than in her photographs. Her pale skin was marred by deep lines at the corners of her

61

mouth and eyes. Her dramatic makeup—black lines around the eyes and bright red lipstick—seemed clownish, although Angel had to admit it was perfect for television and newspaper photos. But the woman was still beautiful. A magnificent bitch, Aldo had called her, and he was right.

There were no sign of recognition in Lucia's eyes, either, of that night when she had watched Gian-Carlo and Angel on the terrace. But, although their affair was a well-kept secret, Angel was certain that Lucia knew about it. The woman was definitely the kind of wife who would find out where her husband was spending his nights.

Angel looked back at Gian-Carlo. His eyes were still blank but polite. She wanted to rip open his shirt and show everyone the scratches she had gouged into his skin while delirious with pleasure. She wanted to scream, "I did this!" The intimate, knowing looks exchanged between Gian-Carlo and Lucia added to her humiliation. They were treating her as if she were a little girl with a crush on a man who merely found her amusing.

She felt Aldo's hand on the small of her back and knew he was warning her not to make a scene. He had predicted that this would happen. Aldo was right more often than she wanted to admit. She knew a messy scene would hurt her more than Gian-Carlo or Lucia, but she wasn't going to let them get away with this. She had a point to prove, and before the night was over she was going to prove it.

Angel swiftly took in the expressions of the men who were facing her. The two politicians were dripping with lust, but they were too timid to do anything. The tall thin man with wire-rimmed glasses, introduced as Dr. Uccellini, looked at her with pure hatred. He was probably the kind of person who thought orgasms should be illegal. But the industrialist was still eyeing her breasts, and the actor had managed to slip closer to her, a smile playing at the corners of the handsome American's mouth as if he were imagining the two of them in bed.

The industrialist had money and power, and Gian-Carlo knew him well. The actor was younger and much more attractive. Which one would make Gian-Carlo more jealous?

It was close, but Angel decided on the actor. Especially since he looked as if he'd be the better lover. Men obsessed with breasts were usually only fun for the first ten minutes of lovemaking.

"Tell me, Ron," Angel said, turning to face the actor and excluding the rest of the group, "don't you wish you had more opportunities for serious work? You're so wonderful in the films you do, and you're obviously a very talented actor. It must be frustrating never to get the chance to use the full range of your talents."

Ron gave a slight bow, acknowledging the compliment. "I would like to stretch my wings a bit. But, at the same time, I'm happy that my films bring so much pleasure to people. I think it's wrong to assume that if the public likes something it must be worthless."

"No shit," contributed Aldo. "That's my opinion exactly. I'm always saying, if the people want tits and ass, then they've got every right to see tits and ass. Who are we to act superior just because we might prefer something else—like thighs or cunts or something?"

Angel and Ron both laughed, while the others in the group stared uncomfortably at the floor.

"Aldo," Angel chided him, "actors can handle talk like that, but you're embarrassing all these stodgy politicians." She and Ron exchanged a complicitous glance as they tried to suppress their giggles.

"Angel," Ron said, holding out his hand, "may I have the honor of introducing you to some of my friends? Though I'm sure everyone else will hate me for stealing you away."

"I'd love to," Angel gushed, taking his hand. "But what about—" She glanced pointedly at the slim young woman in mauve chiffon who was obviously Ron's date.

"Sheila will be fine. Won't you, Sheila?" Ron added, his eyes issuing a warning to the young woman who, until Angel's arrival, had probably considered herself pretty and vibrant.

With a brief wave of her hand to serve as a good-bye, Angel allowed Ron to lead her away from the group.

Two hours later, two hours spent charming the cream of Roman society with Ron Blackstone at her side, Angel allowed herself another look at Gian-Carlo. She had flitted past him several times, but now that the party had settled down, they were both stationary. He was a few yards away in a group that included his wife and Franco Uccellini. Angel judged them to be just outside of hearing distance. She was alone with Ron, lounging beside him on a tapestry-covered couch in one corner of the large room.

Angel curled up closer to the actor and slid one bare leg over his knees. "Tell me more about your career," she whispered, pouting seductively for Gian-Carlo's benefit.

"You're sure you're interested?" he asked.

"Of course." She ran her fingers down his red silk tie. "Tell me all about your triumphs."

"Well, my first big break was *Raiders of the Sun*. It wasn't a great role, but I had two really good scenes. Did you see it?"

Angel murmured a reply that could have passed for assent. "What came next?" she breathily asked.

"*Duel at Midnight Corral*. Even though it did okay, I wasn't right for a western."

"God, no. You're much too sophisticated. Who would want to get dust all over a face like yours?"

He smiled, nodding. "Yeah. Then I got the second lead in *Broken Hearts*. I played the lead's best friend, but all the reviews said the heroine should have picked me. Right after that I was signed for *The Deadly Exocet*, and I've been playing Brad Bradley ever since. Despite the fact that I've played him in five pictures so far, I still manage to find something challenging in the role every time. You know what I mean?"

Angel whispered that she understood. She raised her knee so that it was only an inch or two from his crotch. God, she thought, didn't this man care about anything except his career? She should have gone for the industrialist. At least he'd be fondling her nipples while he talked about his latest big deal.

Quickly checking to make sure that Gian-Carlo was still watching, Angel leaned forward, pressing her breasts against Ron's arm. "You're great in love scenes."

He nodded. "And it's hard, too. Some of those actresses are real dogs up close. It takes a lot of talent to make it look real."

Angel nearly gave up. Was he gay? Why had he spent the whole evening with her if he wasn't interested? Forcing herself to look as if he had just made an amusing and risqué remark, Angel gave a deep seductive laugh.

"You're really getting to be a big star here, aren't you, Angel?" Ron asked, finally getting to the point. "You don't mind if I tell my press agent we met here and hit it off, do you? It would help the Brad Bradley movies in Italy, and it would improve your career chances in the U.S. Maybe we could even get someone to take a few shots of the two of us together."

Angel didn't notice Gian-Carlo until he was leaning over her. His sudden presence took her breath away.

"Come with me," he whispered. "Now."

Angel forced herself to give him a slow, relaxed smile, her fingers still holding Ron's tie. "Is it important? Ron and I were just discussing our . . ." She hesitated, then winked at Ron. "Careers."

Gian-Carlo grabbed her wrist. "Now."

Angel coldly held his eyes. Beneath his anger, she saw hunger and fear. She had won.

She dropped Ron's tie, slid her leg off him, and stood up. She gave the actor a friendly wave. "Patriotism calls," she explained.

Gian-Carlo led her directly to a door at the side of the room. When she looked around, she saw that Lucia was watching them. Angel grinned.

Lucia's face froze. She touched Dr. Uccellini's arm and whispered something to him.

Gian-Carlo grabbed Angel's hand and pulled her through the door and along a hallway. He stopped at a small bedroom where some of the guests had left their coats. Once they were inside he locked the door. The only light came from a small dim lamp.

"What will we do if people need their coats?" Angel asked playfully, fingering a sable that was on one of the two beds.

"They can freeze. Don't play with me, Angel. What's going on between you and that stupid actor?"

"What's going on between you and that stupid wife?"

He was angrier than she had ever seen him before, but he had to pay for humiliating her in front of his wife.

"Lucia's getting old, isn't she?" she continued. "Dry and wrinkled. Is her cunt dry and wrinkled too?"

He took a deep breath. His fists were clenched. "You're talking about the mother of my children."

"If she's so goddamned wonderful, then why is your back covered with scratches from my nails?"

Abruptly he turned to face the wall and pressed his forehead against the silk covering. His black suit pulled tight across his broad shoulders.

"I can fuck anyone I want," Angel whispered. "You have no claim on me. Not as long as you live with her."

He didn't answer her.

"That's only fair!" she yelled.

He turned to face her. She stepped back, startled by the pain in his dark eyes.

"Fair!" he screamed out. "What kind of idiotic talk is that? How can you use a word like *fair* to describe people like us? Fairness is for peasants. My God, Angel, don't you understand anything? *I have to have you.* I have to worship you, devour you, I need to possess you completely, body and soul. And you talk about fairness? Fairness between Angel Concelli and Gian-Carlo Cassieri?" He held out his hands, his fingers outspread, as if he wished he could physically force her to understand.

"Angel, don't you understand what's happening between us? Look at us! This isn't a courtship, I'm not going to come to some civilized arrangement with Lucia and then present you with a nice diamond ring. If you think that, then you don't know yourself any more than you know me. We aren't like other people. Ours is a contest between giants. I have to own you and I know I never will. I crave you, I am you, God, sometimes I even wish you were dead so that I could be free of you, except I know your memory would cannibalize me until I was destroyed too. And if that's not the kind of love you want, Angel, I don't know what you can do. Because it's too late. It's too late for both of us. If we'd never met . . ."

He shook his head, dismissing the thought. "No, we had to meet. Don't you see? We had no choice. Even if we had started out on opposite sides of the planet, we still would have found each other. And the same thing would have happened. This pain, this agony, this incredible, useless love. But for God's sake, don't expect *fairness* from me. Ask for my soul, but don't ask me to shrink down to the level of peasants."

Angel was trembling. She didn't know what to say. He was frightening her. He was too dramatic. Although she was obsessed with their love too, she didn't want it to be what he had described. She needed more than passion. If he was right, then what would their future be? Where would she be in six months, or a year, or in ten years' time? Wouldn't there be days when she wanted someone to like her as well as love her, someone she could be bored with, someone to listen to music with on a rainy Sunday afternoon?

"I don't know," she whispered, feeling the heat of their angry, frightened bodies in the small room. She felt as if she were smothering; she wanted to smash the window open with her fists. "I don't know if that's what I want."

Without warning, Gian-Carlo took her arm and pulled her over to the mirror. In the dim light she could see them side by side. A commanding, attractive man and a beautiful, glamorous woman. He moved behind her. He caressed her bare shoulders, then ran his hands down over her breasts to her hips. A possessive gesture. He slid his fingers back up to her shoulders and tugged at the thin straps on her dress. Slowly he lowered the top, exposing her full breasts. Their eyes met in the mirror.

"What do you want, Angel?" he said finally.

She couldn't speak. She couldn't think.

"Now," he said. "Make up your mind now."

His hands were still on her. His touch seemed to burn her skin. She knew he would demand everything from her. And give her less. She looked into the mirror and saw two ordinary people, a little more attractive than most, perhaps, but frightened and lonely like everyone else.

She blinked and looked again. This time she saw two giants. He was right. They belonged together.

He was waiting. She took a deep breath, then glanced over her shoulder at the pile of coats on the two beds.

"Is your wife's coat here?" she asked.

He hesitated. If he said no she wouldn't be able to tell if he was lying. But he told her the truth.

"Yes."

"Which one?"

He pointed to the ankle-length white mink cape stretched across the nearest bed.

The top of her dress still around her waist, Angel walked over and picked up the luxurious thick cape. She rubbed it over her face and bare breasts before flicking it out and letting it fall to the floor. Then she stepped onto it, digging into the skins with her stiletto heels. She eased her dress down to her ankles and kicked it away. Naked except for her long black gloves, she slowly stretched out on Lucia Cassieri's fur.

Someone knocked on the door. Angel stared at Gian-Carlo, waiting to see what he would do.

"Is someone in there?" a woman's strident voice called out. "I need my coat." The woman tried the door knob.

Gian-Carlo slowly undid his tie and then tossed it into the corner where Angel's dress had landed. He began to unbutton his shirt. Angel smiled, watching him closely.

The door rattled as the woman tried to force it open.

Gian-Carlo stripped his shirt and jacket off. His fingers moved to his belt.

"Take your time," Angel murmured. "After all, we're not peasants."

12

THE wind raised the long lace curtains and held them suspended in the dark room.

In the next room Angel shivered in her sleep.

A sudden violent gust whipped out the curtains. One of them wrapped around an empty wineglass and knocked it to the floor.

The crash pulled Angel awake. She sat up in bed, indistinct images of flight and pain flooding her mind. She rubbed her eyes to free herself of the disturbing dreamworld.

The apartment was very cold. The wind was whining in the next room. She slipped her legs over the side of the bed and slowly pulled herself up. Half asleep, she stumbled into the living room. The window was wide open. She shook her head, angry at herself for forgetting to shut it. In the moonlight she noticed the pieces of shattered glass. Stepping carefully around them in her bare feet, she tried to close the window. It was always hard to shut. She yanked hard on it before it gave way and slammed down. Still not fully awake, she returned to her bed and huddled under the blankets.

She was balanced on the edge of sleep when suddenly she remembered that she *had* closed the window before she went to bed. The memory had too many details to be false. Just before she went to bed she had recalled that the temperature was expected to plunge during the night. So she had gone back into the living room, turned on the light, and pulled the heavy window down, cursing when she ripped one of her long nails.

She touched the broken nail.

She imagined a dark figure climbing over the windowsill, walking softly through her living room, moving into the bedroom, standing over her while she slept . . . She pulled the blankets up to her chin. He could be crouching in the shadows, waiting. Who?

But the apartment felt empty. The only sound was her own ragged breathing. But if she was wrong, if he hadn't—

She was too terrified to move. Silently she counted to ten, and then to twenty, trying to concentrate on the pointless endeavor, while her nerves felt stretched and raw and tears bit at her eyes and throat. She had to act, but like someone fleeing in a nightmare, she couldn't make her body obey her mind's command.

Finally, with a violent force of will, she lunged for the telephone and pulled it onto her bed. The clock's glowing red digits told the time. Three-fifteen. She could call—

The police. And tell them what? That a hysterical actress had forgotten to close her window?

Gian-Carlo? She didn't even have his home number.

In a lonely life, Angel had never felt so lonely before. There was no one. Except—

Too desperate to think about the consequences, Angel carefully dialed a nearly forgotten number.

It rang for a long time. She closed her eyes and imagined the nearly empty villa, the ringing echoing through the rooms. A light would be switched on. A hand would finally reach for the receiver.

"Yes?"

Overcome with relief at the familiar voice, Angel started to cry. "Grandma?" she managed to whisper, holding the phone to her wet face. "Grandma, it's Angel. I'm frightened. Will you help me? Please?"

There was a long silence. Angel waited patiently in the cold room, refusing to hang up.

Finally the clipped and precise words came. "Please do not disturb me again. You are not my granddaughter. Angel is dead."

For a long time Angel held the lifeless telephone, sobbing in the dark, terrified that someone would step out of the shadows and make her nightmare come true.

13

"ANGEL is dead." Ellen Brenner's luminous blue eyes filled with tears. "I actually said that to her. I will have to live with that for the rest of my life."

The cloudless sky was beginning to darken over the lush garden behind the villa. Seated in a white wicker chair, Stevie studied the gracious woman who claimed to be her grandmother.

Ellen Brenner was obviously not poor; a villa with two live-in employees—Stevie had been introduced to the husband and wife team of chauffeur/handyman and cook/maid who ran the household—required quite a bit of money to maintain. And the villa's furnishings and artworks, as well as the generous selection of books, were those of someone who was cultured and educated.

Stevie couldn't remember her father saying anything about her maternal grandmother except that she was dead. Although she had often wondered about her family history, Stevie had respected his reluctance to talk about the past, believing that her mother's death had created a painful block.

And now this woman was insisting that not only was she Stevie's grandmother, but that Claire herself had lived longer than Stevie had been told and was Angel Concelli's mother.

The old woman pulled out of her painful reverie and resumed her story.

"I remember that night. I was alone here. Gina and Rafael were visiting relatives in Parma. The telephone frightened me. I have few friends. And then I heard Angel's voice asking for help. I was amazed. I detested the girl. I had told her that I never wanted to hear from her again. That, as far as I was concerned, she was dead. And so that was what I repeated to her. Then I hung up. I lay awake until morning, wondering if I had made a mistake. But the last time I had seen her was still so clear in my mind. And . . . I suppose I would have had too much pride to call her back, even if I had known her number."

Once again, Stevie had a sudden urge to return to Boston, to leave all this behind. Her father and mother were dead. She had never even met Angel Concelli. Why should she allow their ghosts to disturb her peaceful life?

The old woman smiled apologetically. "I know I'm confusing you, Stephanie. After our meeting this morning, I told myself to start at the beginning and tell you everything in the order it occurred. But I find it difficult. Please make allowances for an old woman who has lived a more unpleasant life than she would have liked. I promise I'll try. You have to be told these things, and I'm the only one who will do it."

Part of Stevie wanted to beg the woman to keep her secrets to herself. She was afraid of the truth. The past was the solid ground she walked on—each unexpected revelation was a crack in the earth. But it was already too late to stop. If she didn't learn the answers now, the questions would eat away at her for the rest of her life.

Stevie leaned forward. "I was told that my mother died when I was a baby."

Ellen Brenner nodded. "It was a terrible lie. But I understood why your father decided to tell you that, at least back when it all started. The truth hurt him so much. He found out everything so suddenly. It must have been a terrible shock. Late one night, without warning, your mother announced that she was in love with another man. An Italian, he called himself an artist, but he was—in plain English—a bum. She was flying to Italy with him the next day. If it hadn't been for you, I think your father would have killed himself that night. He told me later how he sat at the kitchen table till dawn, a razor blade in front of him, wanting to open his wrists. But he couldn't forget you, innocent and vulnerable, sleeping quietly in your room."

Stevie grasped the arms of her chair. It couldn't be true. Like a small child, she cried out the first thing that came to her mind. "Why didn't my mother take me with her?"

Ellen took a deep breath, but she couldn't bring herself to speak.

Stevie whispered the only explanation that wouldn't destroy her universe. "Was it my father? Wouldn't he let her?"

Ellen's voice dropped to a whisper. "This is a very important moment in both our lives, Stephanie. I am at a crossroads." She looked into Stevie's eyes. "I can lie to you and save you pain. Or I can tell you the truth and hurt you. For reasons you will understand when you know the complete story, I feel I must tell the truth. The pain will be horrible. But I have learned the damage that lies can do. I try only to tell the truth now. No matter what the consequences are." She paused, waiting for Stevie's reaction.

Stevie took a deep breath. But there was really no choice. Without realizing it, she had left her options behind when she stepped on the plane to Rome. "Tell me the truth," she said.

Ellen nodded. "First, I will have to digress. I was always proud of Claire. She was beautiful, witty, a vibrant, exciting person. Your father was a good, solid man. I thought they were a perfect match. He would give her stability, she would bring excitement to him. Of course, now I know that life doesn't work like that. He wanted to turn her into a less adventurous person; eventually she hated him for being dull and ordinary. I don't know when she started seeing other men. I doubt the Italian was the first. Perhaps he wasn't even the first one your father suspected. But he was the first one your father had to acknowledge, maybe even to himself. I have learned that people have an almost infinite capacity to lie to themselves. We perform so many mental tricks to help ourselves believe the lies. It is fear, fear of loneliness, of change, of pain. And, despite their problems, your father loved many things in his marriage and his life. He loved having a beautiful wife, an adorable baby, that little house in the suburbs—which Claire saw as a prison. I think at first Claire wanted to keep that life too. Perhaps as an anchor. She could risk more, knowing that she always had somewhere to return to. I don't know if she loved your father—that is not a judgment other people can make about a marriage. I'd like to believe that she loved you, at least in her fashion. But Claire should never have had a child, she should never have married."

Ellen didn't look up and see the tears running down Stevie's face. The young woman felt as if her very existence was being negated.

"Her leaving was only a question of time. And it was like Claire to make a quick break. Not because she was impulsive. The very opposite. She tried too long to stay with him, to stay in that little house. And when she left it was out of desperation. She felt that if she didn't go that very night, she would go insane. She had reached her limit. The Italian was unimportant. A means rather than an end. Italy has its seductive powers—the liquid sun, the indigo sea, the golden earth. Good food, cheap wine, laughing people. A myth, but one with more truth in it than most myths."

As Stevie sat there in the garden, the setting sun warm on her face, a cool glass of bright red bitter by her side, she tried to make this new Claire become real in her mind and replace the one she had created to comfort herself. She had spent so many years believing in her carefully constructed fantasy of a sweet, loving woman, the perfect mother, a woman who would have turned down the apple and banished the snake from the Garden of Eden.

Not someone who would abandon her daughter and husband for a cheap affair.

Stevie suddenly felt older. Her childhood was slipping away. For the first time in her life she saw her parents as human beings instead of paragons, two flawed and lonely people, no better than everyone else.

"I didn't hear from Claire for fifteen years," Ellen continued. "She had sent me a short letter when she left for Italy. When your father decided to tell you she was dead he gradually cut me out of his life as well. I think he wanted to pretend that Claire had never existed. That you were his alone. I used to think that if she ever went back to him he would greet her with a shotgun. As you know, he was not a violent man, but he hated her, love turned sour, and that hate swirled around inside him for so long, with no release. An acquaintance in Boston sent me his obituary. I must admit I was happy that he had finally been liberated from his pain."

Stevie stared in amazement. She couldn't believe this woman was talking about her father, Matthew Templeton, that calm, gentle man who had seemed so free of demons. And yet, at that moment, Stevie knew she had been pushing certain memories out of her mind, blocking out the nights when she had awakened to hear sobs coming from her father's room, times when he had sat for hours staring into space, until Stevie had gently prodded him alert and helped him to bed. But in families—especially a family of two—members quickly learn to accept the other one's faults and eccentricities as normal.

"After fifteen years Claire wrote me a long letter. I had been living in England for some time. My husband, your grandfather, died when Claire was a baby." Ellen shook her head. "Fifteen years. Claire said she was working as a waitress in Rome. And that she was lonely and afraid of getting old. She wanted to see me. It seemed a surprisingly honest letter for Claire. I remember sobbing with relief when I read it. I had wondered so many times if she was dead, if my only child had died without my knowledge. And, being Claire, she saved the most important news for the end. *I have a daughter. Her name is Angel. I want her to meet you.*"

Ellen gave a small smile. For a second her sad eyes were filled with the wonder and relief she must have felt when she received that letter.

"I flew to Rome the next morning. I arrived at their tiny apartment on the sixth floor of an old firetrap on the Via Tiburtina. The squalor was incredible. Garbage in the hallways, filthy children covered with scabs. Like any decent mother, I would have taken the bread from my own mouth to give to my daughter. It broke my heart to know she was living like that. When I knocked on the door there was a long silence. And then I met Angel."

Ellen broke off. She reached for a lace handkerchief and brushed her eyes with it. She struggled for a moment, unable to speak.

"If you want to wait until tomorrow—" Stevie offered.

"No, no," Ellen said. "I must tell you. Since Angel's death I've been tormented by the fear that I might die without telling this. I owe Angel too much to let that happen. Someone must know what her life really was. I'm sure you've already heard a great deal about Angel's magic. Well, it wasn't apparent that day. She was exceptionally voluptuous for a girl her age. But to me, she wasn't a future Italian goddess. She looked like a Roman tart. She had on a tight sweater, ridiculously high heels, and a skirt that barely covered her behind. Her face was covered with makeup. Her hair was in one of those absurd European messes, those hairdos that make a girl look as if she just climbed out of bed. She wasn't the granddaughter I wanted. I wanted my legacy to be a girl like you, modest and well-behaved. Matthew's daughter, not Claire's. And Angel must have seen the contempt on my face. It took me a long time—too long—to realize how perceptive she was. I treated her like something subhuman. There was a lot of bigotry in it, I realize now. My little half-Italian grandchild, not as good as the all-American one. God, the obscenities we let ourselves believe. Humans have such a foul need to feel superior. I didn't even tell Angel who I was. Claire was at work. So I gave her a note for her mother with the name of my hotel. My God, I couldn't even put my arms around the girl and tell her I was her grandmother."

Ellen sighed before continuing. "Claire arrived at my hotel

alone. It's a shock for a mother to see that her child has aged, even after a long time apart. Once our children have mastered tying their shoelaces and crossing the road alone, we want to pretend they're exempt from the ravages of time, that they're immortal. My beautiful young daughter was a middle-aged woman. It broke my heart. We talked for hours that night. I never even asked her where Angèl was.

"Claire told me she had taken the name of the man she'd run away with, Angel's father, even though they'd never married. But this Concelli had died, and since then she had had to work at menial jobs to support herself and Angel. I asked her why she waited so long to contact me. She said she was ashamed. I understood that. Later it was what kept me from getting in touch with Angel, at a time when she must have needed me most. Fear of the brief discomfort of a few opening minutes makes us deny ourselves years of happiness. I gave Claire some money and told her to find a good apartment. I said I would stay in Rome to be close to her. I admired her pride and strength, raising her little Italian daughter alone, working so hard. I think I saw Angel as some kind of foster child, like those starving children in magazines, instead of my own flesh and blood."

Ellen pulled herself upright in her chair and looked at Stevie again. "There is one more thing about that night. This will hurt you, Stephanie, but you must know the truth about your mother. She didn't love you any more than she loved Angel."

Stevie frowned. Her mother had stayed with Angel and abandoned her. How could she ever imagine that Claire had loved her more?

"Before Claire left I asked her if she wanted to see the last picture Matthew had given me of you. The one I showed you this morning. Claire turned away from me. I thought she was trying to hide her feelings. I thought I knew how painful it was for her to be separated from you, how much she missed you. I put my hand on her arm. Claire, I said, take the photograph with you. She pulled away from me. I couldn't see her face when she spoke. 'It's been so long, Mother,' she told me. 'I hardly remember Stephanie. It would be like looking at a picture of a stranger. I honestly don't care anymore.'"

Stevie gasped and doubled over as a sick, violent pain ripped through her. "Stop it, stop it, stop it!" she cried, pounding her legs with her fists. "You're lying. You must be lying. My mother loved me. She loved my father. She died when I was a baby. She loved me, she loved me, she loved me!"

Stevie was barely conscious of Ellen's movement into the house. In the garden alone, miles from anything she knew of as home, Stevie fought the bitter pain of a past she hadn't known was her own life. "It's not true, it's not true," she whispered, as she tried to keep reality away, rocking back and forth like a child in her mother's arms. "My mother loved me," she whispered again, blinking back tears. She covered her face with her hands. In her heart she knew that the old woman's quiet words couldn't be denied, but this first, killing pain was too much to bear. In time she would let herself look at the truth, but not now, not here, when it cut like hot acid in her eyes.

A figure moved in front of her, blocking the sun. Suddenly she felt cool fingers on her arms, pulling her hands away from her face. She looked up. He was a shadow against the light.

"Angel," he whispered, his voice harsh with emotion.

"No," Stevie whispered. "I'm—" But who was she? Not Stevie Templeton, the young woman from Boston whose loving mother had died when she was a baby. And not Angel, the beautiful Italian girl opening a door to her cold and distant grandmother on a hot Roman afternoon. "I don't know who I am," Stevie sobbed, tears streaming down her face.

"Get out of here!"

The man's hands dropped from Stevie's arms. Stevie looked at the open door to the villa. Ellen Brenner was standing on the steps with a glass of water in her hand. "Get out of here!" the old woman repeated.

The stranger stepped back from Stevie and turned to Ellen. "I had to see her," he said.

"Leave her alone," Ellen shouted. Her voice filled the quiet garden. Angrily, she moved toward him. "You destroyed one of my granddaughters. You will not destroy this one. Get out of here now!"

Gian-Carlo Cassieri took one last look at Stevie, his eyes full of passion and need. She stared up at the mysterious, attractive man who had come to find her. But he was mistaken; she didn't exist. She felt as if she were fading like her past, as if, at any moment, she might disappear into the evening sky. She nearly reached out for his cool hand again. There was something solid and whole about him. Maybe he could help her, maybe he could tell her who she really was.

"Get out of here!"

And then he was gone, slipping into the shadows beside the villa.

14

HER limbs felt heavy and weak. Stevie rolled over in bed, wanting to go on sleeping for hours, except that sleep had been a terrifying place, where she dreamt that strangers were chasing her down long, dark corridors. Just as hundreds of hands reached out to grab her, raw fear had pushed her awake.

She groaned and decided that she might as well get up, make some breakfast, and get ready for work. She opened her eyes and peered around the dark room, searching for her alarm clock.

A terror worse than in the nightmare shot through her. She didn't know this room. And this was real; she wouldn't wake up a second time. Fighting hysteria she reached over to switch on the lamp beside the bed. She blinked at the strange surroundings.

Finally she remembered she was in Ellen Brenner's villa in Rome. There was nothing frightening about the cosy guest room. The matching curtains and bedspread in a blue and yellow floral print were reminiscent of a garden on a sunny morning. But as the events of the day came back to her she felt she really had awakened to a nightmare.

She checked her watch and found that it was nearly midnight. Although she had slept for several hours, she thought there was a good chance that Ellen was waiting for her downstairs. Quickly, she washed and, still wearing Toni's light wool dress, went down to the sitting room where she and Ellen had had their first conversation earlier in the day. Her sense of time was completely skewed; it felt like years since this woman had handed her those three earth-shattering photographs.

Ellen was sitting in a high-backed chair, a heavy white shawl pulled round her shoulders over her black mourning dress. "I hoped you would come," she said when she saw Stevie in the doorway.

Stevie moved to a chair facing the older woman. They hadn't spoken since the incident with Gian-Carlo Cassieri. Too disturbed to continue their conversation, Stevie had gone upstairs to rest. "I'm very confused," Stevie admitted. "I don't know what to think about all this. It's too much of a shock."

"You'll have plenty of time for thinking later." The old woman looked pale and tired. "But you must know the whole story first. Please, let me continue. It's very important."

Reluctantly, Stevie nodded. Her body was tense and aching after the restless sleep. But Ellen was right. She had to find out the whole story.

"When I found Claire again, I moved to Rome, to this villa. I gave Claire enough money to enable her to get a better apartment and leave her horrible job as a waitress at a dirty little trattoria. I invited them to live with me, but Claire declined. I understood. I don't think children should be shackled to their parents for life. But I saw them every Sunday. Claire would bring Angel here and we would have tea, usually in the garden, and talk. Claire told me of her hobbies, the music she liked, the books she was reading. Angel was quiet. Claire made her dress nicely for the visits, girlish clothes, pretty dresses. The child never wore makeup and her hair was pinned back. She seemed a blank to me, a nothing. I confess we ignored her most of the time. She would sit staring out at the flowers and trees. I never even wondered what she was thinking during all those hours when we chatted on. I never asked Claire about anything that might upset her—her abandonment of you and Matthew, that Roman she ran off with, why she didn't contact you after all this time. After all, you were practically an adult by then."

Stevie tried to match this information with her own history, placing Claire and Angel at this villa at the same time as she was finishing high school and going to college. But it didn't seem real. She couldn't shake the belief that her mother had died in Boston. That was reality; this rambling story had to be a disturbed old woman's bizarre fantasy. Yet Ellen Brenner seemed so sane and honest, offering confessions that seemed to hurt her almost as much as Stevie.

"You might think I was a coward," Ellen continued. "I suppose I was. But I was so desperate to have Claire in my life again, to have family after all those years alone, that I was terrified of upsetting her, of driving her away. I was willing to let our reunion, our entire relationship, be on Claire's terms. And I played that game for a year and a half."

Ellen pulled the shawl closer around her shoulders. Watching her, Stevie felt cold too, although the room was quite warm.

"And that was why I refused to believe Angel when she arrived that day. It was very early in the morning. She started banging on the door like an insane person. Gina, my maid, called me. At first I hardly recognized the girl. She was wearing tight, revealing clothes again, and her hair was in that awful rat's nest. Her makeup was smeared from crying. I remember thinking, this whore cannot be my granddaughter. She demanded a drink from Gina. I had never seen her take anything stronger than coffee before. And it was only after she was sitting down that I saw the scratches and bruises. Saw, and didn't see. Because, despite the black eye and bruised jaw and red welts on her neck, I refused to believe her story."

Ellen was shivering. She pulled the shawl tight again, although the cold was coming from inside her.

"She told me—" the old woman's voice broke, "she told me that Claire was a liar. Her words rushed out, half in Italian, half in English. I could hardly understand her. She said Claire had told me a complete pack of lies. I remember noticing that she called her mother Claire. I hadn't realized that. It is odd what the mind fixes on. She said that Claire was a slut. That she had had four husbands—or men she must have claimed were husbands because, of course, she had never divorced your father—since she came to Rome, and countless other men. 'When I was eight,' Angel said, 'she stopped making me call them uncles.' She said that was how Claire had survived, through men and their money. The jobs had only been temporary, to get her through to the next man. She said Claire only wrote me because she felt she was losing her looks and she wouldn't be able to attract men much longer."

Ellen shook her head. "Why is it so much easier to believe that your granddaughter is worth less than your own daughter? I don't know. But I couldn't believe what Angel was saying. I asked her why she had come to me, why she was telling me such filth. She was crying. She told me that her mother had brought a man home the night before. He saw Angel sleeping on the couch, and he told Claire he wanted Angel instead. He grabbed at Angel. She told me he ripped her blouse open and squeezed her breasts so hard she nearly fainted. And Claire started screaming. She ordered Angel out of the house. Angel. Not the man."

Ellen halted. She rubbed her pale forehead with the back of her hand.

Stevie waited, thinking of Angel, Angel standing in this very room, with this woman whose soul was ravaged by memories of her mistakes.

"Angel said she begged her mother to let her stay. She argued that it wasn't her fault and she had nowhere to go, no money, nothing. Claire opened her purse and pulled out forty thousand lire, about fifty dollars, and threw it at her. Angel admitted that she lost her temper then. She screamed at her mother, letting out all the rage and pain that had been building up in her. She called her mother a slut, a worn-out whore, an old hag. The man Claire had brought home was watching them. Like a stud waiting to see which bitch would win him, Angel told me. Finally Angel threw the worst insult she could think of at Claire, the one she knew would hurt the most because it was true. She said that men would rather have her than Claire, that Claire was only making her leave because she couldn't stand the competition." Tears were streaming down Ellen's face. "Claire went insane. She charged at Angel, scratching, hitting, pounding her with her fists. As soon as she could get away, Angel grabbed the money off the floor and ran out."

Ellen took a deep breath. "She ran to me."

Moved by the pain on the old woman's face, Stevie said, "You couldn't have known what the truth was. Don't be so hard on yourself. You didn't know that Claire would lie." As she spoke, Stevie realized that this Claire, this horrible woman, was supposed to be her mother. But she couldn't be. There had to be two Claires. Just as there was Stevie—and Angel.

Ellen shook her head. "I can't let myself do that. I can't give myself excuses. I knew the truth. I knew I was lying, lying because it was easier to hurt a teenage girl, a little foreigner, than risk losing my own beautiful daughter. I could handle losing Angel, but I thought I would die without Claire. And in the end, of course I lost them both. That day I was almost as cruel to Angel as Claire was. A little more generous, but then I had more to be generous with. I wrote her a check for five hundred thousand lire, about six hundred dollars. And I told her I never wanted to see her again. That she was a liar and a tramp. I said I could figure out the truth for myself—that her mother had obviously caught her with a man, probably not for the first time—and kicked her out. I remember watching her pocket the check. I told myself, if she had integrity, if she had class, she would refuse it. My God, how could I be so unfair? A teenage girl who suddenly found herself all alone in the world, and I expected her to turn down the only assistance she would get. At the same time I never questioned the fact that

Claire was willing to accept substantial amounts of money from me with barely a thank you. At the door Angel turned to stare at me. She was such a wild looking creature. Beautiful, yes, but in such an obvious way. I could see its power—at least for men— but it wasn't the kind of beauty I trusted or admired."

The old woman paused, remembering. "I've heard people say that she looked like sex. It is a difficult thing to say about one's own granddaughter, but I suppose that is as accurate a description as any. But it made me uncomfortable, and I blamed Angel for it. I attributed it to her foreign blood, and not to her life with Claire. When she turned to me at the door—the last time I saw her in person—her eyes were full of pain and frustration and anger. It hurt to look at her. She said, 'Why can't you see Claire for what she is? Why can't you see the truth? I thought you would help me.' I answered, 'I've given you a lot of money, Angel. You should be grateful for that, instead of telling me lies about your mother.' And that was the last time I saw her."

Ellen huddled in the large chair, her shawl wrapped around her. She gave a deep sigh, as if a load had finally been removed from her shoulders. And yet she seemed oddly emptied out, a shell. Stevie wondered how much the pain, the need to confess, had been sustaining her, driving her on, getting her through each day.

"What did Claire say to you?" Stevie asked. She wasn't thinking of Claire as her mother. This had to be a story about other people, about strangers.

Ellen's voice was a thin, tired whisper. "She didn't know that Angel had come to see me. She told me that she had sent Angel to a good school near Firenze. After a few months, she stopped mentioning the child altogether. But once I had heard Angel's story, it was harder to close my eyes to the truth about Claire. It was in her eyes, in her walk, in her manner. I suddenly noticed how she lit one cigarette from the butt of the last one. How she always had to have a drink in her hand. How she stared in the mirror checking every little line, applying more makeup, trying so hard to look young and attractive. And there was such a harshness about her, with her calculated lies. Telling me she spent her time rereading Proust, when she must have come to me straight from some man's bed. We saw each other less frequently. I was sick of the part I was expected to play. The generous old fool, a figure of contempt. After awhile, I gave her a lump sum of money instead of an allowance. I couldn't take the lies anymore. And yet—" She pulled the shawl tight again. "Five years later, when Angel called me wanting help, I turned her down. I had seen her first movie. She was so sexy and cheap, falling out of her clothes. I closed my eyes to her beauty and her pain. I couldn't stand it. I still needed my lies. I needed distance, thinking that would save me, when of course it only made everything worse. For me. It is presumptuous to think I might actually have helped the poor child."

Stevie rubbed her eyes. She felt both restless and exhausted. Ellen's story was spinning around in her head, raising as many questions as it answered. She wished she could get away for awhile and forget everything. Standing up, she began to pace around the large room. She felt as if the villa were crowded with ghosts—people acting out the past again and again, unable to change it, unable to show charity and love.

Her own past had been so safe and calm, living with her quiet, loving father in Boston, attending school with her friends, studying hard to become a teacher. Whores and movie stars, Roman villas and tenements, death and haunting memories, all seemed unimaginably foreign. And yet this gulf only existed because she and Angel Concelli had had different fathers; without that, their lives might have been the same, either one or the other.

Too restless to sit down again, Stevie moved to the window at the front of the villa. She pulled back the curtain and looked out into the night. Stars were scattered over the silent countryside. Cedars and pine trees swayed in the darkness. And—

A car was parked in front of the villa. A man stood leaning against it. Stevie had seen him twice before. In a black-and-white photograph, sitting next to Angel Concelli. And earlier that afternoon, in the garden, when he had placed his cool hands on her arms.

87

He was waiting for her.

He was Gian-Carlo Cassieri, a name in the newspapers, one of the most powerful people in Italy.

"What about Angel's father?" Stevie whispered.

He saw her at the window. He began to move toward the house, but like everything else, that had to be a dream.

"Was Claire telling the truth when she said he was dead?" Stevie continued, staring out at Gian-Carlo. "Or was that another lie?"

Ellen was slow to answer. But Stevie didn't notice the hesitation. Gian-Carlo Cassieri was coming closer, his eyes on her, on Stevie Templeton. She felt mesmerized, a rabbit held in a snake's gaze. And yet— He was waiting for her, coming to her.

"Angel's father was Matthew. Matthew Templeton."

Stevie nodded, watching Gian-Carlo move across the dark lawn toward her. Then the words sank into her consciousness and she spun around to look at Ellen.

"Late one night," the old woman whispered, "about a year after Angel left, Claire had too much to drink. That was when she admitted the truth. Angel was Matthew's daughter. She was your sister."

15

Two young men were feverishly repairing the hairdo and makeup of Anna Maria Poli, the hostess of a popular live afternoon talk show. Her guests were Angel, a young Frenchman who had written a novel, and a middle-aged man who was out of breath after his tap-dancing routine. "Make me more beautiful than Angel!" commanded the gaunt blonde in a red sequined sheath. Then, throwing Angel a saccharine smile, she added, "Just joking, of course, Angel darling. No one could look better than you."

When the red light lit up on the camera, Anna Maria's shrill voice switched to melodious stage tones. "Welcome back, my friends. My guests and I are looking forward to the next act just as much as you are. Their latest single is number one in North America and England, and rising fast on the charts here at home. I want you all to meet the new sensation from England, that wonderful rock group, BARF!"

Angel stared at her nails, refusing to applaud a group of un-washed louts who considered crotch-scratching showmanship.

Three young men, pale and pimply, ambled out to the center of the orange-and-yellow set. The studio audience, mainly bored housewives, responded weakly to the flashing applause sign. The lead singer belched into the microphone and checked that his fly was closed while the rhythm guitarist struggled to pull a guitar over his spiked hair.

Angel leaned back. "God, this show had better make my movie a hit," she whispered to the tap dancer. "If not, I'll kill my pro-ducer for ordering me to do it."

The numbing music was giving her a headache. She was sick of answering inane questions, and there were at least twenty more interviews scheduled over the next few days. Her first starring movie was opening on the weekend, and Aldo had arranged the maximum advance publicity to whet the public's interest. He was sure that this picture would catapult her to superstardom.

Suddenly a young man from the talk show staff rushed out onto the other side of the stage, waving a piece of paper and yelling Anna Maria's name. As he ran toward the hostess he cut in front of BARF! who were in mid-song. The group's lead singer didn't no-tice the interruption.

Anna Maria hissed an obscenity at him when he handed her the message.

"Amateurs," she muttered as she unfolded the paper. Then her face turned white. "I can't believe it," she gasped. "I never thought I'd be so lucky. A scoop!"

She jumped to her feet and ran out to the center of the stage. The nearly comatose members of BARF! barely stirred when she yanked the live microphone away from the lead singer.

"Ladies and gentlemen, a terrible tragedy has just occurred." She paused to wet her lips and fluff her hair. "One of Italy's lead-ing political figures, a man we all admire and love, has this very afternoon been shot by an unknown assailant. At this moment—and we are the only station with this news—he lies hovering be-tween life and death. The moment we learn of any change in his condition, we will relay the news to you. And now, to honor the man, I will return to my panel of guests and discuss his tremendous accomplishments."

Ignoring BARF! who were still pouring out their song into dead microphones and amplifiers, Anna Maria swept back to her chair. Turning to her three guests, she asked in a solemn tone, "Tell me, my friends, what has Gian-Carlo Cassieri meant to you, personally, as Italian citizens?"

Angel jumped as if pins had been stuck in the soles of her feet. As the news slowly sank in, she stared blankly around the studio, half expecting to wake up from a nightmare.

"Actually, I'm from New York," the tap dancer was saying.

"Although I am, of course, a Parisian," the novelist offered, "I would be glad to offer an analysis of the role political figures play in modern life. Assassination in particular—"

Anna Maria cut him off. "We are very lucky to have Angel Concelli with us today. Angel, like Gian-Carlo Cassieri, is for many Italians a symbol. Of freshness, of vitality, of Italy's future. Angel, what do you think Gian-Carlo's death would mean for our country?"

Angel slumped forward and dropped her head in her hands.

"Angel?" Anna Maria prompted. She picked up a pencil and poked the young actress in the arm. "Did you hear me?"

Angel knew it couldn't be true. If he was dead, if he was in pain, she would know it. She would have felt the bullet entering her flesh at the exact moment it entered his. It was some kind of trick, a stupid lie. "Gian-Carlo," she whispered, "tell me you're all right. Tell me you're alive."

"I'm afraid you'll have to speak up," Anna Maria snapped.

For a second Angel let herself imagine that the worst had happened. He was gone, he was dead. She saw his body riddled with bloody holes, his sightless eyes staring blankly at the ceiling.

No. He couldn't have left her all alone. She had already had too many years of living with no one to love. She stumbled to her feet. She had to find out the truth.

91

She hurried across the stage, ignoring Anna Maria's cries. The camera followed her until she disappeared backstage.

"Well," Anna Maria said when she finally waved the camera back to her, "we can see how the news has upset Angel Concelli, just as it has hurt all of us. Now perhaps the young Englishmen from BARF! would like to join our panel and offer their opinions on this shattering event."

Backstage Angel pushed through the curious crowd until she reached a telephone. She dialed the private number for Gian-Carlo's office.

When his secretary answered, she whispered, "This is Angel Concelli. Tell me how he is."

"I can't say anything," the secretary replied. "I've been instructed to—"

"This is Angel Concelli!" Angel shrieked. "Tell me or I'll have you fired, you idiot!"

The secretary hesitated, then decided the smartest course of action would be to give Gian-Carlo's mistress the telephone number of his hospital room and deny that she had given it out.

Angel struggled not to cry as she dialed the hospital. Staff from the talk show were staring at her, but she didn't care. As soon as the phone was picked up she poured out her questions.

"Is he all right? Will he live? Is he in pain?"

A woman delicately cleared her throat. "Who is this?"

"It's Angel. Angel Concelli. Tell me, is he all right?" Angel clenched her fists, trying to steel herself for the worst.

Lucia Cassieri took a deep breath before answering. "Miss Concelli, the state of my husband's health is none of your business. But, if you insist on learning his condition, I refer you to the media, which will be issued regular bulletins. Please do not call this number again. And, should you know any of my husband's other whores, I would be grateful if you passed this message on to them."

16

As soon as Aldo's white Porsche pulled up in front of the television studio, Angel staggered out of the doorway, wiping her eyes with the back of her hand. She blinked in the bright sunlight.

"Come on, *cara*," Aldo told her as he helped her into the car. "I'll take you home."

She looked at him as if he were insane. "Not home. To the hospital. I have to see Gian-Carlo."

The producer, dressed in a beige linen suit and straw hat, walked back to the driver's side. "You'll never get in," he said as he climbed in beside her. "I'm taking you home."

"Please, Aldo," she begged, starting to cry again. "It's important. If I don't find out how he is I'll go crazy."

Aldo shoved the car into gear and pulled out into the traffic, narrowly missing another car. "All right, if you really want to see that prick, I'll take you there. But I can tell you how he is. He's fine. The whole story's a crock of shit."

93

"He's fine?" Relief filled her like a powerful drug, but it was quickly tempered by distrust. Aldo wasn't above lying when it suited him. "Who told you?" she asked suspiciously. "They said at the studio that he was rushed to the hospital in an ambulance. And no one knows whether he'll make it, not even the doctors."

He ignored her question while he passed several already speeding cars. "You won't like this, Angel. I know you think he's a wonderful man who wants to help the world—"

"Christ, Aldo," she interrupted, "I'm not that naive. I know he's not Mother Theresa. But he's not as bad as you say."

"He's probably worse. Look at the facts, Angel. The guy came out of nowhere. He married Lucia Battistoni, whose father had the money and connections to take him wherever he wanted to go. He's backed by the kind of people who don't want their names known. Try to pin the guy down—you can't. He never says exactly what he'll do if he comes to power. He trades on people's hopes and fears. He tries to convince the left he's a leftist, the right that he's on the right, and everybody in the middle that he's a moderate."

Angel sulked for a moment. Then she reached over and pulled his handkerchief from his jacket pocket. She blew her nose and tossed the soiled handkerchief out the window. "He just doesn't fit into a slot, that's all. He's something new."

"The people behind Gian-Carlo Cassieri don't want something new," Aldo argued. "What they want is as old as time itself. Privilege and power. And Gian-Carlo—handsome, charismatic Gian-Carlo—is their way to get it."

"Come on. He's not a puppet."

Aldo sped past a stop sign. "A well-paid puppet, who gets the chance to pull a couple of his own strings now and then, with Franco Uccellini pulling the rest. And I don't even want to think about who's pulling Uccellini's strings."

Angel glared at him. "How can you say that? Gian-Carlo must be doing something right if the terrorists tried to assassinate him."

"Terrorists?" Aldo snorted. "Grow up, Angel. You think there's only one kind of terrorist? That everybody who goes out with a gun and tries to take justice into his own hands is trained in the same place—in Libya, or the U.S.S.R., or even somewhere in Texas by the C.I.A.? Or that being on a hit list means you're necessarily a good guy? Hitler was on a couple of hit lists, too. Anyway, I know who shot Gian-Carlo, and he wasn't a terrorist. And, before you work yourself into a nervous breakdown, I do know for a fact that he's okay. I checked before I came to get you. All he has is a flesh wound in his shoulder. But I'll bet you when he appears in public he'll look like death warmed over."

"You're absolutely sure it was just a flesh wound?" she cried. "Who told you?"

"I've got connections, Angel. Word got out fast. It wasn't an attack, it was an accident. One of the security guards at Gian-Carlo's estate was cleaning his gun while Gian-Carlo was in the garden. It went off accidentally and grazed Gian-Carlo's shoulder. A doctor patched it up with some disinfectant and a Band-Aid. Then Gian-Carlo's backers heard about it and decided to play it up for political gain. They made him put his bloodstained shirt back on and rushed him to a private hospital. Now they're spreading the rumor that it was a masked assassin. The left are supposed to think the right did it, and the right that it was the left. The way these things work, ten groups will have already claimed responsibility. Anyway, it's bound to get him a lot of sympathy. People love public figures who nearly gave up their lives for their country—war heroes, survivors of assassination attempts. Now that Gian-Carlo's one of the select few, there'll be no stopping him."

Angel clenched and unclenched her fists, taking in the information. "Give me a cigarette, Aldo," she finally snapped.

"I don't have any."

"Why the fuck not?" she screamed. "You always have cigarettes!"

"What are you mad at me for?" he said, glancing at her angry face. "I'm just telling you the truth."

"Yeah. If it *is* the truth."

Aldo didn't bother to answer her. Angel looked out at the passing buildings. In about ten minutes they would reach the hospital.

"So what if most of the story is fake?" she suddenly spat out.

"Everybody does something lousy to get ahead. That's how the world works. Just because Gian-Carlo plays a few games with publicity doesn't mean he wouldn't make a good prime minister. I'm in no position to act self-righteous, and neither are you."

But Angel's eyes had filled with tears. She honestly didn't care if Gian-Carlo wanted to screw the Italian people. What enraged her was that he hadn't got a message to her first. He should have known that when she heard the news she would go insane with worry. He had treated her as if she were a nobody. *One of his whores.*

"Anyway," she continued, turning her anger on Aldo, "what's it to you if I want to believe Gian-Carlo? My personal life is none of your business."

Aldo looked hurt. "I care about you, and not just because your contract is money in the bank to me. And be honest. You care about me too. After all, I was the one you called from the television station. I just don't want you to get hurt by this guy. Don't kid yourself that you've got a future with him."

"Shut up!" she screamed. "I do have a future with him!"

Aldo sighed. "Angel, come on, he couldn't marry you even if he wanted to. Do you think Italians—or any other country—would take him seriously as a politician if he divorced Lucia and married an actress like you?"

Angel threw Aldo a haughty look. She pulled herself up in the leather seat and crossed her legs. "Is that so? Well, I'd like to remind you that Nancy Reagan used to be an actress. And she was *his* second wife."

Aldo laughed so hard he almost lost control of the car. He slapped the steering wheel, roaring. "Oh, Angel," he managed to get out. He put his arm around her shoulders and pulled her against him, then kissed the top of her head. "Angel, you're as far from Nancy Reagan as anyone can get."

She gave a reluctant smile. "Yeah, I guess you've got a point there. Still, don't write me off, Aldo. I'm a lot tougher than I look."

Aldo was forced to slow the car in the congested streets near the hospital.

"We'll never get there," Angel complained. She switched on the radio to find out the latest news about Gian-Carlo.

A reporter was broadcasting live from outside the hospital, where a crowd estimated at fifty thousand had gathered to wait for word on the politician's condition. "All eyes are riveted on the balcony of Gian-Carlo Cassieri's room," the newsman reported, "waiting to see if the charismatic political figure will live or die. Will yet another possible savior for our country be snuffed out by the forces of darkness? Wait, the door is opening! It is Lucia Cassieri, Gian-Carlo's wife. She is addressing the crowd. It's hard to make out exactly what she's saying from where we are, but I believe she's telling everyone that her husband needs rest. She is telling them to go home. That there is nothing they can do. She is about to leave. Wait! I see someone else coming to the balcony doors. A man in a wheelchair. Yes! Yes, it is Gian-Carlo Cassieri himself! Gian-Carlo has come to greet his followers! He is obviously in great pain. His left arm and shoulder are completely bandaged. The crowd is cheering. People are weeping. My God, the man is incredible. He is actually pulling himself to his feet. Yes, with his wife's help, Gian-Carlo is standing. He is waving back his doctor. He is raising his good arm to the crowd."

Angel shut the radio off.

"Still want to go to the hospital?" Aldo asked in the suddenly silent car.

Angel stared out the window for a minute without answering. Then she took a deep breath. She ran her fingers through her thick blond hair, straightened her short skirt and smoothed her tight sweater.

"Take me somewhere nice," she said, finally, pulling a mirror from her purse so she could repair the damage to her makeup. "Let's try a fancy restaurant first. And then dancing—a club with a lot of men." She stared at her reflection in the small mirror. "I feel like some raw meat and a fuck."

17

In the morning Stevie lingered in bed listening to the wind rustling the leaves outside Ellen's villa. After a leisurely bath, she brushed her hair dry at the open window, enjoying the view of the quiet garden. Her luggage had already been picked up from the airport and brought to her room. She decided to wear a comfortably familiar cotton shirt and jeans. When she finally went downstairs to have breakfast in the sunny dining room, Gina, the quiet, middle-aged maid, volunteered that Ellen was in her room. Alone at the table, Stevie hungrily consumed three sticks of bread smothered in marmalade and cup of cappuccino. She sat facing the doors that opened onto the garden. The day was sunny and warm, and the sweet perfume from the flowers seemed to fill the entire house.

When she finished her breakfast, she asked Gina for a pen and paper and then returned to the table to write a list. It was time to get organized; she had a lot to do.

1. You *must* call the school today. Classes begin in three weeks.
2. Start looking for an apartment.
3. Buy three dresses and a pair of shoes.
4. Send flowers to the Contessa to thank her for letting you stay at her place.

Satisfied, she put down the pen. It was a reasonable amount to tackle in one day. Even with the late start, if she left the villa immediately she should get everything done. Sight-seeing could wait until the essentials were out of the way. She had always been a practical person.

She asked Gina to tell Ellen that she would be back in time for dinner. On her way to the door, she started to worry that she had wasted too much time. There was so much to do. Enough to keep her busy for at least several days. Much too busy to think.

She opened the door and stepped into the heavy, midday sun.

Gian-Carlo Cassieri, his eyes hidden by dark glasses, was waiting at the wheel of his black Alfa Romeo on the other side of the road. As soon as he saw her, he reached over and opened the passenger door.

She stared at the car. She couldn't believe he had waited there all night. What did he think? That she was going to walk right over and get into a stranger's car?

She turned away and started walking briskly down the sidewalk. Then she realized she didn't have the slightest idea of how to get into Rome.

Feeling foolish, she stopped, conscious of his eyes on her. If she turned back and went into the villa, what would he think? That she was afraid of him?

She sighed and turned to face him. After all, it was obvious that, despite her excuses, unconsciously she wanted to see him. She waited for him to speak first.

Instead, the powerfully built man stepped out of the car and crossed the road toward her. His magnetism was almost frightening. When he reached her, he slowly lowered his dark glasses. His bloodshot eyes were ringed with dark shadows. He stared at her for a moment, but unlike everyone else she had met in Rome, he didn't seem to be comparing her to Angel. Then, to her surprise, he smiled. "Thank you for coming out to see me," he said.

Stevie shrugged, embarrassed. "I was just . . ." She waved her hand, not knowing what to say. "Going shopping, actually."

"Then I can drive you into the city," he immediately offered.

She swallowed. This wasn't what she had had in mind. But what could she say? That she was afraid to be alone with him? He was one of this country's most important political figures, and she was just a nobody.

"I, uh . . ." she stammered, blushing.

He looked amused. "I hope you weren't planning to walk. It's a very long way."

Her fear did seem ridiculous. And what was she basing it on? Just some wild rumors repeated by Nick and the Contessa. Although his all-night vigil was a little unusual, if he had loved Angel a desire to meet her sister was perfectly reasonable. Since Ellen had made it clear she wouldn't let him in her home, what else could he do except wait around for Stevie to come out?

"All right, I guess," she said, feeling a rush of relief that she had found the courage to say yes. She had to admit she wanted to know more about this intriguing man who had waited for hours to meet her.

"Wonderful," he said, his eyes still staring into hers. There seemed to be a question in them, as if he expected something from her.

Then he turned and started toward the car. She glanced back over her shoulder, almost expecting her grandmother to open the door and order her back inside. But no one was there. She followed him to the car.

He held the door open for her, an old-fashioned courtesy no man had performed for her before.

When he slipped into the driver's seat, he grinned at her. "Better wear your seat belt. You'll need it in Roman traffic."

She laughed. "So I've already noticed."

In such close quarters his charisma was almost tangible. She had never been so close to such a handsome, magnetic man. She

was embarrassed to admit that his presence made her a little dizzy, like a fan who suddenly found herself alone in an eleator with
her faorite movie star.

Gian-Carlo started the engine "I haven't introduced myself. My
name is Cassieri. Gian-Carlo."

"I'm—"

"Stephanie Templeton," he said, smiling down at her. "Yesterday your grandmother called and asked me to keep the crowds
away from the apartment where you were staying. Laura Barberini's place." He smiled again. "You see, I already know everything about you."

"Signore Cassieri," she said, "if it's too much trouble for you to
drive me—"

"Gian-Carlo," he corrected. "And there is nothing I would
rather do than show you Rome. But first—" He steered the car out
into the road. "First, I'm going to take you to see Angel."

Steie caught her breath. Was he insane? He had to know that
Angel was dead. She looked at his face for some clue to what he
had meant. He was staring straight ahead at the road as if nothing
were wrong, a slight smile on his lips.

She felt for the door handle. But the car was moving too fast.
Then her eyes fell on a newspaper that had been shoved on the
floor.

The headline was as huge as the one that had announced Angel's death.

Angel Uccisa! "Angel Murdered."

Stevie slowly raised her eyes to the mysterious man behind the
wheel. If he was a murderer, she had walked right into his trap.

GIAN-CARLO parked the car on a narrow street. Stevie looked
around, wondering why he had brought her to this ordinary
place. Clotheslines crowded with dripping laundry stretched from
one side of the nearly empty street to the other. A small boy with
open sores on his thin legs was playing with pebbles in a nearby
doorway.

Neither of them had spoken during the drive into Rome. She didn't know the reason for Gian-Carlo's silence, but, dazed and fearful, she had planned dramatic escapes from the speeding car that she would never have had the courage to try. Now that she could easily run away, her fear was ebbing. This quiet, domestic street with its wet clothes didn't look like it held a murderer's lair.

Gian-Carlo reached in front of her and opened the glove compartment. He took out a pair of dark glasses and a soft brown hat.

"Put these on," he said, handing them to Stevie, "so people won't stare at you."

She held the blue-rimmed glasses for a moment. Somehow she knew they had belonged to Angel. The plastic frame was stained with sweat and makeup. Her sister's sweat and makeup.

Shutting out the disturbing thought, she slipped them on her face. She pulled on the hat, tucked her hair in at the sides, and turned to Gian-Carlo for approval.

He nodded. "They'll help, although people may still recognize you. Romans are notoriously hard to control, and I can't promise anything. But we don't have far to go. It's just around the corner to your left. I'll go first to make sure everything's all right. Follow in about two minutes."

He hesitated, staring at her. Stevie wondered how many times he had seen Angel in these glasses and this hat. A chill ran along her spine as she remembered his words. *I'm going to take you to see Angel.*

He slipped out of the car and walked quickly along the street. In this shabby neighborhood, his perfectly tailored dark suit and flashing gold cuff links were an incongruous sight. She remembered that he was a well-known politician in the middle of an election campaign. She kept her eyes on him—an incredibly handsome man with the bearing of a born leader—until he disappeared around the corner.

Alone, she wondered what insanity had possessed her. Why was she doing whatever this stranger asked? Why wasn't she using this opportunity to escape?

But the questions made her nervous. She didn't want to analyze her behavior. There was something flattering, very flattering, about the attention he was paying her. After all, she was plain little Stevie Templeton from Boston and he was Gian-Carlo Cassieri.

And, despite his puzzling actions, she couldn't seem to stay afraid of him.

She remembered the moment in the garden when he had found her crying. When his hands had touched her arms, she had felt that he could help her understand all the mystery and confusion. She had almost felt that she needed him.

Maybe for once in her life trusting her instincts was the right thing to do.

She pulled down the sun visor and looked into the vanity mirror.

The effect of the disguise startled her. She was anonymous, a fair young woman with an oval face and a wide mouth. It could have been Angel Concelli. But it wasn't. It was Stevie Templeton in another woman's hat and glasses. Yesterday she had worn Toni's dress. This was no different. They were objects, pure and simple. The props of life.

Except that these had belonged to her dead sister, and the man who had kept them was waiting around the corner.

It had been at least two minutes since he had left. She reached for the door handle. If this was a trap—

They were in a heavily populated area. She could scream and kick and run away. She wasn't helpless.

But if she didn't go, she would probably never see him again. He would dismiss her as a rude American.

She got out of the car and walked past the thin boy who was still piling one small pebble on top of another. He glanced up at her and said, "*Ciao,* Angel."

As soon as she rounded the corner she felt like a melodramatic idiot. Angel's name was in huge letters on the marquee of a small cinema. Their destination was just a movie.

Inside the dingy, faded lobby she slipped the sunglasses into her purse and pushed open the creaking door of the darkened theater. The movie had already started. On the screen a tall, gray-haired man was shouting at a bent old woman in a black dress. As soon as Stevie's eyes adjusted, she located Gian-Carlo in the back row. She made her way along the narrow aisle and slipped into the seat next to him.

"She'll be on soon," he whispered. "This was her second movie, her first big role. The movie is nothing, but Angel's wonderful. Wait. You'll see."

Only five other people were present, scattered near the front of the theater.

Then Angel appeared, above them all, more beautiful than any woman had a right to be. The golden, luminous actress who was gliding across the screen in a thin white cotton dress seemed more alive than anyone Stevie had ever met. She wasn't an icon or a myth; she was a real person. Her death was impossible; life couldn't be that unfair. Steie forgot where she was, forgot the man sitting beside her. She was alone with her sister, her full sister, a being conceived one night in Boston in the room her father had slept in until his death, conceived while Stevie slept in her crib across the narrow hall.

Stevie thought of the life the two of them might have shared growing up together, playing in the small backyard behind the modest bungalow, fighting over their dolls, whispering late at night, running side by side into the living room on Christmas morning to find their presents brightly wrapped under the tree. To Stevie, to Angel. Love from Mom and Dad.

Instead there had been all those lonely days and nights, holidays when she and her father had gone through the motions surrounded by silence. Tears were running down her cheeks; she groped for a tissue and wiped them away. She imagined a picture of herself with Angel, their arms around each other, laughing at a shared secret. Sisters.

But it was a humbling thought. Although their features and builds were similar, on Angel the raw material became something spectacular, while all Stevie possessed was a pleasant face and a reasonably good figure with a bad slouch. A photograph of them side by side would devastate her ego.

She sensed that Gian-Carlo was looking at her. At the dull, plain sister. He touched her shoulder. She didn't want to take her eyes from the screen, but he cupped her chin and slowly turned her face toward him.

His black eyes possessed her face. Angel's face, except that it wasn't, it was only hers. She wanted to hide. But his eyes were worshipping her as if she were the beautiful one. His fingers lightly stroked her cheek, sending waves of pleasure through her body. He looked at her mouth.

In the movie Angel was laughing, a bawdy, abandoned laugh.

"Help me," Gian-Carlo whispered, moving toward her.

And then his lips were on hers. His soft, strong mouth was tasting her, making love to her. She felt herself dissolving, melting into his flesh.

Had Angel felt like that when he kissed her?

Stevie shut her eyes, trying to forget Angel. His mouth was everything. She felt as if no one had kissed her like that before, as if no one had really made love to her.

His mouth was becoming harder, his kisses more demanding. Stevie couldn't stop. She couldn't push him away. For whatever neurotic, self-destructive reason, she wanted him as much as he wanted her.

Suddenly Angel's scream filled the theater.

The couple jerked apart and stared up at the screen.

Angel was holding out her hands, yelling, *"Stop, stop, stop."*

Gian-Carlo softly moaned.

There was a gunshot.

Angel grabbed her chest. She fell to the floor, blood spilling out between her fingers.

Gian-Carlo whispered, "It didn't have to happen."

His tense face was illuminated by Angel's light. No, Stevie reminded herself, by the light shining through a colored piece of film. What did he mean—it didn't have to happen? Was he trying to tell her something about Angel's death?

Angel's eyes briefly fluttered open. "It didn't have to happen," she whispered to the man standing over her with a gun. "I loved you, and only you."

Gian-Carlo abruptly stood up, walked quickly along the aisle, and left the theater.

Stevie stayed behind, watching her sister die.

18

STEVIE walked through Rome for hours, barely conscious of the famous sights she had been longing to see. Her mind was on Angel. And Gian-Carlo Cassieri.

It was dusk when she came upon the massive ruins of ancient Rome, the tremendous beauty of the pale marble dazzling in the setting sun. She stopped and stared out at the wreckage of a distant civilization. It was a sobering sight, and yet it was oddly exhilarating, as if the vast entertainment of time and folly were condensed before her eyes.

They came to this, she thought. Magnificent rubble. And, if the current civilization didn't blow the planet to oblivion, what would be left of it in two thousand years? Images of a beautiful blond woman captured on celluloid or some more advanced medium for the preservation of the past? Records of the career of a politician who had—perhaps—led Italy for a short time in the latter half of the twentieth century?

And of Stevie Templeton? Nothing.

She slumped down on a stone bench. She had stopped in a coffee bar to read the newspaper story about Angel's death, spreading the thin newsprint out over the stainless-steel bar while she sipped a cappuccino. It was sleazy journalism, unsubstantiated rumors and speculation. The paper hadn't even had the courage to name names. But everyone had to know that the man they described as Angel's possible murderer could only be Gian-Carlo Cassieri. With the election in nine days a story like that could ruin him if people believed it. Which made it all the more suspect. At the same time she knew that just because politicians had enemies didn't mean they were necessarily innocent.

But, now that she had met Gian-Carlo, she couldn't believe he had murdered her sister. She was sure he had loved Angel, a love that was still torturing him. That was why he was following her, why he had kissed her in the darkness of the theater. He needed Angel to be alive, to feel her warm and breathing in his embrace.

And yet, wouldn't a murderer—one who had acted in passion and lived to regret it—feel the same longing, the same obsession?

Perhaps. But so did everyone who had lost a loved one. She had felt the same way when her father had died, wanting men she passed in the street who bore even a faint resemblance to him to turn around and reveal themselves as Matthew Templeton, miraculously restored to life. She wanted his death to be a hoax, reversible, the sawed-in-half lady made into one again.

Stevie stared out at the graceful marble arches climbing high into the sky, the clutter of ruins spread out before her. How many millions of people had seen them, how many generations?

It was too humbling a thought. She wanted to feel important, instead of just another corpse-to-be.

She realized it was getting late and she should head back to her grandmother's villa. But at this moment, she wished she could walk through Rome forever and never face reality again. She was tired of hearing about the past, about her parents' mistakes. She hadn't come to Italy to discover a painful history. She had expected her year here to be—except for the excitement of her surroundings—quiet and a little dull. She would make friends with the other teachers and dedicate most of her time to her students.

Of course, in the back of her mind she had hoped she would meet someone and fall in love. Like everyone who was alone, she wanted that, dreamed of it. So far she had only had two serious relationships. The first one was with a restless young man she had met in her first year at college. Then one day Patrick wasn't there anymore. Leaving a note saying that he had to find out more about life before he settled down, he'd headed westward. A year later—a year filled with boring dates spent drinking watery beer and watching bad movies while some oaf tried to grope her thigh—she had met Jan. He was Patrick's opposite, earnest and stable and just a little bit dull. A lot like herself, she had acknowledged in her more honest moments. After three years, when they didn't love each other enough to get married or dislike each other enough to break up, she had finally understood why Patrick had left. Safety isn't enough. To stay with someone just because you know they'll never leave ultimately becomes an insult to yourself.

Whenever she had fantasized about falling in love with someone in Rome, the man was always an American, someone about her age, with similar interests, probably another teacher. Someone she could return to Boston with and live what she considered a normal life. Rome was meant to be an interlude, an extended vacation. She had never imagined falling in love with a man whose entire world was different from hers.

A marmalade cat sat licking itself clean on an ancient slab of marble. The cat stared back at her, looking as timeless and peaceful as the ruins.

Night was falling quickly. It was getting cold. She was still wearing the dark glasses to ward off Angel seekers. She remembered Gian-Carlo taking them out of the glove compartment and handing them to her, his long, tanned fingers holding the delicate frame. She remembered him walking toward her the night before, coming across the lawn, pulled by her image—or Angel's image. And then her grandmother had revealed Claire's biggest lie, and

Stevie had turned away. Gian-Carlo had waited there all night, while she cried herself to sleep in a room upstairs, unable to believe that her mother had actually stolen away her unborn sister, kept Angel a secret even from the man who had fathered her.

Stevie knew that the powerful feeling she felt for Gian-Carlo couldn't be love, but she couldn't get his face out of her mind, she couldn't stop thinking about his mouth on hers. She wanted to put her arms around him and make love to him for hours. Real love was something different. Love was when you became someone's friend, when you shared interests and values. When you slowly grew together, built a solid life, and helped each other through the struggle of daily living.

The other kind of love—that wild, destructive passion of literature and movies—was not for someone like Stevie Templeton.

It was for someone like Angel. And Gian-Carlo Cassieri.

Stevie shut her eyes, hating herself. Hating all her limitations and fears. Hating herself for picking dark blue dresses and shoes with sensible heels and coats designed for warmth over style. For being a schoolteacher.

For not being Angel, that sad, tormented, magnificent girl, who must have lived a lonely, terrifying life. But Angel was the lucky one. She had known passion. She had been loved by Gian-Carlo.

Stevie looked down at her feet, planted firmly on the ground. She was wearing gray sneakers, good ones, Reeboks.

She smiled. If she had worn high heels today her feet would be covered with blisters by now. At least there was one thing to be said for being the one who wasn't glamorous, the dull one, the shadow, the one Gian-Carlo could never want, even though he had kissed her the way no man had ever kissed her before.

19

THE glass ashtray flew past Gian-Carlo's head and crashed into the wall behind him.

"Angel! Stop this!" he yelled, shielding his face with his hands.

"You mother-fucking prick!" Angel growled. She grabbed a lamp, ripped the cord out of the wall, and heaved it at him with all her strength. Gian-Carlo ducked. Before she could pick up anything else, he rushed forward and trapped her in his arms.

"I told you I was sorry!" he cried.

"Fuck sorry!" she yelled, trying to squirm free. She attempted a kick to his crotch, but he was too close. "I'll murder you, you son of a bitch!"

When he looked into her cold green eyes he realized she might actually mean it. To calm her down, he tightened his arms around her. "It's only been three weeks," he said. "And you don't understand what my life's been like since the assassination attempt. The increased security—"

111

"Assassination attempt?" she snorted. "Don't feed me that crap. I'm not one of those idiots stupid enough to vote for a fraud like you. When the next election comes I'm voting for a real man. That other one, whatever his name is. You know, the short one with the cheap suits. Aldo told me how the whole assassination thing was faked."

"Not the whole thing," he said. "I *was* shot, although I admit it was accidental and the wound wasn't as bad as we made it look. Believe me, it wasn't my idea to capitalize on it. Uccellini decided we had a lot to gain."

"That cold-faced prick. You shouldn't listen to him."

Gian-Carlo smiled affectionately. "I don't like him any more than you do. But he knows a great deal about politics."

She was still enclosed in his arms, but she had stopped struggling. He kissed the top of her head. "I really am sorry," he said, gently massaging her back while he spoke. "And as a matter of fact I did try to call you when your movie opened, but your line was always busy."

"You're lying," Angel whispered, "or you would have said that when you came in the door." She knew that if she allowed one lie, it would be followed by another one, and another; the lies would never stop. But at least he was finally here. She put her head on his shoulder and confessed what had been bothering her most. "You should have let me know about the shooting before it was announced to the press. I was terrified. I made an idiot of myself on Anna Maria Poli's show."

He caressed her silken blond hair. "Everything moved so quickly." He kissed her forehead. "And Lucia was there. I didn't have a chance."

The memory of Lucia calling her a whore revived Angel's anger. She shoved him away. "How can you claim to be capable of running the country if everyone orders you around? You're obviously weak and incompetent."

His face froze. "Politics is a complicated business, Angel. If you want to get back at me for the pain I caused then throw another lamp, but don't ever question my honor or my abilities."

Angel shrugged and walked over to the long white couch. She put her bare feet up on the gray marble coffee table and stretched her arms out along the back of the couch. She had moved into the apartment two days earlier. It was Aldo's present to her, a year's lease paid up on a furnished luxury apartment in the Viale Parioli. She knew he had done it to appease his guilt over the unfair contract she was still tied to. But it was a nice gift. Better than flowers.

With the new apartment and the opening of her movie, the last three weeks should have been the best in her life. Her performance had drawn rave reviews, and the movie was breaking box-office records with lines around the block at every showing. To get Gian-Carlo out of her mind she had started dating feverishly. There was certainly no shortage of interested men. But no one excited her the way Gian-Carlo did. She had gone to bed with several of them, but their lovemaking had only made her miss Gian-Carlo more. One of the idiots had even had the nerve to sit up in bed afterward and shout, "I can't believe it! I actually fucked Angel Concelli!"

And yet, now that Gian-Carlo was here, she wondered if they were better off apart. Their relationship was too one-sided. Here she was a star, and she was waiting around for the phone to ring like some ugly little waitress with thick legs. Surely somewhere in Italy—in the world—there was a man who could compete with Gian-Carlo Cassieri. Maybe she just needed more than three weeks to find him.

"Gian-Carlo," she said, dropping her head back on the couch, "I think you should leave."

He frowned, looking at her as if she had spoken in another language. "Angel, you must be joking. *Cara,* I . . ." At a loss for words, he moved toward her.

"Don't touch me." She massaged her aching forehead. "Please don't touch me."

He stopped in the center of the room and waited for an explanation.

She didn't know what she really wanted. But if he touched her it would be decided. They would go to bed, and then it would all start again. Sex and fights, snatched slivers of time, and now the lies. She wasn't sure she could take the strain much longer. She couldn't seem to get used to it; it was getting harder instead of easier. Maybe they should stop before things got even worse. At least now she could still imagine a life without him.

She looked up at him. He was wearing a blue silk shirt, open at the neck, and perfectly tailored black trousers. His legs were apart and his strong hands were at his sides. A thin veil of sweat covered his tanned face. Her eyes were pulled to his mouth, his flesh. It was a Saturday night. She wondered what Lucia was doing, what lies he had told to get free.

Angel covered her face with her hands, overcome with depression. It was as if she had tumbled into a deep dark pit, and the walls were too steep for her ever to climb out.

"I can't do it," she whispered. But she didn't know what she meant. That she couldn't give him up, or they couldn't go on this way?

"We need each other," he said softly. "You know that."

She thought of the days stretching ahead, days when she would be all alone, wanting him, wanting someone who cared. Days when he was at home with his family.

"I get so lonely," she confessed. She looked down at the floor. She couldn't meet his eyes while she was telling the truth. "It eats away at me. I walk around talking to myself, praying the phone will ring, that you'll call, you'll show up at the door. When I come home at night I want someone here to listen to boring stories about my day, about the cameraman who said something silly, or the makeup girl's gossip about other actresses. And there's no one."

She stopped, trying to decide whether to continue. But the words that had been building up inside her rushed out on their own before she could make up her mind. "Sunday afternoons are the hardest. They always have been, ever since I stopped living with my mother. We used to go to my grandmother's every Sunday afternoon and sit in her garden and drink tea. Can you believe it? Tea, in Italy. And now, on Sunday afternoons, I crave family. It comes like a physical longing, like hunger. And then sometimes . . ."

She faltered, losing her nerve. She was already telling him too much, confessing things she had never spoken aloud. But he claimed to love her. He claimed to care. If she couldn't tell him, then there would never be anyone she could tell. She took a deep breath and forced herself to continue. Her voice sounded small and distant, as if it were someone else's.

"I know where my mother lives. Sometimes on Sunday afternoons I drive there. I don't go in. She wouldn't want to see me. I just sit in the car and look up at the apartment building. Sometimes I see her through the window. Once she came outside and walked down the street. She never looks in my direction. I just stay in the car, alone. And then, after awhile, I go home."

Angel was crying, the quiet tears of an old loss, a wound from years ago. She looked at her hands, small and thin on her knees.

"I wish I had my own family. A husband and children. I know I don't seem the type. I know I'm flashy and shallow and I fuck around like a slut. I am a slut, I suppose. My mother once told me that sluts are made, not born, and I try to take some consolation in that. But I wish I had my own family to spend Sunday afternoons in the garden with. And knowing you has made it so much harder. I used to dream I'd meet someone, a man who loved me, who would overlook everything that's wrong with me and ask me to spend my life with him. That imaginary man was the last thing I thought about every night before I went to sleep. I loved him more than anything, even though we'd never met. I knew he was the only man in the world I could truly love. I just had to wait until he came along. And now the pain is so much worse, because I've found the man I want. He's not a dream—he's you." She took a deep breath, shivering slightly. "And every Sunday afternoon I think of you in your garden with your family, with your wife and children. And you know what?"

She raised her eyes then and looked straight at him. She wanted him to know that every word she was about to say was true.

"Now when I go to bed at night I pray that your wife and children will die. I pray that they'll be in a car and it'll go sailing off a cliff. Or that terrorists will ambush them. Or that—"

"Stop!" he screamed, finally driven too far. It was an animal scream, a parent's cry. His eyes were brimming with tears. "Please don't torture me, Angel."

She stared at him for a moment without speaking, and then lowered her face, rubbing her forehead with a rhythmic, desperate gesture.

In the silence that followed he walked over to the bar and poured himself a drink. He leaned against the wall and gulped it down. Angel remained on the couch, staring at the floor. Finally Gian-Carlo steadied himself enough to speak.

"Don't you think I hate this too? It's hell, Angel. I wish I'd never met you, and at the same time I thank God for the privilege of loving you. I have to separate my life, break it down the middle. When I'm with Lucia and Roberto and Francesca all I can think of is you. And when I'm with you I want to tell you how Roberto is doing at school, and about the time Francesca called me at the office to say her tooth had come out. I want to show you their pictures. I want the three people I love to be together. Instead I hae to watch myself so I don't say anything that might hurt one of you. I have to hold in my thoughts, my joy and love, because it would be cruel to let it out. I wish I didn't love you, Angel, just like you must wish you didn't love me EVERYTHING WOULD BE EASY then. But giving you up would be like giving up my own life. I wake up terrified that you'll move to Los ANGELES YOU'LL LEAVE ME bEHIND That you'll fall in love with someone else, someone who can offer you a complete life, children, the home you want. I wish misery on you, Angel. I wish your loneliness on you. I want you to be unhappy, I want you to stay mine I wish an empty life for the person I love." He hesitated. Then he whispered, "Just as you pray for my children's deaths."

For several minutes, neither of them spoke. Angel felt exhausted and drained. She wondered if they really needed each other as much as they thought. What was this fierce emotion that bound them together? Was it really love? Could love be this vicious, this hopeless?

Gian-Carlo was the one to break the silence. "It will never get better, Angel. We'll only ever have a snatched life, time stolen from other people. We'll both tire of it. We'll probably end up hating one another. If we're lucky."

Angel exhaled. She rubbed her eyes and then slowly stood up, stretching her cramped, tired body. She looked across the room at Gian-Carlo. He was watching her, waiting for her decision. Too tired to think, she shut her eyes. Standing there, unable to see him, she could feel his body. It seemed to pull her. She wanted to go over and slowly undress him; she wanted to make love to him inch by inch. Her nipples were hard, the insides of her thighs were already wet. If he left the room, silently, without a sign, she would know he was gone, she would feel his absence. For the rest of her life, she would feel his absence.

She gave a small shrug, giving up. She started for the bedroom, unbuttoning her blouse.

"Angel."

She didn't stop.

"Angel!" he yelled after her. "Angel, listen to me! I'll leave if you tell me to. This is the time. When we both have the courage to be honest."

In the bedroom she stripped off her clothes and yanked the satin cover from the huge bed. The curtains were open and the lights were on. She looked out at the bright windows in the buildings across the street. Naked, she stared at people going through the motions of their lives. They were all in pain, she thought, from something. Disease, heartbreak, loneliness, fear in all its forms. Why should she be lucky? Why should she be the one person on earth exempt from pain?

She knew when he was in the doorway. She stayed at the window while he undressed; she didn't care who saw them. Finally he came up behind her and led her to the bed. The lights were still on.

He crouched over her, staring into her expressionless eyes. "Tell me," he whispered. "Tell me again."

Then he dropped down on top of her, opened her legs, caressed her, and felt how wet she was. Waiting, he stared at her.

Angel spoke slowly, still meeting his eyes. "I hate your wife. I hate your children. Roberto and Francesca." She had never said their names before. "I pray for their deaths."

He whispered, "You want me that much?"

"Yes." Then she kissed the tears from his hot face and felt his need inside her, masquerading as sex.

20

Too impatient to take the elevator, Angel ran down the stairs, her heels clattering, and hurried past the sleeping concierge, an obese old woman who responded with indecipherable grunts whenever any of the residents took the trouble to wake her.

The day was overcast and cool. Angel pulled up the collar of her faded denim jacket. Her hair was hidden by a brown scarf, and her bloodshot eyes were pale without makeup. No one would recognize her as Angel Concelli, but she hadn't chosen the outfit to evade fans. It was how she always dressed on Sunday afternoons.

Her car, a battered red Citroën, was parked outside the building. Inside it, she lit a cigarette. The previous night, with its furious lovemaking that had lasted till dawn, seemed light years away. Already their confessions felt embarrassing—pointless words, better left unsaid.

She leaned back with her eyes shut and slowly smoked the cigarette. She wished her mind would go blank, that all the throbbing, pushing thoughts would disappear. She didn't want to admit what she was about to do; she just wanted to do it. She wondered if this was how a heroin addict felt when reaching for another fix, an alcoholic pouring his first drink in a month. *This isn't happening. I'm not really doing this.*

He opened the door and slid into the seat next to her. She didn't open her eyes; she knew who it was. Although she hadn't expected him to come, it was as if she had been waiting for him, smoking the cigarette because he was late.

"Where's your family?" she snapped as she butted out the cigarette in the overflowing ashtray. She felt full of rage—as angry as if she were the one he had abandoned on a Sunday afternoon, the one whose rights came first.

"Shut up," Gian-Carlo said. He sounded exhausted. Neither of them had had much sleep. "Sometimes we're so stupid, Angel. Both of us."

At that moment they were both stunned by the sudden flash of a camera. The young and brash photographer grinned triumphantly, waved his camera, and strutted away. Angel wondered which of them he had been watching, or if he had chanced on the scene and rejoiced in his luck.

She glanced at Gian-Carlo to see how he was taking it. His face was impassive. "I'm sorry," she whispered. She meant it.

He shrugged. "I don't care. At least today I don't care. Tomorrow I will. So I'll worry about it then."

"Thank you for coming."

He nodded and gave her a small smile. He held out his hand, signaling a truce. She slipped her fingers in his, grateful for the warmth of his touch.

"Shall we go?" he said.

She stared at him. Then, like a small girl seeking permission, she asked, "Is it all right?"

His fingers tightened. "Anything is all right, Angel. I love you."

Blinking back tears, she started the car. It was a long drive to the apartment building where her mother lived, a long lonely wait outside, hoping to catch a shadow of the woman who had raised her. Such a pointless journey, she thought, like carrying flowers to an empty grave.

Angel had never imagined that anyone would love her enough to come along for the ride.

21

STEVIE stepped back to get a better look at the new dress in the triple-sided mirror.

"It's you," the saleswoman in the high-fashion store announced.

"Me?" Stevie replied, amused. Since the almost-emaciated woman was wearing an eye-straining black-and-white suit with shoulder pads large enough for a football player, Stevie didn't give her opinion much weight.

Yet the crimson silk dress, body-hugging except for the skirt, which swirled out below the hips in layers of the gossamer material, was beautiful. The long tight sleeves emphasized the low scooped neckline. It wasn't quite Angel Concelli, but it certainly wasn't Stevie Templeton. And it would cost a month's rent on her old apartment in Boston.

"Perhaps something in dark blue," she said, glancing over at her drab clothes heaped on a chair in the changing room. And in a less expensive store, she added to herself. This was not what her father would have expected her to spend his insurance money on.

"Nonsense," the saleswoman replied. "Red is your color."

Stevie looked at her reflection again. She had spent the day transforming herself; the dress was meant to be the crowning touch. She had already paid more money than she wanted to think about to have her hair and makeup done. The short loose hairstyle and flattering makeup had made an enormous change. She kept waiting for the attractive image in the mirror to be replaced by the old Stevie Templeton.

She knew the desire to improve her appearance—which had possessed her like a demon when she woke up that morning after her long day walking through Rome—stemmed from the feeling that she was the ugly sister, the one the prince pushes aside in his search for Cinderella. But she wasn't trying to become Angel. If anything, the short hairstyle diminished their resemblance.

In fact, she was starting to see that feeling inferior to Angel was only part of this impulse. Lying awake the previous night, she had realized that her father had always pressured her to look plain, pushing her toward unflattering clothes and hairstyles, until she finally believed they were the only appropriate ones for her. The poor man must have been terrified that she would turn into Claire, the beautiful wife who ran away with a Roman lover. His fear had taken away her self esteem; she had wasted so many years thinking of herself as ordinary, even unappealing. But this pretty woman in the mirror was definitely Stevie Templeton.

She swirled around, watching the skirt flare up, flattering her legs. And they were very nice legs. She imagined Gian-Carlo taking her in his arms and dancing across the room with her.

"I'll need shoes too," she instructed the saleswoman. "And some casual dresses. In bright colors."

Stevie was modeling the red dress and the matching delicate red sandals in her room before dinner when there was a knock on her door. She opened it to her grandmother. She had spent very

123

little time with Ellen since their first night together. She wanted to be alone to digest the revelations, but she was also uncomfortable with her grandmother's violent dislike of Gian-Carlo.

"Stephanie," Ellen began, sounding angry, "I promised I wouldn't lie to you, so I'm going to tell you the truth now. Gian-Carlo Cassieri is at the door. I want to tell him to leave. But since he's here to see you, I cannot in good conscience do that without first receiving your permission."

Stevie's heart pounded as she thought of Gian-Carlo waiting for her at the bottom of the stairs.

Ellen continued. "I saw you leaving with him in his car yesterday, and I want you to know that I strongly suspect he is responsible for Angel's suicide. Men that ambitious can be very ruthless. Of course in a moral sense he can't be held solely responsible. Your mother and I are not blameless. Nor is Angel herself. But you would be wise to stop seeing him."

Stevie's heart fell. She wanted to see Gian-Carlo, but she couldn't go against Ellen's wishes. She was a guest here, and Ellen was her grandmother. Sighing, she smoothed the red silk dress. If Gian-Carlo didn't see her again, he would always remember her as a plain, dowdy girl. But maybe that was justified, since her new clothes were only window dressing. Inside she would always be Stevie Templeton, wallflower.

What would Angel have done?

She would have run down the stairs to her lover.

Stevie imagined herself running into his arms. She remembered his kiss in the movie theater, his taste, the heat of his lips.

She was an adult. She could make her own decisions. What right did this old woman—this absolute stranger—have to order her around? Why couldn't Ellen Brenner mind her own business?

"You can't tell me what to do!" Stevie said suddenly.

As soon as the words were out, she felt guilty. She was wrong to take out years of repressed rage on this well-meaning woman, when the real targets were her father and herself.

"I'm sorry," Stevie said. "And thank you for caring about me. But it is my life, and I have to make my own decisions."

Ellen stared sadly at her granddaughter. "I believe that he is an evil man."

"I don't believe in evil," Stevie quickly replied.

Ellen sighed. "You're young yet. You'll find it soon enough. In your heart first, that's where we all discover it for the first time, curled and ready. But go, then. Go and find out what life's really like."

The old woman's cynicism startled Stevie, who reached out and touched Ellen's wrinkled hand.

"I'm sorry to upset you," Stevie whispered. "But I need to do this."

"I know." Ellen grimaced. "I might not like the truth, but I can accept it. Actually, the perverse thing is that if you didn't go I would probably think less of you. I'd hate to find out you were too much like—" She stopped.

Stevie sensed what her grandmother had been about to say. "Like my father, you mean."

Ellen gave a small smile of respect for Stevie's honesty. "Yes. But don't be too much like Claire, either. Or Angel. Moderation does not get sufficient respect in this world of ours."

Stevie kissed her grandmother on the cheek. She walked down the stairs to meet Gian-Carlo, feeling the cool silk sliding over her legs. He was wearing a beautifully tailored gray suit. He looked tanned and relaxed; the shadows had gone from under his eyes. His face lit up when he saw her in the dramatic red dress.

"Perfect." He held out his arms. "I've come to take you to dinner."

"MORE champagne?" Gian-Carlo asked, filling her glass before she had a chance to answer. "You were telling me you're a teacher?"

They were at a corner table in the Ristorante Pontevecchio, a large, fashionable restaurant. Gian-Carlo's back was to the other diners, but Stevie couldn't help noticing that almost everyone in the crowded room was staring at them.

"Yes," Stevie answered. "I'll be teaching English here for a year.

125

I visited the school this morning, and it seems lovely. I think I'll be very happy."

"You must be very fond of children."

Stevie nodded, confused by the conversation. She had wondered where they would pick up after the passionate kiss in the theater and his abrupt exit. She had never expected small talk about her job.

"I have a boy and a girl," he continued. "Would you like to see their picture?"

"I'd love to."

He took a picture out of his wallet. "Francesca is seven, a wild little creature. Roberto is ten. He's too serious for his own good. This morning Francesca told me that she wants to be a clerk in a store." He chuckled. "She thinks they get to keep all the money the customers give them."

"What does Roberto want to be?" Stevie asked, looking at the photo of the delightful pair.

"Prime minister, of course. In some ways I'm an old-fashioned man, but I want my daughter to have as good a life as my son. So I told her she should want to be something big and successful, too. She said she might be Pope, but she'd rather work on the cash register in a candy store."

Smiling, Stevie returned the photo to him.

"It must be wonderful to have children," she said wistfully. She often wished she had children of her own.

"Yes," he whispered, a shadow crossing his face. "Having children changes your entire life." He stared at the picture for a moment before restoring it his wallet. Stevie wondered what had upset him.

Then he smiled at her as if nothing had happened. "What else? I want to know everything about you. About your friends, how you happen to know Laura Barberini, what you think of Rome. Everything."

Stevie blushed. "I'm probably the most boring person in the world."

"Not at all," he said, reaching out and touching her hand. "You don't know how refreshing it is to be with a lovely American schoolteacher."

"I don't think any woman dreams of being called refreshing," she said. "We'd rather be exotic and mysterious."

He laughed. "Men spend the first half of their lives wanting a woman they don't understand. Then they spend the second half hoping to find one they do."

For the next few hours they talked and drank champagne, laughing together. Stevie was impressed. He was kind and perceptive and very easy to talk to, not at all the ogre her grandmother and the newspapers had led her to expect. She didn't know why he had chosen to spend his evening with her, but after several glasses of champagne she was having too good a time to analyze his motives.

When they finally left the restaurant, it was almost midnight. Necks craned as they walked past the other diners, many of whom had lingered over their coffee to catch the Gian-Carlo show. Stevie was amused by the amount of attention she was receiving. These people didn't realize that their lives were probably far more exciting than hers. In a couple of weeks she would be explaining English verbs to a group of fresh-faced boys and girls, back to sensible shoes and one of her dull cotton dresses.

When she and Gian-Carlo hit the cool night air, her head started to spin. The combination of fresh air, champagne, and an attractive escort was almost too much for her. But Gian-Carlo seemed to be in his element. He took her hand and pulled her along the sidewalk, his fingers entwined with hers.

"I love Rome," he said, swinging her hand, "even though I live outside the city for the sake of my children. I love to feel the layers of civilization, that on this very ground great men walked and lived." His smile was dazzling. "It keeps me humble, which is always good for a politician."

He led her into a small piazza with a fountain in the center, where they sat side by side on a stone bench. The piazza was empty; the buildings were dark. She was aware of his body next to hers, his warm hand holding hers. He leaned back and stretched out his long legs.

"I know a lot about humility," she said. "I've been feeling plenty of it since I arrived in Rome." She blushed, afraid he would think she wished she were Angel, when her feelings were much more complex than that. "I don't mean I—"

"You don't have to explain," he said softly, squeezing her hand. "I know you weren't just talking about Angel. I have the same feelings myself. I suppose it's the human condition. We find it so hard to like ourselves. We desperately want to be loved, and yet we never believe we deserve it. You know the most unusual thing about Angel? When she looked in the mirror she saw a beautiful woman. I mean, she saw accurately. She was the only person I've ever met who believed she deserved to be loved. And no one had the decency to love her. No one loved that incredible woman."

A tear slid down his cheek. Stevie didn't know what to say. "You loved her," she finally whispered.

He didn't answer for a moment. Then he turned to her, his face still wet. She was surprised by how calm he seemed. There was a stillness about him she had never seen in anyone, as if he were looking at his whole life without illusions.

"I love her now," he said. "It's always easier to love someone who's dead. They never embarrass you, they never make demands . . ."

He couldn't finish. Stevie reached up and wiped the tear from his cheek with her finger. He grabbed her hand and gently pressed the palm to his lips.

"You cut your hair," he whispered, touching it lightly. He stared at her face. "You're very beautiful."

"No," she said, shaking her head. "No, I'm not." She had never accepted a compliment without complaint. She wasn't Angel.

"I miss her," he said. "I miss her all the time." His hand was on her neck, caressing her pale skin. "You're the only one who understands."

He slowly lowered his mouth to hers. It was a gentle kiss, full of longing. He touched her neck, her breasts. Her nipples were hard; he touched them lightly, acknowledging her desire.

Stevie slid her arms around his neck and let herself fall in love.

22

STEVIE fumbled with the key, dropping it twice before she managed to open the front door of her grandmother's villa. As she staggered into the dark house, she wished the floor would stop moving long enough for her to get to bed.

Suddenly arms were around her. She was pulled into a tight embrace and a mouth was firmly pressed against hers. The kiss only lasted a split second before Nick pulled back and switched on the light.

"What the hell—" Stevie said.

"Forgive me!" Nick cried. He had a huge grin. "But there's nothing more irresistible than a horny woman! Does your unsatisfied appearance mean Gian-Carlo Cassieri isn't quite the legendary stud of popular opinion? Those of us with equipment of average proportions and skills acquired through trial and error rather than divine intervention would be very relieved to find that out. Every man in Italy lives in terror that Gian-Carlo will entice his woman away."

"Oh, shut up," Stevie said, dropping her purse on the floor and falling into the closest chair. "I'm sick of hearing Gian-Carlo attacked by people who don't really know him."

Nick raised his eyebrows. "My, you've come a long way from the Boston schoolteacher who was frightened by the discovery of a strange man in her bed. Or my bed, to be precise. And your new hairdo and dress are very pretty."

Stevie glared at him. Although Nick was an attractive man, she wished he'd leave her alone. He was almost too comfortable to be with. She felt he could see right through her to the nervous little schoolteacher who was pretending to be someone special. "Why are you here, anyway? Especially at—" she glanced at her watch, "two in the morning?"

"You left something at Laura's apartment. When I brought it over, your grandmother was kind enough to invite me to wait for your return. She went to bed a few hours ago. I was starting to worry that you had come to harm, but no woman kisses the way you did unless she's feeling more virtuous than she'd like to."

Stevie gave him a shrewd, hostile glance. "You're reading a hell of a lot into a two-second kiss. And I don't remember leaving anything behind."

He pulled a long yellow scarf out of his pocket and waved it in the air.

"That's not mine."

He shrugged, smiling, and put it back in his pocket. "Well, we all make mistakes. Since I'm here, how would you like to have dinner with me? Tomorrow might be better, since it's a little late tonight. I could pick you up around seven."

Stevie yawned. "What about the Contessa?"

"Why would I invite Laura? *Dio,* one minute you're a sophisticated woman of the world out seducing political candidates to all hours of the night, and the next you're suggesting we need a chaperone for dinner. Stevie Templeton, you're the most confusing woman I've ever met."

She kicked off her shoes, grimacing at the blisters the uncomfortable red sandals had given her, and pulled herself to her feet.

"I'm going to bed."

"Now you're sophisticated again. I know we've been to bed once already, but I still think you're rushing things. I suggest we start with dinner tomorrow. Then, maybe the next night . . ."

"Goddamn you," she muttered as she passed him. She reached out and punched his arm.

"Sadistic, too!" he cried, jumping back. "God, is there no stopping this woman in her pursuit of debauchery?"

When Stevie reached the first step of the wide staircase, she turned back and leaned against the railing.

"I don't want to go out with you," she said.

He came over and stood in front of her. He put his hands lightly on her waist. Without thinking she ran her fingers through his hair. "You need a haircut, Nick."

"Why don't you want to go out with me, little one?"

Her drunkenness was already turning into a hangover. She longed for aspirin and an ice pack.

"I don't remember," she said. "But it's a good reason."

"Is it because of him?" Nick asked quietly.

She bit her lip, afraid to answer.

"You can tell me the truth, Stevie."

She waved her arm, almost toppling over. Nick's hands tightened around her waist to steady her. "I don't know the truth. I don't know anything. But he makes me feel . . ." She shrugged. "Like I'm a different person."

"No doubt," he coldly replied. "But never mind. I can't invite you to tell the truth and then punish you for it. You will take care of yourself, won't you?"

She nodded.

He stared at her for a moment, then pulled her against him. He kissed her again, an ardent, lingering kiss, the kind of kiss that would normally be a prelude to sex. When he finally pulled back they were both breathing heavily.

"You are a magnificent kisser, Stevie Templeton. Who taught you to kiss like that? Wait!" He held out his hand. "Don't tell me. I suspect I wouldn't like the answer."

She grinned. "You're a nice man, for a cad."

He looked shocked. "Why am I a cad?"

"I'm too drunk to remember."

"Drunk and sleepy. Go to bed. I always seem to be telling you to go to bed. And never inviting you. You're probably too tired to be much fun anyway. But don't forget me, *cara*. Actually, I won't let you. I'll be in touch. And remember you have my phone numbers if you need me." He gave her a quick parting kiss and then let himself out of the villa.

Stevie turned and slowly mounted the stairs in her stocking feet, her expensive crimson dress looking as limp as she felt. Her lips, and other parts of her body, were still tingling. Dragging herself up the stairs, she marveled at the fact that two gorgeous men had kissed her with passion tonight, yet here she was, off to bed alone. Obviously, she didn't have this femme fatale business figured out yet.

23

"RUN away with me, my love. I've stopped caring about what the rest of the world thinks."

Angel took a deep breath before replying. "I . . . I can't. There's something I haven't told you. Something . . . terrible."

"Nothing about you could be terrible. Please, just say you'll go with me."

"It wouldn't be fair to you. You see, I have . . ." Angel hesitated, reluctant to speak the word. "I have leprosy." She threw the script on the floor. "Jesus, Aldo, does it have to be leprosy? I don't want to get scabs. Can't I have whatever Ali McGraw had in *Love Story*?"

At the head of the long table, Aldo sighed. He and Angel and John Freemantle, the stars of his next production, were meeting in a room at Cinecittà Studios to run through the partially completed script.

"Angel, *bella*," he said, "I've hired the hottest writer in Europe.

I'm paying him more than my own nephew is getting to be coproducer. We've got to trust his judgment. And remember, this is only a rough draft of the first four scenes. I'm sure he won't actually make you have scabs. I picked him because I thought this would be good for your career. Show your range. You know, that you're more than a pair of tits."

"Lovely though they are. Tits to die for, in my considered opinion," said the voice across the table.

Angel grinned at her new leading man. John Freemantle, an English stage actor in his mid-forties, had accepted the role in Aldo Guerritore's latest movie because, as he put it, it was the only good-paying job he could find anywhere on the planet and he was sick of working for peanuts on the stage. Aldo was thrilled at the chance to inject some class into his latest project at a reasonable cost.

"Tits so magnificent," the Englishman continued in his booming, trained voice, "that I would venture to suggest they would even look good covered in scabs."

In the doorway a compact young man with jet black hair slicked back from his forehead cleared his throat to attract their attention.

"If you've all finished with your miscellaneous crap, I would be happy to enlighten the well-endowed Miss Concelli on the merits of my script."

Ben Gasperini was wearing a well-cut pale linen suit and a black T-shirt. Handsome in a dark, brooding manner, his small figure radiated a brittle energy.

"I'm not the leprosy type," Angel drawled.

Ben snorted. "If it was good enough for Ben Hur's sister then it's good enough for you."

It took them all a moment to realize it was a joke. Then Angel fell back laughing and John Freemantle gave Ben a welcoming nod.

Ben yanked a chair back from the table. He turned it around and set it down next to Angel, then sat astride it and leaned toward her. "I like the idea of leprosy," he said, the words coming so quickly she had to strain to distinguish them. "Celluloid flesh decaying. Though I might let her live. She could just be stringing her lover a line to get rid of him."

"Rid of me?" John said, feigning horror.

"I'd rather live," Angel told the writer. "I died in the last one. I wouldn't want to make dying a habit."

"I saw that film," Ben said. "It's why I agreed to write this script. You've got charisma, but I really don't think you've got any talent."

Angel shrugged. "Better charisma than talent. More money in it."

"Wise words from one so young," John said.

"Fuck money," Ben announced.

John rolled his eyes.

"If you're a serious artist," Angel said, "then why is it that in the scenes we've been given so far I appear in a bubble bath, a bikini, sheer lingerie, and, for the traditionalists, naked on a bed?"

Ben's grin was surprisingly boyish. "Because I get to be on the set during filming," he confessed, his cheeks flushing pink.

One of Aldo's assistants, a young man in baggy jeans with a cigarette dangling from his mouth, slouched into the room and handed Aldo a newspaper. Aldo took one look at it and let out a howl of despair. "Angel, *bella,* how could you do this to me?"

"What?" she asked.

He pushed the newspaper down the table for her to see. On the front page of *Il Tempo* was the photo that had been taken of Angel and Gian-Carlo in her car the day before. Angel looked tired and tense, Gian-Carlo brooding and angry.

"Not flattering," John said, squinting at it across the table. "Who's the gentleman?"

No one bothered to answer the Englishman. To Italians, the question was idiotic.

Under the picture the paper had printed a second one showing Gian-Carlo with his family. It was a publicity photo, staged to show the Cassieri family as a model of respectability and marital bliss. Gian-Carlo and Lucia were smiling into each other's eyes like two love-struck teenagers. Lucia was holding a solemn Roberto's hand.

Francesca, adorable in a white lace dress, was looking up at her handsome father.

Angel stared at the newspaper in silence. No one disturbed her while she read the accompanying article, which speculated on the possible relationship between Gian-Carlo and "sex-bomb" Angel Concelli. But a shot of them naked in bed would have been no more incriminating than the photograph of them in the car, their faces reflecting the particular anger and pain that is reserved for lovers.

Finally Angel looked up at Aldo. "It's okay, Aldo," she said softly. "It'll sell more tickets to the movie." But she knew her haunted expression in the photo was more upsetting to him than any threat to their careers.

Ben, who had stood up to read the paper over Angel's shoulder, was shifting restlessly from foot to foot. Unable to keep his opinions to himself any longer, he blurted out, "Gian-Carlo Cassieri is just a corrupt old fart."

"Maybe," Angel sighed, looking down at the newspaper. "But he's the corrupt old fart of my dreams."

"What do you mean you can't see me?" Angel screamed into the telephone.

Since her dressing room wasn't ready yet, she was using one of the telephones in the huge rehearsal studio. It was after seven, and everyone else had gone for the day. She and Gian-Carlo had arranged to meet when she finished work, but he had just broken the news that they would have to stay apart for several weeks.

"I thought you loved me!" Angel continued, remembering the previous afternoon when they had sat in the car outside her mother's home.

"Of course I love you," he answered. "But we have to be careful. Paparazzi will be following both of us."

To release her anger, Angel shot out her fist and smashed it into the wall next to the telephone. Gian-Carlo didn't ask about the noise. Feeling a little foolish, she sucked her scraped knuckles.

She should have waited until she saw him again and pounded it into his face. Why couldn't the bastard love her as much as he said he did?

"Please," he continued, "try to understand. We both have too much to lose. I was talking it over with Uccellini this afternoon. Now that I'm head of the party—"

"Oh, great. Just what we need. An adviser for our love affair. How incredibly romantic."

Ben Gasperini opened the door on the other side of the room and sauntered in. When Angel saw him she automatically took a more seductive pose, leaning against the wall with her shoulders back and her pelvis out. She kept her voice down, hoping Ben wouldn't be able to make out what she was saying. "So much for our grand passion, Gian-Carlo. Can you imagine Romeo and Juliet playing it cool because of what everyone thought?"

"You're obviously unfamiliar with the play. And Romeo didn't have two children."

"You bastard!" she screeched. She didn't care if Ben heard her. "Your kids have nothing to do with this. Don't use them as a fucking excuse. If you want to be president of the universe and married to a black widow spider, then say so. Don't use those kids to keep me in my place."

She slammed the phone down and looked over at Ben. He was staring at her like a fly caught in a spider's web. She was glad; her ego needed it. She wet her lips and tossed her hair back. Neither of them moved for a minute, letting the sexual tension build. Then, slowly, he walked toward her, swinging the latest draft of the script.

When he reached her he stood too close. She glanced down and saw that he already had an erection.

"Have a fight with the old fart?" he asked. He couldn't suppress a cocky grin. He looked like a teenager, an eager, horny boy with one old prophylactic in his wallet.

Angel shrugged. "What difference does it make?"

"Plenty. Want to go somewhere?"

"Where?"

"Anywhere."

"And?"

"Fuck."

"Are you any good?" she asked, lowering her eyelashes.

"Better than old farts with politics on their minds."

Angel sighed. Although she had goaded him to this point, her ego wasn't really that desperate. If she went home alone she could go to bed with a magazine and some chocolates. The alternative was to have this rather nasty boy humping over her, squirting out his bodily fluids with whoops of joy, while Gian-Carlo spent the evening with his real family.

"Sorry," she snapped, tired of games, even the ones she had started. "I can't tonight."

Ben's mouth tightened. He moved closer, pushing up against her. "Why not?" he whispered between clenched teeth.

Angel glared at him. He was a bore and a pest, and she shouldn't have led him on.

"I have to wash my hair. You know how girls are."

She put her hands on his chest and gently pushed him back.

"You don't know what you're missing," he said.

She suspected she did. But, remembering that she had to work with him for the next several months, she smiled. "Maybe I'll find out before the movie's finished. And thanks for the offer."

She started toward the door and had nearly reached it when she heard Ben's footsteps behind her. He swung her around and pushed her back against the wall. Then he kissed her, a generous, seductive kiss, with none of the horny clumsiness she had expected.

When they came up for air she smiled at him.

"You're not as much of an asshole as you pretend to be," she said.

"Yeah, I know," he said. "Few of us are."

He was caressing her face, admiring her beauty. It felt good. Maybe he would be better than chocolates and a magazine after all.

"I guess my hair can go another day."

He laughed softly. "Your place or mine?"

"Mine. You probably live in a rat-infested garret and invest all your money in Miami condos."

"Currency futures."

"Close enough."

He kissed her again, rubbing his pelvis against hers, letting her feel his erection. "One thing, Angel, before we go. I don't want to be a one-night stand."

"Hey, don't worry," she whispered, nibbling his ear. "I'll probably fuck you right up to the wrap-up party. And then you can move onto the star of your next picture."

"You don't think we're a match made in heaven, the beauty and the brain?"

"I hate to be the one to break the news, but you're not really that good-looking."

He jabbed her in the ribs and then pulled her close. "Don't sell me short, Angel. I'm not used to coming second."

Angel studied the intense young writer. In her heels, she was at least two inches taller than he was. "Sell you short? You're three feet tall!"

He blushed, turning bright red. He was a strange mix of bluff and reality, a boy and a man. But then she was only twenty-two herself, although she felt much older. It might be nice to be with someone young for a change, to party and flirt, without the intensity and pain. Without saying good-bye at three in the morning when her lover crept out of bed to go home to his wife and children.

"You're not married, are you?" Angel suddenly asked, feeling frightened.

"Is that a proposal?"

"Not yet." She moved her hand down between his legs. "But let's go home and you can audition for the part."

24

ANGEL ran her fingers along Ben's naked back.

A technically perfect lover, he was skilled and inventive, as if he had memorized every book on the subject. She wouldn't have been surprised if that was exactly what he'd done. He seemed to be trying to prove something—his worth, his appeal, his right to be successful and wanted. It made him the ideal one-night stand, but too neurotic for anything more. Even if she were shopping around for Gian-Carlo's replacement, Ben wouldn't be the one.

The phone rang again. Someone had called at least fifteen times during the five hours they had been in her apartment. She was certain it was Gian-Carlo. He couldn't let their affair end any more than she could.

"Why don't I answer it for you?" Ben asked, his voice muffled by the pillow pressing against his face. She was sitting cross-legged beside him, naked and sleepy after the lengthy round of sex. "Could you scratch my left shoulder?"

"What would you say to him?" She moved her long red nails to his shoulder.

"I'd tell him that I made you come twelve times."

"Give or take a few."

"Twelve."

"You counted? That's disgusting." She dug her nails deep into his pale skin, enjoying the howl of pain that coincided with the cessation of the telephone's ring. "How do you know I don't come fifty times with him?"

"Everybody knows politicians are lousy lays."

Angel dropped down beside him on the rumpled bed. She whispered in his ear, "Do you really want to know what he's like in bed?" She rubbed her breasts against him. "Want me to tell you what the competition can do?"

With one swift move, he pushed her onto her back and swung on top of her. His dark brown eyes flashed with anger. "No. I just want you never to fuck him again."

Angel shut her eyes, remembering the passion of Gian-Carlo's lovemaking, the sense, when she was in his arms, that she was clinging to the edge of a cliff.

"Don't even think about him," Ben barked out. "I wish I could fuck that guy right out of your head."

"Why?" Angel asked, bored with his absurd jealousy. "I'm only another conquest to you. You don't love me. Hell, you don't even know me. I'm actress number forty-seven, one who counts for extra points because my career is going well, a name to cross off a list. This week Angel Concelli. Who's next?"

"Burt Lancaster. I want to have all the greats. You know that's not true, Angel. And what about your motives? Are they honorable? You're in bed with me because some aging politician is afraid of what the voters will say if they find out he's fucking a common whore like you."

She had been close to tears for so long that she hardly noticed it when she crossed the edge and actually started to cry. The tears pushed their way out of her eyes and slid down her temples onto the satin pillow. Ben was kissing them away, begging her forgiveness, but it was like a kitten trying to lick away a sorrow it couldn't begin to comprehend. The phone started to ring again. She counted the rings, thinking of nothing else. Five, six, seven. By not answering it, she was hurting herself more than Gian-Carlo.

"Please, Angel," Ben pleaded, "say you forgive me."

Ten, eleven.

"There's nobody else like you in the whole world," he continued.

Thirteen, fourteen, fifteen.

"I love you, Angel. I knew it the minute I saw you in that god-awful movie. It's why I took this project. Just to be near you. I love you, I really love you. And you're the only woman I've ever said that to."

Nineteen, twenty. And silence.

She was suddenly conscious of Ben's weight pinning her down.

"What did you say?" she asked, blinking up at him. "I wasn't listening."

At three in the morning, Angel finally got Ben to leave. When he argued at the door that he should stay the rest of the night so they could go to the studio together in the morning, she realized with a shudder that their affair would soon be gossip all over the set. Then the paparazzi would be onto it. But at least it would take some of the heat off the rumors about her and Gian-Carlo. People would probably conclude she was just someone Gian-Carlo had sampled for a quickie, which would be far less damaging to his career than talk of love.

The phone had been silent since a little after one. Still naked, she flopped down on the bed, too exhausted and depressed to straighten the stained sheets. But an hour later, when the phone finally rang again, she was wide awake, staring at the ceiling.

"Ciao," she said, trying to sound nonchalant.

"Angel. Don't ever do that to me again. Do you hear me? Ever."

He was unfair. If she did something that hurt him she was being selfish and shallow, but everything he did was allegedly for a good reason. She didn't want to fight, though, she wanted to roll over and discover him buried in the sheets. She wanted to go to sleep with her cheek pressed against his warm shoulder and wake up in the morning with him still beside her.

"Hanging up on me was bad enough," he went on, "but refusing to answer your phone was really childish."

"I was out."

"Don't lie to me."

"Okay, I won't! I spent the night fucking someone else. Here, in this bed. The same one we use. I came—he tells me—twelve times."

"Only twelve?"

Angel smiled. "You bastard. When did I ever come twelve times with you?"

"My goal is quality, not quantity. I love you, Angel. Will you see me tomorrow? And the day after? And the day after that?"

She stretched out on the bed and raised one leg to admire it. "Everybody loves me tonight. It's about time. I've been waiting all my life to become popular. Where are you? In the master bedroom? Is Lucia snoring next to you, her false teeth in a glass by the side of the bed?"

She had driven past his house once, an enormous, sprawling structure surrounded by a high wire fence.

"I'm in my den."

"I'm naked on my bed. Alone. Alone now, anyway, since lover boy went home for a change of clothes."

"Angel."

She sighed. It was his demanding tone, the one that told her he was going to ask for more than she wanted to give.

"Angel, I'm very sorry for what I said. And you know I couldn't really have gone days, let alone weeks, without seeing you. But you have to promise me something."

Her chest tightened and her mouth went dry. She knew what he was going to ask. It was too unfair, too one-sided. "Don't say it," she whispered. "Don't even ask."

"Angel, I have to. I love you. Do you know what it does to me to think of you making love to someone else? I satisfy you, don't I? You don't need other men."

"I do," she whispered. She couldn't begin to tell him how much she needed someone else, how much she wished she could purge the desire for him and only want another man. Even neurotic, boyish Ben would have been better than a lover whose real life had nothing to do with her, and never would. "I need someone. Right now, I need someone. And you're not here, are you? What am I supposed to do?"

He was silent. She hoped he would say that he'd be right over. But that was impossible, even if he'd wanted to. It was nearly morning, and she had to be at work by six-thirty.

He took a deep breath. "You like making love to me, don't you?" he asked. His voice was husky and low; it was as if he were whispering in her ear, his hot breath running down her spine.

She wanted him. She wanted him so much it hurt. Her desire was stronger than any and all of her twelve orgasms with Ben.

"Do you want me now?"

She nodded, knowing he already knew the answer.

"Do you need me, Angel? The way I need you?"

"Don't do this," she whispered, rolling over onto her stomach, pressing her body against the oversize pillow. "I can't take it."

"Don't you want to feel my hands on you right now? My mouth?"

"Please, stop," she begged. She moved her hand to her breast. The nipple was hard. "You're being cruel to me."

"Open your legs," he whispered.

She opened them, pushing her pelvis against the pillow, pretending it was his body.

"Tell me you need me, Angel. Tell me! I have to hear it!"

"I need you," she whispered. "You know that already."

"Tell me you won't let anyone else touch you."

She was crying, crying too much, crying every day. "I can't," she said. "I get lonely. Gian-Carlo, try to understand."

"You can promise. You have to. Feel me making love to you, Angel. Feel my hands, feel my mouth, feel all of me. Right now. Then tell me you'll never have another man."

"Please," she begged. "Try to understand."

He hung up.

25

STEVIE pushed away the untouched plate of sausages. She couldn't even look at them without gagging. Her stomach was on fire, her head was pounding, and her nerves felt as if they had been transplanted to the surface of her skin.

She had never had a good head for alcohol. And now, when she had so much to think about—Gian-Carlo, Nick, her grandmother's revelations—all she wanted was to lie in a dark room and wait for her body to recover from an excess of champagne.

Gina came into the dining room, her feet pounding like an invading army.

"Gian-Carlo Cassieri is here to see you." The usually polite maid scowled, expressing her disapproval, and added, "Again."

Stevie frowned as her swollen brain slowly processed the information. It was eleven o'clock on Sunday morning, only nine hours since he had dropped her off at the door after their dinner together. In Boston she couldn't even get a date, and in Rome two spectacular men were paying her unexpected visits at the oddest hours. Toni was right—Rome was the place to be.

She suddenly remembered that she looked awful. In addition to the ravages of the alcohol, she wasn't wearing makeup, her hair was uncombed, and she had pulled on her oldest shirt and jeans.

"Tell him to wait, Gina. Please." Stevie rushed out of the room. She snuck up the back stairs, did a quick repair job on her face and hair, pulled on a skirt and blouse of sea-green silk that she'd bought the day before, and made it back downstairs in less than ten minutes.

The night before had apparently done no harm to Gian-Carlo. He looked relaxed and handsome in a cream suit and white shirt.

"Sorry to keep you waiting," Stevie gasped, trying to catch her breath after the whirlwind change.

He surveyed her with approving eyes. "It's always a pleasure to wait for a beautiful woman. Within reason, of course."

"Well," she countered, "my beauty is certainly within reason, though I'm not sure about the wait."

He laughed. "You're so different from Angel."

"Why wouldn't I be different from her? We were raised by different people, in different countries. The only thing we have in common is blood."

"Only blood," he said, raising his eyebrows. "What an American remark. I wonder what Angel would have said if she had found out about *you*."

Stevie stared at him for a moment. Sometimes he seemed to read her mind and understand her deepest fears and insecurities. "I've wondered that, too," she admitted. "Would I have mattered to her at all? She's so special, and I'm . . ." She couldn't finish the sentence.

He took her hands and pulled her closer to him. "You take modesty to such absurd extremes. Of course you would have mattered to her. Though I suspect that Angel would have been frightened by the discovery that she had a sister."

"Frightened? Of me?"

"Not of you in particular. But to Angel your existence would have meant there was one more person in the world with the power to hurt her, to reject her."

"I would never have—"

He interrupted. "Don't be so certain. Angel could be very trying, even for those of us who cared very deeply for her. She was a simple girl with a complicated life. Simple girls can be difficult. They don't understand the messy compromises the rest of us make. Sometimes I felt she wanted me to say that I'd run off to a deserted island with her where we could live on berries and nuts for the rest of our lives." He shrugged. "But she would have hated that as much as I would. By the second day she would have been complaining that the island didn't have air-conditioning."

Looking into his attractive dark eyes, Stevie could sympathize with her sister's position. She had already had a few daydreams in which he announced he would leave his wife, withdraw from politics, and go back to Boston with her. Of course, for her they were only daydreams; but if she were as beautiful and fascinating as Angel, she might have expected more.

"There must be something other than the extremes of a demanding political career and a deserted island," she said, trying to think of Angel and not herself. "Another option."

He nodded. "Yes." He sounded bitter. "Once I even thought we had found it. But—" He shook his head, cutting off his words, then abruptly changed the subject. "But why are we wasting our time standing here? Come on, my car is outside."

"Where are we going?" Stevie asked.

He smiled down at her. "Why don't I surprise you?"

"Actually, I don't like surprises," Stevie said, feeling nervous despite herself.

"Don't worry. I know you'll like this one." He read the fear in her eyes. "You're not afraid of me, are you?" he added.

Her grandmother's voice—*I believe that he is an evil man*—seemed to whisper in her ear.

Stevie smiled brightly so he wouldn't read her thoughts. "Of course not. I can't imagine anyone being afraid of you."

He grinned and squeezed her hand. "At last. A woman who understands me."

"Now, this isn't our real destination," Gian-Carlo said as he led her along the dark corridor. Except for a few guards, the government building was deserted on a Sunday. "But I thought you might like to see my office first."

"I'd love to," Stevie said, excited by this backstage look at the world of power.

A young security guard with a gun in a shoulder holster was standing at the end of the hall. Gian-Carlo nodded at him, then ushered Stevie into the wood-paneled room where he worked. He leaned back against the door while she looked around.

"It's very impressive," she said, taking in the enormous oak desk, the forest green leather furniture, the modern paintings on the wall. Dark brown velvet curtains kept the bright sun from entering the dimly lit room.

"Sit down," he said, nodding at his own chair. "See what it feels like."

"Really, I couldn't," she said. "And you must be incredibly busy, with the election so soon. I've been taking up too much of your time." Since she was enjoying his flattering attentions, she hadn't let herself think about his other obligations. But this forbidding office reminded her that an extremely important and powerful man had been wasting hours of his precious time with her.

Gian-Carlo gestured at the chair again. "Please," he said. "I have all the time in the world."

Stevie shrugged and slipped into his chair. Sitting behind the huge desk, she felt like a small child who had sneaked into the secret, important world of adults.

Gian-Carlo walked to the front of the desk. "I wish I could just hand the whole job over to you. You efficient American women always look like you could take on anything."

Stevie grinned. "Not me. I'm just a schoolteacher. I wouldn't know where to begin."

149

He stared at her for a moment. "You're beautiful," he whispered.

Stevie lowered her head, allowing her hair to fall forward and hide her embarrassment.

"No," Gian-Carlo whispered, coming around the side of the desk. He put his hands on her arms and swiveled the chair so that she was facing him. He knelt beside her, then gently pushed her hair back behind her ears. "Your face is too beautiful to cover up."

Her heart was pounding so hard she was afraid he would hear it. He dropped his hands to her shoulders. His palms were hot through her silk blouse. Her breath was shallow and quick. She remembered the kisses in the piazza, his hot, demanding mouth, his body pressed against hers. All night long she had tossed and turned, imagining a scene like this.

He touched the top button on her blouse. His eyes remained on hers as he slowly undid it. "Do you want me?" he whispered.

Stevie caught her breath. His fingers had moved to the second button. "Yes," she whispered.

He put his hands under her arms and suddenly lifted her out of the chair and set her down on the edge of the huge desk. His eyes hadn't left hers. His hands slid over the silk covering her breasts.

He stepped back to look at her. "Undo your blouse," he said. "Open it for me."

"I . . ." She hesitated.

"Please," he whispered.

Her fingers moved to her blouse. While he watched, she slowly undid the remaining buttons. She was only wearing a thin camisole underneath. It had a row of tiny pearl buttons down the front. She unbuttoned them one by one, conscious of his eyes on her hands. When she finished, she was too shy to open it herself. She looked up at him, hoping he would understand.

Gian-Carlo stepped forward. He put his hands on her shoulders and gently lowered her down onto the desk. She stared up into his eyes. Then his hands moved to the camisole. Without looking down, he opened it. He kissed her mouth, slowly, his hands still holding her clothes open. Her bare breasts rubbed against his shirt. Then his mouth moved along the curve of her jaw, down her throat, onto her breast. His tongue touched her nipple. He made her feel like the most desirable woman in the world.

"Angel," he whispered.

Someone pounded on the door.

26

TENSE and embarrassed, Stevie pulled back the edge of the velvet curtain and looked down at the traffic outside Gian-Carlo's office.

While she had quickly buttoned up her clothes, Gian-Carlo had answered the door. A man she couldn't see said he needed to speak to Gian-Carlo for a few minutes. Gian-Carlo gestured for her to wait and then slipped out.

She wished she could go home and never see him again. When he had whispered Angel's name, she had gone from feeling desirable to shabby in a split second. What kind of dream world had she been living in? Nick and her grandmother were wrong: there was nothing dangerous about Gian-Carlo. But spending time with him was a mistake. She couldn't seem to stop herself from falling in love with him. But the woman he wanted was Angel, not plain little Stevie Templeton.

"How do you like Rome?"

At the sound of the woman's voice, Stevie dropped the heavy curtain and slowly turned around. She felt like a little girl caught snitching candies by someone with a large ruler.

Lucia Cassieri looked just like her newspaper photographs. She was wearing a dazzling white bouclé suit, her black hair pulled tightly back from her face. A lesser woman would have been destroyed by such a severe style, but Lucia looked stunning. She had an aura of power and control, a woman who could do and have whatever she wanted.

Stevie squirmed, feeling more than ever like a child who had misbehaved. Her green silk outfit, wrinkled after the episode on the desk, looked cheap and juvenile next to Lucia's sophisticated ensemble. Stevie wished she had worn jeans and a cotton shirt, taking herself completely out of competition.

"Rome is beautiful," Stevie said, finally answering the surprisingly innocuous question.

Lucia raised one eyebrow. "Undoubtedly. It makes one feel . . . small, though. Insignificant."

Stevie knew Lucia had never felt small and insignificant. "I'm pretty small and insignificant to start with," she said, deciding to be honest. She had nothing to lose. This woman was only further proof that she had never had a chance of winning Gian-Carlo. Maybe Angel had, but not Stevie Templeton.

"Nonsense, my dear," Lucia replied politely as she sat down in one of the leather chairs and crossed her slim legs. She studied her perfectly manicured nails. An enormous diamond ring flashed in the light. "Do you like my husband's office?"

"Yes, of course," Stevie said, blushing as she remembered lying beneath him on the desk. She felt as if Lucia knew what had happened, but of course that wasn't possible. "But I didn't mean to intrude," she added.

Lucia smiled as if Stevie had said something amusing. "I'm sure you didn't, Signorina Templeton," she remarked dryly. "Few of us actually *want* to intrude in other people's lives."

"I meant . . ." Stevie sighed. She couldn't handle all the undercurrents in the conversation. But it was her own fault, for getting involved with a married man. "I just meant I'm sorry."

"I'm glad to hear that."

Stevie avoided the woman's piercing eyes. She wished she could snap her fingers and instantly transport herself back to Toni's apartment in Boston, where her best friend would undoubtedly be chattering away about matters of absolutely no consequence.

Lucia broke the silence. "I understand you never met your sister."

Stevie shook her head.

Lucia nodded, as if the question had only been posed to confirm her sources. "I only met her twice. Early in her career and again not long before she died. She was a lovely child. Beautiful." Lucia's mouth tightened, and she suddenly looked much older. "It is a pity she had to die."

Lucia turned her mesmerizing, intelligent eyes on Stevie again as if she were trying to determine whether the American had understood.

"Your sister," Lucia continued, "was not a careful person. I hope that isn't a trait you also inherited."

"I'm too careful," Stevie replied quickly, envying Angel's courage and spontaneity. She couldn't imagine Angel being intimidated by this woman. And who was Lucia to talk? She didn't exactly look timid herself.

Lucia smiled. "I wonder. Would you be here if that were true?"

Stevie blushed. The woman had a point. Although she had thought this was merely a sight-seeing expedition, she had certainly been pleased and flattered when Gian-Carlo turned it into something more.

"Just don't try to live your sister's life. I know it must be tempting. But remember how her life ended." Lucia cleared her throat. "You wouldn't want the same sort of thing to happen to you."

"It could never—" Stevie began.

Lucia interrupted, rushing her words now. "My husband will be back in a moment. I'm going to leave now because I don't want an embarrassing scene. I know young people hate receiving advice from their elders, but I really must offer some. Remember one thing, Signorina Templeton. We were all very pleased when we heard of Angel Concelli's death. She was mourned by no one who really knew her. I'm sure that is not the death you want for yourself."

Then, as quietly and quickly as she had arrived, Lucia slipped out of a second door at the side of the office.

Before Stevie had a chance to figure out what Lucia was trying to say—other than *hands off my husband*—Gian-Carlo returned. He looked haggard as he came in the door, but his eyes lit up when he saw her. The armed guard was standing in the shadows behind him.

She wondered if he would expect them to resume their love-making. She wished she had gone home when she'd had the chance.

Instead, he smiled at her from the doorway. "Come on. Get your purse."

"I should be getting back—"

"This is important," he insisted. "We still have our second stop to make."

"Really, Gian-Carlo," she said, "I can't—"

"I'm going to take you to see someone you haven't seen in a long time." He ran his fingers through his hair, looking tired again.

"I'm going to take you to meet your mother."

27

"DON'T pinch me," Angel snapped.

The plump wardrobe girl standing behind Angel silently mouthed an obscenity. She grabbed both sides of the strapless black dress and yanked them together, then tried to force the zipper up. It wouldn't budge. The girl pushed harder, digging the zipper into Angel's skin.

"Ouch! Stop that or I'll have you fired!"

The girl exhaled loudly. "It's not my fault you've put on weight since we took your measurements, Signorina Concelli."

"I have not," Angel growled. "You just don't know what you're doing."

"Why don't you try holding your breath?"

"I can hardly breathe now!" Angel screamed. "You must have made a mistake!"

"Now, now, ladies," John Freemantle said, preening before the

156

mirror in a dapper blue suit. He straightened the yellow silk kerchief in his breast pocket. "This should be white—it's tacky to
have the kerchief match the tie—but never mind, the audience for
this movie will never know. Angel darling, I hate to be anything
less than a gentleman, but you do appear to have put on an ounce
or two. Perhaps a touch too much pasta and champagne?"

Angel groaned. "God, don't mention food. My stomach hates
me."

The wardrobe girl, out of hostility more than professional enthusiasm, made another violent attempt at the jammed zipper. Angel howled with pain.

"*Basta!* I'm the star of this picture. Nobody's treating me like
that." Scowling at the unperturbed wardrobe girl, Angel turned
and stalked out of the room.

John followed her into her dressing room. "How tasteless," he
murmured, surveying the pink and mauve decor, which Aldo considered appropriate for any female star. "My wallpaper is littered
with ducks and shotguns. I keep wanting to hide under the bed.
It's my notorious sympathy for the underdog. I suppose our il-
lustrious producer thinks all Englishmen have an unseemly taste
for the blood of small animals."

Angel was slumped in front of the large mirror on her dressing
table. "I'm losing my looks," she said. "I'm twenty-two and I'm
already losing my looks."

John sat down on a pink wicker chair that creaked and sagged
under his weight. "Darling Angel, I don't mean to speak out of
turn, since we've only known each other a little more than six
weeks, but I do suspect you may be, as we English say, preggers.
Which may present some difficulties for your portrayal of the virgin cum nymphomaniac our Ben has created. God, where is
Nabokov when we need him? Well, dead and rotting, or at best
arguing grammatical points in a White Russian heaven. But back to
the matter at hand . . . Are you listening to me, Angel dear?"

Angel was still examining her unusually pasty complexion in
the harshly lit mirror.

"I thought pregnant women glowed," she said.

157

"Lightbulbs glow. Pregnant women vomit and get hemorrhoids. How far along are you?"

"I'm not pregnant." She stared into her dull eyes. "I am not pregnant," she repeated with more conviction.

"This isn't a line reading, Angel, this is real life. How far along are you?"

She shrugged. "A month, I think. My period was due two weeks ago."

"Which would make you six weeks pregnant, due to the ridiculous system used to calculate these things. I've never understood how the medical profession can claim that a woman was one week pregnant a week prior to conception. But never mind. I suppose this means the father can't be our magnificent screenwriter, who has been discreetly and in the most gentlemanly way letting everyone on the set know he had the honor of sampling your considerable favors five weeks ago. Twelve orgasms, too, I understand."

He shook his head in simulated awe. "My ex-wife, bless the bitch, didn't come that many times in the entire six years of our marriage. Well, not with me, anyway, and there were extenuating circumstances. But I keep getting distracted from the problem at hand. Tell me, what is your response to this allegedly blessed event? Do you actually want to have one of those demanding little creatures who will cover you in snot and shit?"

"I don't know if I want the kid," she answered. With a final scowl at her appearance, she started layering blusher on her pale cheeks. "But I definitely want its father."

"Was this, then, a planned act? A premeditated attempt to increase the population of our overcrowded planet?"

"God, no." She was making up her eyes, but her face still had a pallid, tired look. "I'm just careless. And I hate all that gunky stuff. I don't even know exactly when it happened."

"Oh, to have a sex life so active! But you're sure of the father?"

"Absolutely," she nodded. "I only fuck someone else when we've had a fight."

"I never realized what an old-fashioned girl you were. So you're going to tell the man of your dreams—presumably a certain well-known politician—and hope he offers to leave wife and kiddies and risk his entire political future to make you an honorable woman and give your joint love child a name from the paternal side of the family tree?"

Angel met his eyes in the mirror. Colored contact lenses made his a disconcerting shade of blue. "Love conquers all and everyone lives happily ever after," she said. "That's what happens in movies, isn't it?"

"It depends on the scriptwriter, but usually no. The unwed mother gives up the baby for adoption and then lives a dreadful life, usually drunken and desperate for money."

Angel pinched her cheeks in a final attempt to make herself look healthy. "Then thank God this isn't a movie. Because I expect a happy ending."

"Angel, darling." John moved his chair closer and slipped his arm around her shoulders. "To be serious, which is rare for me, if I can do anything to help I will. Money, names, a place to go. Anything. Don't let this destroy your life. You'll have many opportunities to have another child. With someone who really loves you, who wants to spend his life with you. If you have this child . . ." He shook his head. "The mind reels at the possible complications. The scandal, the media drooling over every detail. The paparazzi would turn the poor kid's life into a living hell, as well as yours."

Angel stared down at her abdomen. Gently she placed her hand on it, as if she expected to feel some movement, a heartbeat, the first kick of an almost infinitesimal baby.

"I wouldn't be able to have this baby again," she whispered, tears coming to her eyes. "A different one, maybe, but what about this one here, the one Gian-Carlo and I made together? Can I really tell it to go away?"

John was silent for a moment. Then he pulled her against his chest in a rough embrace. "Oh, Angel, darling, I'm so sorry. I had no right to pressure you. Do whatever you want. Those bastards out there don't matter. Go to Cassieri. Tell him. Maybe I'm selling him short; maybe you will have a happy ending."

She pulled in one corner of her mouth, trying not to cry, if for no other reason than that she didn't want to redo her makeup.

"Sure," she said. "And Santa Claus will bring me a nice Christmas present." She touched her abdomen again. "Welcome to real life, kid. And don't expect it to get any better."

28

"ANGEL, *carissima,* listen to reason."

"Fuck reason!" she screamed. "Fuck everybody! For once, *I* want to come first. Angel Concelli, loser. I want my wishes to matter. Did you make Lucia get an abortion when she was pregnant?"

"Lucia has nothing to do with this."

Angel paced back and forth on the plush white rug in her oversize living room. Gian-Carlo hovered by the door, hoping for an opportunity to escape.

Angel paused to glare at him. "You're a bastard, Gian-Carlo. I knew it all along. I don't know why I let myself get involved with you."

He held out his hands in a gesture of peace. "Angel, think this out. What else can we do? How can you have this child? It will destroy both our lives and the lives of my children. And the child

161

will only suffer. We're too famous. I'm not some accountant who could quietly leave his wife."

"Do you want to leave your wife?" Angel shot back.

"In some ways, of course! I love you, you know that. But things aren't that simple. I have a duty to my country, to the people of Italy."

Angel collapsed in a chair and covered her face with her hands. "What am I doing here?" she whispered. "Why am I even taking part in this absurd discussion? This man doesn't love me."

"Angel, of course I love you." Gian-Carlo came over and knelt in front of her. "*Cara,* I wish everything could be different. I wish I could say the things you want me to say. I would love to live with you, with our child. But it's too late in my life. I burnt my bridges long ago. You're right, I should never have drawn you into this affair. But I wanted you so much. Needed you. Is that so terrible?"

"Yes," she howled, throwing back her head and raising her fists to the ceiling. "Yes, it's terrible. You can't make someone love you and then abandon them when things get rough. That's the definition of a bastard, Gian-Carlo. You're selfish, greedy, inconsiderate, cruel . . ." She choked back a sob. "Our child!" she wailed. "Stop for one fucking second and try to imagine our child. What would it be like? What kind of person would it grow up to be? What would its existence mean for the two of us, for the love we're supposed to share? Don't you see? We would be bound together forever. I could stop worrying that one day you'll just cut me out of your life and never see me again. I wouldn't be the lesser love, the one on the side. I hate coming second to Lucia. God, I hate knowing you've had children with her, that you share a complete life with her. With me, in the end it's only sex. There's nothing solid, nothing lasting. Do you know how much that hurts me? I want to be closer to you than anyone ever has. I want to share everything two people can share. I want to be your family, Gian-Carlo, and I want you to be my family. With a child we could do it, we could pull it off. We'd have a reason for risking everything, for hurting people. It wouldn't just be our own selfishness. It would be for our child. But you won't . . ."

She covered her face with her hands again. Gian-Carlo, still on his knees in front of her, gently pulled her fingers apart so she would look at him.

When she saw tears in his eyes, her heart filled with hope. She had finally made him understand.

"You're right," he whispered. "The pregnancy does make us closer. Together we've made a new life. And even if I lose you to another man someday, I'll always know we had that ultimate intimacy, our bodies locked together in passion, creating a new being. In this, mere men and women become gods. I know in the end you'll understand that you can't have this baby, but even the abortion won't take this closeness away from us. We'll always know that, however briefly, we were part of a miracle."

Angel stared at him in silence, her face blank.

He leaned forward, pressing his palms against her thighs. "Angel, tell me you feel closer to me, too."

Before he realized what was happening she jerked up her knee and slammed it into his chest, knocking him off balance. Gasping for air, he landed on his back. "I should kill you!" she screamed, leaping to her feet. "I should get a knife and ram it into you!"

In agony, he clutched his chest and moaned for help. His face was gray; beads of perspiration had broken out on his forehead. Angel stared down at his writhing figure. "I loathe you, Gian-Carlo. You know what I'm going to do? I'm going to marry someone else." She kicked him in the leg to make sure he was listening. "I'm going to marry a man who worships me, and I'm going to tell him it's his baby. Together we're going to raise your little bastard. No one will ever know you're the real father. And, listen to me, Gian-Carlo, listen carefully: this kid is going to be magnificent. Better than the two wimps you and Lucia produced. You'll spend the rest of your life regretting this."

"Angel," he moaned, "please, you have to understand—"

"I already understand. And that's why the next time you see me I'll be Mrs. Ben Gasperini."

She stepped over his prostrate figure and walked to the door.

"One more thing," she said, turning back, "when you leave take everything that's yours. This is the last time you'll see my apartment. My husband-to-be is the jealous type. He wouldn't want any of my old lovers coming around to bother us."

"Angel," he wheezed, struggling to sit up. "I'll talk to Lucia. I'll see what I can do. Give me some time."

Her eyes were cold. "It's too late, Gian-Carlo. Are you so fucking stupid? Can't you see that you finally went too far?"

He managed to straighten his pained body. He struggled to his knees, his face still ashen, and held out his arms. "Did you think it would be easy for me to hurt my children? To destroy my career? Angel, I wish I could be this perfect man you want so much. But I'm only human. Don't leave me now. Please. I'll find a way. I'll do whatever you want."

Their eyes met and held.

Angel slowly realized what had finally happened. Gian-Carlo Cassieri was on his knees, begging her, offering to do whatever she wanted.

"Please Angel," he whispered.

As if she were moving in a dream, outside the rules of time and space, she turned and put her hand on the brass doorknob. She saw her fingers squeezing the cool knob; she saw the door slowly opening. She seemed to float into the hallway. She could fly away if she wanted to; she could be free of him.

She decided to risk one final look. He was crying; he was on his knees and crying. She marveled at the sight; it was a miracle, like a statue of the Virgin Mary with teardrops of blood pouring down her cheeks. Gian-Carlo, offering her exactly what she wanted. The vision pulled her forward; she felt as if she might tumble across the room and into his arms. He would kiss her and make her dreams come true. It would be different this time; she had heard his promise. All she had to do was say yes, and the future was hers.

Instead, another word forced its way out of her mouth just before she shut the door.

"Liar."

29

"Is it far?" Stevie whispered. It was the only question she had the courage to ask. All the others that had rushed through her head while Gian-Carlo maneuvered his car along the coastal road south of Rome toward her mother's home were like grenades, too frightening to touch.

"We're nearly there," he answered.

She shivered in the brisk sea breeze. The afternoon had turned cold, and heavy clouds threatened rain. Beside them, the Tyrrhenian sea looked polluted and icy, a far cry from the fabled Mediterranean parade ground for exhibitionist starlets and sun worshippers. This barren, cruel landscape was an Italy she hadn't been exposed to, a harsh place where for centuries people had struggled to survive.

Claire Templeton, the woman Stevie had mourned for as long as she could remember, lived here. How many nights had she cried quietly in her room for her lost mother? She couldn't begin to count them.

She glanced at Gian-Carlo's profile. He hummed softly, a popular tune that was playing on radios wherever she went. He seemed pleased with himself. She couldn't begin to understand his latest action. Sometimes he was as clear to her as her own mind, but this time he had shocked her with a bizarre, inexplicable twist.

Grief had to be the reason. Lucia was wrong when she said no one had loved Angel. Perhaps she couldn't bear the truth, that her husband had loved Angel. He was obviously a man in mourning. That was why Stevie couldn't stay angry with him, even though he had called her by her sister's name. She knew grief, knew it well from her father's death. People caught in its pain deserved kindness and patience.

Gian-Carlo slowed the car and turned up a narrow driveway. Stevie looked down at the floor. She was afraid to look at the house. Her heart was rushing at what seemed like a thousand beats a minute.

He turned the engine off. Stevie wiped her sweaty palms on her skirt and slowly raised her eyes to look at the house.

It was a small stone building, constructed in a simple square with space for three rooms at most. A peasant's house, like many they had passed on the way. The only oddity was its isolation, perched on a small ridge overlooking the sea with no other buildings in sight. There wasn't even a car.

Gian-Carlo moved to open his door.

"Wait," Stevie said. Her heart was still racing. "I need a minute."

"Stephanie." He put his hand on hers. "Trust me. I know this is the right thing."

"I'm not sure," she whispered. The plain dwelling terrified her like a haunted house in a horror film. Not without reason, she thought, since this one did contain a ghost. "For so long, I thought she was dead," Stevie admitted, "I can't seem to—"

Gian-Carlo sighed. "You have to see her. She's your mother." He got out of the car and walked around and opened her door for her. When she looked up at him, he smiled down at her. His eyes were reassuring. He really believed this was the right thing.

Reluctant to make a scene, Stevie followed him to the house. His loud knock echoed in the silent landscape. The wind had picked up; her skirt whipped against her legs. The first drops of rain struck her face. Stevie stared at the wood door, praying it wouldn't open.

Let her be dead, she thought. *Let Gian-Carlo be wrong, let my mother be dead.* Then she stepped back, frightened by the harshness of the wish.

Gian-Carlo knocked again. He waited patiently, confident someone would come.

"Let's go," Stevie whispered. "No one is here."

"She's always here," Gian-Carlo replied. "I made inquiries. She never leaves the house."

"She must go shopping, go into Rome . . ."

"A woman in the next village tends to practical matters."

"Gian-Carlo, I can't—" Stevie's heart was thumping so hard she thought she would faint. She turned to look at the pounding sea, trying to calm herself, but the relentless crashing of the waves only added to her rising fear.

The door opened. But she couldn't turn around, she couldn't look.

Gian-Carlo spoke first. "I've wanted to say this for a long time. I was afraid I might never have the chance. Signora Concelli, I've brought your daughter to see you."

He put his hand on Stevie's arm, signaling her to turn around. She stared at the sea, thinking of years of false grief, of lies and lies and lies. Her dead mother: when Stevie was a child, she had thought her head would explode from images of that giving, gentle flesh turning to dust in a Boston cemetery. So many times she had wondered why her father wouldn't take her there, why he wouldn't let her see her own mother's tombstone.

"Stephanie," Gian-Carlo prompted.

The woman in the doorway hadn't spoken.

Stevie howled. A wild, inhuman cry that burned her throat, as years of suppressed pain spilled out of her. She knew that if she turned around she would throttle the woman. She would put her fingers around the bitch's neck and strangle her dead on the spot.

She wouldn't be satisfied until the eyes went blank, the flesh started to rot, and those fucking, useless bones finally crumbled away.

Her scream didn't seem to belong to her. It continued to spin out of her mouth and over the sea. If she turned around she would kill, she would kill her own mother.

You will first discover it in your own heart.

She ran, stumbling down the steps to the road, ran like a wild beast, trying to escape from the monster who had brought her into this world.

30

STEVIE stumbled into the dark bar. The driving rain had plastered her hair to her head and turned her silk outfit into a dishrag. She had flagged a ride from a truck driver near her mother's house, but he had only taken her about half a mile. A sudden thunderstorm had drenched her while she trudged along a deserted stretch of road.

When she spotted the bar in the distance, she rejoiced, but now that she was inside and her eyes were adjusting to the gloom, she was having second thoughts.

It was a small dingy place, thick with cigarette smoke and dust. The other patrons—a depressing selection of the worst Italy had to offer—were all men, and each one appeared to be taking a detailed inventory of her physical assets. She tried to straighten the clinging wet skirt, but it was a hopeless task.

Glancing back at the door, she wondered if the storm might be

169

a better bet. But she couldn't walk any farther. Her expensive sexy shoes had collapsed, and her already aching feet were becoming bruised and swollen. Beauty certainly had its price. She limped over to the bar and leaned across the counter to address the bartender, a huge man with a black mustache and contemptuous eyes.

"Per favore," she said, "I need to use a telephone."

He smirked and threw a knowing glance at his customers, as if to suggest that she had asked for his sexual favors instead of a telephone. "You need to, do you?" he crowed.

She took a deep breath. This was no time to come up against the infamous Italian machismo. She made her voice firm. "I am an American." Someone behind her snickered, but she ignored it. "I'm lost. I need to make a telephone call."

"You're not lost," the bartender said, waving his arms to make sure everyone caught his performance. "I know where you are!"

"Very amusing," Stevie muttered over the roar of laughter that greeted his wit. "You should have your own television show. Now would you please tell me where the telephone is?"

He put his hands on his hips to show off the beefy muscles and unimaginative tattoos of hearts and birds bulging out below the sleeves of his stained T-shirt. After a long silence, during which he presumably made some point that Stevie preferred not to identify, he gestured to the back of the bar. She dropped her ruined shoes on the floor and walked past the gauntlet of leering eyes in her stocking feet.

At the telephone, she ignored her audience and took a moment to decide what to do. The obvious choice was to call a taxi and go back to her grandmother's villa, where a hot bath and change of clothes would be bliss. But she wasn't ready to face her grandmother yet. Ellen had stressed the importance of truth and then kept from her the biggest secret of all—the fact that Claire was still alive.

There was only one other person who could help her. She rummaged in her purse and finally found the card tucked away in a corner. She dialed, praying the Contessa wouldn't answer. Laura

170

Barberini was one of the many things she wasn't ready to think about.

"What is it?" he barked.

"Oh, Nick, the least you could do is sound friendly," she wailed, close to tears. "Do you know how hard it was for me to make this call?"

"Stevie, I'm sorry," he said in a softer tone. "I didn't expect it to be anyone I knew. I'm in the middle of some work. Laura's gone off to Milano and I told the servants to go home. I thought it was some tedious friend of Laura's calling to gossip. Gossip about you, I might add, since you're the current hot topic in Roman society. Where are you, *cara?* What's wrong?"

"I'm . . ." She looked around the oppressive bar. The tables and walls were filthy. The men looked rough and violent, and they were all staring at her.

"I don't know where I am," she said, starting to cry. "And I'm wet and cold and terrified."

"*Cara,* please don't cry. Let me speak to someone there. I'll straighten everything out."

"I can't," she whispered. "They're all men. And I'm afraid of them."

"My God, the predicaments you get yourself into. What kind of place is it?"

"A bar. In the countryside somewhere. There's nothing else around. And I got caught in the rain."

"You Americans carry sight-seeing to such extremes. Get the bartender."

"I'm afraid to."

"Get him."

Since she couldn't offer any alternative, she put the receiver down and walked back to the counter while the men watched in silence. She was starting to feel like the floor show. She whispered to the bartender, hoping no one else would hear.

"A gentleman on the phone would like to speak to you."

"What!" he bellowed, stepping back and waving his arms again.

171

"Who wants to speak to me? A gentleman? No gentleman ever speaks to me!"

The patrons all laughed, and the bartender beamed at his social triumph. Stevie stared around her at these hostile, foreign creatures. Why did they want to humiliate her? What had she ever done to them? Life was too difficult, one pointless cruelty after another.

With a sigh, she slipped onto one of the high stools and put her head down on the counter. "That's it. I give up," she moaned. "I hate Italy. I want to go home."

A heavy silence followed her remarks. She shut her eyes, wishing she could fall asleep and wake up in her old apartment in Boston, the jangling alarm erasing an ugly dream of a trip to Italy.

A rough, warm hand touched her arm. *"Signorina,* I'm so sorry," the bartender said. "We were just having a little fun. We didn't mean to make you cry. Here, have a cappuccino. It will make you feel better. Giorgio, get the lady a towel. Enzo, we need a handkerchief. A clean one. And go get my wife. Tell her we need some dry clothes. They'll be too big, but they'll keep her from getting pneumonia. I'll talk to the gentleman on the phone."

The transformed bartender patted her arm again. "Don't worry," he whispered so the others wouldn't hear. "I'll fix things with your boyfriend. You just drink the cappuccino and get warm."

Stevie was trying hard not to sob. They were too kind. She had misled them; she had misled everyone. She had just remembered why she was here. It wasn't a dream, and she would never wake up. She was the monster, not these men. She was the one who wanted to kill her own mother.

"We all want to kill our mothers," Nick said. "Our fathers too. Don't feel so guilty."

They were sitting at a table in the back of the bar eating a magnificent meal that had been prepared by the bartender's wife. Stevie was wearing a heavy sweater and a wool skirt that were several sizes too large but comfortably warm and dry. In faded jeans and a blue V-necked sweater, Nick looked even more attractive than usual.

"Nick, it was a horrible feeling. I knew if I turned around and looked at her I would squeeze the life right out of her. I've never felt anything like that before."

Nick raised his eyebrows. "Never? You and your father must have had a very unhealthy relationship. Didn't you ever fight?"

She thought about it for a moment, then shook her head. "No, not really. We were always polite with each other."

"Now that's sick," he told her, waving a fork that was dripping with tomato sauce. "In my family we're always threatening to kill each other. You couldn't have grown up with much love in your house if you felt you had to tiptoe around each other."

Stevie sighed. "I don't know. It seemed normal. Who knows what other families are like? When I was growing up I certainly didn't think we had any problems. I'm just starting to realize how much deceit there was, how much suppressed pain. I can hardly believe that my father lied about my mother. I understand why he wanted to lie, why the truth was painful. But I'm amazed that he convinced me. If he was that good a liar, then how do I know what other things were lies? Where did it stop? Maybe he didn't really love me, maybe he had another name, a secret life, a drug problem, girlfriends, gambling debts. How do I know? What was true and what wasn't?"

"I think," Nick said gently, covering her hand with his, "that one lie was probably all he could handle. In my experience, people find it very hard to maintain a lie. After all, he told you his story about your mother when you were very little. He probably thought that when you were older he would explain the truth. But how could he pick the right moment to break the news? And each day it must have been harder, because the lie was further entrenched in your lives. Be kind to his memory, Stevie. He told the lie to protect you, not to hurt you."

She remembered her father. He had always been kind to her, generous and forgiving and gentle. If, perhaps, he had encouraged her to be too timid and conservative, that wasn't a serious fault. She had suffered far less than Angel. And, unlike Claire, Matthew had had his reasons.

"You're right. I'm just confused. When I found out that one of my parents was a monster, I leapt to the conclusion that they both were. But my father didn't leave me. He didn't abandon me for some Italian lover."

"Hey!" He held up his hands, horrified. "Italian lovers are not to be dismissed so easily. Something I hope you haven't found out yet. But don't be too quick to judge your mother, either. You haven't heard her side of the story."

In her mind she returned to that tiny house by the sea, heard the door opening, Gian-Carlo's voice echoing in her ears. The same hatred filled her; she wanted to kill. "I won't hear her side," she told Nick, her eyes cold with anger. "EVER I don't want to see her."

He shrugged. "It's up to you, *cara*. Not Gian-Carlo, not me, not your grandmother. It's easy for an outsider to say that a reunion is the right thing. But I don't know what I'd do if I were in your shoes." He glanced down at the oversize sneakers their hosts had presented her with. "Well, they'd probably fit me better. But take your time. Nothing has to be done today."

"I'm worried about Gian-Carlo, too," she said, changing the subject. "He seems to be neglecting his election campaign—not just neglecting, forgetting it completely."

"The media agree. There is a lot of speculation about the attractive American he's spending his time with when he should be out campaigning. I don't know if you're aware of it, but last night when he was out squiring you around, a crowd estimated at somewhere between fifty people and five hundred thousand—depending on who was doing the estimating—was waiting for him. He stood up a lot of people to take you out to dinner."

Stevie was surprised at the news. She had been too preoccupied to read the papers.

"And today," Nick continued, "he was supposed to tour orphanages and old age homes instead of arranging family reunions.

174

I believe certain members of his party would like to see him replaced, but they're afraid it's a little late in the game for that. The
most terrifying possibility—and a surprisingly likely one, due to
several unappealing traits of the principal opposition parties—is
that he might actually get the most votes. Who wants a disturbed
incompetent running their country? Well, there have been plenty
of them in the past, but at least they've usually tried to hide their
disturbance. Gian-Carlo is almost flaunting his."

"Come on, Nick," she said. "It's not fair to call him disturbed
and incompetent. He's just upset about Angel's death."

Nick frowned. "*Cara,* I think you're being naive. Maybe you
should stay away from him when he's like this."

She stared down at the table, thinking of Gian-Carlo. During her
walk through the rain she had thought about ending their strange
relationship—but what had he done that was so terrible? She
couldn't blame him for her own romantic delusions.

She shook her head. "Staying away from him would be cruel. I
think he needs me right now. And I am grateful to him. He's the
only one who's really told me the truth, both about my mother
and about who Angel really was."

Nick exhaled. "I agree that he probably needs help, but maybe
seeing you is just making it worse. He has to forget Angel, or at
least accept her death."

"You might be right. But . . ." She sighed, deciding to be honest. "I think I might need him, too. Maybe we need a little insanity
together. Joint grief, I suppose, for a woman he loved and I didn't
get a chance to love. I'll never be able to meet Angel, but somehow when I'm with him I feel close to her. And I guess I make
him feel the same way." She looked down, remembering his
kisses, his voice whispering *Angel.*

Nick reached across the small table and touched her cheek. "Is
that the only reason you're seeing him, *cara?*"

She looked at Nick's handsome face, flushed from the cheap,
strong wine. His sparkling blue eyes were warm and affectionate.
He was the easiest person to talk to she had ever met.

"No," she said, because she couldn't imagine lying to Nick. "It's not the only reason. I'm selfish, too. A man like Gian-Carlo wouldn't give me the time of day if it weren't for my connection with Angel."

"A man like Gian-Carlo!" He threw his fork down on the table. "He's not fit to clean your shoes. But enough. Come on, let's get out of here." He shoved back his chair, threw a wad of money on the table, and grabbed her hand.

"Where are we going?" she said, glancing at their unfinished food. "And what about my clothes?"

"I'll come back tomorrow and straighten everything out. Come on!" He pulled her to her feet and started to lead her out of the restaurant.

"Where to?" she repeated.

He swung around to face her. Their bodies were almost touching. He stared into her eyes without saying anything. Then he pulled her into a tight embrace.

"Back to my bed," he whispered hoarsely in her ear, pushing his body hard against her. "I'm sick of playing games."

"Bravo! Bravo!" The sound of applause and cheers drowned out her attempt at a response. Stevie realized that their conversation had been entertaining the patrons of the bar all evening. The men were on their feet, cheering Nick's action. He grinned down at her sheepishly.

"How's that for machismo?" he said. "And you thought I was just a dull lawyer."

"Never dull, Nick," she said, laughing. "Never dull."

31

ANGEL prepared for her performance.

In her dressing room, she applied the understated makeup the scene required. For her costume she chose jeans and a half-unbuttoned blue cotton shirt. She wanted to look eager and innocent, a young woman experiencing the first flush of love and desire—in essence, the sexiest virgin on earth. Having read Ben Gasperini's script, she knew exactly what his weakness was, and fortunately she was a better actress than people gave her credit for.

It was late in the day, and the usually crowded Cinecittà restaurant was almost empty. Ben was sitting alone. At the table next to him John Freemantle, Aldo Guerritore, and a handsome young man she didn't recognize were deep in conversation.

Ben rubbed his shadowed eyes with his fists. Five espresso cups and the script in progress were in front of him. He looked like a boy who had taken on too much and was afraid he would finally be found out. Angel was several yards away; he didn't know she was watching him. He ran his fingers through his black hair, picked up a fresh pencil, and held it hovering over a blank sheet of paper. He finally wrote one word, paused to sip his espresso, then scratched the word out.

She could love him. It wouldn't be the same kind of love she felt for Gian-Carlo. She wouldn't feel consumed and obsessed. It would be a friendly love, the kind articles in women's magazines described, involving compromises and the importance of communication. And at least she wouldn't be alone on Sunday afternoons. She would be with Ben in their home, with Gian-Carlo's child.

Ben angrily squeezed a sheet of paper into a ball and, without looking up, threw it as hard as he could. Angel was in the right position; she merely had to hold out her hand to catch it. She tossed it back onto his table.

When he saw her his face lit up like a little boy's on Christmas morning. She had wasted her time on the makeup and clothes. He wanted her, no matter what. She wondered briefly what woman he saw when he looked at her, what person he changed her into in his mind. An earth mother, a sex symbol, a madonna/whore? Or a nice kid who needed Ben Gasperini to set her straight?

She walked over to his table, giving him her movie walk, with a slow swing of the hips. He grinned and put his pencil down; he probably already had an erection. Except for discussions about the script, she had ignored him since their encounter in her bed. Her mind had been on Gian-Carlo and the increasing suspicion that she was pregnant; Ben had only been a one-night stand. And now she was going to propose marriage to him.

"Ben," she said, leaning over his table so that her cleavage would erase any doubts he might have about the wisdom of such a rash act. "I . . ."

He waited, his childish face open. He kept looking from her breasts to her face with an idiotic smile, as if he couldn't choose between two delicious flavors of ice cream.

Her words would make all his dreams come true. His current

dreams. But what would happen later, when it fell apart? When he learned she didn't love him? When, in a fit of anger, she screamed that the baby wasn't his?

"Ben . . ." she tried again, while he waited patiently.

Who did he see? Who was Angel Concelli to him? What would happen when he found out the truth?

"I . . . I wanted to tell you something."

"If it's about the night we—" he began.

"It isn't," she said, cutting him short because she wanted to get this over with as quickly as possible. "Well, in a way I guess it is."

"I'm working on a scene for the movie where I use the experience. The passion, the fear, the obsession."

She stared at him. What passion, fear, and obsession? They had just fucked for a few hours.

"It's the best thing I've ever written," he continued. "I can't wait until you read it. It's my tribute to what we shared."

She shut her eyes for a moment, trying to identify her reaction to his words. Was it anger? An attack of conscience? No, that wasn't it. Finally she put her finger on it. Boredom.

She straightened up slowly, like someone with a back problem, and pulled her shirt closed. "That's nice, Ben," she said, patting his hand. "Let's talk another day, okay? I'm kind of busy now."

Without giving him a chance to reply, she stepped over to the next table. Aldo and John Freemantle smiled up at her. The young man who was with them nodded. The eyes of all three men were bloodshot and bleary, and the table was littered with empty glasses. This wouldn't be easy, but she knew it was her only choice.

"Did you mean it when you said you'd do anything to help me?" she asked the Englishman.

"Of course, my darling Angel," he assured her, slurring his words. "What would you like?"

"Will you marry me?"

John's smile froze. But, talented actor that he was, he quickly regained his composure, despite Aldo's distracting behavior. The producer was gasping for air and pounding the table.

John took Angel's hand and pressed it to his lips. "Angel, much though I would love to be someone's white knight, you would be making an enormous mistake."

"That's not true," she said. "I've really thought it over."

Suddenly the young man who was sitting next to John stood up. He picked up his drink and threw it in John's face. The English actor didn't move. The young man pushed past Angel and stormed out of the room.

"Jesus," she said. "What a jerk! What the hell made him do that?"

John took a handkerchief out of his pocket and dried his face. "Jealousy," he answered finally. He looked down, avoiding her eyes. "And if you'll excuse me, I'd better go after him. I spent six weeks talking him into joining me here. I wouldn't want him to catch the next plane out."

John stood up. He kissed her lightly on the cheek. "I'm sorry, my love," he whispered. "But trust me. This is for the best."

Angel watched him walk away.

"Angel, you idiot!" Aldo shouted. "How could you even think of marrying him?"

She shrugged. She didn't want Aldo to know about the pregnancy. He already spent too much time worrying about her.

Ben Gasperini rose from his chair at the next table and walked over to her. His fists were clenched. "You bitch," he whispered.

She stared at him, her eyes full of tears. "I'm sorry," she said. "I'm sorry for everything. God, I'm sorry for living."

She turned and ran out of the room.

ANGEL slammed the door shut in her apartment and went to the bar. She poured herself a drink and then carried the bottle of scotch to the couch. She emptied the burning alcohol into her mouth. She poured a refill and gulped it down too, needing to feel the alcohol hit her blood and cancel out reality.

Had she really been planning to marry a stranger? Had she really been that desperate?

The third one she sipped slowly, relishing it, grateful for its offer of false peace. She wondered what the alcohol was doing to the fetus. Her hand instinctively tightened over her abdomen. But the gesture expressed hatred as much as love. The desires to destroy and protect merged into one horrible sensation. It was as if the unborn child had made promises to her and then callously broken them, set her up for more pain than before. And yet she still wanted the promises to come true, she wanted the baby to come into her life and love her and make her happy.

But it didn't work that way. They weren't dolls, they were real people with real needs. What life could Angel Concelli's child have?

Angel remembered the day, when she was fourteen years old, that she had finally worked up the courage to ask her mother who her father was, only to end up screaming that her mother should have had an abortion, should have stopped the pain then, before she was born.

She patted her belly. She would protect her child. She would save it from its mother and father, and all the rest of the crap that made up their lives.

"An abortion," she whispered. Her pulse quickened. The word felt like a snake in her mouth. Her eyes filled with tears. Could she really go through with it?

She imagined her daughter in fourteen years' time, asking who her father was, why she never saw him, why her mother was a slut who took off her clothes in bad movies.

Her hand shaking, she poured herself another drink. "It's okay, *bambina*," Angel whispered. "I'll just be doing what my mother should have done for me."

32

SOMETHING, someone, somewhere, sometime.

No, she had it wrong.

One, two, three, four. Sheep jumping over fences, deep breathing, alcohol, and pills. *Let me sleep,* Angel thought, and then felt herself drifting off, as if a higher being had finally—now, when it was too late—agreed to grant her one wish.

Then she remembered the nightmares. She couldn't survive another nightmare. She sat up in bed. She had to stay awake. It was late, and she had to go to work in the morning, but sleep was dangerous. Sleep could hurt her. Sleep would make her remember—

One, two, three, four.

His fingers were cold. The room was cold. He said his name but she didn't catch it. She would die not knowing the name of the man who had taken her child away.

He accepted major credit cards.

He wasn't evil. He wasn't the horrible devil he became in her nightmares. There were no horns, no sharp teeth, no skeleton grin. He hadn't killed her baby first and then turned on her, his hands on her throat, laughing, saliva dripping onto her face, punishing her there and then for the arrogance of her act.

"Gian-Carlo," she whispered in her dark bedroom. "Why did we have to do it this way? Why couldn't you have loved me more?"

She reached for the phone—for the hundredth time in the three days since the abortion—and started to dial his number. She needed him. She needed someone to hold her and caress her hair and tell her everything was all right. She needed to feel loved and wanted.

So do axe murderers, she thought, so did Hitler.

She dropped her hand.

She mourned not only her child, but also the better life she had almost had, with a family of her own and someone to love her. Now there was nothing but loneliness forever, and the horrible knowledge that she was responsible for it, that she could have changed things if she had only had a little more courage.

She reached for the bottle of brandy on the floor beside the bed and took several quick gulps. Then she picked up a sleeping pill from the dish on the bedside table and washed it down with another generous swallow of liquor. She glanced vaguely around the room, wondering what other escape she could try. Her fingers automatically moved toward the phone, but she stopped herself, staring down at her hand as if it belonged to someone else.

"You're alone," she said. "Remember that, Angel, you're alone." She took a deep breath. She closed her eyes and immediately recalled the doctor's office, the table she had stretched out on, the stirrups she had placed her bare cold feet in. She remembered his fingers pushing into her. "Alone forever," she said.

One, two, three, four.

She took another deep breath and finally, forgetting that she was supposed to punish herself, let herself fall asleep. It was dreamless, the first good luck she had had in a long time.

33

A SHAFT of sunlight cut through an opening in the curtains. Stevie groaned and rolled away from what was, to her throbbing eyes, a blinding light.

"Good morning!"

"Go away," she growled over her shoulder. Her mind was too dull and sleepy to identify the annoying speaker, but she knew she didn't want to see anyone who sounded chirpy. "It's not morning yet."

Nick sat down on the side of the bed in one of Laura Barberini's spare rooms and brushed the golden hair back from Stevie's eyes. "It's almost noon. And I have to go and do some work."

"Noon?" She opened one eye to peer at him. He was wearing a dark blue suit and an immaculate white shirt. "Are you sure? It feels like three A.M."

"Quite sure. And you look great when you first wake up."

She yelped and pulled the covers over her head. At the sound of muffled words, he tugged down the blanket to find out what she was saying.

"I look awful," she was ranting. "Go away and come back when I'm presentable."

"Can't I wait?" He gestured at her clothes, which were piled on a chair across the room. "I love talking to naked women," he added, grinning down at her. "Are you sure you're not too hot with that blanket on?"

"No!" she shouted, then clutched her forehead. "My head is splitting. Two nights in a row of drinking are too much for me. I think I need a lobotomy."

"By the way, I called Ellen Brenner and told her you were safe with me. Well, with me, anyway, since I didn't want to lie. She seemed relieved. Apparently she prefers me to your other suitor."

"And would your grandmother prefer me to your other lady friend?" Stevie shot back. Now that she was sober, the decision to spend the night in the Contessa's apartment seemed unbelievably stupid. And how could Nick have the nerve to court her—or whatever other euphemism was appropriate—in his girlfriend's home?

"If my grandmother were alive," he said, "she would tell me to marry the lady friend—a charming phrase—who could cook the best pasta. Whereas I, of course, judge all my lady friends, and there have been many more than two, by different standards altogether. One can always hire a cook. But a beast in bed—that's much harder to get. Stevie! What happened? You look so sad."

She shook her head, unable to answer.

He touched her cheek. "I was teasing you. You must have known that."

She couldn't tell him what she was thinking—that Gian-Carlo had whispered Angel's name and that to Nick she was only a diversion while his real lover was out of town. All her inadequacies loomed huge: she felt plain and dull and second-rate and was sure she would never have a chance with the kind of man she wanted.

"When does Toni's mother get back?" she asked. At least she could find out when this artificial pursuit would end.

He shrugged. "Laura comes and goes. Why? She wouldn't mind you staying here."

"I think I'll go home now." She started to sit up and then remembered she was naked. It was like a replay of their first meeting. She was once again the inhibited girl from Boston encountering the free-spirited Italian who was willing to have sex with whatever came his way. She probably had more in common with Gian-Carlo than with Nick. At least he only wanted Angel.

"I need my clothes." Her cheeks were hot. She wished these men would leave her alone; she wasn't any good at sophisticated little games. "I don't want you to see me naked, Nick, and if that makes me a prude, then I guess that's what I am."

"Stevie." He put his hand on her bare shoulder. "What have I done? How have I hurt you?"

"Please," she said, pronouncing each word slowly and carefully, "please would you get my clothes. Or else leave the room so that I can get them myself."

His eyes darkened. He was silent for a moment, his face closed and hostile. Then he slowly stood up.

"For Christ's sake, don't treat me as if I were some kind of boor!" he exploded. "If nothing else, last night must have proved that I'm a gentleman. I had a drunk, passionate, beautiful woman on my hands, and I had the good manners to send her straight to bed rather than take advantage of her. Give me some credit for that, though God knows I'll probably regret it for the rest of my life. But, to be honest, I didn't want to make love to someone who would rather have Gian-Carlo Cassieri in her bed."

He strode across the room, snatched up her clothes, and tossed them onto the bed before moving to the door. "Let's get everything clear, Stevie Templeton." His eyes were cold with rage. "I know that finding out about your mother and everything else is very hard for you. I know you're confused and frightened. I can even accept—but just barely—that you find the attentions of a man of Gian-Carlo's stature flattering. But, despite what I might have tried to make you believe, I am not a patient man. I won't wait forever for you to make up your mind about what you want.

I've never come second to any man before, and I don't like it. And especially not when the man is an asshole like Cassieri. So do what you please—it's your life—but don't expect me to be there no matter what. Don't think I'll take whatever Gian-Carlo leaves behind. Because I'm worth a fucking lot more than that." He slammed the door so hard the paintings shook on the walls.

Stevie shivered on the bed, stunned by the force of his anger. She felt completely lost. How could he expect her to ignore his relationship with the Contessa, especially when he was so angry about Gian-Carlo? These men were all impossible. Or else the level of sophistication was just too far beyond what she was or ever wanted to be. *La dolce vita* wasn't for her.

There was only one solution. She would get dressed—she stared at the borrowed clothes and realized she would have to borrow another of Toni's dresses—and take a cab to the airport. She could leave Rome forever. It would be easy; there was nothing and no one to stop her. She could step back into the past as if nothing had happened.

But if she did? She would miss—

Ellen's peaceful wisdom. The old woman's lovely, sad face. The eerie closeness she felt to Angel, not all the time, but in sudden, stunning bursts. She would miss Rome itself, this seductive, frightening masterpiece where people actually lived their daily lives. She would wonder about Gian-Carlo and her mother, wonder what she might have meant to them if she had stayed. Most of all, she would miss Nick.

She picked up the white-and-gold telephone beside the bed and placed a long-distance call. It was answered on the twelfth ring with an obscenity. "No friend of mine would call at seven in the morning!" the woman continued in a deep, attractive voice.

"Toni? Is that you?"

"Stevie!" her friend shouted. "What the hell is going on? My mother says you're having an affair with the handsomest man in Italy and that you've found a whole lost family. And you haven't even sent me a postcard!"

"Toni, I have to know something."

"My recipe for lasagna?"

Stevie smiled; she had missed her friend more than she realized. "No, silly. About your mother. And Nick Funaro. How close are they?"

"Nick?" Toni thought for a moment. "My mother's as close to him as she's ever been to anyone. Closer. She couldn't live without him."

Stevie shut her eyes. It was even worse than she had expected. "Okay," Stevie replied softly, getting ready to hang up. "That's all I wanted to know."

"That's all you called for? Just to find out how important my mother finds Nick Funaro? Stevie, any wealthy Roman could have answered that for you. It's how all rich Italians feel. Their lawyers mean more to them than their lovers do."

"Wait." Stevie's heart was thumping hard. "Say that again. The last part."

"Your brain is slowing down, Stevie. Maybe you should wear a hat when you go out in the sun. I said that Italians value their lawyers more than their lovers. After all, lovers cost them money, and good lawyers show them clever ways to increase it. We're not a stupid people. What's all this about?"

"Have you ever met Nick?"

"No. But my mother tells me he's handsome and smart. Handsome's a bonus, smart would be enough for her. Why are you asking about Nick? Do you want to hire him?"

"Toni, don't be an idiot! I don't want a lawyer. I just wanted to know where I stand."

"Lawyers can find that out. Is there something involving an estate? I hear you had some movie star sister who was murdered. My mother says it's the juiciest gossip she's ever heard. And that you're dating the man who might have killed her. But I told her that was unlikely. You've always been for gun control and nuclear disarmament. By the way," Toni purred, "I met a gorgeous doctor the other night. Cold hands, but other than that he's perfect. It's amazing what a knowledge of anatomy can do."

"Toni!" Stevie yelled. "Don't change the subject! I think I'm in love. I don't know what to do."

"A lawyer can't help you with that. But are you sure a murderer is a good bet? He could be sent up for twenty years. You've got good bones, but you'd still lose your looks in that much time, and so would he. It wouldn't be the same when he got out. Maybe you should try dating Nick. My mother says he has a fierce case of the hots for you. Stevie, are you still there?"

Stevie leaned back and gave a deep sigh. This was just like the old days, but better. She snuggled up against the soft pillows and settled in for a long talk with her friend.

"Yeah. I'm still here. What else did your mother tell you Nick said about me? And what's this doctor's name? And I forgot to tell you that I got my hair cut. It's short, but kind of full. Nick says I look a lot better."

34

STEVIE paid the taxi driver and walked up the steps of her grand-mother's villa. As she was about to open the door she noticed a dark blue car parked about fifty feet away under a large tree. Someone was sitting inside.

She hoped it wasn't Gian-Carlo. She wasn't ready for another encounter with him. She squinted, trying to make out the shad-owy figure at the wheel. Perhaps he was a neighbor, although she couldn't imagine why someone would sit in a car on a hot after-noon. Shrugging, she went inside. Her first priority was to con-front her grandmother.

She found Ellen tending the flower beds in the garden, her khaki pants and cotton shirt streaked with soil. Stevie stood at the open kitchen doors. "You lied to me," she said. "My mother is alive."

Surprised, Ellen slowly straightened up. "But I never told you she was dead."

190

Stevie exhaled. "All right, you didn't lie in so many words, but you must have known what I assumed."

Ellen studied the patch of marigolds she had been working on. "I don't know what to say, Stephanie. You're right, of course. I should have mentioned it. But it's been so long since I had anything to do with Claire that in any practical sense she is dead to me. Of course I assumed she was alive, but I only found out for certain last spring when there was some brief, unpleasant publicity. Angel's third movie catapulted her into—"

Ellen paused to search for a word.

"I suppose it's called superstardom these days, but that seems a rather juvenile term for such a powerful phenomenon. In interviews she credited the writer of the film, a young man named Ben Gasperini. He does seem talented—he recently published a critically acclaimed novel. But the revelation of her liaison with Cassieri obviously had a lot to do with it. People love a scandal, preferably one that involves sex. As for the film, I never saw it, so I can't comment on it. But right after its release the press were like vultures feeding on her life. I'm lucky they never identified me. In any case, some enterprising reporter did manage to track Claire down. He showed up at her door and requested an interview. Claire never had patience with fools, and she smashed his camera and spat at him. He left to get the police, and by the time they returned to her apartment she was gone. Gone for good, it turned out. She had left everything—her clothes, all her personal belongings. Angel refused to comment on the incident. In a few weeks the press were already concentrating on more interesting developments in Angel's life, and Claire was forgotten. As, apparently, she wanted to be." Ellen shrugged. "And I've tried to forget her too."

Stevie swatted at a passing fly. She wanted to be polite, but Ellen's explanation was ludicrous and inadequate. How could a mother forget the existence of her own daughter?

The way Claire had forgotten her.

With a dizzy feeling, she remembered standing beside Gian-Carlo on the stone step in front of Claire's house, staring out at the violent, gray sea.

"She lives in a tiny house by the sea," Stevie told her grand-mother. "Completely isolated. I can't imagine living like that."

"The guiltier one feels the more isolation one needs. The sight of other people reminds one of so many past mistakes and missed opportunities." Ellen's mouth tightened. "By all rights, Claire should be on a mountaintop somewhere in India."

The cynicism disturbed Stevie. "She's your daughter. My mother."

Ellen sighed. "I'm not a forgiving person, Stephanie. I don't even wish I were. Which is just as well, since I'm much too old to learn something that difficult. Besides, Claire doesn't care where I am. Or where you are. We have to remember that. We can't beg people to love us."

Stevie thought of her life with her father. The lessons then had all been simple and easy to understand. Be polite. Give your seat to old people and pregnant women. Wash behind your ears. Eat a balanced diet.

We can't beg people to love us.

She couldn't imagine Matthew Templeton saying such a thing. And yet there had been a night when his pregnant wife sat at the kitchen table in their small house and told him she didn't want him, she wanted someone else, she was going away forever. He must have begged her to stay, begged her to give him another chance. Begged her to love him.

"Why did she take Angel away from my father?" Stevie asked. "Why didn't she wait until the baby was born and then leave Angel behind too?"

Ellen began gathering up her garden tools. "Stephanie, I can't answer all your questions. I don't know the answers myself. With Claire, I was always afraid to find out the truth. It was easier to accept the lies. If you really want to know, then there's only one way to find out."

They looked at each other. Despite the heat, Stevie shuddered. She felt tired and small, a hungry, sleepy child who wanted some-one else to take care of everything and make all the decisions. But she was on her own, and an adult. She straightened her spine and pushed back her shoulders. "I can't see her," she said. "I want to know the truth, but only because I'm hoping it will be something different from what I already know. I keep thinking if I hear the whole story, if I understand everyone's reasons, then I can have all my myths back. I can believe my mother and father loved me and each other."

Ellen nodded. "But you can't ask a question thinking you have any control over the answer. Once it's asked you have to accept the consequences."

"I suppose I just have to get used to not having all the answers," Stevie said and sighed. "No matter what the truth is, I'll never find it out. I can't see that woman. I think I'd kill her if I did."

"Fortunately," Ellen said, leading the way back into the house, "we kill fewer people than we want to. I could have wiped out thirty or forty myself if I'd followed my inclinations. And that's excluding incompetent salesclerks and bad drivers."

Stevie laughed. "You sound like Nick."

In the sunny, spotless kitchen, Ellen washed her hands at the sink and then filled the kettle for tea. "A charming young man," she said over her shoulder. "If you don't watch out I'll give you some advice. I might start sounding like your grandmother."

Stevie helped herself to a cookie on the counter. "I keep wondering what my life would have been like if I'd known you all along. And known about Angel and my mother. I always felt so alone. My father was such a quiet man. I used to long for someone to talk to. Sometimes I would even imagine I had a sister who shared my room. Though," she said with a grin, "not a sister like Angel. One I could compete with."

"An Angel raised by Matthew is hard to imagine," Ellen replied. "Even harder, now that I'm getting to know you, is a Stephanie raised by Claire."

Stevie had no trouble imagining such a scenario. "I know what that would have done to me. It would have destroyed me. My God, look what she did to Angel. She should burn in hell for that alone."

The phone rang. Ellen picked it up, then listened in silence.

After a moment she opened her mouth to speak, but changed her mind. She held the receiver out to Stevie.

"Is it Gian-Carlo?" Stevie whispered, hoping it wasn't.

Ellen reacted as if Stevie had said something stupid. Her eyes hardened. Then she suddenly covered her face with her hands and began to move her head from side to side. She was weeping.

Stevie put the phone to her ear.

"Stephanie?"

She had never heard that voice before.

"This is Claire. Your mother. I want to see you."

Stevie couldn't speak. She had started to cry too, the silent tears of panic. She looked helplessly at Ellen, but the old woman was lost in her own pain.

"You know where I live," Claire continued in an abrupt, cool voice. "I'm always home. Come whenever you can."

Mother, she thought. She imagined a beautiful woman smiling down at her. Stevie stretched out her tiny arms to touch the perfect face. *Mommy, I love you.* The woman gently lifted her up and pulled her close with all the force of a mother's love. Had such a scene ever occurred? Or had Claire always hated her, always been counting the minutes until she could get away?

"If you don't want to come, I'll understand. It may have been too long for both of us." And then, without waiting for Stevie's answer, Claire hung up.

Stevie, her own face wet, stared at her sobbing grandmother. "Why did hearing her voice make you cry?" she asked. "You said she meant nothing to you now."

With a sudden violence that made Stevie cry out, the old woman swept the delicate china teacups off the counter and onto the floor. "It's time to grow up, Stephanie," Ellen shouted while tears continued to pour from her eyes. "Are you so naive that you can't tell when a person is lying? My God, she's my own child, my baby girl. I wanted the same thing you do. I wanted that monster to love me. But she never could. Even now, she only called to talk to you."

Humbled, Stevie got down on her knees and began to pick up the shattered china.

35

"ALCOHOL makes me a better actress. It takes away my inhibitions."

Aldo groaned. "Angel, you could use a few inhibitions!" He had dropped by her apartment to discuss their next movie, but when he found her with a drink in hand at eleen in the morning he had launched into a lecture on the dangers of her increased consumption of alcohol.

"Anyway, be glad it's only booze," she argued, sinking down into a large white chair. She was wearing a tight, stained T-shirt and bikini pants.

"And sleeping pills," Aldo pointed out.

She shrugged. "It could be worse. I could use cocaine like everybody else in the film business."

"The only reason you stick to booze and pills is because I don't pay you enough for cocaine. So don't try to make something noble out of it. You're not the Mother Theresa of chemical consumption."

Angel pushed her dirty tangled hair behind her ears. She wasn't wearing makeup, and her face was swollen and pale. "Give me a break, Aldo. I get depressed. I need something."

Aldo knocked some magazines and dirty clothes off the couch and sat down. On the marble coffee table there were several unwashed glasses, ashtrays overflowing with cigarette butts, and two half-eaten slices of pizza that had been left to decompose.

"What happened to your cleaning lady?"

"She quit. I haven't had time to find another one."

Aldo shook his head at the filth. "Jesus, Angel, don't you have any self-respect? You can't go on like this."

She stretched, pulling her T-shirt up over her flat stomach, and yawned. "Why not? Why should I make an effort? Who's it for? Nobody gives a damn about me."

"Cut the self pity. I care about you. John cares. Ben cares so much he wrote you a part any other actress would have killed for. Jesus, Angel, you're the biggest star Italy has. People would rather see you than the Pope. In *One Woman's Story* you were magnificent. You even acted. And every woman who saw it thought it was her story too. You broke hearts, Angel. You made them cry. People love you."

In reply, Angel grabbed a newspaper up off the floor and flung it across the room. It landed at the producer's feet. He had already seen the item; it had been featured the week before in one of Rome's many gossip publications.

"Does *she* love me?" Angel cried. "My own mother won't admit she knows me. They haven't figured out who my grandmother is, but she'd do the same thing. And my father didn't even want me to be born. He didn't want a little bastard around to make the neighbors talk."

"I don't see my family either," Aldo told her, folding the newspaper before he placed it on the cluttered table. "My wife doesn't give a damn about me. She spends all her time in Paris or New York spending my money. My parents are dead. My sister thinks I'm the devil incarnate for giving people the privilege of seeing your tits. You can't have everything, Angel. Don't a few friends and the adulation of millions count for anything?"

She bit her lip in a reluctant grin. "Okay. It's better than noth-ing." Then her face fell again. "But I can't help it if I'm unhappy. If I'm lonely, I'm lonely."

"You're lonely because you won't see anyone. Fix yourself up. Go out. You're in demand at every party in Rome. Men will fall all over you."

Angel reacted as if he had physically threatened her. She pulled her bare legs up and wrapped her arms around them. "Christ, Aldo, you know I can't do that. I might run into him. It's been over six months. If I saw him again I'd go crazy."

Aldo stared at her in despair. "Angel, look at yourself. You're going crazy now. Maybe if you saw him you'd find out he didn't matter anymore."

She picked up the drink she'd left beside the chair. Aldo was disturbed by the desperation in her drinking, the raw need she revealed in the way she held the glass and gulped quickly with a guilty bravado.

"He does matter," she said, once the alcohol had provided its false strength. "I think of him all the time. I wish I could stop, but I can't."

"There are a lot of men out there. Don't destroy yourself, Angel. Don't throw it away."

Angel stared down at her empty glass, wishing he would leave so that she could get another drink without risking a lecture. Fi-nally the desire for the drink won out and she pulled herself shakily to her feet and walked over to refill her glass. With a de-fiant glare at Aldo, she drank it standing beside the bar. She wiped her mouth with the back of her hand. "Why shouldn't I throw my life away? Who wants it? Who will miss me when I'm gone?"

Aldo was startled by how pale and thin she looked; she had changed a great deal in the past few months. He remembered the young girl who had come into his office, the beautiful girl who had knelt naked between his legs not just for her career but also to make him happy. She had class.

"I'd miss you," he said softly.

"Sorry, Aldo," she told him. "You're not enough."

"Want to go to some kind of spa? A drying-out place? They've

197

got a lot of classy joints these days. Everybody goes. It's good publicity. I'll even pay."

She shook her head. "To tell you the truth, I don't want to get cured. I'd rather be drunk and lonely than well adjusted and lonely. I kind of like the idea of going out in a blaze of piss and vomit."

The heavy man picked up his hat and, awkwardly, rose to his feet. He was tired of arguing, and the visit was becoming increasingly painful. "I left some scripts on the table by the door. Pick your favorite. I might as well leave, since I don't seem to be doing any good."

Angel was still holding the empty glass. She reached for the bottle of scotch, then stopped, her hand hovering over it. "Aldo?" she whispered.

"What?" He felt helpless and angry. He wanted to take her by the shoulders and shake some sense into her. But he knew it wouldn't do any good. She'd probably just spit up on him.

"Will you stay a little longer?" She sounded like a little girl. "I'll have a bath and maybe we can call out for some lunch. Would that be okay?"

Aldo wanted to give her a big hug and swing her around the room. But, to protect his suit, he settled for a huge smile. "Sure," he exclaimed. "Why don't we go out to a restaurant and make a real day of it?"

She shook her head. She looked frightened again; he had gone too far. "I can't do that. I might see him. But we'll order in something nice. I haven't had anything but pizza for a couple of days. You'll stay with me?"

"Angel, *bella,* of course I'll stay with you. I want you to be happy."

She tugged at the bottom of the stained T-shirt as if she had just realized how bad she looked. "Let's be realistic, Aldo. I think lunch is all I can manage. Happiness seems—" She struggled for an image. "Like mountain climbing or knitting. Something for people I have nothing in common with." She sighed. "I think I was born to bleed my veins out into a hot tub someday. But I'm just not ready for it yet."

She gave a small shrug and fell silent for a moment. Then, as if she were confessing a weakness, she blurted out, "I can't quite give up hope. Not yet. But I'm working on it, Aldo. I'm working real hard."

"It's Aldo Guerritore. You owe me, and I'm calling to collect."

"What do you mean, I owe you?"

"I set you up with Angel Concelli, along with fifty other gorgeous broads. I've given a piss pot full of money to your organization. How the fuck can you have the nerve to ask if you owe me? You owe me your goddamned foreskin, you bastard. You owe me your mother's cunt."

There was a nervous cough. "Calm down. What do you want? I'll listen to anything reasonable."

"I'm not in a mood to be reasonable, you scum ball. Why the fuck haven't you called her? It's been six fucking months. The kid is falling apart."

Gian-Carlo sighed. "It wasn't working. She wanted me to give up too much. You wouldn't believe what she expected."

"If Angel Concelli isn't worth a few sacrifices, then what is? Are you insane? Do you know how lucky you are to have a broad like her crazy about you?"

"I've got a wife, a position—"

"Who doesn't? But you can't hurt her. Do you hear me? You can't walk all over her. Call her, see how she is. Buy her dinner. Fuck her, if that's what she wants."

"The last time I talked to her she said she never wanted to see me again."

"Broads only say that to men they can't live without. To the rest of us, they say I hope we can still be friends. You're a big boy, Cassieri. You know that. Look, the kid's in really bad shape. I can't help her. You have to try."

Gian-Carlo hesitated. "Maybe she just needs a little more time. She'll get over me."

"Are you over her?" Aldo shot back.

Gian-Carlo fell silent.

"You're not, are you?" Aldo answered for him. "You still smell her on your fingers. You go and see her movies again and again. You think about her in bed with other men and you want to scream. When you fuck Lucia you pretend it's Angel so you can get it up. Am I right?"

"Aldo, it won't do any good. We'll just start it up again. We'll destroy each other."

"Don't be so melodramatic. You can reach a compromise. Lucia's sophisticated. Angel's getting more mature. She won't expect the whole works now. Anyway, she'll probably be in Hollywood in a year making it with Warren Beatty. Just help the kid out now. Be a gentleman. Take her some flowers. And lingerie. I always found women like nice lingerie."

"I'll think about it, Aldo. But I'm not sure you're right."

"Of course I'm right. And don't think about it too long. But call first. Give her a chance to get her hair done and buy a new dress. And listen, Cassieri, and remember that I'm not a man to make idle threats. If you don't do something, I'm going to have your balls served up on toast."

Aldo hung up. Proud of himself, he smiled down at the picture of Angel he kept on his desk.

"I'm glad to help you out, *bella*," he said out loud. "Like I keep saying, I feel like a father to you. You're not as alone in this cold, cruel world as you think."

36

GIAN-CARLO was still asleep in the dark bedroom. At the window, Angel shivered in the night's chill. Although she was exhausted, she couldn't sleep. It was four in the morning, the hour when party-goers have already staggered home and workers are catching a little more sleep. A time when only lonely people and lovers are awake.

She turned and looked at Gian-Carlo asleep on her bed. Her heart contracted at the sight of him. Her mouth went dry. She loved him too much. Or wanted him too much, if there was a difference. The afternoon before, when he had finally called, she had been terrified of saying the wrong thing. That would be a new element in their relationship—the fear that she could go too far and frighten him away. She would have to become more of a mistress—or a wife—a woman calculating her position, her rights, before she asked for anything. She would have to be careful not to step out of line. She was no longer the pursued. That was gone forever. What they had established in the last six months was that he could live without her; she couldn't live without him.

In the darkness she went back to the bed and lay beside him. They were both naked, sticky and aching from too much sex. They had licked every inch of each other's body, pushed and prodded, sucked and bitten, with all the raw need of people who know they can't get sex like this anywhere else, from anyone. It was like the last fuck of a lifetime, all desperation and little love.

She wasn't sure when she started talking aloud, when the internal monologue became an accusation. But she needed to prove that she didn't need anyone, even if it was like trying to prove that gravity doesn't exist and the sun sets in the east.

"For some reason I always imagine him now as a boy. A little you, instead of a little me. It's only been six months since the abortion. I would still be pregnant. I never realized how long it takes before, in real time. I'd be big now." She ran her hands over her flat belly. "It wasn't like in the movies. The place was clean and the doctor was polite. At one point, when I got really scared, I pretended you were in the waiting room. I pretended that if things got bad I could call your name and you would come running in. Later, after it was over, I had a different fantasy. That I would be lying on the table, the doctor would be getting his equipment ready, and you would suddenly come bursting through the door. You would pick me up in your arms and tell me you loved me, you wanted me, you had already left Lucia and handed in your resignation. I want you and our child, you told me. Sometimes, in my fantasy, I went with you. Other times I was cruel. I made you stand there while the doctor did it, I made you watch your baby die. After all, fathers go in delivery rooms now. Why shouldn't they watch their little bastards—their mistakes— get aborted? You can't just hang around for the good moments. You can't pick and choose."

Her voice had risen. The anger was raw. "You were wrong to leave me alone. You were wrong to treat me as if the problem was only mine. You hurt me forever. I mean, the damage is done. I can't fix it. The pain will fade a bit, but I'll never really be the same again. That was our child. We're healthy, we've got money, and we're supposed to love each other. And yet we killed it. We chickened out. We put everybody else before that little boy. We told him that their feelings were more important than his life."

She stopped, wanting to get back on track. She sighed and resumed her story. "When it was over they gave me a sedative and some pain pills and sent me home. They were very nice. It wasn't like in a bad movie. The bad movie was in my head. I needed you, Gian-Carlo. You must have known that. It was your kid, too. I don't know what they did with him. What do you do with some blood and a bit of tissue? I couldn't ask. I was afraid they'd think I was crazy. And what answer wouldn't hurt? What did I want to hear? That he had never existed? Would that have been better?"

She knew he was awake. With nothing more to tell, she lay next to him in silence, her arms at her sides, not quite touching him. After a minute, when Gian-Carlo was certain that she had finished, he tried to answer her.

"You're right, I should have been with you," he whispered, "but you didn't even tell me you were having it done. Remember, Angel, you said you were going to marry another man and raise my child as his. And even if I'd gone, our lives wouldn't be worth living if the press had found out about it."

"Are they worth living now?" she asked quietly. "And why do all those other people matter so much? Why do we always have to put them first?"

"Because they have power. They control us."

"Sure, there'd be a brief scandal. But soon another story would come along, a better one. Especially if we were happy. The press isn't interested in happy people."

He turned on his side and caressed her face, looking down at her in the dim light. "Would we be happy, Angel?" he whispered. "You and I? Without our work and the adulation it brings? Can you honestly see us living quiet lives, just for ourselves?"

Angel shut her eyes. She knew he wouldn't like her answer. "Yes. Yes, I can see us doing that. I would like that very much."

"You know you couldn't give all this up."

Angel harshly laughed. "Give up having strange men masturbate while looking at my picture? And young girls putting on low-cut dresses and high heels so they can be just like Angel Concelli? And being so lonely I think my head is going to split open? Yeah, Gian-Carlo. I could give that up."

"Then you don't know yourself."

She wished she could force him to say different words, to say he felt the same way. "Don't make me cry," she whispered. "I don't want to cry."

He lowered his head and began to kiss her breasts.

Angel Concelli's breasts, she thought. Men who had seen her movie that night had gone home wishing they were married to her, wishing they could kiss breasts like this instead of their wives' tired, sagging chests. And their wives were dreaming of Gian-Carlo Cassieri, a powerful, handsome man, the answer to every woman's dreams.

He moved down, his mouth raining kisses on her flat babyless abdomen. If she hadn't had the abortion, their child would have been too big for him to lie on top of her. She would have had to turn on her side for him to enter her from behind.

"Make me forget everything," she said, wanting sex to be the ultimate drug, better than alcohol, better than pills. "Make my brain stop working."

He pulled her legs apart, stretching them wide.

She clenched her fists, trying not to hate him. "Make me think you're worth it," she whispered.

37

At nine o'clock in the morning, Stevie parked her grandmother's car in front of Claire's house.

Instead of one of her flattering new outfits, she was wearing a cotton shirt and jeans. When she finally met her mother she wanted to make it clear that she was Matthew's daughter.

She looked up at the house. Its stark simplicity was forbidding. It was the home of someone who didn't care about the opinions of other people.

She tried to collect her thoughts and contain the sense of rising panic. Surely not knowing the answers to her questions had to be worse than finding out the truth. How terrible could Claire be? No matter how many mistakes she had made, she was still another human being with fears and disappointments like everyone else. Nick was right; she had to listen to Claire's side of the story.

As Stevie opened the car door, a brisk, cold wind from the sea whipped around her. She climbed the stone steps slowly, her hands shoved into the pockets of her jeans. Her body seemed to be rejecting her brain's decision. Her heart was pounding; she felt dizzy and weak. All her nerves told her that it wasn't too late: she could still change her mind. She could run away.

But she would be running away from her own life. She knocked on the plain wood door.

Claire opened it almost immediately and stepped back to usher Stevie inside.

Stevie hardly glanced at her mother. She wasn't ready to look at her; that would have to wait. Instead she concentrated on the house. The room was almost empty. There was a cheap couch covered in rough white cotton, some books sitting on the tile floor, and two wood chairs. The only decoration was an unframed reproduction of a Cézanne—a still life of a blue vase with flowers—tacked to the wall above the couch.

Claire stood behind her. Stevie took a deep breath. She was with her mother. They were alone together in her mother's home. It was miles from Boston, miles from the cemetery where Claire should have been.

"Please sit down. Would you like tea? A habit I picked up from my mother."

Stevie's eyes stung with tears at her mother's simple statement. She'd never had the chance to pick up any habits from her mother. "Nothing. I want nothing." She pushed herself forward and perched on the edge of one of the wood chairs. Out of the corner of her eye she saw Claire take the other one. They faced each other like enemies across the small room.

Stevie forced herself to look up.

Claire was beautiful. Like Angel's, her beauty was compelling and brutal. Her pale graying hair fell straight to her shoulders. She wasn't wearing makeup. She was in a plain blue cotton dress, her feet bare.

Stevie folded her hands in her lap. This woman had carried her for nine months. Stevie had come to life inside her womb. She had been delivered, screaming and bloody, from between this woman's legs.

Claire was the one who spoke first. "You look so much like Matthew. So . . . in control. How is he?"

"He died," Stevie said. "Ten months ago. A heart attack." She blinked back tears; she still missed her father very much.

Claire looked down, but her face didn't change. "It all seems so long ago," Claire said. "I don't remember much about those days, except that I was exhausted and angry all the time. I thought you and your father were the cause, but as it turned out I spent most of my life exhausted and angry. You were what is known as a good baby. Which is unfair, since it suggests that children who cry when they're hungry and wet are bad. I don't know if it was your nature to be well behaved. I suspect I terrified you into silence. I think that, even as an infant, you were afraid that if you cried too much, if you were too demanding, I would leave. Giving you that fear may have been the worst thing I did to you. Leaving was the best. You should thank me for that. A baby knows when it isn't wanted by its mother."

Stevie stared at her mother in shock, but Claire's face remained expressionless, as if they were talking about the weather.

"Angel once told me I should have had her aborted," Claire continued in the same steady voice. "Perhaps I should have done that with you too."

Stevie's head jerked back. She couldn't believe this woman. "How can you say such a thing?" she cried.

Claire tipped her head to one side and stared at her distressed daughter as if she were observing an exotic creature in a zoo. "I'm sorry to startle you," she said. "But I assumed you came here because you wanted the truth."

Stevie squirmed on the hard chair. She felt as if she were the victim of some cruel psychological experiment. "Jesus Christ," she cried, "you sound like Ellen! Can't the two of you ever be kind enough to lie?"

Claire laughed. "We did lie to you, Stephanie. That's what did the most harm. I can't repair the damage, but at least I can tell you the truth now. And you already know it in your heart. We always know when we're not wanted. The lies only make it worse."

Stevie felt an almost unbearable tension building inside her.

She didn't know what she had wanted from the woman sitting across the room, but it certainly wasn't this. She had to force herself to remain still. She wanted to get up and kick her and punch her. She really did want to kill her own mother.

Claire started to speak in a soft, intimate tone, as if they were good friends sharing secrets. "I was the wrong person for my life. In fact, it's only recently that I finally found the right life. We make such important decisions when we're twenty, when we're so eager to leave home and start our own lives. We marry stupidly, whoever happens to come along just as we're desperate to start living like grown-ups. I knew my marriage to your father was a mistake on my wedding night. I tried to become a different person, but of course it didn't work. It never does. People were hurt in the process. But do I deserve to burn in hell for that?" She made the question sound both real and trivial. "How much do I owe you, anyway? How much more than life was I expected to give you? My life too?"

"You don't understand," Stevie whispered. "You don't realize how much your leaving hurt us."

"Matthew was an adult," Claire said crisply. "He was responsible for his own life."

"I wasn't!" Stevie screamed, "I was a baby!"

Claire shrugged. "What do you want, Stephanie? To nail me to a cross? For not loving you enough?" She gave a harsh laugh; for the first time she sounded like the woman Angel had described to Ellen, a woman who had been with hundreds of men. "It doesn't work like that, kiddo. You have to take me as I am. Or you can leave."

Stevie tried to think, tried to stop the pain long enough for her brain to work. Here was the woman she had worshipped, the woman she had cried for when she was alone at night, wishing she could come back to life and make everything perfect. But her real mother wasn't a saint, she was an arrogant bitch with no sense of responsibility.

Stevie pulled herself to her feet.

Claire's face was defiant, her eyes as blue and cold as the sea outside. Neither of them spoke. They were the same height; they had the same bones and skin. But in every other way they were different.

Stevie turned and walked to the door. "Good-bye," she called over her shoulder as she pulled it open. "I'm sorry I came. I'm sorry I disturbed this right life you finally found. After all, I'm only your daughter, one of the many inconveniences you left behind."

Outside, with the door safely shut behind her, Stevie inhaled the biting sea air. She tried to feel free but she couldn't. Instead, she was lonely and terrified. As she walked back to the car, she found herself wishing she could erase all knowledge of the real Claire and find some way to restore her fantasy of that other one, the gentle, loving mother whose only sin was dying too soon. But it was too late. These strangers in Rome had taken away all her illusions. And now she had to find some way to survive the truth.

38

"COME back. Please." Claire stood barefoot in the doorway.

Stevie leaned against the car. "Why?" she asked in a tired voice. She wanted to go home to her grandmother's villa. Continuing their conversation would be both pointless and self-destructive.

"I have to talk to you." Claire shouted so she could be heard over the waves. "We can't leave it like this."

"I don't think I can take anymore." Stevie took the car keys out of her pocket.

"Of course you can," Claire insisted, rubbing her arms to keep warm. "You're strong. You can take more than you think."

Stevie glared at her. "That's what people say when they're about to hurt you."

Claire smiled. "You're right, of course. But please, let's try. Why don't we make a deal? I'll hurt you, and then you can hurt me."

Her mother's audacity amazed her. "Could I go first?" Stevie asked dryly.

Claire shook her head, still smiling. "I don't trust you to stick around. I'm afraid you'd hurt me and then leave."

"Sounds familiar," Stevie muttered. "Like mother like daughter."

"Come on." Claire shivered in the cold sea wind. "We're both freezing. I'll tell you things you'd rather not hear, and then you can tell me things I'd rather not hear. And maybe when it's all over we'll find we like each other."

Stevie recoiled. "Oh, no. Don't expect that. I could never like you." She couldn't believe she was saying this to her own mother, but if anyone deserved a cruel truth instead of a polite lie it was this woman.

Claire held out her hands. "Then what have you got to lose? This won't be like listening to a lover confess indiscretions you never suspected. You already know I'm worthless. I'll just be filling in the details. But don't make me beg. Or freeze. My toes are turning blue."

We can't beg people to love us.

Stevie wanted her mother to beg, wanted this woman to beg her to stay. But she didn't have whatever it took to go for the jugular. With a shrug, she pocketed the keys and started back toward the house. "I don't need to know everything," she said as she passed Claire at the door. "I don't want you to tell me things just for your sake. Only say the things that matter."

"Oh, Stephanie," Claire said with a laugh, shutting the door, "you sound so much like Matthew. I'd almost forgotten how ridiculous his demands could be. He was always expecting people to stay where he put them. And we never did. With the exception of you, of course. But it must be hard to be the last one out. You end up with a disproportionate share of the guilt. I know I always consoled myself with the fact that I'd left you behind to keep him company."

Stevie sat on the same wood chair. "Couldn't you have stayed? Can you honestly say you had to go?"

Claire looked amazed, as if Stevie had asked her if she could fly. "Of course I couldn't have stayed," she replied, choosing the couch over the chair this time. She curled her legs up and massaged her cold toes. "I was pregnant. What if the child hadn't been his? How do you think Matthew Templeton would have felt about raising a little Italian bastard? And, by the time Angel was born and her baby blue eyes turned that incomparable Templeton green, it was too late to go back. I don't mean he wouldn't have accepted me. I can't possibly know that. But it was too late for me. I had found a life I preferred. It would have been like going back to prison. Sex was very important to me. I suspect it's important to everyone, even people who don't have a sex life, but I know for a fact it was important to me. I understand that children hate to hear that about their own parents. But how else can I make you understand my life? I suppose I chose sex over you, Stevie. If that makes me a horrible person, then a horrible person I am."

Claire shrugged, as if she had confessed to a minor character flaw such as impatience or vanity. "I'm sure you're not a virgin. And, unless you're the luckiest woman on earth, you must know there is nothing worse than bad sex. Why do you think people get divorced? The reasons they provide are at best half-truths or euphemisms. Incompatibility. Mental anguish. Conflicting interests. It's because they want another partner in bed. So did I. I hated sex with your father. So I broke his heart and abandoned you. So I'm a human being. Are you so sure you wouldn't do the same thing? If you live in dread of that moment when the lights go out, when you can't get away with claiming another headache, then life isn't worth living. But if someone makes you feel wonderful in bed, then all the rest is easier to take. Is that so impossible for you to sympathize with?"

Stevie stared at Claire. Her mother looked calm, relaxed, almost expectant, as if she had just explained a simple point that would clear up all the misunderstanding between them. But Stevie didn't want to understand. What child would want to hear this? That her mother had left her for sex, for orgasms, to have strange men pushing into her?

Stevie started to laugh, but it was hysterical and uncontrollable, terror welling up inside her and pouring out as laughter. She had the same disconcerting sensation she had felt during her first con-

versation with Ellen, as if the earth had tilted, as if right had
turned into wrong.

"You can't relate to this at all?" Claire asked, leaning forward.
"Am I that foreign to you? Haven't you ever done anything selfish
just for sex?"

The laughter stopped as abruptly as it had started. But Stevie
still felt out of control. She couldn't think straight; her emotions
were in charge. She pulled a tissue from her pocket and wiped
her eyes. "Could I have a drink?" she asked. She looked around
the room, but she couldn't see a liquor cabinet. "Anything strong
will do. I'm not fussy."

Claire shook her head. "I'm sorry, there's no alcohol here. I
gave up smoking and drinking a couple of years ago. For that
matter I gave up sex, or it gave me up. It does start to lose its
charms as the years go on."

"Then you must regret—" Stevie began.

Claire shook her head. "I have no regrets. Not even about you
or Angel. I did my best. If it wasn't much, how am I to blame? I
left you and hurt you. I kept Angel and hurt her. What should I
have done differently? You see, I can't look back on my life and
imagine how I would have lived it if I'd been a different person.
That would be hating myself. This is just who I am."

Stevie decided that the woman must have some flaw that made
it impossible for her to understand how other people really felt.
But someone had to make her know how much damage she had
done. She had to be punished. Stevie took a deep breath and then
began to speak. It was her turn to do the hurting. "I used to cry
for you. I thought you were dead. I thought if you could come
back everything would be all right. My father cried too. He was a
lonely, bitter man. I imagined you as a wonderful woman. As a
good mother. I thought—"

Stevie stopped. Claire's face was blank. There was no sign of
pain.

"How can I hurt you?" Stevie cried, meaning it.

"Do you really want to?" Claire asked. She sounded curious.

Stevie studied the beautiful woman. What would her life have been like if Claire had stayed? Her parents would have argued. The fights would have escalated. Stevie would have hid in her room, trying not to listen when Claire came home, disheveled and late, and Matthew confronted her with his suspicions.

She had never had a chance at a nice life like the ones on television, in which the smiling children trade cute quips with their happily married parents. Instead, two people who didn't love each other had conceived a child, and then another one. The children had suffered. Claire was right: preventing their births would have been the only way to prevent the pain. There was nothing to be gained by attacking Claire now. Especially as Claire was like the weather, impervious to the fools who curse it.

"Apparently, I don't want to hurt you after all," Stevie said finally. Her chest was tight; the room seemed hot and dim. "Not anymore. But I might need to." Her head was moving from side to side, she couldn't seem to control it. "How else do I get rid of my pain?" She didn't realize that she had started to scream. Somehow she was on her feet, her clenched fists pumping at the air. "What the fuck am I supposed to do with it?" she shouted at her impassive mother. "Can you tell me that? Do you have the answer to that one, Claire?"

"I have no regrets. I can't. My memory is too good."

Stevie and Claire were in the small kitchen. Holding a chipped china mug of tea, Stevie was still struggling to understand her mother.

Claire continued. "For instance, I remember lying awake one night beside Matthew. You had woken from a nightmare, and after I got you back to sleep I stayed awake. I suspected I was pregnant. I honestly believed it was my lover's child, not Matthew's. I wanted to think my baby had been created from pleasure, and not from one of those silent, cold couplings in the dark when Matthew demanded his rights. And I wanted an excuse to leave. By pretending I wanted to be a good mother to Angel, I allowed myself to be a bad mother to you. And I thought that even if it was

Matthew's child, then it would be a fair division—he would have one and I the other. I was terribly lonely. I could never talk to him, and you were only a baby. I knew I wasn't in love with the other man I was seeing, but I did enjoy his company. And he had offered to take me to Italy. It seemed a gift from God, a solution to all my problems. So I ran, and I didn't let myself look back. You say Matthew cried after I left. Well, I cried when I was there. It's true I was selfish. But aren't you being selfish to suggest I should have stayed? Why am I any worse than you?"

"Because you're my mother," Stevie answered, although the truth sounded feeble.

Claire shrugged. "Maybe when you're a mother you'll see things differently. Maybe not. So many mothers swear they never hate their children. They never admit how they feel at four in the morning when the child has been screaming for hours and they're desperate for sleep, how they start to imagine what a relief it would be to slam that tiny skull against the wall and lie down on the bed and sleep for as long as they want. Until I started seeing other men I used to be afraid I'd kill both you and Matthew some night when I couldn't take it anymore. I felt—it was odd—I felt like I was being squeezed all the time, that my life was forcing me to become tinier and tinier. There was a whole life there, a family, a home, and in some sense I was the center, and yet I didn't believe there was room for me. The place I was supposed to live in felt too small. I couldn't shrink down to fit it. I started to feel that only some violent, horrible action would free me from that house in Boston, that family that felt so wrong for me. That was when I started looking for other men. At least, while in their arms, I could let go. I could feel whatever I wanted, and not just the right things, the acceptable things. I could have passion and pleasure. I needed that. I did my best, Stephanie. I really did. But I wasn't the right mother for you."

Stevie tipped her mug, watching the tea swirl in a slow, irregular circle. She knew it wasn't always easy to be a wife and mother, but that didn't justify Claire's behavior. She was sick of her mother's selfishness. For revenge, she said the cruelest thing

215

she could think of: "Did you do your best the night you beat Angel because a man found her more attractive than you?"

Claire stared down at the wood table. For the first time Stevie saw the emotion she wanted to see in her mother's eyes. There was pain; there was fear and guilt.

"I shouldn't have done that," Claire whispered. "We had stayed together too long, Angel and I. I should have given her to Ellen to raise, but I always resented my mother for wanting me to be dignified and dull. She hated the person I really was. And you don't know what it was like to live with Angel. What it's like to live with someone who is a better version of yourself. Men always wanted her. I had to work for it, I had to be nice to them." She sighed.

"Angel once told me that the tragedy of my life was that a vibrator wasn't good enough for me. I admit I was jealous of her. I wanted to be as special as she was. I always had a good face and body, but I never had the magic. I shouldn't have attacked her, but watching her was like looking at my own mortality. I was getting old, my options were shrinking, and yet I'd never amounted to much. I had spent my life trying to attract men, and I hadn't even been very good at it. I suppose I should try to sound fashionable and enlightened and say I wish I'd done something worthwhile instead of looking for my worth in the arms of men. But that would be a lie. And I've neer liked glib psychological explanations for why people are the way they are—you know: 'I was compensating for the fact that my daddy died when I was a little girl,' or 'my mommy didn't love me enough.' I only wish that I'd seen who I was earlier, that I hadn't dragged so many innocent people into the mess I made of my life. But, as I said, then you and Angel would never have been born."

Stevie looked around the spare kitchen. Everything in the small house was simple and plain. It was not the home of someone who entertained guests. "What do you do now?" Stevie asked. "What is your life like?"

Claire leaned back, cradling her teacup. "I look out at the sea. I read a bit. I don't get lonely anymore. That went away gradually. If you don't need anyone, then why risk the pain?"

216

"Then why did you call me?"

Claire smiled to herself. "The way you looked when you ran away from here the other day. That desperate, angry howl, as if I were evil incarnate. You couldn't even bear to look at me." Her face softened as if she were remembering something sweet Stevie had done. "For the first time, I thought we might have something in common. When you were little, I used to go down in the basement of that dreadful house, close the door, and scream as loud as I could. I thought I could scream my demons away. But of course I couldn't. Instead I ran."

"I came back. You didn't."

Claire raised her eyebrows. "Of course I did. I phoned you, didn't I? It just took me a long time." She grinned. "I was never good with children."

Stevie exhaled. "I don't know if you're sane or crazy. You say such monstrous things in such a straightforward manner."

Claire paused to pour herself another cup of tea from the blue china pot. "I've lived alone for a long time. I'm not used to censoring my words for other people's consumption. And, as I said, I presumed you came here for the truth. Now tell me about your life. Tell me what happened after I left."

Stevie didn't know where to start. How could she describe her whole life to the mother she had never known? And she didn't believe that Claire really cared. She shrugged. "It was the life you ran away from. Boring, safe, conventional. I liked it. It suited me."

"Oh, no," Claire said, refusing to accept that. "Rome suits you. You look like someone who has just burst out of her shell. You have that eager, hungry look. Angel and I were born that way. It took you longer, that's all."

The comparison made Stevie want to throw her cold tea in Claire's face. "I'm nothing like you," she snapped. "I believe in love. I believe in making sacrifices for people I care about."

Claire was slow to reply. She sipped her tea for a minute while Stevie listened to the sea outside, smashing against the rocks. This was her mother's entire life—this small house, these insistent, deadening sounds.

Finally Claire put down her cup. "Love? Show it to me, Stephanie, and then I'll believe in it. Not lust, or need, or fear. Show me something pure and unselfish. A mother's love? It runs out about halfway through labor. And sacrifices? I thought I made them. But apparently it wasn't enough. At first I thought Angel killed herself just to hurt me. And then I realized that I was only a small part in her life. It's cruel, isn't it? Suicide? Like my running away. You take some desperate action purely because of your own needs, and the people left behind only see what it did to them. They don't understand the horrible pain that drove you to it. They don't understand that you never really had any choice at all. Poor Angel. But at least she got her peace earlier in life than I found mine."

Stevie felt dazed and exhausted. Their conversation was so peculiar that she felt as if she were being forced to translate from a language she had never learned. She stared across the plain wood table at her mother. Claire Templeton. *She is a stranger,* Stevie thought. Her father had lived a monk's life pining after this exotic woman. Stevie had believed her youth was empty because this person wasn't there to share it. But Claire really had nothing to do with them; the tragedy wasn't her absence, it was the false image they had made of her.

Stevie realized it was time to leave. She pushed back her chair. "I might come back," she said as she stood up.

Claire smiled. "If you wish."

"I might not."

Claire looked down. She shrugged as though it made no difference to her.

When Stevie opened the door she was surprised to see the bright sky. She felt as if it should be the middle of the night, but it was still early in the day.

Stevie hesitated. She felt cheated. She had wanted so much from this woman. Love and platitudes, she supposed, the mother she had dreamt of.

"Angel came once with Gian-Carlo Cassieri," Claire volunteered. "The other times she always came alone. She would park outside on Sunday afternoons. Not here. In Rome, at the place where I lived before."

"You didn't go out to see her?"

Claire shook her head.

"Why not?"

"Why didn't she come in?" Claire asked as if it were an equally valid question. "I don't know what we would have said to each other anyway."

When Stevie thought of Angel sitting in her car, watching their mother's home, she wanted to cry. "You're sure she committed suicide?" Stevie said. "There have been suggestions . . ."

"Murder?" Claire supplied. "Perhaps. It takes a lot of courage to kill yourself." She looked past Stevie at the water shimmering in the brilliant sun. "There's a lot to give up," Claire continued. "The simple pleasures, the sun on your skin, a starry night, the wind in your hair. We'll take a lot of pain before we sacrifice that. I'm glad I never did. I'm happy now."

When she saw Stevie's shocked expression she softly laughed.

"Would you like it better if I were miserable? If you had found me living with regrets, begging your forgiveness? Do I ask you to apologize for crying in the night when you were a baby? Why should I apologize for being me? It's too late anyway. We can't change anything."

"But you're so cold. You don't even seem upset at the possibility that Angel was murdered."

Claire shrugged. "We're all going to die. She just beat us to it. That's like Angel. She was always in a hurry, even when she had no place to go."

Stevie stepped back. She looked at the thin woman in the doorway, the house, the barren landscape—freezing it in her mind, like a snapshot. She knew she would never return. Then, without looking back, she walked away.

39

"You're the most desirable woman in the world. Feel it. Believe it. Show me." The photographer, a lanky young man in black leather pants and matching leather jacket, crouched in front of Angel.

On one side of a large room in Cinecittà, where Angel was being photographed for a magazine spread in *Oggi,* Aldo sat watching his star. Angel's behavior had become less self-destructive in the weeks since she had resumed her relationship with Gian-Carlo, but the producer was still worried about her.

The photographer went on snapping Angel's constantly changing positions as she moved quickly around the room in a red silk blouse and a black miniskirt.

"How about this one?" Aldo said. He held up a script. "It's a movie deal in L.A. A beautiful young woman becomes a vigilante to avenge her father's murder. It's a love story. And if you don't like that, I've got an offer for a big American TV series. They want to fire an actress who's asking for too much money. She'll have plastic surgery and come back as you."

"Will I get to exercise my art or do they just want a pair of tits?"

Aldo threw the script on the floor. "Angel, if that's not a joke, I'll—"

She grinned. "Come on, Aldo. You know I can't leave Rome."

The photographer moved closer to her. "I want to feel that you're desperate for my body!"

"Don't we all," the producer said. "Angel, you know that bastard would leave Italy if it suited his career. And the world is full of men who are crazy about you. Men who give sex the importance it deserves. What's wrong with that nice Ben Gasperini? He wrote such a lovely part for you after you broke his heart."

"Ben doesn't want me. He wants Angel Concelli."

"You are Angel Concelli!"

"Only sometimes," she said, pouting at the photographer. She stalked around the room on her high heels, the photographer hurrying to keep up with her.

"And who are you the rest of the time?" Aldo said.

"God, this is perfect!" the photographer yelled. "You're really turning me on."

Angel turned to face the camera. She leaned forward, her hands on her bare thighs, her breasts straining the thin shirt. She slowly licked her lips, looking as if she wanted to make love to the lens.

"Need me," the photographer said. "Show me what you've got."

Angel slowly undid the buttons on her blouse. Coyly she turned her back to him and slid the silk down over her arms. Looking over her shoulder, she winked at the camera. Then, in a quick move, she shrugged off the shirt and tossed it across the room. The photographer caught the image of Angel's naked back, her arms stretched out, the crimson silk shirt suspended in the air.

Her hands on her hips, she swung around to face the camera. Topless, she walked toward the photographer. Shooting one picture after the other, he backed up until he hit the wall. She stood in front of him, her legs apart, her lips open, and slowly raised her arms over her head. Aldo, his face red, was fanning himself with one of the scripts.

"Am I really the most desirable woman in the world?" she whispered huskily.

"Absolutely, baby," the photographer gasped.

"Great." She dropped her arms and turned away. "I'll see you later."

"What?" the confused photographer said. "Where are you going?"

"To give sex the importance it deserves." She picked up her black trenchcoat from a chair.

"Angel!" Aldo protested. "He's not finished."

"Why should I waste it on the goddamned camera?" She buttoned the coat over her bare breasts, then waved over her shoulder as she walked out of the room. *"Ciao."*

The photographer looked stunned. He was still holding his camera. "Do I wait for her?" he asked Aldo.

Aldo shook his head. "Something tells me she'll be awhile."

"Is this Gian-Carlo's office?"

Gian-Carlo's secretary jumped up from her desk when Angel walked in.

"Yes, but he's—"

"Thanks," Angel said, sweeping past the young woman.

"But you can't—"

Angel smiled at her. "Oh yes I can," she said as she opened the door to Gian-Carlo's office and stepped inside.

He was on the telephone, the sleeves of his white shirt rolled up and his striped tie loose at his neck. At her unannounced arrival he looked up in shock from behind his enormous oak desk.

She kicked the door shut behind her.

"Uh, yes," Gian-Carlo said into the telephone. "That's exactly what I thought."

Angel grinned and, unbuttoning her coat, started walking toward him.

"Yes," Gian-Carlo continued, trying to keep his voice steady. He wiped his forehead. "I understand. Look, could I get back to you—"

When she reached him she swung his chair around so that he was facing her. Then she opened her coat and showed him her bare breasts. He waved his hands to tell her to stay back. Grinning, she bent down and started kissing his neck.

"No," Gian-Carlo said into the telephone. His voice sounded strangled. "Nothing's wrong. I just—"

Angel reached for his belt and unbuckled it.

"Franco," Gian-Carlo said, "I promise I'll get right back—"

Angel took the telephone receiver out of his hand and hung it up. She picked up his hands and put them on her breasts. "Now let's get to some real business," she whispered. She pushed back some papers on his desk and slid onto it. She took Gian-Carlo by the wrists and started pulling him toward her.

Suddenly he shoved her away. He stepped back and quickly buckled his belt. "You idiot! he roared. "What the hell are you doing here?"

Shocked, Angel stared at him.

"Don't you read the papers!" he shouted. "We're heading toward another election in a couple of months! And you march in here and start taking your clothes off like . . . like a whore. Anyone could have been in here. Christ, you could have ruined me!"

Her eyes filling with tears, Angel lowered her head and let him shout his abuse. She pulled the coat tight across her breasts.

"Why did you come here?" Gian-Carlo was screaming. "What on earth made you do such a stupid thing?"

She didn't answer him.

"Answer me!" he yelled.

She shrugged. "I guess I forgot," she whispered.

"Forgot what?"

She was still looking at the floor. She wiped her wet cheeks with the back of her hand. "Forgot who I am, I guess. That I'm just a slut. For a moment I thought I was someone that somebody loved."

She stood up. She tried to smooth the papers she had wrinkled on the desk, then gave up. Gian-Carlo was staring at her. She turned and headed toward the door.

Someone opened it before she got there. "What happened? Is your phone out of order?"

The tall thin man with receding hair and wire-rimmed glasses stopped when he saw Angel. She recognized Franco Uccellini from the party where Gian-Carlo had taken her into the bedroom. His cold pale eyes swept over her. He noted the short tight skirt under the half-open trench coat, the stiletto heels, the wild blond hair, as if he were checking off items on a list defining *cheap*.

Angel continued walking to the door. She didn't look back at Gian-Carlo. Uccellini moved to let her pass. "He's all yours," Angel told him. "Though I suppose you already knew that."

40

"RUB it in, Aldo. You were right."

Aldo sat down next to Angel on the long couch he had had installed in his office for naps and infidelities. Much to his regret in the last few months naps had become the more frequent of the two.

"I don't want to rub it in, *bella*." The heavy man patted Angel's knee. She was still wearing the black trenchcoat over her mini-skirt. "I wish I'd been wrong. I want the best for you."

She leaned back and put her hands behind her head. "So get me a movie in the U.S. Make me a big international star. That's what I want. I've got to get out of this country. I don't want to hear his name or see his picture for the rest of my life." She slapped her thigh. "Christ, I just thought of something awful. If he actually becomes prime minister they'll talk about him over there too."

Aldo smiled at her misperception of Italy's position in international affairs. "Not much, Angel. And in L.A. not at all. Are you interested in the picture where you play the vigilante or do you want me to try for something else?"

"Would I get to kill a lot of people?"

He held out his hands. "Nearly everyone in the picture."

"Great. That would suit me just fine right now."

"Good move, kid." He kissed her on the cheek and then pulled himself to his feet. "Let's celebrate. Take off your coat. I'll get the champagne."

Angel wished she had stopped off at her apartment to get dressed instead of coming directly to Aldo's office. Any other time she would have confessed that she was still topless and borrowed one of the outfits he kept on hand for "guests," but the scene with Gian-Carlo had left her feeling embarrassed and cheap.

"In L.A.," she announced, "I'm not going to fuck anybody. I'm going to make them think I've got class."

He selected a bottle of champagne from the well-stocked re-frigerator behind his desk. "In L.A. they don't hold promiscuity against you. It's an altogether healthier climate." He unwound the wire from the cork, then stopped to wipe his forehead with a large silk handkerchief. "Jesus, I'm tired. I work too hard. I keep getting these dizzy spells. Maybe I'll go out to L.A. with you for a couple of weeks. Take a working holiday. Might be nice to sit beside a pool with a couple of Valley Girls. Italian women are so demanding. I fucked a starlet last night who actually complained because I didn't make her come. Jesus, I'm giving her a part in a movie. With two lines! Doesn't she know how these things work? I've got the money—I don't have to be a great lay. She said I was a sexist pig. I explained that when she gets to be a star she can pick up young guys and make them please her. What's sexist about that? Sounds fair to me." He was struggling with the cork.

"Do you need help?" Angel asked.

His face was red. He wiped his forehead again. "I'm not old. I can still open champagne bottles. The damn thing is just stuck."

"Try another bottle. It's only money."

"Only money, she says. Only *my* money." He stopped to catch

226

his breath. "The French make them this way so that men in other countries look like wimps when they're trying to impress broads." He tried it again, pulling with all his strength.

"It's okay, Aldo," Angel said, leaning forward in concern. "Why don't we just go out to a restaurant and have some dinner? I'm really not thirsty."

"Angel," he exploded angrily, waving the heavy bottle at her, "I told you I can open a fucking bottle of champagne. I'm not a helpless old man. I've opened thousands of these in my time."

Suddenly his eyes went blank. It was fast, without any of the drama he would have used in filming it. He slumped to the floor, in a soft heap. The corked champagne bottle landed with a quiet thud at his side.

"No," Angel whispered. She stayed on the couch; she was afraid to move. "Don't do this to me, Aldo."

She waited, convinced that he would come up with one of his absurd lines. He would bound to his feet, champagne bottle in hand, and pull out the cork in a quick, easy move.

His eyes were open but blank. His chest wasn't moving.

"Aldo, please, no." She stumbled to her feet and ran to his side. Dropping to her knees, she grabbed his shoulders and shook him as hard as she could. "Come back, you old fool!" she screamed. She slapped his face. "Don't die on me!"

He was limp and heavy. She bent over him and pressed her lips against his. She blew into his mouth. When nothing happened, she started pounding his broad chest with her fists.

It didn't work. It was as if this thing on the ground, this object, had never been alive, as if she were touching some eerie life-size dummy of Aldo Guerritore. She grabbed his shoulders and shook him again. His head bobbed back and forth. His eyes remained blank.

"I need you, Aldo!" she screamed. "You're my friend, my only friend. You can't die! Get up!" She ran over to the phone and punched in the number for the Cinecittà operator.

"Get someone here! Fast! Aldo Guerritore's sick!"

She dropped the phone on the floor and ran back to him. With

227

mascara streaming down her face, she grabbed his arms and tried to pull his heavy frame upright. "Come on, Aldo. I'll walk you around the room. You'll be fine. Just put your arm around my shoulders." She tried to prop his inert arm around her, but it flopped back down on the floor. "Come on!" she commanded again. "You have to try. Get up!" She grabbed his arms again, but he was too heavy for her.

She crouched beside him and stared down into his blank eyes.

"Damn you!" she yelled, saliva spilling out onto his face. "Damn you for dying on me!"

Then she collapsed sobbing on his chest and slipped her arms around his neck. "Don't leave me here alone," she whispered in his ear, her hair falling on his face. "It's too hard, Aldo. Nobody else cares about me. I won't stand a chance if you're not here to help."

But she knew it was too late. He was already turning cold. She leaned over and kissed him on the mouth. Then she stretched out next to him, her arms around his wide belly, and waited for someone to come and do whatever was necessary for the corpse.

41

STEVIE trudged up the stone steps to her grandmother's villa, dreading Ellen's questions about her visit with Claire. She didn't know if she could find the right words to describe the emotionally exhausting encounter. She didn't even know where to start.

Claire had been so calm and reasonable. Everything she said seemed, on the surface, to be rational. Yet Stevie considered the woman a monster. But she didn't know what other people—even Ellen—would say. Her own response might not be reasonable. In the last few days she had started to see herself through other people's eyes. She had discovered how naive and conservative she was compared with most people. Maybe Claire was normal. Maybe that was the way life really worked, and she just had to get used to it.

The villa was quiet. Stevie knew it would be cruel to put off talking to Ellen. She had been putting off too much: calling Nick, thinking about what she should do if Gian-Carlo called . . .

229

When she heard a sound in the library, she walked over to the open door. Her grandmother was standing with her back to the window, her face pale and lined. She looked very old. At the sight of Stevie she gave out a small cry of dismay.

"Stephanie, I tried to call Nick Funaro. You don't have to put up with this. These men—"

Two men were seated side by side on the flowered couch. She had seen them before. On her second day in Rome they had come to the Contessa's apartment to question her about Angel's death.

"Officers," Stevie said wearily to the two policemen, "surely you must know by now that when Angel Concelli died I was still in Boston. What use could I possibly be to you?"

The smaller one rose. He had done the talking the last time, too. She remembered that his name was Garelli. "We only have a few questions, Signorina Templeton," he said, his voice sharper than she had remembered. His small eyes were bright and hostile. "As a guest in our country, surely you should be pleased to offer any assistance you can. We only ask for an hour of your time, perhaps less. If it might help us clear up the matter of your sister's death, then how can you decline?"

Tired of disagreeing with people, Stevie gave in. She really didn't mind answering a few questions—even though she couldn't possibly help them. Her fear was that they would pry into her parents' lives. What if a leak in the police department—and the Roman police force was said to have no shortage of leaks— led to the story of her parents' lives appearing in headlines across Italy? She also had to be careful that Ellen's name didn't get to the media. The last thing her grandmother needed was a crowd of paparazzi camped out across the street.

"I'm sure it's just a formality," she assured Ellen, hoping she was right. "May we use this room?"

"No," Garelli announced, "We have arranged to take you to our office in Rome."

Although displeased with this rather melodramatic turn of events, Stevie decided it was too late to insist on her right to professional advice. Especially since she didn't know what her rights were under Italian law.

It was a fast drive. The heavier police officer drove through the dense traffic like an escaped madman. Stevie wondered several times if she would survive the trip. At one point they sped up onto a sidewalk and sent a couple of overweight women scurrying for shelter. She speculated on the field day the Italian scandal sheets would have describing Angel's sister meeting such a bizarre death.

At a large unidentified building, which she assumed was police headquarters, she was ushered up a flight of stairs and into a tiny windowless office. Garelli told her to sit in a wood chair. Maltesta, the fat one, remained standing by the closed door while Garelli settled in behind a small metal desk. The desk and three wood chairs were the room's only furnishings. If it was Garelli's office they were in, she knew he wasn't very important. That reassured her; it meant the authorities didn't give much weight to this interview.

Taking a thick file of papers from the top drawer, he set it on the desk before asking his first question. "What is your relationship with Gian-Carlo Cassieri?"

Stevie stared at him in amazement. "I thought you brought me here to discuss Angel," she finally managed to say. "What has Signore Cassieri got to do with this?"

"You are being purposely naive, Signorina Templeton," he snapped. He unbuttoned his heavily creased jacket and folded his small hands on the file. "Gian-Carlo Cassieri has a great deal to do with this. As you have already pointed out, you were in Boston when Angel Concelli died. You obviously cannot provide us with firsthand information about that night or the events leading up to it. You have, however, been seen in the company of Gian-Carlo Cassieri on several occasions since your arrival in Rome. We would like to know everything he has said to you about your sister's death."

Stevie was stunned. If she had known they were going to question her about Gian-Carlo, she would never have agreed to come.

"My private conversations are none of your business!"

The thin man straightened up. His small eyes reminded her of a rodent. "We are investigating a possible murder. If you are withholding information relevant to the case we will lay charges against you. Would you like to see our prison system from the inside, Signorina Templeton? You might find it somewhat less elegant than Signora Brenner's charming villa."

"You have no right to threaten me." She got up from the chair. The room was stifling; her cotton shirt was already clinging to her back. "I won't put up with this. I'm leaving."

Out of the corner of her eye, she noticed the second police officer close his hand around the doorknob.

"Signorina Templeton," the man behind the desk continued smoothly, "you can't really believe that. Of course I can insist that you answer my questions. I'm trying to find out what happened to your sister. We think you know more than you're saying. What do you expect me to do? Say thank you very much, good-bye? Now please sit down again and answer my questions. What has Gian-Carlo Cassieri said to you about Angel Concelli's death?"

Stevie sank back down on her chair. "I really can't help you," she said. "He's only talked about the kind of person she was."

"Nothing about her death?"

Stevie shook her head.

He laughed, a sharp, grating noise. "You expect me to believe that?" he asked, leaning forward. "Are you saying you've never asked him what happened?"

She rubbed the back of her neck; it was dripping with sweat. She wished they would open the door and let in some fresh air. "I already know what happened. It was suicide. There was nothing to ask Signore Cassieri."

He raised his thin eyebrows. "You didn't ask your sister's lover where he was on the night of her death? He didn't tell you?"

She shook her head.

"He didn't volunteer that he was seen leaving her apartment late on the night of her death?"

Stevie stared at him. "No," she whispered.

"Why did he take you to his office on Sunday?"

Her palms were wet. She wiped them on her jeans. "I don't know why. Sight-seeing, I guess."

Maltesta snickered behind her. She felt herself blushing. Garelli gave her a contemptuous look, then signaled to his partner.

"Get him now. Tell him she won't cooperate."

"Get whom?" Stevie asked.

"Shut up," Garelli shot at her. "We didn't bring you here to listen to stupid stories. We're not fools and we don't like to be treated as if we were. You Americans come here expecting to con a bunch of stupid wops. Would you try to get away with this if you were talking to a police officer in the United States?"

Without waiting for her answer, the two men left the room. She leaned back in the uncomfortable chair, relieved to be alone for a minute. She heard a clicking sound at the door. With a sickening sensation, she realized that they had locked her in. She was a prisoner.

While she waited in the small airless room, trying to remain calm, she wondered what the men wanted. They seemed convinced that she knew something, but she didn't. She racked her memory for anything that Gian-Carlo might have said that would implicate him in Angel's death, but she came up blank. Even if someone had seen him leaving her apartment that night, it didn't mean he was guilty. Angel might have called and begged him to come over, then when he arrived he found her dead. Or they had a fight and she took the pills after he left.

The two men had been gone for over ten minutes. The thick file was still on the desk. It probably contained everything they had on the case. She wondered how much they really knew about Angel's death. Was there proof that Gian-Carlo had visited her that night or had his political opponents started the story to cost him the election? She was tempted to take a look. But it was confidential. Garelli must have forgotten to put it away before he left.

Another ten minutes passed, and they felt twice as long as the first ten. She was thirsty. She stared at the blank walls. There wasn't even a calendar. The only thing in the room was the bulging file folder.

She stood up to stretch her cramped legs. She was covered in sweat; her damp hair clung to her forehead and neck. She walked around the tiny office taking deep breaths, trying to keep alert. She wished someone would show up with a cup of coffee. Running her fingers along the desk as she passed it, she touched the file folder. She stopped.

Garelli could have left it open. If someone came in, they wouldn't know that she was the one who had opened it. And even if they did, how could they blame her? If it was confidential, it should have been locked up. Any curious person would look inside.

She flicked the top up.

An eight-by-ten photograph was inside: Angel and Gian-Carlo in bed together. They were naked, the blankets in a tangle on the floor. Her legs were wide, her hands were up above her head. He was kissing her breasts, his hands holding them to his mouth. He was inside her.

Stevie slid it over and looked at the next picture. Angel was kneeling before Gian-Carlo, taking him into her mouth. His hands were grasping her hair. His face was contorted with ecstasy.

In the third one they were standing up. He had pushed her against a wall. Her white satin dress was pulled up to her waist, her panties around one ankle. He was still fully dressed in a tuxedo. They couldn't even wait to undress.

She looked underneath.

The room was dark. The outline of the couple could barely be made out. Angel was on her back. Gian-Carlo was holding her blouse open as his mouth moved to her nipple.

Stevie.

Stevie in Gian-Carlo's dimly lit office last Sunday afternoon.

She knocked the photograph aside.

She was lying on a table, naked and gray, a bruise on the right side of her bloated face. She was in the morgue.

"Signorina Templeton. I'm glad you're having a look at our file on Angel Concelli's death. It might encourage you to answer our questions."

Her eyes full of tears, Stevie turned to look at the tall thin man with wire-rimmed glasses who was standing in the doorway.

42

"I can't help you," Stevie whispered.

"Can't? Or won't?"

She couldn't take her eyes from the last chilling photograph. The image of Angel dead, stretched out like a slab of meat, threw her own mortality in her face. Sex and death, she thought. We are such primitive beings.

She shuddered and then looked at the man who walked over to sit down in the chair behind the desk. Dressed in an immaculate suit of dark gray wool—his cuff links had the dull sheen of real gold—he had the air of a man accustomed to having people obey him without question. "I'd like to leave," she told him. She pushed her damp hair back from her face. "What are my rights?"

He smirked. Behind the thick glasses his eyes were intelligent and cold. "Morally or legally? After all, we are investigating your sister's death."

"I'll handle my own moral dilemmas," she shot back. "I don't need to be preached to by someone who doesn't even have the manners to introduce himself."

"Forgive me," he conceded, bowing his head in a formal manner. "I am Dr. Franco Uccellini."

She frowned. The name was familiar. "What kind of doctor?" she asked. "Medical?"

"Political science and public administration."

"And you work for the police?"

"I work for my country, Signorina Templeton." He made it sound like a sacred calling.

"But what is your specific position?"

He folded his long, narrow fingers on the small desk. After a slight hesitation, he said, "Special secretary."

She finally remembered where she had heard his name. After Garelli and Maltesta had left the Contessa's apartment, Nick had said that they might work for someone named Uccellini rather than the police. And he had added that Uccellini worked for Gian-Carlo.

But that didn't make sense. Why would one of Gian-Carlo's own people be investigating him? Unless this man was secretly working for the opposition. "Special secretary to whom?" she asked, testing him.

He shrugged, avoiding her eyes. "I am an adviser to the government. As you must know, interest in your sister's death has mushroomed into a public obsession. Rumors have started to include members of the government. Since there will be an election in a few days, the questions must be cleared up as quickly as possible. I have been assigned the responsibility of finding out the full story."

Stevie looked at the photograph again. All this political intrigue was pointless; nothing would bring Angel back. These people—the press, the police, politicians—were exploiting her death to further their own selfish aims. "She killed herself by an overdose of sleeping pills. Isn't that the full story?"

He shrugged. "Possibly. But certain details still must be explained, details that have caught the public's imagination. Ashes on her bedroom rug, suggesting something was destroyed. A man's tie draped over the headboard. A bruise—as you must have noted in the photograph—on Signorina Concelli's face. Of course, the explanations are probably simple. A fall could account for the bruise. The tie? Left behind by a gentleman. Or even a new fashion trend for women. The ashes? A suicide note, one that she decided against leaving. But without further investigation, we cannot be sure."

Stevie sighed. Even if his motives were honorable—and she wasn't ready to concede that—there was still something unseemly about this enterprise. It was like taking jewelry from a corpse, and she didn't want any part of it. "And what am I supposed to be able to tell you?"

Uccellini gestured for her to sit down. She hesitated, then walked over to the chair.

"Gian-Carlo," Uccellini began, "is an excellent man and a fine politician, but he had one weakness. Angel Concelli. Even though she is dead, his memory of her is interfering with his judgment. In his distress he has turned to you, her sister and a remarkable physical likeness. It is impossible to believe that he has not talked to you about her death." He gestured down at the photographs. "Particularly during your more intimate encounters. I'm only asking you to share this information with me."

"But who are you representing?" she asked. "You can't just say the government. I'm not that naive. If you're reporting to Gian-Carlo's political opposition—"

He held up his hand. "Surely what is at stake here is the truth about your sister's death. If, for instance, you had information that led us to believe her death was not suicide or an accident, we would reopen the investigation. You wouldn't want your sister's murderer to go free, would you?"

The light from the bare overhead bulb glinted off his glasses, hiding his eyes. Stevie looked at the picture of Angel in the morgue. The poor, lonely girl. What would have happened if she hadn't died that night? When Stevie arrived in Rome people would have pointed out the resemblance. Would the two of them have discovered their connection and become friends?

Stevie looked at the white skin, the blue-veined eyelids, the swollen lips. Could she have saved her sister?

"Signorina Templeton," Dr. Uccellini prompted. His smooth voice was persuasive. "You must help us."

"But I honestly don't know anything," she said.

"You must realize," he said, "that you've put yourself in a very difficult position. You've become confidante to an extremely powerful man who could become a thousand times more powerful in a matter of days. He has become obsessed with you, just as he was with your sister."

She shook her head. "No. You're wrong. He isn't obsessed with me at all."

"Now you *are* being naive, Signorina Templeton." He gestured at the pictures again. "The man is the head of his party, he's running for the office of prime minister, yet he spends an entire night outside a private villa waiting for a glimpse of you. He's married, but he takes you to dinner in one of Rome's most popular restaurants. He brings you to his office and . . ." He didn't finish.

Stevie massaged her forehead; her head throbbed with a dull, sickening pain.

"You're much more important than you realize," his soft insinuating voice continued. He got up and walked around the desk, stopping right beside her. "Can't you see that you're destroying his career, destroying an entire political party?"

Looking up, she caught him staring at her with a cold, calculating look. He held her eyes. "In fact, you're doing exactly what your sister tried to do and failed."

"Not me," she said. "You're wrong."

"You, Signorina Templeton."

The room was spinning. Stevie touched the desk, afraid she would fall. The metal surface was surprisingly cool. "So much has happened since I arrived in Rome," she whispered. "From my first night here . . ." She remembered waking up to discover Nick in her bed. "And people thought I was Angel, risen from the dead."

238

She remembered how terrified she had been of the crowds chasing her through the streets.

"Did Gian-Carlo tell you how Angel died?" He touched her hand. Why were his fingers as cool as the desk? Was she the only one who felt the oppressive heat? "Did he tell you what really happened that night?"

"Who took those pictures?" she whispered. She blinked. The walls seemed to be moving closer. "Who photographed me? Who took the pictures of Angel and Gian-Carlo? Did you do this?"

His fingers tightened around her wrist. He was hurting her. "How much do you know?"

Tears burned her eyes. "Nothing."

"Why do you keep seeing him?"

She didn't answer.

Slowly, he twisted her wrist. "Tell me," he whispered. "What do you know?"

Suddenly the door opened. Uccellini snatched his hand away and stepped back.

"Stevie! I've been looking all over you! Ellen told me those two buffoons took you somewhere."

At the sight of Nick, Stevie nearly cried with relief. "Thank God you're here," she whispered.

With the door open, fresh air quickly filled the small space. A young woman in a tight pink dress and dangerously high heels strutted down the hall with a pile of papers. Real life. Stevie took a deep breath.

"Franco," Nick said, looking fresh and handsome in a white shirt and dark blue pants. He extended his hand to the man behind the desk. "I haven't seen you in ages. Staying out of trouble, I hope?"

Uccellini frowned. After a brief hesitation, he curtly shook Nick's hand. "This is actually a private conversation," he complained, settling into the chair again.

Nick moved the third chair closer to the small desk and sat down in it. He leaned back and crossed his legs. Although Uccellini was the taller man, Nick's easy manner and bright, perceptive eyes allowed him to dominate the room. "I think Stevie would like to have me here," he said in a friendly but businesslike tone. "And I'm sure you won't mind. After all, she is an American citizen, unfamiliar with our customs and laws."

Dr. Uccellini's eyes narrowed. For a moment he looked as if he might protest. But then he rose and walked over to shut the door.

Nick turned to Stevie. "What's going on?" he asked softly. "Are you all right?"

She blinked back tears. "I don't know." She looked down at the photographs on the desk. Uccellini followed her eyes. His hand swooped down and picked them up.

"We were examining these," he told Nick. He smiled, as if he had regained the upper hand. "Perhaps you'd like to have a look at them."

With a flourish he dropped the photograph of Stevie and Gian-Carlo onto Nick's lap. Nick caught his breath. He stared at it for a moment. Then he whispered, "Stevie."

Uccellini dropped a second photograph on top of it. Angel knelt before Gian-Carlo, taking him into her mouth. Stevie realized that the rapid juxtaposition would make Nick think she was the woman in both pictures. Uccellini had purposely chosen the one where Angel's face was most hidden.

"Nick, I—" she said.

"Interesting photographs," Dr. Uccellini said, cutting her off.

"Angel," Nick whispered, identifying the sister in the picture.

Uccellini handed him the two other photographs of Angel and Gian-Carlo. Nick only glanced at them long enough to ascertain that the woman was Angel. Then he returned to the one of Stevie on the desk. The curve of her body and the expression on her face telegraphed her state of arousel.

He finally looked up at Uccellini. "Any more, Franco? Perhaps some snapshots of your wife?"

Uccellini scowled. Nick looked through them again. He hesitated at the one of Angel kneeling before Gian-Carlo. With her face hidden and her hair tangled around his fingers, the woman was hard to identify. He glanced at Stevie, a cold, comparing look.

Her cheeks were burning. She had never felt such shame; it was like seeing the ugliest thing on earth, and it had her face and her name.

"I asked who took them," she said quietly.

Nick shrugged. His shirt was already stained with sweat, and he looked tired. "Does it matter?"

"There's another one," Stevie said. "Taken of Angel after she died."

Obligingly, Dr. Uccellini held it out. Nick took it gingerly and held it by the edges. "A sad end," he murmured. "Such a lovely woman. But doomed, I suppose, from the start. I think that was part of her appeal. We all sensed she was on her way to tragedy, and now we have the arrogance to think that given the chance, we could have been the one to save her."

"You sound as if you were a little infatuated with her yourself," Uccellini observed, glancing over at Stevie as he spoke.

"Oh no," Nick said quickly. "I've always preferred comedy to tragedy. Unhappy endings make me feel cheated." He dropped the photographs down on the desk.

"Back to business," he said. Nick's tone was brusque: a lawyer discussing a client. "Signorina Templeton has been under considerable strain. If you insist on questioning her, then please submit a written request to my office. I will be representing her in this matter."

Uccellini straightened his shoulders. "I'll do that," he snapped. "Your secretary will have it first thing tomorrow morning."

Nick reached out and took Stevie's hand. She got up and followed him to the door. When she glanced back at Uccellini, his smile was slightly ominous. She wished her dealings with him were over rather than just beginning. She never wanted to see him again.

Once they were out of the office, Nick rushed her down a steep flight of stairs, along a crowded hallway, and out into the hot, dazzling sun. His blue BMW was parked illegally in front of the building.

Exhausted, she sank back into the soft leather seat. A cold blast

241

of air-conditioning felt like a miracle. A typical Roman driver, Nick steered the car into the never-ending stream of traffic with more courage than patience.

"Where are we going?" she asked.

Instead of answering her, he pulled on a pair of dark glasses and adjusted the sun visor.

"People in Rome are always taking me places," she snapped. "I'm getting tired of not being consulted. Why the hell can't you say where we're going?"

Suddenly Nick slammed on the brakes. The car screeched to a halt. Stevie looked around for a stop sign, but they were in the middle of a busy block. The drivers behind them were already honking their horns. It sounded like a modern symphony—blaring and arrhythmic.

Nick ignored the commotion and leaned toward her. She could hardly make out his eyes through the dark glasses. "Since you seem to have some aversion to Laura Barberini's apartment, I'm taking you to a hotel. At that hotel, I plan to make love to you for—" He consulted his watch. "Three and a half hours. Do you have any objection to that?"

She stared at him. In addition to the honking horns, about twenty motorists were now shouting obscenities at them.

"Answer me!" he screamed. "Do you have any objection to that plan?"

She didn't know what to say. Her brain wouldn't work. "I guess not," she whispered.

His lip curled with disgust. "Is that all the enthusiasm you can work up? You're ready to strip for Cassieri, but when I proposition you all you can manage is *I guess not*?"

"Nick, that's not fair, I—"

"Do you want to make love to me or not?"

Out of the corner of her eye she noticed that a large man had abandoned his blocked truck and was angrily weaving through the stopped traffic toward them. She looked back at Nick. "Yes. Yes, I want to make love to you."

"Now? At a hotel? You won't change your mind?"

She took a deep breath. "Yes, now. I won't change my mind."

"Fine." Nick turned to face the road again. He stepped on the gas pedal. The enraged truck driver, who had reached the side of the car, jumped back and waved his fist at them.

"We should be there in about three minutes," Nick informed her as if he were discussing dinner arrangements. "Feel free to fondle me on the way. I've got nothing against foreplay." Then he looked over at her and grinned.

Stevie stared at this unpredictable man who was whisking her off to bed with him. She wasn't sure how she had reached this point, but she knew she didn't want to turn back. Testing unfamiliar waters, slowly she extended her hand and placed it lightly on his thigh.

She was rewarded with a huge smile.

43

ANGEL stopped in front of a large mirror on the wall of the Ristorante Pontevecchio to adjust her chin-length black wig. She pushed her sunglasses back up on her nose and fixed one of the straps on her yellow silk dress. "You're gorgeous," she said to her reflection. "But don't let anybody recognize you, or they'll go crazy." She nodded at the curious middle-aged man sitting at a nearby table, watching her. "Shhh," she said, holding her finger to her lips. "It'll be our little secret."

Then she resumed her walk to the table on the other side of the restaurant where John Freemantle was waiting for her.

Halfway there she stopped and leaned against a table where two perfumed women in silk and jewels were having lunch. She picked up a glass of wine from their table and gulped it down. The women exchanged glances that were both embarrassed and amused.

"Excuse me," Angel said, putting the empty glass down. "But it's a long walk to my table."

People were murmuring her name.

She held up her hand and addressed the restaurant. "It's not me!" she said. "Honest."

John rushed over to her and put his arm around her. "Come on," he said. "Let me take you home."

"But we haven't had lunch yet!" she protested. "I'm starving. And I want another drink."

He sighed and helped her back to their table. She fell into her chair.

"Angel," he warned. "I really think you should go home."

"I like it here," she said. "I don't get out enough. Since Aldo died, I'm not allowed to work. His wife owns my contract. She won't loan me out to another producer and she won't make any movies with parts for me. She's only doing it because she never liked me. Hell, she never even liked Aldo."

As she reached for her glass, she knocked it over. The brown liquid soaked into the white tablecloth.

"Oh shit." She stood up and waved her arms. "Waiter! Waiter, I need another drink!"

John covered his face with his hands. "Angel, I'm taking you home. You shouldn't be out in public like this."

"Why not?" she said, dropping back into her chair as an embarrassed waiter rushed over to the table with another drink. "These are my fans. They love me. Didn't you see the way they chased me all around the damn cemetery at Aldo's funeral?"

"Yes," John murmured, "like cannibals sniffing a fresh missionary. Poor Aldo. What's it been, two months now? To my astonishment, I actually miss the bastard. But you must find something to keep you busy. Get a lawyer and fight Signora Guerritore. Contracts as binding as yours must be illegal in this day and age. Feudalism went out a long time ago, even in Hollywood, the least civilized place in the universe. And for God's sake, go to one of those drying-out places."

Angel picked up her drink as if his suggestion had only served to remind her of it. "I never thought I'd be a drunk," she said. "It always seemed so disgusting. But it's not really like that at all. Alcohol comes to life. You smell it across the room, and it's like hearing a familiar voice. Your spirits pick up. You know you're not alone. It's like having a buddy, a best pal, someone who'll walk home with you and stay beside you when you're falling asleep. I don't want to give it up and go back to being alone all the time. I want to be able to open up the cabinet and see all my friends lined up waiting for me. They pat me on the back and say it's okay to be miserable. They hold my hand late at night."

John stared down at his own half-finished drink and burning cigarette. "Angel, given the vices I have so fervently embraced in my life, I am the last person on earth with a right to preach. However—"

"He still sees me, you know," she interrupted. "Gian-Carlo. He keeps saying he's through with me, then he shows up in the middle of the night desperate for a fuck. Even now, when the election is so close. I'm still the only woman who can do it for him."

"But are you getting what you want from him, Angel?"

She frowned, looking close to tears. John realized she was walking a tightrope between euphoria and deep depression.

"It's better than nothing," she insisted.

"No, it isn't. If a man treats you like garbage, you kick him out and find someone better. That's what I do. Life's much simpler than you think it is."

She looked around the restaurant. Her eyes rested on a familiar face. She couldn't place him at first. Then she remembered those cold eyes watching her leave Gian-Carlo's office the day she had gone there from the photography session.

"Oh fuck!" she yelled loud enough for everyone in the restaurant to hear. "It's that prick Uccellini. The one who pulls Gian-Carlo's strings. But who's pulling Uccellini's strings?"

"Angel." John put his hand on hers. "This isn't smart."

Angel knocked his hand away and struggled to her feet. "Hey, Uccellini!" she yelled across the crowded restaurant. "What are you really going to do if Gian-Carlo gets elected? Come on! Tell us the truth! Or are you afraid to?"

Uccellini threw his napkin onto the table and stood up. Without looking at Angel he left the restaurant.

"Hey!" she screamed. "He didn't pay! Waiter! Arrest that man!" She started giggling.

John was beside her, his hand on her elbow. She picked up his unfinished drink and raised it to her mouth.

"We're leaving now," he said, propelling her toward the door. The drink splashed onto the front of her dress. "The paparazzi will be here any minute. This will be in all the papers."

No one was eating; all eyes were on Angel. Word had spread and people had gathered on the street outside. Their faces were pushed against the large window.

Angel finally gave into John's pressure. Still holding the drink, she stumbled out of the restaurant into the hot midday sun. On the curb John hailed a taxi while the crowd loudly discussed Angel's disheveled, drunken state. John ushered her into the back of the taxi. The driver, a huge man in a sweat-stained T-shirt, turned around to see what was happening. His eyes widened when he recognized Angel under the crooked wig. John started to follow her into the car, but she held out her hand to block him.

"Angel," he explained patiently, "I have to take you home. You're too drunk to be by yourself."

Stretching across the seat, she put her feet up and leaned against the far window. She finished the drink and dropped the glass on the floor. "I won't be alone. I'm going to visit a friend."

"Who?"

Several members of the crowd had come forward to peer inside the car. Three old women shuffled onto the road to get a better view. Angel raised her voice so everyone could hear. "I'm going to see my dear friend Lucia Cassieri. We're just like sisters. We're so close we even fuck the same man. You can't get much closer than that, unless you're a dyke."

"Angel—"

She lunged forward and slammed the door in John's face, leaving him on the curb surrounded by curious pedestrians. Out of

247

the back window she saw a man with three cameras around his neck running down the middle of the road toward them.

"Take me to my destiny, driver," Angel said, leaning back again. She yanked off the black wig and shook her knotted hair free.

"No problem, lady," the man replied, starting the car. "Could you just give me the address?"

44

"LET me in, you motherfucker! I've got just as much right to be here as that old cunt!"

The young security guard stationed at the gate to the Cassieri estate stammered in embarrassment. "I'm sorry, I—"

Angel lunged forward and grabbed his lapels. "He loves me, not her!" she screamed into his face. The young man averted his eyes from the hysterical woman. "This should be my home!"

Although Angel had thrown the taxi driver enough money to pay for the trip four times over, he was still parked outside the gate, enjoying his front-row seat while he decided which gossip paper to offer his story to.

"Let me in!" Angel screamed again.

"Signorina Concelli, I'm sorry," the guard said, peeling her fingers from his jacket. "I love your movies. But I have a job to do. And no one is here now except the staff. Please, come back another time."

Angel slumped down at his feet on the gravel road and started to cry. Her black high-heeled shoes were scraped and dusty. One of her stockings had a large tear.

The young guard stared helplessly at the beautiful movie star. He had spent hours fantasizing about making love to this woman. In real life she seemed so small and pathetic, like a child exhausted from a temper tantrum. And yet she was still the loveliest creature he had ever seen. He crouched down beside her. "Let me help you into your taxi. Go home and get some sleep. Tomorrow everything will seem different. Sometimes I drink too much, too. We all do."

Angel didn't answer him. She rubbed her bloodshot eyes and frowned at the countrylike surroundings as if she couldn't remember where she was.

"Please," he said. Gently, he took her arm and tried to lift her, hating to see her lose her dignity. "I won't tell anyone about this. You can trust me. You'll be glad you went home."

At the sound of an approaching car he raised his head, trying to decide what to do. A gray Mercedes-Benz rounded the corner. Lucia Cassieri was alone at the wheel. She pulled to a stop beside the taxi. Her handsome face was expressionless as she took in the' scene. Angel stared blankly at her enemy.

"Get out of here," Lucia commanded the gawking taxi driver without looking at him. He opened his mouth to speak, then changed his mind and backed out. Lucia returned her attention to Angel and the guard.

"Has she been here long?" Lucia asked.

The young man shook his head. "About five minutes. I told her to leave."

"We can't send her off like that. Help me get her into the car. I'll take her up to the house and give her some coffee."

Together they helped Angel into the backseat of the Mercedes. Lucia thanked the young guard for his assistance and drove on to the house, ignoring the drunken woman who had slumped onto her side. At the house, Lucia asked two of the servants to help Angel into the living room. Then she went into the kitchen to order espresso and sandwiches.

In the doorway of her elegant living room, Lucia paused to look at Angel huddled in the far corner of the blue velvet couch. The bright afternoon sun shone through the large window overlooking the carefully tended garden. Lucia's scarlet lips tightened as she studied her husband's mistress. She stepped back to make room for the maid, who deposited a tray in front of Angel.

When the maid left, Lucia sat down beside Angel. She was silent for a minute. Finally, with an almost imperceptible shudder, she patted Angel's knee. "It's all right, dear," she said soothingly. "Things look horrible now, but in a little while you'll see everything more clearly. Have a bite to eat and some coffee."

Angel blinked several times and looked around the large room. Eventually her eyes turned to the tray of food. Like an obedient child, she ate the cheese sandwich and downed the rich espresso. By the time she had finished, she was alert enough to face Lucia. With a dim awareness of the contrast they provided, she ran her fingers through her tangled hair. It didn't help. Her face was streaked with makeup and her thin yellow dress was stained with alcohol. The perfectly coiffed Lucia wore a simple dark blue suit and white silk blouse.

"Would you like more coffee?" Lucia asked.

Angel shook her head.

"How about some clean clothes? And perhaps a shower would do you some good. I can have the servants prepare the guest room for you. You shouldn't go home like this. There are too many gossips in Rome. It is, in many ways, a village."

Angel cleared her throat. She had to speak now; she might never get a chance like this again. She leaned forward until the two women were almost touching. Lucia smiled politely.

"I love Gian-Carlo," Angel said slowly, surprised by how difficult it was to form words. "And he loves me. He's told me that. He wants to spend the rest of his life with me."

Lucia continued to smile as if nothing of consequence had been said.

Angel pushed her hair back out of her eyes. None of this was coming out the way she had planned. For months she had imagined confronting this horrible woman as an equal. But Lucia was like a wall.

"He loves me," she repeated lamely.

"Of course he loves you," Lucia replied. "You're a wonderful child."

"Not a child," Angel answered, frowning. "A woman."

"Yes, you're right. A beautiful woman. I know Gian-Carlo cares very deeply for you."

"You don't understand," Angel cried. "I said he wants to spend the rest of his life with me. He wants to leave you."

Lucia raised one perfect eyebrow. "You're certain of that?"

Angel looked down. She noticed Lucia's enormous diamond ring and gold band. She touched the bare ring finger of her own left hand.

"As you must know," Lucia continued, leaning back and making herself comfortable, "Gian-Carlo is not a simple man. He has many desires and needs. He wants you, but he also wants a family, a chance to serve his country. Sometimes the things we want conflict. It is sad, but not tragic. When that happens, we must try to be wise and do what is best for everyone. If you stop and think, you will realize the truth of this. And there are things you want that would conflict with a life with Gian-Carlo. You are a very talented and beautiful woman. The people of this country idolize you, they are obsessed with you. You have a duty to them, as we all have a duty to those who care for us. And you have many opportunities. The world is yours, Angel. Stop for a moment and imagine your future. The United States, the chance to work with the greatest filmmakers of our time, to meet exciting, talented people, to become an international star. Would you really want to give all that up?"

Angel thought of lying in bed with Gian-Carlo, stretched out on top of him, absorbing the heat from his body. Was anything worth more than that? "I love him," she whispered. "And he loves me."

Lucia nodded. "Yes, but as we get older, we learn to put love in its place. We have no right to destroy other lives because of love. Or even to destroy our own lives. We come to appreciate other kinds of love. Love for our children. Love for the people we can serve."

Angel rubbed her eyes, digging deep, until she was hurting herself. "My child died," she whispered.

For a minute there was silence in the room.

Angel's shoulders sagged. "He made me kill it. I wanted it. I wanted to live with him and raise our baby together. I would have given up everything else for that child. What does making movies matter compared to having your own family? And he even had the nerve to say he was glad he made me pregnant. It made him feel like a man. He wanted to knock me up, but he didn't want to have a child with me. I felt so . . ." Her voice momentarily failed her. "Betrayed."

Lucia stood up. She straightened her immaculate skirt and smoothed her perfectly groomed hair. She slowly walked across the room and came to a stop next to an antique side table. Then she faltered. Her knees buckled, and she grabbed the table for support. Angel was oblivious to everything except her own feelings.

"You were pregnant," Lucia confirmed, her voice cracking on the last word. "You aborted my husband's child."

"I wanted it," Angel sobbed. "I wanted to have a life with Gian-Carlo. He needs me. I know he does. He comes to me in the night begging me to take him back one more time. He said we have a great love, a love—"

"Shut up!"

Still dazed from the alcohol, Angel was startled by the unexpected command.

"Shut up!" Lucia repeated. Her hand groped on the table. Her fingers closed around a delicate crystal vase. Suddenly she raised it over her head and flung it at Angel. Angel cried out and covered her head with her arms just before the vase smashed against the wall a few inches away from her. Fragments of glass rained down on her arms and legs.

"You wretched little bitch," Lucia said, moaning in her rage. "You slut. You actually come here, drunk, to *my* home, the home of my children, and tell me that my husband made you pregnant. That he bragged about it. You tell me he loves you, that he begs you to continue seeing him. *Begs you!* Have you no sense of decency at all? Are you such a miserable excuse for a human being that you don't even know the difference between right and wrong? What silly, mythical world do you live in? What did you think would happen here? That I would acknowledge your greater right, and say please marry my husband, please take him away from me? Did you expect me to pack his things and give them to you? Did you think it would be that easy to destroy another person's life?"

Angel's head was still lowered. She couldn't look at Lucia.

"You've had your chance. You've been seeing my husband for a year and a half. *A year and a half!* If he wanted you instead of me he would be gone by now. I've done nothing to stop him. Do you think I don't have any pride? Do you know what it was like to watch the two of you the night you met, to see him groping around in your dress, sticking his tongue in your mouth? Another slut, I thought, who doesn't even care if he knows her name. There were times when I doubted my initial judgment. When I thought you might really be a rival, a worthy opponent. But in the end, I've been proved correct. Angel Concelli, you are only a slut. Men like Gian-Carlo don't marry women like you. They go to your bed at three in the morning when they're drunk and desperate and want someone who will do whatever they ask. You're an unpaid whore. Look at yourself! Look!"

Lucia pointed at the mirror at one end of the room. Frightened but mesmerized, Angel slowly raised her head. She saw a disheveled, filthy creature with bleached hair, streaked mascara, and ugly shadows under her eyes. Her tight dress—chosen to draw attention to her large breasts—was wrinkled and stained.

"Why would he want you when he could have me?" Lucia cried. "Do you look like a woman he would choose to be the mother of his child? When he made you get an abortion, he was doing you a favor! It was an act of kindness. He saved you from discovering what you really are. But you had to know. You had to go too far, and find out what we really think of you. Now get out of my home. I do not entertain uninvited tramps."

Lucia rang a bell for one of the servants. Angel was still staring at her reflection, lost in her private hell. When the butler took her arm she followed him without resistance. She quietly got into the backseat of the waiting limousine. The driver, who had already been told her address, started down the long driveway.

At the gate, another car was about to enter the property. As the limousine passed it, Angel stared at its driver. But her face was blank, as if she had never seen him before. She was beyond crying, beyond asking for help.

Gian-Carlo stopped and turned around to watch her go. Then, slowly, he drove up to the house where his wife was waiting.

45

"MORE, more!"

Nick groaned in protest. As he rolled over onto his back, the bed creaked and sagged beneath his naked body. "That's the last time I take up with a younger woman. You're exhausting me."

"Come on," Stevie said, climbing on top of him. The tiny hotel room with stained peeling wallpaper and a tile floor was dominated by the large utilitarian bed. The other furnishings were minimal. The management had done nothing to disguise the fact that their rooms were primarily rented for sex.

Stevie gave him a slow kiss. "This is nice," she whispered when they came up for air. "Even if three hours appears to be all you can handle."

He grinned and playfully slapped her bare behind. "See what a good time you could have had your first night in Rome? Instead of jumping out of bed as if I were some kind of monster? I told you I was a great lay."

"And you were certainly telling the truth," she replied, rubbing her breasts against his chest. "What did you say then? Women usually present you with gifts afterward? A car or something? I'm not sure my savings will cover a suitable reward."

"Don't worry," he murmured. He kissed her again. "The first one's on the house."

"This *is* nice, Nick," she said, becoming serious. "I've never felt such . . . such pleasure before. Sex was always tense. I worried about whether or not I was good enough."

"And with me you don't care if you're lousy?" he said with a laugh. "It's all right," he said when she started to protest. "I know what you mean. We fit well together. We're not afraid of each other. That's very important." He hugged her close to him. "I'm glad I found you in my bed, Stevie Templeton."

"I'm not usually insatiable," she mentioned with a smile.

"That's good to know," he answered dryly.

She kissed the corner of his mouth. "It's just that it's so nice to touch you. Among other things."

"Then go ahead and touch," he cried, flinging his arms above his head. "Help yourself to any of my body parts. I love to be taken advantage of."

She ran her hands over his lean, athletic body. "Next time can we go to a hotel with room service? I'm starving but I don't want you to put your clothes back on."

"You're a wonderful woman, Stevie. But what do you mean about next time?"

Her hands froze. "What do *you* mean?" she said, staring into his eyes.

He raised his eyebrows. "We're certainly not going to continue carrying on like this."

"Nick!" She swung off him and jumped onto the floor. "You bastard!"

"No, no, no," he said quickly, realizing she had misunderstood. He propped himself up on one elbow and admired her naked figure. "We'll keep up the sex, of course. *Dio,* I'd have to be an absolute fool to give this up. I meant we won't continue to use hotels."

"We can't go to the Contessa's apartment—"

"Of course not. But mine will be ready in a few days. The renovators are nearly finished. You must have realized I wasn't planning to impose on Laura's hospitality forever. My place will be a little small for both of us, but it will do for the short term."

Stevie's eyes widened. She sat beside him on the bed. "You mean you think we should live together?"

He put his hand on her thigh. "Of course we should live together. Most married people do. Then, in a little while, we might even have a few children." He leaned forward and kissed a small mole on her hip. "All the usual things. I love you. You seem to love me. What's the problem?"

Stevie stared at the pale green flowers on the cheap wallpaper. Suddenly feeling cold, she freed a sheet from the tangle at the bottom of the bed and pulled it around herself.

"I don't know what to say," she said after a few moments.

Nick stared at her. "You say yes. Why wouldn't you?"

She shrugged. "Nick, we hardly know each other."

"Bullshit!" His voice echoed in the small room. "We knew each other the night we met. In the dark, without names or histories or anything. It's easy to know when you've met the right person. Your heart tells you, your gut, your instincts. The mind has nothing to do with it. Do you really care about my hobbies? My middle name? What my birthday is? If you do, then I can tell you all that in a flash. Cars and nineteenth-century French novels. Ferdinand— dreadful, but after a distant relative. August thirteenth. Do you honestly believe such trivia would make you decide you don't want to spend your life with me? Is there any possibility you might say, 'Nineteenth century French novels? But I could only marry a man interested in twentieth century literature!' Stevie, you can be shy, you can be timid, that's understandable, but you cannot use it as an excuse for hurting me. I proposed to you and you acted as if I had asked you to do something horrible. Just because I'm a man doesn't mean I don't have feelings. We write bad poetry and listen to stupid pop songs when our hearts are broken just like women do."

Stevie fingered the thin white sheet. "But can't you give me a little time?"

"For what?"

She exhaled. Her stomach felt tight and tense. "Nick, please . . . so much has happened since I arrived in Rome. I don't know who I am anymore. I don't know who I want to be. When I get up in the morning I honestly don't even know what clothes to put on or how to wear my hair. I'm so sick of the old Stevie Templeton. It's as if I don't fit inside her anymore. I have such cravings to be someone else, a different person, the kind of woman who . . ." She faltered.

Nick's eyes were cold. "The kind of woman who can become the mistress of Gian-Carlo Cassieri?" he supplied in a flat voice.

"No," she whispered. "Of course not. Anyway, he wouldn't—" She stopped. The sheet had slipped; she pulled it up again.

"You mean you're not good enough to attract Cassieri?" he taunted. "You're good enough to be the wife of Nick Funaro, but not to be the woman Gian-Carlo sees on the side when he has a few minutes and a few sexual urges to spare? Is that what you're saying?"

"No, I . . ."

"Then what are you hinting at?" he demanded. "Or do you want me to say it for you? You're thinking that if you live with me you'd have to stop seeing Gian-Carlo. You'd have to stop being his mid-night confessor, Angel's ghost. You can't give that up, can you? Not the chance to fuck a hotshot like that, both of you feeding off your poor sister's memory."

He jumped out of the bed. "I'm sick of this," he said, striding naked across the room to the chair where they had left their clothes. "I don't want to look at your face for another moment."

"Nick," Stevie wailed. "You don't understand."

He turned to stare at her. "Don't I? You told me nothing more happened in his office after that god-awful picture was taken. But tell the truth, Stevie. Have you thought about making love to him?"

She blushed and lowered her head. Her hair fell across her

face. "That's human, Nick. You can't expect me to be any better than that."

"Let me tell you this, Stevie Templeton. I expect my wife—the woman I give my life to—to put me first. In her desires, in her fantasies, and in her bed. I don't want a wife who will ever, *ever,* lie awake at night wishing she'd fucked another man. I don't want her wondering for even one second if he would have been better than I am, if she missed her big chance for the fuck of a lifetime. I don't mean you can't see a Tom Cruise movie and come home hot and bothered. But I don't want you ever doubting your choice."

He was rifling through their clothes, separating them into two piles. "I don't want to win on points," Nick continued, dropping her cotton shirt onto one of the piles. "You know what I mean." He did a cruel parody of her accented Italian. "'Gian-Carlo's better looking, he's got more money, he's got power. But Nick's single, he doesn't have any kids, and he's a nicer guy.' I don't want anyone to settle for me, least of all the woman I choose because I love her more than I ever thought it was possible to love someone. I want all your passion, Stevie, or none of it." He picked up her clothes and carried them over to her.

"Go find him," he commanded, waving at the door as if Gian-Carlo were waiting in the hallway. "Go on. Get that bastard out of your system. Sample the merchandise. Maybe he is a better fuck than I am. Maybe he is what you really want. But if you decide on him, leave me alone. Forever. No calls from you or your grandmother for help, no requests for a shoulder to lean on. I'm not interested in being your babysitter. If you want him, he's all you get."

Stevie shook her head. "Nick, I can explain."

"No," he answered quietly. He took her hands and pulled her to her feet. The sheet fell to the floor. She felt ashamed of her body again, but when they were making love he had made her feel beautiful.

"You can't, Stevie. You said it yourself. You don't know your own mind."

She pushed her hair back from her face. "I don't even know if I'll ever see him again. Or if he'd want to—"

"Stevie, you're such a sweet idiot. Of course he wants to. He's a bastard, but he's not blind and made of stone. And he will see you again if you let him. He needs you to be Angel for him. I suspect he needs your forgiveness. But be careful. And I'm not just saying that because I'm jealous. If nothing else, Franco Uccellini is the wrong person to have as an enemy. You don't understand the kind of games the big boys play." He dropped his hands. "But I can't live your life for you."

He walked back to his clothes and started to get dressed. Stevie slowly pulled on her own sweat-stained things. When they were both ready he escorted her to the door. She realized he meant for her to leave alone. "You're not coming?"

He shook his head. "I'm too upset to drive. I need a few minutes alone."

She nodded, reluctant to leave him. She wanted to kiss him and hold him one more time, but she didn't feel she had the right. She felt as if she had failed at something terribly important, that she had possibly—in a few brief minutes—destroyed her future. "I . . . I do love you, Nick. Today was wonderful."

His smile was stiff. "But apparently not wonderful enough."

She sighed. The last thing she wanted was to hurt this man. "It's not that I think anyone else is better than you are, and least of all Gian-Carlo." When she said that he reached out and touched her cheek. "It's my worth I'm unsure of, not yours. I don't feel like Angel's ghost—I feel like her shadow. On top of that, Claire and Ellen have ripped apart my past." Her voice broke. She struggled to keep from crying. "If I don't know who Stevie Templeton is, then how can I know if I'm worth loving?"

"Stevie, of course you are," Nick said. Because it hurt to keep her at a distance, he pulled her close and kissed her soft hair. "I know I can be a demanding bastard sometimes. Forget my rantings. Take some time to think. I'll wait . . ." He smiled down at her. "Well, just don't make me wait too long. I like you too much to do without you."

Stevie kissed him again, and then he ushered her out the door. Downstairs, when she walked out of the dark lobby into the bright afternoon, she had the odd sensation that she was walking out of light and into shadows. She looked up at the hotel windows. If Nick was watching her, she couldn't see him. She thought of running back inside to say she would marry him. But she would be running to safety, running away from herself. And Nick deserved better than that.

46

IN the garden behind Ellen's villa, Stevie stared up at the stars, hoping that the fragrant flowers and clear cool air would help her think. After her eventful day, it felt much later than nine o'clock, but only a few hours had passed since she'd left Nick in the hotel room. When she came back to the villa, she had bathed and changed into a white cotton dress for dinner with her grandmother. Afterward Ellen had gone upstairs to rest, unsettled by Stevie's frank description of the visit with Claire.

In the quiet garden, Stevie was trying to understand her own behavior. She was becoming as much of a mystery to herself as Claire and Angel were. Why didn't she call Nick? She knew she loved him. And he was worth loving; it wasn't a foolish glandular attraction that she would regret in a few months.

But she felt too unsettled, too unfinished to do anything permanent. In some ways, she was in mourning; and no one in mourning can embark on a new life. She mourned the perfect mother who had proved a myth, and she mourned the sister she hadn't had a chance to know. And she still mourned her father, that unhappy man who had taken his secrets to his grave. But probably the person she mourned most was Stevie Templeton, that Boston schoolteacher who had been so certain she knew exactly what she wanted out of life—a quiet routine without surprises or passion. On some level, she must have sensed the cracks in the foundation of her life; she must have been afraid that it would smash open someday, and all the secrets would come pouring out like snakes and goblins.

The stars in the black sky were blank and cold, unrecognizable as balls of fire. It was a world of deceptions, of false impressions, of secrets and lies. But Angel's life must have been even harder. All those accumulated miseries, with no light at the end of the tunnel. Why else would anyone commit suicide?

Gian-Carlo was seen leaving her apartment late on the night of her death.

Garelli's insinuating voice seemed to fill the quiet garden. But he and Uccellini were ridiculous to suggest that a man as kind and gentle as Gian-Carlo could be a murderer. She remembered walking through the empty streets of Rome at night with him, their fingers entwined.

If she never saw Gian-Carlo again, if she married Nick, how would she feel? Could she forget Gian-Carlo, or would she—as Nick feared—live with the regret forever?

She didn't know. She was a woman, with feelings. She couldn't ignore his physical attraction, even though nothing serious could ever come of it.

But far more important than that, she didn't want to give up her only real link to Angel. No one except Gian-Carlo could tell her who Angel was. And there was so much she still wanted to know, so many questions needing answers. Had Angel killed herself because of her hopeless affair with Gian-Carlo? Or was Claire's cruelty the real reason?

Maybe if she found out the truth about her sister, she would find the key to her own life and finally become free of the cage her family had put her in. Then she could start over again as the person she was meant to be, someone strong and confident, instead of a lonely coward hiding out in a garden.

Gian-Carlo's arrival startled her. She had expected to see him again, but not until after the election, which was only a week away. If he wanted to be prime minister, he shouldn't waste any more time on an American girl who happened to bear an uncanny resemblance to a woman he had once loved.

He arrived at the villa around ten o'clock, shortly after she came in from the garden. Dressed casually in a blue turtleneck sweater and black pants, he looked completely free of responsibilities. He leaned against the doorway and smiled at her.

She wished, for Nick's sake, that she could tell him she didn't want to see him again. She wasn't quite ready for that yet, but tonight would have to be their last night together. She would ask him all her questions about Angel and find out the truth about her sister's life and death.

"We need to talk," he said.

She smiled. So often he seemed to read her mind. "I know. Why don't we go in the garden?"

"There's a better place. It will be more private. And I don't want your grandmother coming out and screaming at me again."

Stevie looked out to where his car was waiting. The sky was black; at this time of night in Boston she would have been getting ready for bed, laying out her clothes for the morning. In Italy she was heading out into the night with the man who would probably be the country's next prime minister.

"All right," she said.

When they reached his Alfa Romeo he paused and pointed to a dark blue car parked about a hundred feet away. She thought it was the one that had been there the other day. She hadn't looked for it since then. He lowered his lips to her ear. "They're watching us."

Stevie shivered, remembering the photographs. She wondered if she should tell Gian-Carlo about them, and about Uccellini's possible treachery. She rubbed her cold arms. "Do you know who they are?"

"It's insane. They're my people. I used to control them. Now they think they control me. But if they did," he added in a light tone, "I wouldn't be here with you, would I?"

He held the door open for her. She stared back at the other car. She couldn't make out the driver's face. She wondered how Nick would feel looking at a grainy photograph of her getting into Gian-Carlo's car. But she pushed the thought aside and got into the car. She looked up at the villa. Her grandmother's pale, worried face was visible at one of the upstairs windows. Ellen's eyes moved to the car behind them. Stevie considered going back and telling her grandmother that she would be all right.

But before she could speak, Gian-Carlo started the engine. The car roared off at full speed.

Gian-Carlo maintained the high speed along the road to Rome. He kept checking the rearview mirror. When they reached the city, his driving became erratic. He kept to back streets, made turns without signaling, and circled the same block several times. Stevie glanced over her shoulder; as far as she could tell, he had lost the other car. She was relieved. Even though she was definitely not going to start anything physical with Gian-Carlo again, even a benign photograph of the two of them sitting in a restaurant would have made her squirm after her encounter with Uccellini.

He finally pulled over to the curb on a dark street. They were at the edge of a park. He opened the door for her and then, to her surprise, led her into the park. The soft, swaying trees made a hushing noise. He took her hand; she wrapped her fingers around his. She didn't want to lose him here. He pulled her forward, hurrying around the dark trees, slipping through shadows, following a jagged, confusing path. Bushes scraped her bare legs. A small animal scurried through the grass. A bird cried in the darkness; its wings rustled the leaves.

She was cold in her thin white dress. The only warmth was from Gian-Carlo's hand. He hadn't spoken a word since they'd left the villa. There was a sense of urgency in his manner.

They ran along an uneven stone path, then into the thick bushes again. She held up her free arm to protect herself from the sharp branches. She didn't know why he was running; no one could be following them now. "Where are we going?" she asked.

When he didn't answer, she looked at his face, but there was too little light to make out his expression.

He pulled her down a gentle slope. She saw a gate. Street lights. A small green car slowly passed; the only careful driver in Rome.

"Here," Gian-Carlo said, ushering her out onto the narrow sidewalk. "It isn't far now."

She stumbled after him as he picked up the pace. Majestic golden buildings lined the quiet street. He stopped in front of an ornate building. It had the quiet dignity common to most residences for the wealthy. Gian-Carlo let go of her hand and walked up to the front door. She knew he lived on an estate outside the city, but perhaps he also kept an apartment in Rome. He held the door open for her. She shivered and involuntarily took a step back. She realized she was afraid to go inside with him.

But what exactly was she afraid of? The street was quieter than most, but voices were still spilling from open windows, a young couple strolled along the sidewalk toward her. Gian-Carlo stood waiting, with a polite but slightly impatient smile. After all, Uccellini or his goons were the ones to be afraid of, and thanks to Gian-Carlo's driving they didn't know where to find her.

She followed him inside. The walls of the small lobby were silver marble. Two black leather couches stood on a blue-and-gold silk rug. A fat elderly woman was asleep in the concierge's small office. Gian-Carlo took Stevie's hand again and hurried her up three steep flights of stairs, then along a hallway to a door at the end of it. Pulling a key from his pocket, he unlocked the door.

He stepped into a large living room. "Good," he said. "I told them not to disturb anything."

The thick rugs were white. The white and gray furnishings were in the modern Italian style, sleek and elegant. A fashion magazine was on the floor beside the large couch. Its garish cover, with a pouting woman in a short strapless red dress, was the only clue to the personality of the apartment's resident. There were no other personal touches, no photographs, no paintings, no mementos on the long bare mantelpiece.

"Follow me," Gian-Carlo said. He disappeared down the dark hallway to their left.

He flicked on the light in the bedroom just as Stevie came up behind him. The bed was enormous; she couldn't imagine owning one that size. The silk sheets were a delicate shade of yellow. They were wrinkled; the top one had been pulled back. The bed, a chair, and two small ivory night tables were the only furniture. Like the living room, the room seemed bare and anonymous. Except for a blue tie draped over the ivory headboard. And, in one corner, a small pile of ashes on the soft white rug.

Slowly, Stevie realized that she had seen this room before. In the pictures of Gian-Carlo making love to Angel. And in the newspaper photo of Angel's corpse.

"I can't—" Stevie cried, backing up.

"Of course you can," Gian-Carlo said, sounding tired. He turned to face her and put his hands on her shoulders. She couldn't read his face; it was a cool, handsome mask.

"This isn't right," she whispered. "I have to go."

"We belong here," he said. Then his eyes filled with tears. He wrapped his strong arms around her and pulled her close. He rubbed his face against her hair. His heart was beating against her breasts. "Don't leave me," he whispered.

Still holding her close, he looked into her eyes. "Please don't leave me again," he said. "Can't you see how much I love you?"

Then he pressed his mouth against hers.

47

ANGEL carefully draped the blue silk tie over the headboard and stood back to admire her work. She smiled. It would drive him crazy.

She had found the tie in one of her drawers a few days ago, left behind by some long-forgotten lover. It would be useful tonight. The old tricks still worked. A sexy dress, a souvenir from another man to make him jealous. If all else failed, a blow job. Men were simple creatures.

She started for the liquor cabinet in the living room and then changed her mind. She needed a clear head. It was already seven-thirty. It wouldn't be long now.

She knew that when Lucia and Uccellini reported her drunken escapades to Gian-Carlo, he would convince himself that without a lecture on restraint she would do something even more embarrassing.

But it wasn't that simple. When he stepped into his car to come to her, he would know, as well as she did, that they would end up in bed. That tomorrow at dawn he would tiptoe into his home smelling of her perfume and spent sex.

In her enormous walk-in closet, she sorted through her rack of evening dresses, ruling out one after another for a variety of reasons. Then she found it. The perfect gown. The one she had worn the night they made love on Lucia's white fur cape while an angry old woman pounded on the door. That memory should make him hot, she decided, carefully stepping into the delicate black dress. She pulled the thin straps up over her shoulders and adjusted the tiny bodice to cover her nipples. Despite her recent loss of weight, her breasts were smooth and firm. The dress was a little looser than before, but she still looked good. Better than what he got at home.

She fastened on the diamond earrings he had given her, fluffed out her shimmering hair, and slipped into a pair of black high-heeled sandals. She paused in front of the three-sided mirror for a final inspection. She looked as beautiful as she had the day they met. More beautiful; he would read her sexual knowledge in her eyes; he would remember the things she could do to him. At least the extensive preparations of the last few hours had been worth it. And her new maid service had already prepared the setting; the old woman who from now on would come every day had managed a miracle, transforming an alcoholic's lair into an elegant home.

Angel didn't have to wait long. She was lounging on the couch reading a fashion magazine when she heard his familiar knock. Tossing the magazine onto the floor, she picked up her black lace wrap and a gold evening bag.

She pretended to look for her key in the open purse as she walked out of the apartment. Gian-Carlo was forced to step back.

"Gian-Carlo?" she said, acting surprised to see him. "You didn't tell me you were coming tonight."

His handsome face was lined and pale. Lucia must have given him a rough time.

"Angel, we have to have a serious talk. I can't believe the things I've been hearing."

She shut the door behind her and turned the key in the lock. "I'm sorry," she said over her shoulder, "but could we do this some other time? Someone is waiting for me."

Her appearance finally registered with him. His eyes widened. He had obviously expected to find her distraught and drunk, grateful for a few hours of his company. "Where are you going?"

"Oh, just the usual," she said, waving her hand. She dropped the key into her purse and snapped it shut. "But I really have to hurry. I'm already late."

"Angel—"

She gave him a polite but bored smile. He was wearing a dark blue turtleneck sweater and black pants.

"Angel, give me a few minutes. I don't understand what's going on. This afternoon you—"

She touched his arm lightly; it was the way she would have touched someone she had never desired. "I'm really sorry about that. And please give my apologies to Lucia. I guess the explanation is obvious. I had a little too much to drink. Do you think it would help if I sent her some flowers? Not that you don't have enough out on that enormous estate, but I want her to know how sorry I am."

Gian-Carlo stared at her. "Angel, they said you were out of your mind. In the restaurant, with Uccellini, and then at the house. Lucia told me that—"

"Was I that bad?" she interrupted, her eyes round. "I really will have to watch those long liquid lunches with John. As I said, I'm very sorry, and you can be sure it won't happen again. Now, if I could get on my way?" She looked pointedly toward the iron gates of the ancient elevator.

"No, of course you can't leave. We have to talk. Where the hell are you going, anyway?"

"I told you," she replied. "I have an engagement."

He looked at her. "That dress— We once—"

She smiled politely while she patted her hair. "Once what, Gian-Carlo?"

"You remember. At that party. On Lucia's fur cape. You wore the same earrings, too."

She frowned. "Are you sure? I thought I wore something red that night. Oh well." She shrugged. "What difference does it make? All water under the bridge, isn't it? God, we were so foolish back then."

"Angel, how can you say that? Remember what we said to each other that night?"

She wrinkled her forehead. "Let me see. That was the night I met Ron Blackstone, wasn't it? He's in town again doing promotional work for his latest movie."

Gian-Carlo grabbed the purse out of her hand and took out her key. "Open the door," he said.

She pursed her lips. "I told you that I'm in a hurry."

His face darkened with rage. "I said open the door!"

"Please," she said in a stage whisper, glancing around, "don't make a scene. My neighbors will hear you."

He slammed his palm against the door. "I told you to open it!"

Angel sighed in exasperation, shrugged, and unlocked the door as if she were placating an ill-behaved child. Once they were inside, Gian-Carlo resumed his angry questions. "Who are you seeing? How can you wear that dress to go out with another man?"

"Calm down." She walked away from him and dropped her purse and the lace wrap on the couch. "It's only a dress. And why wouldn't I go out with other men on evenings when you're not available? You must have noticed by now that I'm not the monogamous type. I do like variety." She looked over her shoulder and smiled. "Sometimes even on the same night."

"You whore!"

Briefly she lost control and winced at the word. But she recovered quickly and answered, "Hot-blooded is a better term. I like sex. Speaking of which, I really must be going."

"You're not going anywhere!" he shouted.

"Who's going to stop me?" she said, picking up her purse again and starting toward the door.

He lunged forward and slapped her hard across the face. She stumbled back, trying not to lose her balance. Her hands flew to her cheek. The hot, stinging pain drew tears to her eyes. "You bastard! You really hurt me!"

"Bitch!" he growled. He grabbed her arm and twisted it behind her back. He pushed her down the hallway toward the bedroom. "If you need sex, then call me, not someone else!"

"What's wrong?" she angrily laughed. "Are you afraid of the competition?"

He pulled her arm tighter.

"That's it!" she yelled. "I'm never fucking you again!"

In the bedroom, he shoved her down on top of the yellow sheets. Before she could get away, he dropped down on top of her and pinned her to the mattress. "Yes, you're going to fuck me," he roared. "Whenever I want!"

"Like hell I am!" she screamed.

He spotted the tie on the headboard. He stared at it without moving.

"What's wrong?" Angel asked in a cold voice, although she knew what had caught his eye. "Change your mind? Or can't you get it up as often as you used to?"

"Shut up. Whose tie is that?"

She grinned. "Oh, that's— A memento, I guess. Does his name really matter?"

He stared down at her with raw fury in his eyes. She matched it, letting him see how deep her own anger went. "This is what you want," she whispered. "It was your choice. You were the one who decided I was only going to be something on the side."

He stared at her. Then, abruptly, he rolled off her and lay beside her.

Angel waited for him to make the next move. She couldn't have counted the number of times they had made love here, the number of shared orgasms they had reached in this bare room. Their faded passion seemed to crowd the closed space like ghosts.

A thousand Gian-Carlos and a thousand Angels eternally coupling inside these four pale gray walls.

Gian-Carlo turned on his side and looked down at her. The anger was gone from his eyes. He reached out and lightly touched a lock of her hair.

"Make love to me, Angel." His voice broke. "I don't want to force you. Make love to me as if I were the only one."

She hesitated, afraid to lose ground. Then she saw the tears in his eyes. As helpless as he was, she held out her arms. He moved on top of her. Slowly, she began to undress him, pulling his blue turtleneck sweater up over his chest.

48

"I NEED you," Angel whispered again and again. She forgot her resolution to be distant and cold. She let herself free, let herself tell the truth with her body. After she undressed him, she kissed him everywhere; she paid tribute to his body, letting him know how much she loved him, how desperate she was to be loved in return.

Her brain emptied; thought was a foreign thing to their simple, driven, lovemaking. She crouched beside him on the bed, the yellow sheets soft beneath her knees, and took him in her mouth. He held her hair back from her face, watching her. She gave him pleasure, yet it became an act of selfishness. The line that separated them had gone. The pleasure spilled out and filled the room; it was the air they moved in, the air that gave them life.

He caressed her full breasts, he ran his fingers along her tensed thigh. She let her hair fall onto his belly and tasted his desire.

He took her shoulders and guided her onto her back. She had to kiss him; she opened her mouth and licked and sucked with a greedy frenzy. She held his mouth against hers; she needed more. His fingers slid across her wet inner thighs. She raised her knees and wrapped her long legs around him. Finally, he moved inside her.

She turned her head from side to side, moaning and crying. This was the way it should be every time; this joy destroyed all the petty lies and anger. She dug her fingers into his back and felt him swelling larger. She grabbed the headboard and raised her body. He bit her face; he scratched her; she seized his mouth, tasting their blood. He pushed inside, again and again. This was everything she wanted; this was love and joy. She pulled her legs apart. He wrapped his arms around her heaving body and held her as close as he could. She was sobbing. It was too much pleasure; she could never come back. He cried out her name. *Angel,* it was Angel he loved, Angel he needed. She came, crying with relief, letting the spasms of pleasure tell her that she had finally found the only place where there was peace.

They lay naked together, covered in sweat and semen, their bodies almost as close as one flesh. Angel felt as if the sky had slipped into the room with them. She was surrounded by stars and the soft, quiet night. So this is happiness, she thought, smiling. Without opening her eyes, she saw Gian-Carlo. He was finally hers. The arguments were finally over.

"Gian-Carlo?" she whispered, although she felt absurd using his name. Where did he end, and where did she begin? She almost believed that if she relaxed enough, if she gave into her feelings without hesitation or fear, she would become part of him, one soul united with another. Out of habit, she had been going to say she loved him, but she realized the declaration would be silly. Tonight words were unnecessary. He had to know that for the first time in her life she felt completely loved.

He shifted his weight, a tiny shift, his head turning. She felt it as if her own body had moved. This love was such a gentle miracle. "What were you going to say?" he whispered.

She couldn't find the words. But it didn't matter. He could read her mind, as he had read her body. He had to know and share the peace she had finally found. She had been silly to use tricks like jealousy. It was honesty that mattered, the honesty of their bodies joined in a communion of love.

"I know," Gian-Carlo told her then. His lips were next to her ear. "We can't see each other anymore. This was our last time."

They hadn't turned the lights off. Angel opened her eyes and looked around the room to situate herself in time and space. It was about nine o'clock. She was in the apartment that Aldo, poor dead Aldo, had paid for. On the floor was the black dress she had been wearing when Gian-Carlo arrived.

No.

She was in Rome. Rome, a city. Her name was—

She was a woman, twenty-three years old, an actress—

She was—

She couldn't hold onto reality. It hurt too much. She stumbled out of bed, opened the drawer on the small bedside table, and began searching through the clutter for her bottle of sleeping pills.

"What are you doing?"

"I . . ." she said. But her voice sounded unfamiliar. Someone else was speaking. Angel Concelli, the actress, the woman who lived here. Not the person in pain, not the pure animal being who was desperate and lonely, searching for oblivion.

She couldn't find the damn pills. She yanked out the drawer and dumped its contents onto the floor. On her hands and knees, she looked through the jumble of jewelry, bottles of cream and perfume, tissues, magazines . . .

"Angel, what is it?"

With a deep sigh of relief, she picked up the bottle of yellow pills. She needed three to get to sleep. In the morning everything would be different. The pain wouldn't hurt as much.

"Angel, stop overreacting," Gian-Carlo was saying. "It's time to be reasonable."

Strengthened by the pills in her hand, she was able to look at him. She stared at him as if she were seeing him for the first time. He was a forty-five-year-old man, getting a little slack in the middle, with gray hairs beginning to dominate the black. She was seeing too accurately today—herself as a whore in Lucia's mirror, and her magnificent lover as an aging, tired man. The truth hurt too much.

He read her eyes and pulled up the sheet to cover himself. "Our relationship has become pointless," he snapped. "We're not good for each other anymore."

Although she knew that anything she said would only add to her pain, she couldn't stop herself from trying to make him understand. She sat down on the edge of the bed. She was holding the small plastic bottle of pills in both hands.

"The night I wore the black dress," she began haltingly, "you told me we weren't like other people. You said we had a great love—a contest of giants, you called it. You said we would probably destroy each other, but we had no choice." She saw the shadowy room in the luxurious palazzo, Gian-Carlo slowly lowering her dress while they watched each other in the mirror. "I was terrified. But I believed you. I believed we were each other's destiny, that I had no choice." She turned to look at him. His face was gray and oddly narrow, as if he had lost weight in the last few minutes. Would she have loved him if he had looked like that— broken and small—the day they met? "Are you telling me that was only a line to seduce me? That all this pain has been for nothing?"

He leaned back against the wood headboard and shook his head. "I wasn't lying to you, Angel. I was lying to myself. I almost wish—" He stopped himself.

"Tell me," she ordered.

He shrugged. His usually noble features looked injured and old. "I almost wish that they had discovered us that night, when we were making love on Lucia's cape. I wish they had broken down the door and settled it once and for all. You'd be mine now."

Angel caught her breath. "It's not too late," she whispered. "We can still tell them all to go to hell."

He shook his head. "I can't, Angel. You must realize that by now."

"You said we were giants," she insisted. She leaned toward him. She wanted to touch him, to start again, to prove they could do whatever they wanted.

He sighed and ran his fingers through his hair. "Maybe you are. But I'm not. I never was. I'm a frightened, aging fool, who only ever craved power and money and a beautiful mistress. I want to love you completely, like a great love, but I don't have it in me. I worry about Lucia, my children, the gossip columnists, Uccellini and the people he represents. Do you know what happened this morning? I came into my office and found an envelope with pictures of us on my desk." He covered his eyes for a moment. "I nearly had a heart attack. I was terrified. I thought my entire career was over."

Angel sat up straight. "What pictures?"

He sighed, as if he were sorry he had raised the subject. Then he shrugged. "I'll show you. Maybe then you'll understand." He got up and went to the chair where he had left his jacket. He took a folded envelope out of the inside pocket and handed it to her.

Angel took out the three photographs—in the first one she was on her knees in front of him; in the second they were in bed together; in the third he had pushed her up against the wall and pulled her dress to her waist—a record of their most intimate moments. She stared at them in horror. "Who took these?" she asked when she could speak. She held up the one that showed the two of them on her bed. "My God, this wasn't taken from the window! They must have put a camera in this apartment!"

Gian-Carlo exhaled. "In the apartment next door. I had it taken out a few weeks ago."

She squeezed her eyes shut, trying to think this through. "If you had it taken out, then you must have had it put in." She waited for him to provide another explanation.

"I . . ." He walked away from her and sank into a chair on the other side of the room. "It was foolish. But I hated not knowing what you did when I wasn't with you. You were always bragging about other men. I hoped you were only lying to make me jealous. So I sent some people to install surveillance equipment. In your old apartment it was just a microphone. That time the whole thing was nearly a fiasco; the idiots went in when you were asleep. When I found out you were moving here I made sure I had the best. Professionals. I wanted to be in control."

Angel stared at him. "You mean you saw me—"

He waved his hand. "It wasn't like that. I received reports." He looked down. "I told myself I had to do it to make sure you didn't repeat sensitive things I had confided to you."

"Like the way you want your cock sucked?"

"Angel, don't be vulgar."

She stared at the photographs again. She had revealed as much of her body in movies, but this intrusion, this attack was obscene. And Gian-Carlo had done it.

"You spy on me!" she sobbed. "You photograph me fucking and doing God knows what else, and then you accuse *me* of vulgarity! You bastard—"

"Angel, I told you. I'm not a very strong person. I claim that the reason I want power is to help other people, but I only abuse it. I spy on the woman I love. I skim off money. I—" He shook his head, unable to continue. "But that's not the point of the photographs I received today. They weren't part of the regular reports. They're a warning from Uccellini, telling me to stay in line, not to jeopardize things when we're this near to our goals. I'm being told how easy it would be to destroy me."

She flung the three photographs onto the rug. "I don't give a fuck who sent them, or why! How could you do this to me! What right did you have?"

"Right?" he asked softly. When he looked at her across the room, his eyes were clear and honest. "We may not be giants, but it has been a contest, Angel. Wouldn't you have done the same thing if you'd had the opportunity? Wouldn't you have put cameras in my bedroom?"

She sighed. There was so much he didn't understand. "I didn't have to," she answered. "I was already there. Bound and gagged in the corner, watching you make love to your wife. That's what being the other woman means."

"Oh, Angel, I'm sorry," he said, tears filling his eyes. "I wish I could change things, I wish I could erase all the mistakes and start again."

She looked up, suddenly hopeful. But, as much as anything else, his aging body with those wrinkled genitals that she had sold her soul for told her he would never do it. She was still holding the pills. Her fingers tightened around the smooth bottle. She was only twenty-three years old, but she felt a thousand and one.

"What now?" she asked him. "Are you suggesting that we never see each other again? Do you honestly believe we could do it? Especially the way I am now. I'm a drunk, Gian-Carlo. I pulled myself together tonight just so I could hurt you, but most of the time I'm a stinking, delirious alcoholic."

He leaned forward. "You don't have to be, Angel. The whole world is yours."

"Oh shut up!" she screamed, saliva running down her chin. "For God's sake, don't tell me how lucky I am! I had enough of that crap today from Lucia!" She jumped up and went to the window. She pressed her naked body against the cold glass. It didn't matter if people saw her. After all, how many men in her lover's employ had already watched her making love on film, had listened to her gasping out in pleasure?

And heard her sobbing when she was alone and lonely.

"Destroy them," she whispered, rubbing her forehead against the window. "Those pictures."

"But these are only—"

She turned and let him see how disgusted she was. "Destroy them! Now! Burn them and never mention them again. And I want the rest of them destroyed as soon as possible. Everything. I want my privacy back."

He walked over to his coat and took out a lighter. Then he looked around the room, trying to locate a place to burn them.

"Anywhere!" she yelled.

"But the rug—"

"Fuck the goddamned rug! Burn the pictures!"

He knelt down next to the photographs. They burnt quickly,

shriveling and shrinking into ashes. Then he blew on the small flame to put it out.

Angel leaned back against the window. "Good," she whispered.

"I'll see that the rest are destroyed, Angel. Don't worry."

She nodded, although she knew he couldn't fulfill such a promise. But at least a gesture had been made. And tomorrow seemed far away. Suddenly she felt exhausted. She walked over and sank down onto the bed. She was still holding the pills. They were her lifeline, her only source of solace.

"Don't go home yet," she pleaded. It didn't matter that it was Gian-Carlo; she would have begged anyone to stay. "Let me take my sleeping pills first. Wait until I'm asleep."

He nodded, his eyes filled with concern. "I'll get you some water."

She shut her eyes, feeling as if she could sleep for days. But sleep was such a seductive liar; once she was alone it would scamper away and hide. But she had her pills.

When Gian-Carlo brought the glass he placed it on the bedside table and then sat beside her. "You'll go to Los Angeles and become a big star," he said. "You'll forget all about me."

"Shut up," she whispered. "Just shut up if all you can say is crap."

"Angel, I . . ." Gian-Carlo stopped himself. There was no reason to pretend. She was right: neither of them would have this kind of love again. Everything would be pale and cold after this violent, searing heat.

"I can't promise you anything," Angel was saying.

He looked at her lovely profile. Even now, she was the most beautiful woman he had ever seen.

"I can't promise I'll behave in a civilized manner." She gave him a small, regretful smile, an old friend confessing her weaknesses. "Tomorrow morning at dawn you might find me outside your bedroom window screaming for you, demanding you make love to me. I promise nothing, Gian-Carlo. Even if I could still control myself—which I can't—I'm not sure that restraint is the right thing. Doesn't love count for anything?"

She touched his shoulder; a heartbreaking caress. He wondered how he could give her up. But it was his only choice.

"What if we *were* giants?" she asked suddenly. "Would we give up so easily? Would we shake hands and say good-bye and then meet again in twenty years to compare notes on how lonely we'd been, how many regrets we had accumulated? Is that what a giant would do?"

"Giants . . ." he began. He remembered saying that to her, but he didn't know if he had believed it even then. He had told too many lies to know the truth anymore. "You tell me, Angel. What would we do if we were giants?"

She dropped back onto the bed and slowly smiled. He smiled too, touched by this sign of happiness in the woman he adored. "If we were giants," she mused, "we would live happily ever after. Or else we'd die. Those are the only two options for real giants."

He stared down at her. She was transcendently beautiful at that moment, pale and slender on the primrose yellow sheets.

"Let's die," he said.

She blinked at him. It took a moment for his words to sink in. Then her eyes filled with terror. "No," she whispered. She licked her dry lips. "Don't even say it, Gian-Carlo. Say you love me instead. Say you'll run away with me. Say we can be happy."

Awkwardly, she pulled herself into a sitting position. She put her hands on his shoulders and stared into his eyes. "Change your mind," she begged. "Gian-Carlo, say we can live."

But he didn't answer her. He was too busy thinking about death and all the pleasures it would bring.

49

In Angel's bedroom, Stevie tightened her arms around Gian-Carlo's broad shoulders as he kissed her. His hands slid down her back, pressing her against him.

She knew she shouldn't be doing it, but he was irresistible. She refused to let herself think of Nick, Lucia Cassieri, Angel, or even tomorrow.

He pulled back and smiled down at her. His eyes seemed to shine with love. If she wanted to stop, she had to say so now.

How much would she hurt this vulnerable man if she walked out of the apartment? How much would she hurt herself? Before she could decide what to do, his cool fingers took her hand. He led her into Angel's dressing room.

She gasped when she saw the glittering, exotic clothes in a rainbow of colors. She ran her fingers along the row of delicate shimmering gowns. They looked impractical to the sister who had never purchased anything without checking the cleaning instructions.

"Here," Gian-Carlo said. He held out a fragile black dress. To Stevie, it seemed less substantial than a slip. "Put this on."

She didn't know what to do. Gingerly, she took it from him, almost expecting it to dissolve in her hands like candy floss. "I can't," she whispered.

The dress weighed nothing. She had thought her new crimson dress was dramatic and daring; compared to this it seemed like a housedress for a middle-aged matron.

"I'll wait in the bedroom," he said.

"Really, Gian-Carlo—" she protested.

He reached out and touched her cheek. Then he bent forward and kissed her softly on the lips. "Please." His voice was low and urgent. "For me."

He gave her one final pleading look and left the room, shutting the door to give her privacy.

Alone in the room, Stevie moved to the triple-sided mirror, her lips still tingling from Gian-Carlo's kiss. Her face looked flushed and tired. Dark shadows were under her eyes; her hair was limp and dull. As usual, she found Stevie Templeton nothing special.

The resemblance to Angel was confusing. Their features were the same, but Angel was never anything less than a great beauty. Sometimes, when she looked at her sister's picture, she wanted to trade ten years of her life for one moment of that beauty, one moment when she could feel spectacular.

She looked down at the black dress in her hands. She could imagine Angel in it, that creamy skin and glistening gold hair against the jet black gown. To look like that must be . . .

She held the dress up against her body. Even the thought of trying it on embarrassed her. Gian-Carlo would probably laugh at her. She couldn't do justice to the dress. It was for movie stars and princesses, magical women with special lives and dashing lovers. Women like Angel Concelli. Not for the sister who didn't count.

She studied her face, trying to see Angel's face, trying to see a beautiful woman. She remembered the crowds chasing her through the streets chanting *Angel, Angel* . . . She remembered them falling to their knees and stretching out their arms. How would it feel to be worthy of so much love? To be the kind of woman a man wanted so much he was willing to risk everything for one night with her?

Without letting herself think, she pulled her cotton dress over her head. The black gown was too flimsy to be worn over anything. She peeled off her underwear and then kicked her shoes across the room.

Naked, she went to the makeup table that took up the far wall of the changing room. She surveyed Angel's collection of cosmetics. It was like being given carte blanche in the makeup department of a major department store; Angel had obviously spent more money on makeup than Stevie did on food. She sat down and carefully painted black lines around her eyes, layered on mascara, covered her eyelids with shimmering silver, and painted her lips a seductive wet red. She brushed her hair, fluffing it out as much as she could, and pinned it up at the back with two jeweled clasps. For the final touch, she fastened on a pair of diamond earrings that were on the table.

She turned to the black dress again. If she couldn't do it justice now, she never could. She carefully stepped into it and pulled the narrow straps over her arms. She walked past the glittering collection of dresses to the full-length mirror.

It was Angel Concelli.

No, she hadn't quite succeeded. Something was missing. A sexual arrogance, perhaps, a sense that she could deliver on the promise implicit in such a sexy look.

But she was still a thousand times more captivating than she had ever imagined she could be. She felt a sweet lift of joy as she ran her hands over the clinging dress, imagining men surrounding her, women staring at her with envy. It was wonderful to leave Stevie in a crumpled pile of clothes on the floor.

"Thank you." Gian-Carlo was standing in the doorway.

Her heart was pounding. She couldn't pretend that she didn't know what this was leading to.

He moved behind her and put his hands on her shoulders. She looked at the reflection of his tanned face, his enigmatic eyes, his strong mouth. He was the most handsome man she had ever seen. And, in the mirror, they belonged together.

He caressed her bare shoulders. "You're so beautiful," he whispered. He lightly kissed her neck. His fingers continued to stroke her skin. "You don't know how it feels for a man to see other men eating a woman up with their eyes, and to know that he's the one she chooses. That whenever he wants he can make love to her."

His hands tightened on her shoulders. He pulled her back so she was leaning against him. Stevie took a deep breath, trying not to faint. She really was beautiful; she could see it in his eyes. He touched her, his fingers light on her arms, her neck, her breasts. He kissed her hair. Then he gently slid the thin black straps down her arms and lowered the dress to her waist. Stevie saw her bare breasts in the mirror, Gian-Carlo's hands caressing them, his fingers holding her erect nipples.

She was Angel Concelli.

His hands were on her hips. He tugged the dress loose. It slid to the floor. She stood naked against him, watching his eyes worshipping her. He caressed her again, running his hands over her hot bare skin. She could feel him hard against her. Then he slowly turned her around. He put his hand under her chin and raised her face. She tried to read his eyes. But they were full of wonder and regret, emotions she didn't really understand. She had led a sheltered life, and all that protection had done its damage.

"Undress me," he whispered. "Make love to me."

Stevie's arms were at her sides. Her nipples barely touched his chest. Then his mouth was on hers as he caressed her body. His kiss was slow and demanding; his hands skimmed across her, teasing, arousing, as if he had made love to her a thousand times before.

Trying to think of nothing but physical pleasure, she raised her arms and tugged his sweater up over his chest.

50

THE lights were blazing in the cool, silent bedroom. Gian-Carlo lay next to Stevie on the huge bed, marveling at this miracle, his love reborn.

He caressed her smooth body. With nothing to prove but his love, he was taking his time, tenderly giving her as much pleasure as he could. Naked from the waist up, he pressed his chest against her breasts.

Stevie made herself stop thinking about her sister, about guilt, and Nick, and playing with fire. Instead, she shut her eyes and let the exquisite lovemaking happen like a dream. It was a dream, one every woman had had—sex with a movie star, a handsome stranger spotted on a street. Gian-Carlo Cassieri. A man who would never have wanted her in real life.

But this was real life.

This was a real man pushing against her. He was heavier than she expected; suddenly she felt smothered and trapped.

"I love you," he whispered. He was kissing her, biting her lips. "Tell me," he commanded. "Say it too."

But she didn't love him. Not the way she loved Nick.

She felt his saliva on her face, his sharp teeth. This was Gian-Carlo, the man she couldn't resist.

"Please," he repeated. "Stop being cruel. Say you love me."

She couldn't say it. She couldn't lie. She wanted him, it felt like love, but it wasn't. Love had a future.

He took her hand and pulled it toward his belt.

Suddenly she yanked her hand free and squirmed out of his embrace. Before he had a chance to react, she slid across to the other side of the bed. She covered herself with the loose yellow sheet. "Gian-Carlo, I'm so sorry. I don't know what I was thinking. God, how could I have done this!"

In shock, he stared across the bed at her. She braced herself for his anger. But instead there was only sadness, two tears in his black eyes. He shook his head. "Angel, why are you doing this?"

"I'm not Angel!" she cried. "I'm Stevie!"

"Angel," he held out his arms, "I know I've hurt you, but I'm a different man now. I see all the mistakes I made. I should have taken you out in public instead of coming here all the time. I should have been proud of you. Even if it meant sacrificing everything else, I should have chosen you. You were right about everything. We should have had the baby. We should have run away. But this time I've proved it. I've proved you're more important to me than politics, than everything else in my life."

Stevie thought of her sister's love for this man. How Angel must have longed to hear these words.

That was why Stevie was here, that was the only right she had to this passion. Her sister's love, not hers.

By wanting Gian-Carlo, she had only proven how little she thought of herself. And, caught up in her own neuroses, she had fed the poor man's misery by playing these stupid games with him. Ashamed, she blinked back tears.

Gian-Carlo leaned toward her. "Angel, I'll prove how much I've changed. You'll see. This time I'll do it."

"Gian-Carlo, it's all right," Stevie said to calm him down, wishing this were finished, wishing she could go home and wash this man off her skin. But she had to be patient. His mental state was far more fragile than she had allowed herself to see. After going this far with him, she had to handle him gently. "You'll be okay," she said. "By tomorrow everything will be fine."

"Yes," he whispered. He reached out and caressed her bare arm. "I brought the pills. We'll take them together."

Stevie shivered. She remembered that he had been here the night her sister died. In this apartment, on this bed. She had been wrong about so much. Could she have been wrong about her sister's suicide too?

She pulled the sheet up to her chin. "Why don't we get dressed and go somewhere to talk?" she said, trying to keep her voice steady. "We should get out of here."

He shook his head. "You don't understand. It's going to be different this time."

Stevie slid back until she was against the wall. She looked around, getting her bearings. But he was between her and the door. The telephone was on the other side of the room.

"But I need your help," he continued.

Stevie pushed back her hair. Her hands were trembling. She shut her eyes, wishing she were somewhere else, that she wasn't made up to resemble her sister, naked on her sister's bed while a man called her by another name.

"Gian-Carlo—"

He moved toward her. He put his hands on her shoulders. His dark eyes were glazed. His fingers dug into her skin. He was seeing Angel.

"We'll do it right," he whispered. "This time, we'll both die."

51

ANGEL was huddled in the corner of the bedroom, crouched naked on the rug with her arms wrapped around her knees. Her wide eyes followed every move Gian-Carlo made.

Sitting on the bed beside the small night table, he poured some of the sleeping pills into the palm of his hand and began dividing them into two equal piles. "There are enough," he assured her without looking up. "We won't wake up in the hospital, looking foolish."

Angel didn't say anything as she watched him count the pills out, one to the neat pile on the right, one to the pile on the left.

She couldn't move. She felt as if she would never move again. She was amazed that she could even breathe, that air continued to pass in and out of her lungs, that her heart beat with the steady pounding that banged in her ears. "No," she whispered. She had actually spoken. What had she said? "No," she repeated, for her own benefit as much as his.

Gian-Carlo continued dividing the pills as if she hadn't said anything.

"No," Angel said, raising her voice. She rubbed her hands over her knees, feeling the skin that had been toughened by childhood falls. "I don't want to."

Gian-Carlo emptied the remaining pills into his hand. "But you were the one who made it clear that this is our only solution. What other choice do we have?"

Angel's eyes were pulled to the neat piles of pills. Her death, waiting for her. "I'm not ready," she whispered. "Maybe . . ."

He sighed. "Maybe what?"

She thought of a thousand things at once. Of children she might someday have, a little boy and girl, and she would swing them up and hug them close, and on beautiful sunny days they would all run through the long green grass in a field far away from here. And there would be sun showers and rainbows and laughing at silly jokes. And dancing, she loved dancing, and wearing a pretty new dress, and stretching when she woke up in the morning, and the taste of a rich espresso at her favorite coffee bar.

They were clichés. And they were also the principal reason for living.

"I don't want to die," she said.

He shook his head. "If we don't do this what's going to happen tomorrow or the day after? Another embarrassing scene in public? I've already had to pull strings and pay money to kill a lot of stories, but I can't stop them all. You'll be laughed at. And so will I. Can't you see the headlines? Drunken actress loses control in public. Falls against table in restaurant, spills drink down her dress, screams and swears like a fishwife."

Angel shrank back, pulling her arms tighter around her legs. He made her sound like such a horrible person. Someone so ridiculous she didn't deserve to live. "I can change," she whispered.

"You know you can't. And neither can I. This is what we've been leading up to since the day we met."

"We have?" She thought of the baby, the baby that would have made everything different. She would have stayed alive for her child, to look after it, to love it and make it happy.

292

"Did you think, for even a moment, that we'd live happily ever after together?"

For a thousand moments, in all her dreams and fantasies. But how could she admit she had been foolish enough to think he could love her as much as she loved him?

"I don't want to," Angel whispered. "I'm frightened."

"I'll help you." He stood up and held out his hand.

She didn't move. She stared at him, the beautiful man she had loved for so long.

His bare feet were silent on the thick white rug as he walked toward her. She remembered the night they met, when he stepped out of the shadows and came toward her across the dark terrace. Now, his voice was soft and gentle, pulling her in. "We may not be able to live together, but we can die together. Angel, I know this is the right thing. We'll hold each other and slip into the next world. Maybe we'll be lucky. Maybe we'll wake up holding hands in a beautiful place." He was standing over her.

Her tongue darted out and flicked across her parched lips. She was thirsty, but the glass of water next to the pills on the bedside table terrified her. "It won't be like that," she said. "It will be painful and ugly. Our bodies don't want to die. They'll fight back."

"Angel." He knelt before her. She felt the heat of his body. "Do I have to do it alone? Is that what you want? For me to die so you can be free? If it is, don't be afraid to say so. I'll understand."

"Oh, no," she cried. "Gian-Carlo, I love you."

He put his hands on her shoulders. She shivered at the touch of his fingers.

"Then come with me," he whispered.

"I'm afraid. I'm not sure this is the right thing."

"I'm sure. And I'll help you. We'll do it together."

She looked over at the pills, the neat yellow mounds. There seemed so many of them, more pills than she could possibly swallow. "Gian-Carlo, can't we try something else? Can't we—?"

"I wish we could!" he interrupted. "But look at us! Our love has become an embarrassment. We're a joke, Angel. Is that how you want it to end? Or do you want to offer a final proof of our love, a marriage in death because those bastards won't let us have one in life?"

"I . . ." She covered her face with her hands. The bruise on her cheek was tender. Tonight was the first time he had hit her. "I don't know."

"I love you more than life," he whispered. "If you can't say the same thing, that's all right. I don't want to pressure you. I'll die alone if I have to. But let me do it here. I want to be with you until the very last second." He stood up.

She lowered her hands and looked up into his dark fearless eyes. Since the day they had met, she hadn't been able to imagine a life without him. That was her downfall, and she knew it.

She got to her feet, using the wall for support. She brushed away his hand when he offered to help.

They stared into each other's eyes as they both waited for her decision.

"All right," she whispered finally, wondering for the first time if she had ever really loved him at all, or if love was something else, something kinder, a thing that Angel Concelli had never had a chance to know.

52

MEMORIES of Claire flooded Angel's mind. She wondered why her mother should come to her now, forcing her way in, insisting on the last word. Claire, beautiful, cold Claire, with her men and her selfishness.

Then Angel's mind turned to her father, that shadowy figure who had given her life. She had finally erased the fantasies of a kind, loving man who wouldn't stop searching until he found her. She had had enough one-night stands herself. If one of them had resulted in a pregnancy, what would that child have meant to the father? What had her baby meant to Gian-Carlo? Bad news, a skeleton in the closet. No one was out there trying to find her. There was no reason to put off death.

"Will it be easier for you if I go first?"

She jumped when Gian-Carlo spoke. It was odd, she thought, as she looked at him sitting beside her on the bed. He was her reason for doing this, and yet now, at the end, he hardly mattered.

"Do you want me to go first?" he repeated.

Her mother had kicked her out and never shown the slightest desire to see her again. Her grandmother had said that as far as she was concerned, her granddaughter was already dead. Aldo, poor, exploitive Aldo, the person who had treated her the best, was already gone. Would anyone miss her? Only her fans, missing a myth. If she had died alone, would Gian-Carlo have mourned her? She glanced at him. No. He would be too relieved. The burden would be gone, the mistress who had turned into a monster.

She shrugged. "I'll go first."

He put his hand on hers. "I want you to know—"

She interrupted him, snapping, "Just give me the fucking pills."

"Angel—"

"Shut up!" She picked up the water glass and grabbed a handful of the yellow pills.

The first pill felt hard on her tongue. She nearly gagged. But, forcing her mind to go blank, she washed it down with water. She wiped her mouth on the back of her hand, feeling a slow rush of relief. She could do it. One, and then another, and then another. And then she could lie down, close her eyes, and be finished.

"I love you," Gian-Carlo whispered.

Ignoring him, she took the second pill and swallowed it easily. She grabbed the third, eager to get this over with.

It was on the tenth that she lost her nerve. She spat it out onto the rug and started sobbing. She doubled over, clutching her stomach, and cried like a child. She didn't know if it was animal fear or better judgment that made her body rebel. But she was trembling and sweating. If she had had the energy to move she would have flushed the pills away.

"Angel," Gian-Carlo whispered at her side. "Talk to me. Say something."

Even if she had had something to say, she was crying too much, ugly, racking sobs. She felt his hands on her arms and didn't have the strength to resist when he pushed her down on the bed. He took the almost empty glass into the bathroom.

She stared up at the white ceiling, beyond thinking, beyond

reasoning, while tears rolled down her face to the silk-covered pillow. She didn't turn her head when he returned with the re-filled glass and picked up several pills.

He sat down beside her and pressed a pill against her lips.

She shook her head.

"It's too late for us, Angel," he whispered. "You know that as well as I do."

She kept her lips and teeth clamped shut. She was afraid that if she tried to speak he would push the pill inside.

"I'll help you," he whispered, leaning over her. "I'll be strong enough for both of us."

She stared at him with a blank, dull hatred. She could feel the pill against her mouth, his thick fingers holding it there.

"I see our death," he whispered. "I see a lovely garden where we'll be together. I see happiness for us, more happiness than we've ever known."

She was looking at a stranger, a fool.

He tried to push the pill between her lips, but she wouldn't let him.

"I'll be with you soon," he said. "Wait for me there, in the garden."

Her eyes had dried. She had no tears left. She wondered if it was too late to make a new life for herself, leaving this man behind, making friends, acting, traveling.

But she had lost her will to fight. The next pain would be too much, the next betrayal would drive her to this point anyway. It was a matter of weeks, or even days. And the next time she would be alone. No one would hold the glass and say sweet inanities.

"Angel, please," he was begging. "Don't make me do it alone."

She tried to remember believing that she loved him. It was tied up with sex, that foreign, violent act that seemed so silly now.

Almost laughing at their stupidity, she finally opened her mouth and let him feed death to her one pill at a time. She shut her eyes, forgetting her murderer, and thought of Claire again, giving her spoonfuls of cereal with sugar coating, which Angel had swallowed like a good girl, hoping to earn some love.

53

"Angel," Gian-Carlo said, "I love you."

Stevie wrapped the sheet around her. She slid off the bed and walked over to the open dressing room. Quickly, she slipped into Angel's black evening gown, afraid that the sight of her in her own clothes would be too great a shock for Gian-Carlo. She didn't want to trigger anything she couldn't handle. She returned to the bedroom and sat down on a chair across the room from the bed.

"I'm Stevie," she said wearily. "Not Angel, Gian-Carlo."

He stared at her, frowning as if he couldn't quite make out her features. "Angel, I love you," he said. "And I can prove it. I brought the pills. This time, I won't be a coward."

Stevie sighed. "Gian-Carlo, maybe you and Angel had some kind of suicide pact and you chickened out and let her go through with it alone, but don't expect me—"

He shook his head. "It wasn't like that. I knew I wasn't going to take the pills. I'm not sure when I realized that I'd found a way to get rid of her. Maybe at first I really planned to die with you. I don't know. But after you . . . You . . ." He squeezed his eyes shut, then opened them again and looked at her. "Angel—"

"Stevie!" she screamed. "Angel's dead! That's what this is all about, isn't it? That's why we've both been behaving like idiots."

She took a deep breath, trying to contain her impatience. "Gian-Carlo," she continued, "you're welcome to tell me anything you want. But you must accept that I'm not Angel."

He sighed and pushed his hair back from his forehead. His shoulders slumped forward. Stevie saw sanity return to his eyes. He knew who she was. She breathed a deep sigh of relief. Maybe this nightmare was finally over.

His voice was flat and empty of emotion. "We couldn't seem to end our affair. It wasn't just Angel. I couldn't give her up. I thought if she was dead I'd get her out of my mind. I didn't know—" He waved his hand. "How much I'd miss her. Do you understand?"

She nodded.

"She was very brave," he continued. "She started taking the pills quickly, one after another. I offered to go first, I even offered to die alone, but only because I knew she wouldn't let me. But then, after she had swallowed a handful of them, something happened. She changed her mind. She wanted to stop." He looked down at the place where Angel had died. He slid his hand across the smooth sheet where her body had lain.

"I made her take them. I pushed them into her mouth. I had no choice. I had to think of the election, Lucia, my children. I was already planning what I would do when she was unconscious. How I would wipe my fingerprints off the glass and the pill bottle. I would go down the back stairs. I said she had to do it for our love, for us. I told her she would wake up in a beautiful garden. I told her to wait for me there." He covered his face with his hands. He was crying.

Watching him, Stevie felt nothing. It was as if she were watching a movie; it had nothing to do with her. He would cry, and then,

299

when the scene was over, he would get up and go back to his dressing room where he would memorize the lines for his next scene. She knew that what she was feeling was shock, that she wasn't ready to handle the truth of her sister's death. It was so much easier to see it as the simple suicide of a beautiful woman with a tragic life. Or even premeditated murder by an ambitious politician or his ruthless backers. Anything would have been less painful than the truth, this petty, foolish act, two people who had gone too far and hadn't the courage or the strength to pull back and start again.

"Help me," Gian-Carlo whispered.

Stevie didn't move. She had no reason to help him. Anyone could have been in this room with him, witnessing this scene. It had nothing to do with her. He was her sister's lover; but who was her sister? Another stranger.

"I deserve to die," he said. "I gave Angel more than half to make sure she wouldn't live. I kept feeding them to her. Her eyes were wide open. She watched me put them into her mouth. What if she really is waiting for me on the other side?"

Stevie sighed. "That's absurd. She's dead, that's all. She isn't going to walk into this room and call us to account. And that's a lucky thing for us. We've all exploited the poor girl. Now let's leave her alone. If you want to kill yourself, don't do it because you think Angel expects it of you. Even if you believe in an afterlife, it can't be like that, with the dead staring down at us, still obsessed with all our pettiness. Surely they have better things to do."

She realized he wasn't listening to her. He had taken the pill bottle from his pocket. He held it in both hands, as mesmerized as if it were a snake, its head reared up, its tongue flicking out.

"Gian-Carlo, please put that away."

He shook his head. "She wants me to die. It's fair." He opened the bottle and started lining up the yellow pills on the bedside table.

Suddenly Stevie felt tears biting her eyes. Something inside her had opened up, and she was overcome by a powerful realization of what had actually happened to Angel. A healthy young woman with so much to live for had been pressured into death by this man, here in this room. Her sense of loss and helplessness was overwhelming. It was as if Angel were dying now, in front of her, and there was nothing she could do to stop it.

Gian-Carlo looked up at her.

In a moral sense, and possibly a legal one, he really was her murderer. If he hadn't been so selfish, Angel would be here today. Stevie felt a sudden rush of hatred, a surge of anger so violent she had to grip the arms of her chair to keep from attacking him. The shock had gone. She felt the full reality of her sister's death, Angel trusting this bastard, opening her mouth, believing his final stupid promises. He had killed her slowly, without passion; he didn't even have anger as an excuse. He wanted to be free, but free from what? From a few embarrassing scenes in public—in other words, from Angel's love. The bastard should have realized how lucky he was.

Stevie's heart was pounding. She wondered what would happen if Angel *could* walk into the room. Angel in her black dress and diamond earrings, her eyelids painted silver, her mouth a slash of red. Angel alone with her murderer.

Stevie stood up. She smoothed the shimmering dress over her thighs. "Give me the pills," she said.

Trembling with rage, she walked over to the bed. Gian-Carlo stared up at her. Stevie picked up the first pill.

"Thank you," he whispered.

She shook her head angrily. "No! Say you don't want it."

"But—"

"Say you don't want it!" she screamed.

His eyes met hers. He understood. "I don't want it," he whispered. "I don't want to die."

She held the pill against his lips. "You have to," she told him. "You have to die. For Angel." She took a deep breath. "For me."

He parted his lips. She pushed the pill in quickly. He swallowed it eagerly, without waiting for water. Stevie reached for the next yellow pill.

54

STEVIE picked up the empty pill bottle and wiped it clean with a corner of the sheet. Then she hesitated beside the bed. Gian-Carlo's face was finally calm. There was something childlike about him now. She felt as if she should tuck a blanket around his shoulders and leave a light burning so that he wouldn't be frightened of ghosts in the dark.

She glanced around the room, checking to see if there was anything else to take care of. But everything looked exactly as it had when they'd arrived. She turned toward the dressing room to change into her own clothes. But she stopped in the doorway and looked back at Gian-Carlo's inert form. She was held by the image of their encounter earlier, when she had lain naked beside him. It wasn't a memory she was proud of.

But the night was carved in stone. She would just have to live with the guilt and regrets. As she turned to go into the dressing room, someone banged on the apartment door.

"Cassieri!" a voice shouted. "Are you in there?"

Stevie hesitated. She glanced back at the bed.

"Stevie!" Someone slammed against the door. She ran down the hallway and pulled it open.

Nick grabbed her into his arms and held her close. "Thank God you're all right!"

Lucia Cassieri and Franco Uccellini were standing behind him. Gian-Carlo's wife was wearing a plain black coat, her hair loose to her shoulders. Stevie met her eyes, then looked away.

Lucia pushed past Stevie and Nick into the apartment. Stevie tried to pull free, but Nick held her tight. "I was so worried—"

"Nick," she said, "it's not what you think—"

"When your grandmother called," he interrupted, "and said that Gian-Carlo had sped off into the night with you and another car was on his tail, I—"

"Nick—"

Lucia screamed from the bedroom. Stevie pulled away from Nick and ran down the hallway after her. "He's all right!" she shouted. "I only gave him five pills!"

Uccellini and Nick hurried after the two women into the bedroom. Lucia was kneeling next to the bed, Gian-Carlo's limp hand in hers.

"He wanted me to give him more," Stevie explained quickly, "but I pretended he'd had them all. He was confused. I kicked them under the bed. Then he fell asleep."

Uccellini rushed forward and checked Gian-Carlo's pulse. After a few moments he said, "She's telling the truth. He'll be fine."

Lucia sighed. Without her jewels, her tailored clothes, her carefully tended hair and face, Gian-Carlo's wife looked much older. But she also looked like a real person. "Thank you," she whispered to Stevie, her eyes full of relief.

Stevie remembered that she was still wearing Angel's skimpy black dress. Embarrassed, she wrapped her arms around herself. "There's no reason to thank me," she said.

Lucia smiled at her, but her eyes were sad. "You stopped after five."

The gratitude made Stevie squirm. She remembered her bitter

hatred of Gian-Carlo, the almost overwhelming desire to kill him, to take Angel's revenge. She shrugged. "It wasn't a particularly noble act. I think I stopped because of the consequences. For me, not for him."

Uccellini was struggling to raise Gian-Carlo to a sitting position. "We have to get him out of here," he said.

Nick brushed past Stevie and walked over to the bed. He hadn't looked at her since Lucia had screamed. Together he and Uccellini managed to get Gian-Carlo up. The politician's bare chest sagged. Without speaking, Stevie went into the dressing room and got his turtleneck sweater. She held it out to the two men. Nick ignored her, but Uccellini took it. Stevie stood beside Lucia and watched as Uccellini slapped one side of Gian-Carlo's face, then the other. Gian-Carlo's body jerked. His eyes fluttered briefly and then closed again. Uccellini hit him again, harder this time. Gian-Carlo twitched and opened his dazed eyes. He looked around the room, but his bewildered face told them he was still heavily under the influence of the pills.

Stevie hesitated, then decided she had to speak. "He . . . he confessed. He forced Angel to take the pills. She didn't want to die."

Lucia looked down. Uccellini and Nick ignored her.

"He's guilty," Stevie insisted. "He murdered her."

Finally Uccellini turned to look at her. "What do you want us to do? Have him charged with murder? Your testimony—only hearsay evidence—would never stand up in court. And Angel Concelli's sister would be considered biased even if the circumstances weren't—" He looked around the room before adding, "Difficult to explain."

Stevie blushed. "I thought you wanted to know the truth."

Nick finally spoke, but he didn't look at her. "We'll never know the truth."

Uccellini sighed. "And don't pretend a politician in your country couldn't get away with murder, Signorina Templeton." He stared at her for a moment. "You might not believe this, but I honestly don't like that anymore than you do."

"What will happen about the election?" she asked.

Lucia spoke. "We'll announce that he's ill. Another candidate is ready to take his place. In politics, the individual really doesn't matter much. Gian-Carlo has never understood that. He has some ridiculous notion that he's a giant. But the best one can hope for is to be in the right place at the right time and then not make too great a fool of oneself."

Stevie looked at Gian-Carlo. She tried to imagine his future. Even if he fully regained his sanity, the rest of his life would be bleak and empty. His political career was finished. He would never get over his guilt and the loss of Angel. He would live out his own punishment. As she stared at the unimpressive figure Nick and Uccellini were trying to revive, she discovered her hatred was gone along with her obsession. He seemed insignificant, a foolish middle-aged man who had lost control of his life because he had loved a beautiful young actress either too much or not enough.

Uccellini and Nick helped Gian-Carlo to his feet. They dragged him past the two women. Stevie watched Nick leave, wondering if he would come back or if she had lost him for good.

Lucia interrupted her thoughts. "I know you don't understand why I stay with him," she said as the men left the room. "I must seem like a very foolish woman."

"It's not my place to say," Stevie answered.

"People think I use him as an outlet for my own ambitions. That is absurd, of course. Italy is not as liberated a country as it should be, but there are certainly ways in which I could attain power for myself. That's not why I need him."

In the hallway, Gian-Carlo stumbled. Uccellini and Nick pulled him up again. They managed to get him through the apartment door.

Lucia smiled sadly. "I love him. That's my reason. It's stupid, but it's the only one I have." Without looking at Stevie, Lucia turned and followed the three men out of the apartment.

When she was alone again, Stevie went into the dressing room. She picked up her clothes and carried them over to the three-sided mirror. She still looked like Angel, dressed like a butterfly, diamonds shimmering at her ears, the black silk dress tight and revealing. Angel, the sister she would never meet.

Her eyes filled with tears. She felt a raw, searing pain, an enormous, devastating grief. She missed Angel terribly, as if Angel were part of her own self that had been ripped out and tossed away like garbage.

"I wish I'd come a little sooner," she sobbed to her reflection, to her sister. "I wish I'd had a chance to know you. I'm not saying I could have saved you. But . . ." Her voice broke. She took a deep breath. "But I would have tried. Angel, I know I would have loved you." As she cried, Angel's makeup dissolved on her face, leaving Stevie behind. She reached up and unfastened the diamond earrings. She took out the jeweled clasps and smoothed her hair back into her own more conservative style. She slipped off the black gown and carefully replaced it on a hanger.

She put on her own clothes, turning back into herself like a butterfly into a caterpillar. The quiet, sad girl who was now in the mirror was Stevie Templeton. Since her arrival in Rome she had come to know herself better—and to like herself less. That was something she would have to think about.

She heard the door to the apartment open again. She walked into the bedroom. Nick was standing in the hallway. "I didn't expect you to come back," she said.

He shrugged, his eyes cold. "I nearly didn't."

"I . . . I've really made a fool of myself."

He put his hands in his pockets. "You won't get an argument from me."

She wondered how she could ever have preferred Gian-Carlo to this sexy, gentle man. If she lost him, it would be the biggest loss of her life.

"My first day in Rome," she said, hoping he could understand, "when those people crowded around me . . . I knew I wasn't worthy of it. But Angel was. And when I saw her picture . . . she was so beautiful. A movie star. I felt . . . like Angel was the privileged one. Now I know that's not true."

Nick was staring at her. He still hadn't moved.

"I'm sorry, Nick."

He didn't say anything for a moment. Then he waved his arm. "Come on. It's almost morning. I'll buy you some breakfast."

She walked across the room toward him. When she reached him he pulled her into his arms and buried his face in her hair. "I was so worried about you, *cara*. I've never been so worried in my life. I showed up at Cassieri's place screaming my head off. Uccellini was already there. He was the one who followed you and Gian-Carlo. Lucia thought of looking here." He smiled at her. "God, you're a gutsier woman than I thought. I never expected to find you standing there in a sexy black dress like Angel's avenger. You Boston girls can be pretty surprising."

"Do you still want to marry me?" she asked.

"What the hell," he said, smiling down at her. "I always wanted an unpredictable woman."

"Gian-Carlo and I didn't—" she started.

"It's okay," he interrupted. "I don't need to know all the details." He pulled her close again. "As long as you're mine from now on."

"Come on, Nick," she whispered. "You know Gian-Carlo never had a chance against you."

Epilogue

It was Sunday afternoon.

Stevie knelt on the damp grass in front of the gray marble head-stone.

ANGEL CONCELLI

She placed a bouquet of white roses on the ground. There were many flowers in various states of decay. The fans still came, fewer every day. But Angel was only a myth to them, a flickering image on a screen, a glossy picture in a magazine.

"I'll come again," Stevie whispered. She looked out across the cemetery at the other mourners scattered around, clutching their bundles of flowers, bending their aching knees to leave a tribute to someone they had lost. She remembered what she had said to Gian-Carlo. Surely the dead had better things to care about than the petty intrigues of those they had left behind.

But Stevie knew she would continue to visit the cemetery. Pilgrimages were for the pilgrim, not the shrine, and it was about time she paid her sister a little respect.

She stood up and started back toward the waiting car. When she opened the door, she was greeted by Lucia Cassieri's voice. Nick smiled at her and turned up the volume on the radio. A news program was rebroadcasting Lucia's announcement that Gian-Carlo had withdrawn from the campaign due to illness.

"That's my girl," Nick joked before turning off the radio. "A man spends one night with her and he has to check into a hospital to recover. I hope I survive our wedding night."

Stevie smiled. Then she looked back at Angel's grave.

"Are you all right, *cara*?" he asked.

"Don't worry," she answered. "I'll let her die. Soon."

"Take your time," he said, pulling her close for a few moments. "We're in no hurry. By the way, did I tell you about the engagement party Laura is planning for us? She insists it will be the biggest social event in Roman history, a claim that will be hard to live up to unless she's planning on hiring some lions and Christians to provide entertainment. But she's a harmless . . ."

He had started the car. As they drove away Stevie looked back, keeping the tombstone in sight for as long as she could. But then Nick rounded a corner, and Angel was gone.